"Giordano keeps the tension in check with an anonymous narrator whose affection for his eccentric relation can't be disguised."

—*Washington Post,* "6 Beach Reads That Will Bring You
More Pleasure Than Guilt"

"As types of amateur sleuths go, the category of lusty Bavarian widow has been woefully underrepresented—until now . . . Fans of international mysteries or just those who fantasize about good wine and languorous meals on the Italian coast will devour this mystery debut."   —*Booklist,* starred review

"There's a new star in the mystery firmament, and her name is Auntie Poldi. Mario Giordano has created a character who will be the envy of every novelist, mystery and otherwise."

—Alan Bradley, author of
The Sweetness at the Bottom of the Pie

"This book is absolutely delightful. Reading it felt like a mini-vacation to Sicily, full of colorful characters and all the twists and turns I crave in a mystery . . . If you're looking for a book to read on the beach, this one is perfect!"   —*Book Riot*

"Giordano's wit and his formidable heroine's wisdom combine to make this debut a smash." —*Kirkus Reviews,* starred review

"The most enchanting novel I've read in ages! *Auntie Poldi and the Sicilian Lions* is a lush, sexy, and slightly madcap romp, much like Auntie Poldi herself. Mario Giordano has a gift for eccentric storytelling, snappy dialogue, and sly wit, making this a tart and delectable treat that you'll press on all your friends. I can't wait for the next installment!"

—Amy Stewart, author of *Girl Waits with Gun*

Auntie Poldi and the Vineyards of Etna

Also by Mario Giordano

Auntie Poldi and the Sicilian Lions
Auntie Poldi and the Vineyards of Etna
Auntie Poldi and the Handsome Antonio
1,000 Feelings for Which There Are No Names

Auntie Poldi
and the Vineyards of Etna

MARIO GIORDANO

Translated by John Brownjohn

Mariner Books
Houghton Mifflin Harcourt
Boston   New York

First Mariner Books edition 2019

First published in Germany in 2016 as *Tante Poldi und die Früchte des Herrn* by Bastei Lübbe AG, Köln

First English-language edition published in Great Britain in 2018 as *Auntie Poldi and the Fruits of the Lord* by John Murray (Publishers), a Hachette UK company

hmhbooks.com

Library of Congress Cataloging-in-Publication Data
Names: Giordano, Mario, 1963–author. | Brownjohn, John, translator.
Title: Auntie Poldi and the Vineyards of Etna / Mario Giordano ; translated by John Brownjohn.
Other titles: Tante Poldi und die Früchte das Herrn. English
Description: First US edition. | Boston : Houghton Mifflin Harcourt, 2018. | Series: An Auntie Poldi adventure ; 2
Identifiers: LCCN 2018033130 (print) | LCCN 2018050389 (ebook) | ISBN 9781328918949 (ebook) | ISBN 9781328919021 (hardback) | ISBN 9780358299622 (pbk.)
Subjects: | BISAC: FICTION / Contemporary Women. | FICTION / Humorous.
Classification: LCC PT2667.I5617 (ebook) | LCC PT2667.I5617 T3513 2018 (print) | DDC 833/.92—DC23
LC record available at https://lccn.loc.gov/2018033130

Printed in the United States of America
DOC 10 9 8 7 6 5 4 3 2 1

Auntie Poldi and the Vineyards of Etna

1

Tells of water, mongrels, shadows and deliziosi, *and of the family's worries about Poldi's inner equilibrium. Poldi is now a star in Torre Archirafi and has tasted blood, which means that a clash with Commissario Montana is almost inevitable. Once the call of the genes rings out, however, Poldi is not to be deterred by heat, showers of volcanic ash or German tourists.*

Someone had not only cut off the water supply to the whole of the Via Baronessa but poisoned Lady. Thirst and murder—in other words, my Auntie Poldi's two pet hates. They upset her inner equilibrium even more than the sight of a handsome, immaculately turned-out Sicilian traffic cop.

Lady was one of two friendly mongrels that belonged to Valérie, my Auntie Poldi's neighbour. A stumpy, shaggy, yappy mutt with a pronounced underbite, she used to hunt Femminamorta's rats with her twin brother Oscar and welcome visitors to the property. Everyone, simply everyone who knew Lady, had loved her because she generously gave her heart to them all. Whenever visitors came calling, she would go crazy with eagerness to make the acquaintance of strangers or celebrate a reunion with friends. She even endeared herself, in the space of a tail-wag, to Valérie's misanthropic French relations. The workers at Valérie's palm plantation could be heard calling "Lady!" all day long, followed by Lady's hoarse, delighted response. Until one morning, when her shaggy little body was found in the courtyard, stiff as a board. Poisoned bait, according to the vet.

So it went without saying that my Auntie Poldi, being the obstinate Bavarian she was, had to rebalance things and get them back on an even keel. In other words, get the taps running again, find Lady's murderer and see justice done.

Especially as it mustn't be forgotten that my Auntie Poldi already lived on the knife edge between joie de vivre and melancholy. The least she wanted was to straighten things out, because straightening things out was always something of an aid to getting over her fits of depression.

Auntie Poldi was the widow of my late Uncle Peppe, who, in contrast to his parents and his sisters Teresa, Caterina and Luisa, had not returned to Sicily in the 1970s but remained in Munich like my father. My Uncle Peppe was a Münchner through and through. I can't remember him when he didn't have a stein of beer in one hand and a cheap cigar in the other. He spoke only Bairisch and Sicilian, never ran to regular German or Italian. Uncle Peppe had always been the black sheep of the family, the cool dude notorious for his countless affairs, shady cronies, wild parties, falls from grace, spectacular car crashes, walk-on parts in films, bankruptcies and hare-brained business ventures. My favourite uncle, in other words. All that stabilised him somewhat was his marriage in later life to a certain Isolde Oberreiter, known as Poldi. They were a glamorous couple, Peppe and Poldi, svelte as rock stars, chain-smokers, boozers, open-handed and generous and, according to my mother, the most caring friends imaginable. At some stage I recall my parents saying that Peppe and Poldi were getting divorced, and they didn't seem particularly surprised. Uncle Peppe remarried the following year; then he died and we lost touch with Poldi. A few years later we heard from Aunt Teresa that Poldi had bought a house in Tanzania, but that was pretty much all anyone knew.

And then, out of the blue, Poldi reappeared in Munich. Having inherited her parents' small house, she sold up, burnt all her bridges and, on her sixtieth birthday, moved to Torre Archirafi, a peaceful little town on the east coast of Sicily between Catania and Taormina, intending to drink herself to death in comfort within sight of the sea. Suicide with a sea view was her plan, nobody quite knew why. All my aunts did know was that someone had to do something about it, and "someone" included me because, in their view, I was as good as unemployed. Thereafter I flew to Sicily to spend one week a month in Poldi's guest room at No. 29 Via Baronessa, working on my family epic and helping to dispose of her liquor supplies.

Although in the past few months Poldi had temporarily thwarted death thanks to solving her handyman Valentino's murder, her romantic encounter with Vito Montana (Polizia di Stato's chief inspector in charge of homicide cases), her friendship with her neighbours Valérie and sad Signora Cocuzza, my aunts' efforts and, last but not least, her own love of the chase, we all know the way of the world: peace reigns for a while, the worst seems to be over, the sun breaks

3

through the clouds, the future beckons once more, your cigarette suddenly tastes good again, the air hums with life and the whole world becomes a congenial place pervaded by whispers of great things to come. A simply wonderful, universally familiar sensation. And then, like a bolt from the blue, pow! Not that anyone has seen it coming, but the wind changes. Fate empties a bucket of excrement over your head, chuckling as it does so, and all you can think is "Wow, now I *really* need a drink!" And the whole shitty process starts again from scratch.

So it was no wonder my aunts became alarmed when Poldi still had no running water after two weeks and Lady was murdered. No doubt about it, the wind had changed and the ice was growing steadily thinner.

"You must come!" Aunt Luisa told me on the phone. "Right away!"

I tried to wriggle out of it. "I can't," I said. "I'm working on an ultra-urgent pitch for TV. A pre-watershed, parental-guidance thriller. Not my genre, exactly, but it could be a slam-dunk."

"Just a moment." With a sigh, Luisa handed the receiver to her sister Teresa, who's the boss in our family.

It was obvious what that meant: game over.

I heard Luisa whisper something in Italian, then the gentle, still-youthful voice of my Aunt Teresa.

"How are you, *tesoro*? Making progress with your novel?"

I might have known.

"I'm getting on pretty well," I prevaricated. "The first chapter's as good as finished. All I need is a bit of . . ."

"You're frittering your time away," Aunt Teresa told me gently. "What you need is to concentrate on essentials."

She had a point.

"And you could keep an eye on Poldi at the same time."

I said nothing, and Aunt Teresa switched to Italian, the invariable sign that a storm was brewing.

"She's fond of you, you know."

"Eh?"

"She is, for some reason. We often talk about you."

"In what way?" I asked suspiciously.

Aunt Teresa didn't pursue the matter. "This television thing—is it very important to you?"

Direct hit, holed below the waterline.

I landed at Catania at lunchtime next day, was regaled by Teresa with *spaghetti al nero di seppia,* and meekly answered all the aunts' enquiries about the welfare of the family members in Germany. That evening I was back on the sofa in my Auntie Poldi's house in Torre Archirafi. And the strangest thing was, I felt thoroughly at home and far closer to my mess of a family saga than I had for a long time.

"You're developing a little tummy" was the first thing Poldi said when she came to the door.

"Thanks a lot! I'm glad you're glad I'm here again."

She ushered me inside. "I'm only saying. A little tummy suits any man. As long as it's firm, that's all. Bear this in mind for your novel: doesn't matter whether you're talking about art or sex, it's all a question of proportion."

I ignored her aphorism and scanned my surroundings. There was one reassuring feature: her plan to drink herself to death with a sea view seemed to be in abeyance. I could detect no caches of empty liquor bottles, the house made a clean and tidy impression, the potted plants on the terrace had been adequately watered, and the fridge was full of vegetables. No signs of neglect. But, as I said, it was a knife-edge situation, a somnambulist's dance on the rim of a volcanic crater. Not even the aunts seriously expected Poldi to remain stone-cold sober from one day to the next, but she really did drink no more than a bottle of Prosecco a day, plus half a litre of beer at lunch and a little *corretto*—coffee with a shot of cognac—in the afternoon. She was looking as fresh as a daisy. Titivated and fragrant in a billowing silk caftan, with her wig skilfully dressed, she undertook a daily *passeggiata* along the esplanade. On Mondays she went down to the beach, on Tuesdays she accompanied Uncle Martino to the fish market in Catania or sunned herself at the Lido Galatea with Aunt Luisa, on Wednesdays she took classes at Michele's language school in Taormina, on Thursdays she took tea with Valérie. Fridays meant bed with Commissario Montana, Saturdays gin rummy with Signora Cocuzza and Padre Paolo, on Sundays she occasionally went mushroom picking with Teresa and Martino, and at all times she relished the new-found local notoriety she had earned by solving the Candela case in such a spectacular fashion. What am I saying, local! Even the *Augsburger Heimatkurier* had interviewed her on the subject.

In short, my Auntie Poldi was on a roll. Ever since she figured out who killed her handyman, she was the star of Torre Archirafi. Everyone asked her for selfies and sent her wedding invitations. She even attended Mass regularly, Padre Paolo officiating, because this more or less accorded with her new social status in the town. She had also acquired a Vespa. Not just any old Vespa, either, but a restored PX 125 cc, decorated like a *carretto siciliano* by my cousin Marco, who has a talent for such things. It was adorned with traditional designs like those on Sicilian donkey carts, which make even Indian tuk-tuks look drab and boring: ornamentation in vivid colours, plenty of curlicues and, in this particular instance, artfully airbrushed illustrations of Poldi at work on the Candela case.

"Don't tell me," I said a trifle enviously when she showed me the Vespa, "restraint is a sign of weakness."

"Hey, don't go thinking I've lost the plot. I like colourful things, that's all. Vanity doesn't come into it. It's just a tribute to our traditions."

"*Our* traditions?"

"Being Sicilian is a question of heart, not genes, and I know a thing or two about matters of the heart, believe you me. I've always known I was Sicilian in an earlier life—Masai and Sicilian, I just sense it. Kate told me that back in Los Angeles."

"Which Kate would that be?"

"Why, Kate Hepburn, of course. Not a lot of people know this, but she had the gift. Fantastic woman. Crazy, but all heart. Hey, maybe I should go to a fortune-teller and do a regression, what do you think?"

My Auntie Poldi wasn't the type to put things on the back burner—or put up for long with thirst and unsolved murders.

And that was always a source of trouble.

October is one of the loveliest months in Sicily. It's when summer opens its fist again, letting a little breeze into the house and allowing you to breathe again; when the light becomes as mellow as my Aunt Caterina's limoncello and you take a sweater along in the evenings, just to be on the safe side; when the shacks and timber decks on the Torre Archirafi's esplanade have disappeared along with the charivari of children's cries, raucous laughter, flirtations, minor dramas and covert glances at suntanned skin; when you're still receiving envious text messages from home about the weather you're enjoying; when waiters in bars become talkative again and the first snow falls on the heights of Etna; when the grape harvest is in progress somewhat lower down, between Trecastagni and Zafferana, and you're faced with the alarming question of whether the local café has run out of *granita di gelsi,* or mulberry sorbet. But this October was different. Still as hot as a molten glass bubble stubbornly pressing down on the whole island and intent on withering the last remaining wisp of greenery. A sirocco from North Africa was blowing half the Sahara across the Mediterranean, sandblasting throats and the bodywork of cars, and migraines and forest fires were rife. What exacerbated the situation was Etna's continuous activity. For weeks now, the main crater had been surmounted by a column of smoke more than a thousand metres high, and spectacular eruptions and streams of lava were on display every night. The Mongibello, the mountain of mountains, groaned and snorted every minute of the day and night, emitting muffled salutations from the bowels of the earth that preyed on people's nerves and shook them to the core. When the sirocco took a breather, Etna showered Torre Archirafi with fragments of pumice and particles of volcanic ash until snow shovels were all that could deal with the inches-thick deposit in the streets and on the roof terraces. Sicily was once more giving my Auntie Poldi a hard time. To make matters worse, she had recently been reminded by the persistent throbbing of an old crown, top left, that a visit to the dentist was long overdue. It was only a minor problem, but now that Poldi was more self-controlled drink-wise, that minor problem could not, alas, be solved by imbibing several stiff dry martinis, only by stubbornly ignoring it and taking half an ibuprofen. With the best will in the world, Poldi was not yet ready to undergo any Sicilian dentistry.

As if that were not enough, there came a morning when every tap in the Via Baronessa emitted a dry cough. No need to panic, normally speaking. Sometimes the old water mains are to blame, sometimes just drought. Cuts usually last a day or two at most, and the blue plastic tank on your roof will tide you over. It's a nuisance if the cut lasts any longer. A week, say, or two. Or, as in this case, three. It's even more of a nuisance if the reason cannot be found and if only one particular street is affected, namely yours. To a Sicilian, the situation will usually be self-evident: Cosa Nostra is exerting pressure on one of your neighbours.

The reasons can be many and various. Perhaps the neighbour is to be incentivised into signing a contract disadvantageous to himself. Perhaps he is behind with his payments under an existing contract, and cutting off his water is stage one in a two-stage admonitory process. Stage one: a veiled warning. Stage two: violence directed at you and your family. Then again, your neighbour may simply have been sent a message to keep his trap shut in some current court case. Nobody knows for sure, but the whole street suffers as a result. All the better—it only increases the pressure. Cutting off the water has long been one of Cosa Nostra's most effective forms of coercion. It demonstrates total control. Whoever controls the water supply rules Sicily.

Like everyone else in the Via Baronessa, Poldi had been obliged for three weeks to fetch her water in a jerrycan from the public taps at the old mineral water bottling plant. Not a really satisfactory option, because the four taps were besieged by queues all day long. Even when her turn came, it took Poldi an age to fill her jerrycan, after which she had to tote the whopping thing home or heft it onto her Vespa. One jerrycan was just enough for one person per day. Showering, using the toilet, washing, cooking—everything became complicated. All at once, her daily routine revolved around water alone. The level of water in the jerrycan became a measure of her inner equilibrium, and "full" was only a fleeting moment, a dot on the timescale.

"You've no idea what a thirst I've got," she gasped, mopping her brow.

She did not, however, favour me by removing her wig.

"You'll tell me it's only psychological, of course. I know that myself, but it doesn't help. I could kill for a drink. Like another beer?"

"No thanks," I lied. "So who is it, in your opinion?"

"Who's what?"

"The neighbour the Mafia is putting pressure on."

Poldi stared at me blankly. "What sort of daft question is that? It's *me*, of course, who do you think? The Mafia have had me in their sights ever since I solved Valentino's murder. That's as plain as the nose on your face."

"I thought the Mafia didn't have anything to do with Valentino's death."

"Not directly, but Italo Russo was behind it indirectly. And he, I tell you," she whispered, "is a *capo mafioso,* a boss of bosses."

"Which you can prove."

She gave me a pitying look. "I'm still at the very start of my investigations, but I've got a nose for Mafiosi, arch-capitalistic bloodsuckers and dog murderers. It's an instinct of mine."

Poldi could not be weaned of the idea that Lady's death and the sabotaging of the water supply had only one purpose: to intimidate her.

"It's nearly broken Valérie's heart, and poor little Oscar is down in the dumps. He howls and pines for Lady all day long."

"But why was only Lady poisoned, not him as well?" I asked.

"I wondered that right away, because the pair were inseparable. So what's the only logical answer?"

"Er . . ."

"It's that Lady was murdered deliberately, of course. And why did the killer pick on Lady and not Oscar? Because she was female. Because the message was aimed at me, get it?"

"Isn't that a bit far-fet—"

A brusquely dismissive gesture. "And if I don't catch the bastard very soon, poor Oscar will also be for the chop, believe you me. Anyway, I've already conducted some preliminary investigations."

I got the picture at last. "You mean your hunting instinct has been aroused, eh?"

"My, we're adjusting to the same wavelength. You're slowly catching on. *Benvenuto in Sicilia.*"

No doubt about it, Poldi had tasted blood. She'd heard the call of her father's genes and was prepared, like Detective

Chief Inspector Oberreiter before her, to tread her predestined path: criminology and the pursuit of justice. The only trouble was, there hadn't been another actual murder in the neighbourhood. This, combined with the heat and lack of water and her toothache, was resulting in violent thirst, dire fits of depression and a kind of criminological cold turkey, a withdrawal symptom to which—according to my Auntie Poldi—retired and suspended detectives are particularly prone. Imagine a superbrain functioning at full throttle and someone suddenly pulls the plug. It really can't be good.

"I mean, no top-level athlete can stop training from one day to the next, their heart couldn't take it. They'd go *phut*. It's the same with detectives' brains when there's nothing to detect. They're like dogs with nothing to chase and worry to death. They'll wind up mauling your sweater. Or, as a last resort, some child's arm. So what's left for me?"

It turned out that, as a sort of health measure, Poldi had consequently spent the weeks since my last visit trying to prove that Russo had links with the Mafia. Unsuccessfully hitherto, and no wonder, since her only clue was the photo of a topographical map she'd seen Russo discussing with Corrado Patanè, the building contractor from Riposto. Although Poldi still hadn't located the area in question, she was convinced that Russo had already smelt a rat and was unmistakably telling her to drop her investigation by cutting off the water and murdering Lady. If she didn't, her Poldian logic dictated, it meant *morto sicuro,* or certain death.

"But he's got another think coming, that fine gentleman. Do I look like someone who wets her knickers just because some bighead threatens me? I've already looked death in the face, I tell you. I know I'm not far short of my sell-by date, but till then, my lad, I'm going to pull out all the stops, *amore*-wise, criminologically and in general. And when the time comes — well, I know how to leave the stage. To roars of applause, I mean."

My Auntie Poldi knew a thing or two about *amore*, criminology and death, so she embarked on her investigation of the Lady case with total professionalism. In other words, no one was above suspicion.

She descended on Femminamorta in her dark blue trouser suit, which pinched in places, like a cleansing tsunami breaking on a dirty, jetsam-strewn beach.

"Weren't you a bit too hot in a trouser suit?" I asked. "I mean, in this sweltering heat?"

"Nonsense! It was a must. Why? Because a blue trouser suit is the ideal no-joking-matter look for any woman who's negotiating contracts or arresting or dating idiots of every description. In American crime series they're always worn by grouchy, ponytailed women detectives, know the type I mean? They aren't *your* type, of course. They've no sense of humour. One false word and wham, you're flat on the ground with a knee in the crotch, and click go the handcuffs."

"The trouser suit plus that wig of yours. No joking matter, I get it."

Poldi sighed and shook her head reprovingly.

"Well, what did Valérie say?" I asked, to nudge her back on track.

"What do you think?"

. . .

"*Mon dieu!*" Valérie clapped a hand over her mouth as Poldi, panting and perspiring, flopped down on one of the plastic garden chairs so violently that the seams of her old trouser suit creaked. "You mean everyone's under suspicion, including me?"

"Not you, Valérie, of course not." Sighing, Poldi opened her notebook — a recent gift from Uncle Martino — with a flourish.

It was the kind FBI types always carry on TV, although Martino realised that the private eye in his favourite crime series never needed a notebook in order to register anything. But the PI was a criminological genius, whereas Poldi . . . Uncle Martino wasn't so sure about her, if only because of her drinking.

I have to confess that Poldi's descriptions of Femminamorta — and, more especially, of Valérie — had ignited my imagination with a vengeance. I pictured the old country house, with its pink, jasmine- and bougainvillea-covered walls and dusty interior, its ancient library, faded photographs and crumbling frescos, palm grove and overgrown garden, as an enchanted place where time had stood still — a little paradise, haunted by the ghosts of Bourbon noblemen, where friendly mongrels romped around and destinies were fulfilled. And presiding in the midst of it — or so I imagined, usually at night — was Valérie, as pale and complicated and sensual and ravishingly beautiful as a girl in a French film noir. But although Femminamorta was less than five minutes from Torre Archirafi by car, Poldi seemed disinclined to share this new friend and her little paradise with anyone. Whenever I casually suggested accompanying her there for once, she found some threadbare pretext for leaving me behind. Although I didn't take this amiss — I've several siblings, after all, so I'm no stranger to envy — my imagination redoubled its efforts to conjure up a magical place with a mysterious mistress more splendidly ethereal than Joseph Conrad or Rider Haggard could have devised. So I thought it only fair for me to incorporate Poldi's descriptions in my shambles of a novel. Much later, when I finally got to know Valérie and Femminamorta, I found they fitted her descriptions to a tee.

Valérie had wrapped the little dog's body in a silk cloth and laid it out beside the old, disused wine press, where it was dark and quiet. A good resting place for little Lady, who had had to endure so much pain at the end of her far too short life, for according to the *veterinario*, she must have expired in agony. He put the time of death at around 3 a.m. There was no trace of any poisoned bait near the spot in the courtyard where Lady had been found several hours later.

So Poldi did not believe that Lady had ingested the bait in the courtyard, but that she had been deliberately left there later on. And that, according to her logic, precisely accorded with the motive for the killing. On the other hand, she was well aware that nothing endangered the success of an investigation more than jumping to premature conclusions. Rather than excluding any possibility, therefore, she resolved to begin by exploring all lines of inquiry and assemble facts in a strictly objective and professional manner.

"Did Lady have any enemies?" Poldi asked.

"*Pardon?*"

"I mean, was there anyone who disliked her? Someone she may have nipped or growled at when startled? An inveterate dog hater, perhaps?"

"*Mon dieu,* no!"

Poldi made a note. "Did anything happen yesterday? Anything unusual?"

"No. Why?"

"Think carefully. Any detail could be important."

"No."

Another note.

Professional at work.

"When did you last see Lady?"

"About nine o'clock last night. I fed both the dogs in the courtyard. I could hear them for a while after that because they were squabbling over a rubber toy that kept on squeaking."

Another note. "And then?"

Valérie shook her head.

Poldi closed her notebook. "In that case, I'd now like to question your guests."

"*Mon dieu,* is that really necessary?"

Valérie had inherited Femminamorta from her father, a descendant of the Sicilian landed nobility. She operated a palm-tree nursery on the small property, which after several generations of profligacy, ignorance and mismanagement represented all that remained of a once-extensive family estate. This being far from enough to cover Valérie's running costs, she additionally and not entirely officially ran a small B and B and let her numerous empty bedrooms to guests, whom she regaled with an unconventional breakfast comprising coffee, toast, biscuits, fresh avocados, cloyingly sweet French preserves, and stories of her family.

All the surrounding land was owned by Italo Russo, whom Poldi had it in for and thought capable of any atrocity. Russo, too, raised palm trees, but on a far bigger scale. Not just palm trees, either, but olive, lemon and orange trees, bougainvilleas, strelitzias and oleanders, for supplying to hotels and the owners of sizeable properties. Piante Russo was a nurseryman's empire, but my aunt saw it as an ever-expanding pestilence that threatened to absorb Femminamorta as well.

"Because that," she told me once, "would be the final triumph of an unscrupulous upstart over the degenerate aristocracy."

I never discovered whether all Russo really wanted was Valérie herself. It would have been understandable enough despite their difference in age, but Valérie always firmly denied it, and after all that happened subsequently, I too have my doubts. On the other hand, I can't imagine anyone desiring a piece of jewellery without the jewel. But to revert to Poldi's investigation . . .

"Tell me about your guests," she said.

"They're Germans," Valérie replied. "But—*mon dieu!* —absolutely *delizioso!*"

For Valérie, like Poldi, happiness possessed a simple binary structure, and the whole of human existence was suspended between two relatively distant poles. Between heaven and hell, love and ignorance, responsibility and recklessness, splendour and scuzz, the essential and the dispensable. And within this dual cosmic structure there existed only two kinds of people: the *deliziosi* and the *spaventosi,* the charming and the frightful. Rule of thumb: house guests, friends and dogs are always *deliziosi,* the rest are *spaventosi.* At least until they prove otherwise.

"You see," Poldi told me once, "Valérie has understood

17

that happiness is a simple equation. Happiness equals reality minus expectation. If you don't expect too much, you're less disappointed and happier quicker, get it? The converse is only logical: if you *do* expect too much . . ." She looked at me. "But I've no need to tell you that."

My Auntie Poldi was an expert at boosting one's self-confidence.

However, the *deliziosi* claimed to have heard and seen nothing, nor could Turi and Mario, who tended Femminamorta's palm cuttings, contribute more to the investigation than an expression of their sorrow at Lady's death.

Doris was the éminence grise of a five-strong party of German *deliziosi*, former schoolmistresses from Bad Cannstatt on an educational trip, who had occupied nearly all the vacant rooms in Femminamorta for the past three days. They were led by a retired headmaster from Filderstadt, but, to repeat, Doris generally ruled the roost. An athletic sixty-nine-year-old clad in sensible clothes and hiking boots, she had keen eyes and a firm sense of how the world should be run—and a dead dog wasn't going to upset her world order unduly. Although the other four *deliziosi* were less athletic, they likewise sported sensible clothes and rucksacks as if about to venture into the heart of darkness. At Valérie's request, the little party and their tour guide had duly assembled in the garden, where Poldi was to interrogate them.

Poldi had grasped at once that these *deliziosi* represented a genuine challenge to her criminological neutrality and kind-heartedness.

"You mean because they were anoraks?" I interjected when she brought me up to date on the evening of my arrival. I don't know what got into me—I may have been hoping for a smidgen of understanding—but, to quote Poldi herself, happiness equals reality minus expectation.

To judge by her look of reproof, I was a puppy that had still to grasp the simplest order to "Sit!" "Rubbish!" she exclaimed. "People who call other people anoraks are anoraks themselves. I mean, it isn't a question of fashion or taste or life choices."

"So what is it a question of?"

"The shadows of the past! I realised in a flash that this Doris was just the sort of know-it-all and pessimist that has haunted and harassed me all my life."

I was gobsmacked.

"But, er . . ." I struggled for words. "You shouldn't care about such things. I mean, you're . . ."

"Now you're talking like Teresa." She sighed. "Yes, of course I shouldn't care, but I do, don't you see? It's what's called a backstory wound—make a note of that for your novel. Without a backstory wound your characters will be nothing more than puppets. Whether in life or in a novel, each of us is haunted by a shadow that keeps whispering, 'Don't become like me and you'll be better off!' You can't help this, and you certainly can't choose your own shadow. Where I'm concerned"—Poldi grabbed my half-empty bottle of beer—"I've been haunted all my life by a Doris. *Prosit, namaste*, kiss my ass!"

Criminologically speaking, therefore, Poldi was virtually marking time, and that rather worried her.

"And in other respects?" I said, to change the subject. "How's it going with Montana?"

"Between the sheets, you mean, or in general?"

"In general will do me for now."

"Well, it's complicated." She cleared her throat. "He's jealous."

"Er . . . who of?"

"Of my criminological successes, of course. And also" —she hummed and hawed— "well, of Achille."

Typical Auntie Poldi. I was stunned.

"Which Achille would that be?"

"Like another beer? A *panino*, perhaps?"

"Don't change the subject."

"And don't bully me. I'm getting on a bit and I'm still your aunt, which means I deserve some respect."

There was a brief silence. Then, with a groan, she heaved herself off the sofa, toddled into the kitchen without further comment and returned carrying a bottle of red wine, which she plonked down on the table in front of me.

"Thanks, but no." I made a dismissive gesture.

"It's to look at, not to drink. Don't you notice anything?"

I scrutinised the bottle. Labelled *Polifemo,* it was a Nerello Mascalese from Etna produced by a vineyard named Avola. Neither name meant anything to me, but I'm no wine expert. At a loss, I rotated the bottle in both hands. The label depicted a kind of map of the vineyard; the typography was probably meant to convey a classical impression but looked as if it had been doodled, just before the lunchtime break, by a student intern at a provincial advertising agency.

"Pretty label."

"It is, isn't it?" Poldi beamed. "Vito said so too. Well, then I met Achille, and everything became a bit complicated."

2

*Tells of love at a mature age, of discontinued lines
and chest hair, of ashes and wine, of dreamy places,
the taste of murder weapons, and Montana and his
current case. Poldi gets a brush-off and loses her
temper. She chances on a preliminary clue, meets
two old acquaintances and loses her temper again.
She is rescued, goes up in flames and—no, doesn't
lose her temper, just tells a white lie for which she
pays soon afterwards.*

Until a few weeks earlier, Vito Montana had been morosely and rather bitterly looking forward to the end
of his career as the Polizia di Stato's chief inspector in
charge of homicide cases in Acireale. Morosely because
that was in the nature of the man, and bitterly because a
Roman senator whose toes the cussed commissario had
trodden on in the course of a murder inquiry had engineered
his transfer from Milan to Sicily in order to silence him—
and although Vito Montana was a native of Giarre, he detested Sicily with the fervour of a grand inquisitor. Then he
made the acquaintance of my Auntie Poldi, and, in a curiously touching way, the two of them seemed destined for
each other. Two slightly scratched and dented leftovers from

the jumble sale of life, they had been put on sale once more by a wanton fate. Roll up, roll up, last chance to buy! On the one hand, Commissario Montana of the crumpled suits, a stocky but—by Poldi's standards—well-built man in his late fifties, with a greying beard, green eyes and a permanent frown. A dogged detective by trade and—according to my Auntie Poldi—a sexual force of nature. And there beside him—*ecco là!*—my aunt herself. Only a little older, she was a glamorous, baroque apparition in her wig and Nefertiti make-up, and, booze and depression notwithstanding, still afire with joie de vivre and wholesome Bavarian passion. They made a dramatic, uneasy couple for whom "complicated" wasn't the word. I likened them to two charged elementary particles hurled at one another at the speed of light by fate's cyclic accelerator. In other words, they resembled my great-grandfather Barnaba and his unbearably beautiful Eleonora in the novel I'd made so little progress with in recent weeks. That had to change, and fast.

At all events, Montana's response to Poldi's investigation of the Lady case was a trifle irritable.

"Of course it's awful about poor little Lady, but, *Madonna*, dogs get poisoned every day in this country. Farmers have been putting out poisoned bait to keep strays off their land since the time of the Caesars. We aren't as sentimental about animals as you are."

They were lying together in Poldi's bed in her darkened bedroom. Friday night. The air conditioning was scooping out fug and injecting cool air. Etna growled in the distance, palm trees rustled under a shower of ash, and somewhere across the street a quiz show presenter's hysterical voice rang out, mingled with canned laughter and applause, as if a studio audience were following and commenting on every erotic climax, every sigh, every whispered word that was uttered in No. 29 Via Baronessa.

Poldi stopped winding Montana's chest hair round her finger, pulled the bedclothes over her bosom and sat up. "What exactly are you implying, Vito?"

Montana said nothing, just rolled over and, with great deliberation, lit a cigarette.

Feeling exhausted and mellow after her eruptions of passion and the confluence of two volcanic streams of mature libido, Poldi eyed Montana's hirsute back and wondered if it wouldn't be better to squelch this conversation, which seemed to be taking an unwelcome turn, by applying some gentle massage. However, she was not only curious but spoiling for a fight.

"Well?"

"You're sticking your neck out again," Montana growled. "You're only asking for a heap of trouble."

"You mean you don't see the bigger picture? The conspiracy?"

Montana dragged at his cigarette before replying. "What conspiracy? Look around you. You're popular with everyone."

Poldi looked at him searchingly. "Everyone?"

"I mean, why not enjoy it? You solved a murder. With my help, of course. That always gives one a kick, I know, but then one falls into a trough."

"A trough? What on earth are you talking about, Vito?"

"Don't get me wrong, Poldi, I know the feeling. One wants to keep going, one wants the next kick right away."

Contentedly, Poldi turned over on her back. "Maybe I'll

set up a little detective agency. Everyone keeps sounding me out about it. Agenzia Investigativa Oberreiter, how does that sound?"

Montana stubbed out the cigarette he'd only just lit in Poldi's heavy glass ashtray, looking as if something had spoiled the taste of tobacco, and gazed at her. "There won't be another murder case, Poldi. There won't be another case of any kind. Face facts. You aren't the police and you know it, so your subconscious is trying to fabricate a murder."

"Oh, is that what it's doing?"

"And you'd better drop it."

"So you think I've lost touch with reality? That I'm cracked? That I scent conspiracies everywhere?"

Montana clicked his tongue and gave a slight jerk of the head, the elemental Sicilian equivalent of an offhand negative or a less offhand "Nonsense, that's not what I meant." He reached for her under the bedclothes. "You're a person with a lot of imagination, Poldi, that's all."

He was right, but he definitely hadn't struck the right note.

Poldi thrust aside that nice, warm, beloved hand and sat up straight in bed, giving vent to a barrage of Bairisch.

"Couldn't you please speak Italian, Poldi? I don't understand why you're being so touchy."

With an indignant snort, Poldi quit her satin-draped pleasure island. Naked and perspiring, sans make-up and wig but utterly unashamed, or so I imagine, she confronted him like a living Stone Age Venus of Willendorf.

"I'm not being touchy, I just think you should leave."

A positively Hanseatic display of serene self-control.

"Oh, come on, Poldi, you know what I—"

Before he could complete the sentence, his shirt and suit came flying through the air towards him.

"Right now, what's more. You may take that tone with that Alessia woman of yours, but not with me."

Although rather mean of Poldi, this was emotionally quite understandable. Whether calm or stormy, every relationship, even the longest and most enlightened, brings with it a sediment composed of unspoken expectations, minor wounds, petty fears and unanswered questions. All is well as long as the flow remains unobstructed, but if the sediment forms a sandbank, it divides the river, creates dangerous eddies and, if worse comes to worst, causes a total blockage. Alessia was the sandbank in the river of Poldi's love for Vito Montana. She was Montana's girlfriend. Twenty-five years younger, Alessia was beautiful and clever and temperamental and a hundred other things Poldi worried about whenever she was once more contending on her own with depression and the urge to get blind drunk. Alessia was Montana's convenient emergency exit, but Poldi remained tolerant. I often wondered why she didn't simply go mad with jealousy.

Although quick to take offence, being a Sicilian, Montana sportingly accepted his dismissal. Text messages—irate, conciliatory, wounded, mollifying, irritated, obscene, affectionate—surged back and forth a little later and over the next few days like tides lapping the opposite shores of a stormy ocean, and on the following Friday the couple wound up back in the sack like two teenagers.

Things could have gone on like this forever, if . . . yes, if life were not a state of constant flux and we weren't powerless against it. Sooner or later every spring loses its resilience and goes limp; sooner or later the air escapes from every balloon and someone needs to blow it up again; sooner or later the wheel of fortune turns, and Montana and Poldi were not exempt from this process. But I'm getting ahead of myself.

So Montana and Poldi fell on each other like animals when the following Friday came. Everything went smoothly. The conflagration of lust was followed by a short breather. Montana smoked a cigarette, Poldi fed him with morsels of mortadella. They shared a beer, and she pumped him about his current case. It was only natural, given that Poldi was making no progress with the Lady case, that she should want at least to dip her finger in the honeypot of an ongoing murder inquiry, if only for her inner equilibrium's sake. And Montana, being no fool either, appreciated this. Besides, he was happy to be able to circumnavigate certain sandbanks—certain awkward questions affecting their relationship—in this way.

"I'm not really allowed to talk about it."

Poldi nodded gravely. "Of course not." She gave him a look. "*Madonna*, come off it. Tell me!"

A female district attorney from Catania had been found dead in her second home in Acireale. Hit on the head from behind with a full bottle of wine. Poldi was instantly galvanised. Wine and murder—right up her street.

"Got any photos?"

Montana hesitated. "It isn't a pretty sight."

"Look at me, Vito. Do I look as if anything could upset me now?"

He sighed. "Not here. Not in bed."

Poldi liked it that Montana respected the dead and wasn't a cynic, even though he liked to act the part.

They quickly pulled on some clothes. Montana spread out crime scene photos on the kitchen table and fetched himself a beer. Poldi braced herself for a moment, then looked.

The first photo of the crime scene showed the district attorney's body lying in a pool of congealed blood and red wine and littered with shattered glass. Her name was Elisa Puglisi, unmarried. No husband, no ex-husband, no children. Both parents already dead. A forty-something spinster who had obviously put her career before all else. The cleaning woman hadn't found her until the day after she was murdered.

"But she was quite a dish!" Poldi said when Montana showed her a photo of Elisa from happier days.

A slim woman with a pale, thin face, she was looking straight at the camera, and everything about her—the slightly aggressive posture, the blue trouser suit, the way she held her briefcase, the compressed lips—conveyed determination and disapproval. Everything, that is, except the wealth of dark, untamed curls that overflowed Elisa Puglisi's shoulders.

Poldi turned the photo this way and that beneath the kitchen's overhead light as if this would enable her to see through Elisa's mask and gain some idea of her backstory wound.

"Because mark my words," she told me once, "a detective must always work out what the murder victim is trying to tell them. You, of course, will object that the dead can't talk, but you'd be wrong, they can say a great deal. You just have to ask them the right questions. Like, 'What made you a murder victim?'"

"Are you telling me that, fundamentally, murder victims are always guilty of their own deaths?"

"Nonsense, it's always the murderer who's guilty, but a lot of things may have happened before a murder takes place. What did the victim say or do or fail to do that caused someone to go and kill them? The backstory, know what I mean? You always have to know that."

But the severe-looking woman in the photo did not divulge her secret. There were no witnesses—no one had heard or seen a thing. The perpetrator had continued to batter Elisa Puglisi from behind until the bottle broke, but by then she was dead.

"Wine bottles are robust, you know," Poldi told me in a professional tone. "It's not like in the movies, where they smash at once and the cowboy shakes his head and all's well. Forget that. In real life, the second blow usually desecrates a corpse."

Forensics had discovered neither fingerprints nor traces of DNA on the bottle, and no clues were present on the body or in the apartment.

"A pro," Montana surmised.

Poldi knitted her brow and reshuffled the crime scene photos on the table. "What professional killer kills with a wine bottle?"

"Perhaps it was *meant* to look like a personal matter."

Poldi was unconvinced, especially as she sensed Montana's own doubts.

"She'd had sex a few hours prior to death," he said.

"Who with?"

"We're working on that."

Poldi thought for a moment. "A district attorney, eh? They easily make enemies. Have you examined her cases?"

"We're doing so."

"Can't you be a bit more specific?"

Montana sighed. "I shouldn't tell you this, Poldi."

She looked at him. "But?"

He drained his beer before replying. "Elisa Puglisi headed the DDA of Catania Province."

"The what?"

"The Direzione Distrettuale Antimafia, the anti-Mafia public prosecution department."

"There you are, then!" Poldi said delightedly. "The whole thing's as clear as daylight."

"Nothing's clear until it's clarified," Montana growled. "We're pursuing a number of lines of inquiry, but it's quite possible that I'll soon have the case taken out of my hands by some smart lads from the Direzione Investigativa Antimafia in Rome."

"What a bummer!"

"You can say that again."

"You need my help, Vito."

"Forget it, Poldi."

"I mean, I could—"

"I said forget it!"

He tried to take the photos back, but Poldi wasn't finished yet. Something about them had puzzled her. Not just the look of the corpse, but a detail that had briefly caught her eye without really registering. She carefully examined one photo after another.

Until she lighted on it.

She almost uttered an exclamation, but she had herself under control. She turned the photo ninety degrees and showed it to Montana. "How about that?"

"What do you mean?"

"The remains of the wine bottle. Have you looked at them closely?"

Montana picked up the photo and scrutinised it. "An Etna *rosso*," he said with a shrug. "Nice label. What's so special about it?"

Poldi wondered for a moment whether to tell him, but she hadn't cared for his previous tone at all. "Oh, forget it," she said airily. "A very pretty label, I agree, and such an original idea to use a map of the vineyard. Do you know the Avola vineyard?"

Montana eyed her suspiciously. "What makes you ask, Poldi?"

But Poldi had already stood up. Letting her silk kimono slither to the floor, she went back into the bedroom. "That's enough detective work, Vito. *Namaste*, life beckons!"

"Will you at least tell me?" I asked when she recounted the episode to me later.

"You mean you still haven't caught on?" she cried in amazement. "Why, it's as plain as the nose on your face."

"Then please spell it out for the benefit of the unenlightened."

Poldi disappeared into the bedroom and returned with a photo, which she propped against the wine bottle. It displayed a topographical map that looked vaguely familiar to me. And then I finally caught on.

The label on the wine bottle displayed the same map that Russo and Patanè, who was now under arrest, had been discussing when Poldi was keeping tabs on them in the Valentino case.

"Good for you, Poldi," I whispered, highly impressed.

"It's not a bad wine, that Polifemo," Poldi said triumphantly. "A genuine Etna *rosso*. Robust, dark and elegant, with good length and oomph, a spectacular finish and soft, mysterious almond notes. Liquid commissario, so to speak. Ninety-four Parker points—you don't get that sort of stuff in a supermarket. A disgrace, using such a noble wine for such a nefarious purpose. Like to try a drop?"

"No thanks," I said. "I don't fancy drinking from a murder weapon."

"Well, now you can see how obvious the connection was, can't you? District attorney—Mafia—Russo—murder."

"But don't you think that's a bit . . . I mean, well, farfetched?"

"Lack of imagination is the little sister of timidity. You'll never get anywhere with your novel like that."

It's true, my Auntie Poldi really did have my best interests at heart.

"But what's the connection with this man Achille and Montana's jealousy?"

Poldi tapped the wine label.

"Why, Achille is the owner of the vineyard."

Like so many things in Sicily, the story of winemaking there is one of superb resources, ignorance, greed, mediocrity, neglect, destruction, deliberation, a fresh start and triumph. No one knows that better than my Uncle Martino, because he knows everything about Sicily and fills in any gaps with figments of his imagination. Like everything in Sicily, wine is very ancient, and grown in the furrows of conquest and occupation. According to my Uncle Martino, the Phoenicians brought the first grape varieties to Sicily, but quality wines were not produced there until the end of the nineteenth century. Well, quality . . . Soulless, mass-produced wine for the English market quickly degenerated into the production of cheap Marsala. Sweet enough to make your teeth itch, it was sometimes spiked with almond syrup. You can still get this stuff in souvenir shops, and you're welcome to it. The general ignorance and lousy quality are surprising when one considers the importance attached to good food in Sicily, with its paradisal abundance of foodstuffs and ingredients. But Sicilians drink half a glass of wine at most with their meals, and even Uncle Martino, who would never eat any food but his wife Teresa's, makes do with sour plonk bought in a fifty-litre carboy from a farmer in Randazzo. Yet the conditions for wine-growing in Sicily are ideal, especially on the old terraces on Etna between five hundred and a thousand metres up. The volcanic soil is rich in copper, phosphorus and magnesium, and the ancient drystone walls of lava tuff enclose vines hundreds of years old: Nerello Mascalese, Nerello Cappuccio, Carricante and Catarratto. What with extreme variations in temperature, arduous working conditions, modest profits and occasional volcanic eruptions, local wine growers don't have an easy life, so it may not be surprising that no one took any trouble with Etna wine for a long time. Not good enough for export, little domestic demand—producing it ceased to pay. Financial crises, bankruptcies, wailing and gnashing of teeth, fatalism, forced sales—the old story.

Then, only thirty years ago, came deliberation and a fresh start. Back to basics, so to speak. Viticulturists' associations gambled once more on native grape varieties, which were grown and tended as bushes, and on quality instead of quantity. Or—who would have thought it?—on EU subsidies. It was a success story, because Sicilian wine has since forced its way into the world's premier league and has long ceased to be an insider's tip. Cherries, mulberries, cloves, cinnamon, orange peel, rosemary, thyme, lavender, woodsmoke, stone, caramel, almonds—a sip of Nerella Mascalese can be a trip to the heart of Sicily, for, like its cuisine, Sicily's wine is a sensual, baroque celebration, a superabundance of aromas in a single glass.

"It's a Sicilian wine," Poldi told me before I sampled my first glass of Polifemo, "so don't be surprised if it's a bit awkward and unforthcoming at first. It'll come through all right once you've got to know each other, you can depend on that. It's overflowing with warmth and life, extravagantly generous, loud and explosive and soft and gentle, know what I mean? And then, bingo, it's overcome with melancholy once more. It retreats into its volcanic cave and whispers ancient secrets in your ear. This wine is a Cyclops, I tell you. A force of nature—the sort of man every woman dreams of. So drink up and learn."

No wonder Poldi itched to meet the creator of such a wine.

Achille Avola had inherited the vineyard above Trecastagni from his father. The Avola family had been growing wine up on the slopes of Etna for three generations. It was pretty mediocre plonk until the nineties, when the new ethos and

EU money reached the Avolas, and Achille and his wine achieved their full potential.

Poldi found it child's play to locate the little vineyard. Two clicks of the mouse, a phone call to Uncle Martino, a glance at the road map and *ecco pronto!* Dressed to go with her surroundings, in a red-white-and-green dirndl outfit with plenty of cleavage and a silk headscarf adorned with grapes, she boarded her Vespa one Saturday afternoon and puttered up to Trecastagni.

Whenever I think of Trecastagni I'm reminded of my father, a DIY junkie who loved to screw wooden panelling into every ceiling in sight. When he started thinking aloud about his retirement, he hit on the daft idea of buying a ruin in Trecastagni and single-handedly turning it into an architectural jewel with the aid of cordless screwdrivers, hammer drills, bricklayer's trowels, handyman's enthusiasm and my unskilled but no less energetic assistance.

"All we need is the foundations," I recall him saying. "We'll do the whole thing ourselves. We'll hire a van and fill it with all the things you can get in a proper German DIY store, because they're unobtainable in Sicily, and then we'll drive down there. And in four or five years we'll have ourselves a regular jewel of a house. A jewel, I tell you." Somehow, I was always put off Trecastagni by the idea of spending five years reanimating the corpse of a house there. Wrongly so, because I would now own a home of my own in Sicily and I'd have got to know my father better.

Trecastagni is an idyllic place midway between earth and sky. Airily deposited by a friendly god among some old secondary craters on the east side of Etna, it is one of the twenty or so small towns that ring the volcano like a carelessly strung necklace, largely unspoiled and enjoying mild summers and dank winters. Trecastagni is a place where one gazes out over the distant sea as if it were a cheque to a better future one would never cash. Where Sant'Alfio is revered. Where senior citizens can still chill out in the piazza with their cronies, bemoaning moral decline and their own virility. Where the traffic cops are mustachioed, the girls approachable and mobile phone connections fickle. Where vines flourish, as do the church, mulberries, figs, peaches and all manner of other things. Where gorse has patiently crumbled the volcanic soil for centuries. Where Etna's principal peak looms over the town like a cathedral. Where no Asian tiger mosquitoes whine and no murders occur.

That, at any rate, was Poldi's initial impression when she dismounted from her Vespa in the piazza, relishing the glances of the traffic cop, and treated herself to a coffee in the nearest bar. One of the local senior citizens told her the way to the Avola vineyard, and less than ten minutes later she had pulled up outside a big grey wrought-iron gate. There wasn't much to be seen in any direction. Lava stone walls flanked the road, with cypresses visible beyond them and, farther away, serried rows of vines climbing up the slope to a small secondary crater. Through the iron gate Poldi could make out some vehicles parked beneath the cypress trees, among them a minibus bearing the name of an Acireale travel agent and an old pickup truck adorned with the *Vivi Avola* logo. No sign of life.

Poldi revved her two-stroke engine and sounded the horn. Once. Twice. *Beep! Beeeep!*

"If Italian engineers have understood anything," she told me once, "it's the significance and construction of the horn.

Because the horn is the voice and the heart and soul of any vehicle. The vehicle wants to cut a good figure, wants to sound good without being intrusive or making anyone look foolish. A German horn, by contrast, is always a declaration of war—it suggests that invading troops are already massing on the frontier, so to speak. An Italian horn sounds like a friendly clearing of the throat, a gentle '*Permesso?*' or 'Oh, signore, would you mind waiting? I'm afraid I have the right of way, *grazie, molto gentile.*' With an Italian horn you can compliment a traffic cop on his beautiful eyes. You can even—don't laugh!—make a proposal of marriage with an Italian horn. And the loveliest horn in the world is still the Vespa's, which defies comparison. If Romeo had had a Vespa, he'd be bound to have hooted something to Juliet below her balcony, and it wouldn't have been any less romantic."

Beep-beep! Poldi's Vespa cleared its throat and uttered a hoarse "*Permesso?*" But no one answered, no one appeared. So she climbed off and experimentally rattled the gate, and lo, it was open. Even my Auntie Poldi knows that an unlocked gate isn't an invitation to trespass on private property—in fact, in Texas you can be shot with impunity for doing just that. In the first place, however, Poldi told herself that this wasn't Texas. Second, she was engaged in a murder inquiry and thus semi-authorised. Third, she was already there, and fourth, she was wearing a dirndl, which really wasn't the attire of a burglar or car thief.

It was hotter now that she was stationary, so she removed her headscarf, mopped her brow and thought for a moment. Then, having resolutely pushed the gate open, she got out her mobile phone, closely examined the interior of each of the parked vehicles and photographed their licence plates. She took a particular interest in the white Avola pickup truck. It contained some full wine cartons bearing the same design as the label, together with plastic tubes, tools and an untidy stack of official-looking documents and bank statements. The red plastic baskets in the back were smeared with drying wine must and gave off a sourish smell. Poldi took photos of everything, just in case.

"Because," she pontificated when telling me about her trip to the vineyard, "the same rule applies to love and criminology alike: a bird in the hand is worth two in the bush. That's particularly true of the preliminary attack."

"The preliminary attack?"

"That's what we call the initial investigation when you visit a fresh crime scene and secure any clues. Everything matters, you see. The smallest thing can be crucially important."

"Why did you think of it as a crime scene?" I demanded. "I mean, it wasn't one at that stage."

"I was speaking metaphorically," she back-pedalled. "However, I did grasp that I was hot on the trail of something, and that's when I can't help myself. The hunting instinct takes over when I'm in the zone."

Which was why she failed to see the dogs. All she heard was a kind of hoarse rattle behind her, and by the time she had spun round they were already upon her: a pair of dark brown, pure-bred German shepherds. With genetic programming like theirs, they should have torn my aunt limb from limb, but curiously enough they didn't. They merely menaced her, baring every fang and barking fit to burst.

Poldi screamed and staggered back against the pickup,

but her wig, in obedience to the laws of inertia, mass and momentum conservation, described a graceful arc over the dogs' heads and landed in the dirt.

The German shepherds rose on their hind legs and pinned Poldi against the truck like two bad-tempered cops. She smelt the pet food on their foul breath, stared in horror at their chops and tartar-encrusted teeth, and suddenly grasped that she was dealing with two old acquaintances. That broke the spell.

"GERROFFMEYOUFILTHYBRUTES!"

There followed some choice items from her thesaurus of Bavarian swear words. Poldi hurled them at the dogs with fervour and, miraculously, they backed off, merely uttering a few dutiful *woof*s.

Beside herself with fury, Poldi lashed out at them with each foot in turn. "Piss off, you brutes! Get lost! Hop it or I'll skin you alive!"

Hans and Franz knuckled under.

Bending down, Poldi swiftly retrieved her wig and re-placed her headscarf with equal speed. Just in time, it must be said, because approaching from the direction of the vine-yard was a man in jeans and a lumberjack shirt with the sleeves rolled up. A tall, slim figure in his mid-fifties, he had a full head of hair, albeit grey, and bushy eyebrows. Poldi registered every last detail, even at long range.

"The thing is, I've got an autofocus where men are concerned," she explained to me with a sigh. "I clock them with all my senses, my whole body, know what I mean? Even Bob said that was true."

She inserted a brief pause for me to ask which of her celeb friends she meant this time, but I didn't indulge her.

"Well," she went on eventually, frowning, "I got the whole picture in an instant. Those big hands . . . that splendid Adam's apple—like a second nose or a second . . . Oh well, never mind, you know what I mean. That five o'clock shadow, which gives you some idea how raw your face will look the next morning. Those full lips—well, need I say more? Yes, and those mournful eyes, which cry out for consolation. And the weather-beaten, typically Sicilian olive-wood complexion of a smoker with good genes. I couldn't help visualising him in a police uniform."

In short, the man who came towards her and called off the dogs looked the way Poldi sometimes imagined my Uncle Peppe would have looked at that age. No wonder she caught fire—in spite of Hans and Franz, who were still holding her at bay.

"Everything all right, signora?"

Poldi tweaked her wig straight. "No. Does it look like it?"

The man came closer. Poldi's knees became weaker and the temperature rose with every step he took, though this might have been the effect of post-traumatic stress. The man shooed away the dogs, which promptly trotted off in high dudgeon.

"Those aren't your dogs, are they?"

"No, but I own this property. What are you doing here?"

"The gate was open."

The man gave her a searching look. "You aren't from around here, signora, are you?"

"I'm from Munich."

"So in Germany an unlocked gate is an invitation to trespass on private property?"

His shirt was unbuttoned far enough for Poldi to see the

mat of grey hair on his chest, and although he was almost anorexically slim, his arms looked powerful. His forearms especially, and there were few male attributes Poldi liked better than muscular forearms. His awkward but self-assured movements, the way he cocked his head a little when speaking, the crow's-feet around his eyes—they were all such painful reminders of Peppe that Poldi almost felt sick.

"I called out," she said defensively, quite faint with shock and desire. "I'm . . . I'm a journalist."

"Never at a loss for a lie, even in an emergency," I commented when she described the scene to me later on.

"Well, why not? I was there undercover."

"But . . . I mean, you might have known it would blow up in your face in two minutes flat."

"I'm more the spontaneous type, unlike you."

"I get it. You Epimetheus, I Prometheus."

"What do you mean?"

"You Tarzan, me Jane."

"Are you making fun of me?"

"Never!"

"Pity, and I thought there was some hope for you. May I go on now?"

"*Forza* Poldi!"

"I'm from *Wine and Women*," Poldi swiftly improvised. "We're a new wine magazine for women, and I'm doing a series on Sicilian wines and wine growers."

This seemed to amuse the grey-haired man.

"Do they have to be photographed with their clothes off?"

"Just your shirt off will do," Poldi blurted out. "I

mean . . . no, of course not." She extended her hand. "Isolde Oberreiter. Please call me Poldi."

She felt transfixed as the man clasped her hand and looked deep into her eyes. "Achille Avola. Would you like to see our winery?"

"I don't want to detain you."

"Not at all."

He led her round the slope between rows of harvested vines. The two dogs went on ahead to report.

"You're in luck," said Avola. "Today is the last day of the grape harvest."

"Really? How will the vintage be?"

"We're optimistic. Spring was too wet, but summer didn't let us down." He took a packet of cigarettes from his shirt pocket, tapped one out and proffered the packet to Poldi.

The same brand, the same instinctively casual gestures as Peppe. His hands were stained with grape juice.

"Do you?"

She nodded. They paused to smoke, all alone in the midst of the vines, as if the rest of the world had disappeared and they alone existed. A wonderful idea, Poldi thought. She watched Avola smoking. A gentle breeze blew the smoke from his lips. He pointed up the slope.

"We're standing in an ancient crater—the geologists estimate it's twenty thousand years old. Wine was made here back in the Greeks' day. These are Carricante grapes, by the way."

Poldi remained silent—another rarity. To avoid continuing to stare at Avola, she averted her head a little and noticed that they were not alone after all. A muscular, middle-aged man in a baseball cap was slowly approaching them through the vines. He was holding a metal divining rod out in front of him and looked entirely self-absorbed. Poldi suddenly felt cold.

"What's he up to?"

Avola heeled his cigarette butt into the ground. "I don't have the least idea. Someone must have brought him."

When the dowser got to them, he looked up and beamed. Or rather, bared his teeth. It was a smile that didn't reach his eyes.

"Oh, hi, how ya doin'?"

An American, Poldi surmised, judging by his accent, his pallid complexion and his physiognomy, which incorporated a snub nose and a cleft chin. An athletic type in jeans, polo shirt and New York Yankees baseball cap. Possibly an ex-marine. Mid-forties, she estimated. He would have looked utterly unremarkable but for the spiral tattoo on his left forearm.

He was about to walk on when Poldi laid a hand on his arm. "What on earth are you up to?"

He turned and glanced at her for a moment, as if satisfying himself that she could cope with his answer. "I'm looking for positive energies. I travel the world in search of them. My name is Sean, Sean Torso, from Newton, Iowa." He shook hands with Poldi and Avola, in that order.

Poldi could now identify his tattoo. It was a triskelion composed of three linked spirals. An ancient Celtic symbol, it stood for the Trinity and was also the emblem of Sicily.

"Well," she asked, "have you found any?"

"You bet! This whole area is a positive-energy hot spot. I'm stunned!"

Poldi didn't believe a word the man said. "So what are you going to do with all this lovely positive energy? Bottle it and sell it to Coca-Cola?"

The American's laugh was more of a bark.

"Oh no, I'm compiling a global positive-energy map, one that shows all the positive telluric currents that flow around the earth like a great network. Humanity's last great mystery."

Avola straightened up. "Then we won't detain you any longer, Signor . . ."

"Torso, but call me Sean." He tapped his baseball cap in salute and concentrated once more on his dowsing rod.

Poldi stared after him the way she might have stared after a car that had narrowly missed her. And, like an echo of that unpleasant sensation, the old crown on her top-left canine started throbbing again.

Avola's touch recalled her to the present. It was only the gentlest of contacts with her back, but it instantly set her ablaze, and the chill that had overcome her in the dowser's presence was dispelled in a flash. When Avola was guiding her round a treacherous dip in the ground, she even got the opportunity to stumble a little and bump into him as if by accident—an old trick.

The winery was a disappointment to her, however. The facilities for producing wine, the presses and steel tanks, were housed not in a picturesque vaulted cellar but in a big, three-sided shed with a concrete floor and a corrugated-iron roof. Grape pickers were wheeling in stacks of crates filled with white grapes, to be stripped by a de-stemming machine and then pressed. The stalks flew out into a basket at one end of the machine while, at the other, the must—a foaming mush composed of grape pulp, pips, skins and juice—went gurgling through a tube into a steel vat.

"The must is left to rest for a few hours, then put through the wine press—nice and carefully, so as not to squash the pips."

"Because of the bitterness."

"Ah, as if I needed to tell you that. You know the ropes, of course."

Poldi spotted some pink grapes among the white. "Do they go in too?"

"Try one."

Her eyes widened in surprise when she did so. "It tastes like a strawberry! It's absolutely strawberry-flavoured!"

"That's why it's called a *fragolina*. Under EU rules we aren't allowed to grow them as a separate variety. That's why we blend them with the Carricante. The result is truly wonderful."

Poldi believed him at once. She now believed everything Avola said.

"The thing is," she confided to me later as we sat on the sofa, "I realised at that moment—now don't laugh—that the man was an alchemist. An alchemist of sensuality, and I know a thing or two about sensuality."

Avola halted the de-stemming machine and checked the condition of the must. He issued instructions, hauled in fresh crates of grapes and moved the full steel containers into the shade with a forklift truck. He looked satisfied when he rejoined Poldi, who had spent the entire time admiring him from a distance.

"What would you say to a glass of wine and a tasty *salsiccia*, Signora Poldi?"

He led the way up the mountainside to an old cottage built of volcanic rock, similar to Femminamorta but much smaller.

"This is where I stay during the grape harvest."

"How romantic."

"Well, it's more to do with caution than romance," he said. "Two years ago the barrels containing my entire vintage were stolen. Typical Sicily, and you're welcome to write that."

When they reached the house, Poldi saw there was a long table outside, crowded with people seated together over wine and grilled sausages. She also saw that her recent lie was going to present her with a minor problem.

For at one end of the table, seated among Avola's grape pickers, she immediately spotted Doris and the German *deliziosi*. And at the other end, flanked by Hans and Franz, sat Italo Russo. He stiffened in surprise when he caught sight of my Auntie Poldi, and she could have sworn that he grinned.

3

*Tells of Cyclopes and writer's block. Poldi gives
her nephew a hard time again. She also makes the
acquaintance of a neurotic rebel and a famous
fortune-teller who refrains from telling her something disturbing. She has to continue a wine tasting
on her own, which results in (a) a painful awaken-
ing, (b) a hangover, and (c) a dawn encounter she
would have done better to avoid.*

Poldi told me all this on my very first night back in Torre
Archirafi. It was late by the time she yawned and rose
from the sofa with a groan.

"Can that really be the time already? Well, I'm off to bed.
No, don't get up, stay there and finish off the bottle. I've got
another."

Ignoring my remonstrances — I urged her to continue her
story, not break off at that particular point — she simply
left me sitting there and retired to her bedroom with en suite
bathroom. I heard the sound of water running, heard her
gargle and the hum of an electric toothbrush, followed soon
afterwards by her snores.

I, on the other hand, was wide awake. Or reasonably so,
because the Polifemo was having an effect. Anyway, I was

too wide awake to sleep, so I went upstairs to my den in the attic and tried to tire myself a little by revising my novel—a pretty reliable method. I don't know how it is with other authors, but whenever I open my laptop and look at my mess of a draft, I'm overcome with leaden inertia, paralysing fatigue and a sort of ominous malaise. It's as if I've just opened Pandora's box and am already experiencing the preliminary symptoms of the plague. It's like a general anaesthetic: you're still wondering what's happening when you wake up and your appendix is out. Except that your novel is just as unfinished and messy as it ever was. Nineteenth-century novelists never suffered from writer's block. Take Balzac, for example. He would complete a draft with a final full stop and embark on another novel right away. I, on the other hand, am a walking writer's block, a child of the twenty-first century.

"That's because your generation always had their bottoms blow-dried after their nappies were changed," Poldi told me once. "And because everything was always handed you on a plate. Like another piece of focaccia?"

I'd written nothing since my last visit to Sicily. Not a word, so I was doubly surprised when, in the middle of the night and with a second glass of Cyclopean wine inside me, the adjectives came pouring out of me.

Sicily 1919. In Chapter One my great-grandfather Barnaba had been trampled on by a white donkey. This was, in a sense, his call of the wild, his encounter with nature in the raw. Frantic with rage and hubris, Barnaba pursued the donkey and would have shot it but for a volcanic eruption and a fit of compassion. He had then lost his heart, first to the preternaturally beautiful Cyclops Ilaria, and thereafter to gentle, maidenly Eleonora. He had solved a murder, made a pact with the Devil, hurled his shotgun into the maw of Etna, realised that he had to emigrate to Munich, and much else besides. Great cinema. Myth, history, passion, action, sex, fantasy, poetry, hard facts—they were all there. I was heading straight for international stardom, or almost. Now for Chapter Two. I started writing like a man possessed. I was an adjective machine.

I had a vivid mental picture of Barnaba: so terribly young and poverty-stricken that even little David Copperfield would have pitied him, but—of course—immensely handsome and suntanned and as determined as a bull terrier. He eats a bowl of spaghetti every morning before sunrise, then rows his ramshackle dinghy across the Gulf of Catania to work for a pittance for the hard-hearted and avaricious landowner Grasso, father of the luckless Eleonora. Stoically grinding his teeth, Barnaba endures his master's bullying and humiliation for the sake of Eleonora, who brings him a pitcher of water at midday, when the couple make passionate love in the shade of orange, lemon and mandarin trees. It is a feast of the senses of which they partake in constant fear of being flushed out and torn to pieces by Grasso's German shepherds. To avoid interrupting my flow unnecessarily, I jotted down these love scenes in note form only, intending to develop their imagery in an opulent manner. At nightfall I made Barnaba row back across the bay to Catania and his straw-filled mattress in the house of Signora Spadaro, a widow and fortune-teller who had once been reluctant to take him in as an infant. It should be explained that he had lost his mother in childbirth and been rejected by his father, who cruelly blamed the little boy for his wife's death. Barnaba rightly senses that his origins are burdened with some dark secret. At this point I made another note, because I hadn't the faintest idea what that secret could be. Never mind, I would work it out, preferably with the aid of a birthmark or something. At all events, Signora Spadaro serves Barnaba a meagre supper of olives and wild fennel. She is consumed with desire for him, having seen him grow up into an athletic young man, and has only one thing in mind. When he steadfastly rejects her, she throws him out. First, though, she lays out the cards, which predict a great future for him (marginal note). Signora Spadaro does not, however, tell him this but threatens him with dire misfortune. This leaves Barnaba cold, because after the incident on Etna he's determined to emigrate to far-off Germany and seek his fortune there. No sooner said than done. Barnaba bids Eleonora a tearful farewell (marginal note) and, barefoot and wearing his only shirt and only pair of trousers, sets off on the long and dangerous journey over the Alps with nothing in his hand but half of an ancient talisman presented to him by the Cyclops Ilaria in memory of their night of love. This talisman is associated with a mysterious prophecy (marginal note plus question mark). After an adventurous crossing of the Alps, which involves magical encounters, fights with bandits, wounds, temptations and lyrical campfire scenes (various marginal notes), Barnaba at last reaches Munich, where, it has transpired en route, a distant aunt of his is living. The eccentric Pasqualina, formerly a celebrated artist and spy, sees Barnaba as the reincarnation of her late husband and welcomes him to her apartment in Westermühlstrasse. In the course of a touching scene (marginal note), she asks Barnaba what he intends to do with his life from now on, and he tells her . . .

"Well, what does he tell her?" Poldi asked me when I deposited a printout of the second chapter on the breakfast table late the next morning.

"It's what you call a cliffhanger."

"You mean you ran out of ideas." She eyed me with concern. "And you wrote all this last night?"

"Uh-huh," I said with a shrug. I stuffed a *cornetto* into my mouth and did my best to look cool in the extreme. Just don't ask her what she thinks of it, I told myself.

"Well? What do you think of it?"

Poldi laid the manuscript aside. "Are you feeling all right? You look pale. Got a temperature?"

"I'm fine, thanks. Well?"

She tapped one of my marginal notes. "What does that mean?"

"It's the way I work. First the rough structure and then—"

"What bollocks!" she interrupted. "You don't have a clue. You simply dashed it off. It's utter tosh. Is that really the best you can do?"

"Thanks for the constructive feedback."

"That's right, take offence." She angrily flung my unfortunate second chapter down on the table and rose with a grunt. "You can do plenty better than that. I'm off to the beach at Praiola. Go back to bed. Have a lie-in and then rewrite the whole thing, okay? See you this evening."

But before she left the house, she turned and said, "There was one sentence—you know, where you describe how small and lonely Barnaba feels in his rowing boat out at sea, but at the same time so at one with himself and the world. On the borderline between joie de vivre and melancholy, so to speak. I liked that."

One sentence out of a whole chapter!

Ah well, not bad for a start.

But to revert to the case.

"Donna Poldina, what a nice surprise!" Russo said when Avola was introducing all his guests in turn.

"I can't say the same," Poldi retorted, "considering the welcome I got from those canine killers of yours. And you can let go of my hand."

"What a shame," Russo said softly. He continued to hold her hand, gazing intently into her eyes. "What a lovely dress you're wearing."

Poldi would have liked to interpret the look on his face as ice-cold or lethally menacing. It did in fact convey something quite different — something that disturbed her almost as much as Achille Avola's aftershave.

"Oh," said Avola, "you've already met?"

"Briefly. On the occasion of, er . . . an interview. Signor Russo likes to set his dogs and contract killers on me sometimes."

Before Russo could explode her little white lie about journalism, Poldi swiftly retrieved her hand, took Avola's arm and got him to conduct her to a vacant place at the long table far enough away from Doris and her German *deliziosi*, who were persistently waving to her. She cast her eyes up to heaven and prayed that Doris would not come and sit down beside her.

"White or red?" All at once, Avola was so close to her that his lips almost brushed her ear.

Poldi went hot beneath her wig and headscarf. It was like the onset of a fever that would soon consume her utterly. A vampire must feel something of the kind just before sunrise, she told herself. At the same time, she was feeling far from ill. On the contrary, she felt as sexy and desirable as she had in her heyday, when she first met Peppe.

"Red," she whispered, "but only a teensy drop."

Avola poured her some wine and reached for the dish of grilled sausages. "You're drinking a Nerello Capuccio from last year. It's still a bit too young—a pubescent teenager. It needs another year. I call it Brontes. All my red wines are named after Cyclopes. The whites have nymphs' names."

"How sensual," Poldi said huskily. She sipped her young Cyclops and moved still closer to Avola. She would have liked nothing better than to screw him on the spot, but, being on duty, in a manner of speaking, she tried to gain some idea of the assembled company.

Half of those present were clearly grape pickers from the locality—cheerful, hungry Sicilian peasants with calloused hands who drank only sparingly and discussed the quality of recent vintages like wine waiters in a Michelin-starred restaurant.

The others were Avola's guests. Doris and the *deliziosi* had obviously been transported there for a wine-tasting by a young tour guide. Poldi recalled seeing the minibus with the travel agent's name on the side. Their presence was purely coincidental, therefore, and could be dismissed. Russo appeared to be a close friend of Avola's, because he clearly knew every grape picker by name, chatted jovially with everyone and presided at the head of the table as if the whole vineyard belonged to him. Poldi noticed that he seldom took his eyes off her and resolved to corner him alone somewhere after the meal, as soon as everyone dispersed to pick grapes.

A very nervous young man across the table from Poldi had embroiled the elderly grape picker beside him in a heated argument. The pair were speaking thick Sicilian dialect, so all Poldi gathered was that politics must be involved. The young man did most of the talking. He flapped his hands wildly as if plucking invisible demons out of the air or fending them off, waving them away or squashing them. His most noticeable feature was his pale linen jacket, which looked as suitable for grape-picking as a wetsuit for mountaineering.

"Italy is up the creek!" he said, turning abruptly to Poldi. He was positively incandescent, evidently because he couldn't hold his wine. "This country is just a puppet of the Mafia, a zombie. Andreotti, Craxi, D'Alema, Berlusconi and now Renzi—they've sold us to the Mafia for decades, and the EU has supplied the fuel. The fuel, know what I mean? Were you aware that Italian politicians' salaries are the highest in the world? It's a disgrace! And now this humiliating fuss about African refugees. We've been betrayed and taken for a ride by the whole of the political caste, that gang of corrupt bandits. And we won't form a government with traitors, no way! They can get stuffed, the lot of them!"

"Who's 'we'?" Poldi inquired, more out of politeness than interest.

"The movement!" declared the angry young man. "The Five Star Movement. We stand for the regeneration of Italy."

54

"Ah." Poldi now grasped his connection with the anti-party led by the comedian Beppe Grillo, which forbade its representatives to form coalition governments or participate in talk shows. After the most recent elections, the MoVimento 5 Stelle had long ceased to be purely a protest party and a cooling basin for the overwrought. The party now occupied a quarter of the seats in the Italian parliament and the Senate, and it was the same story in the regional assemblies. No one who aspired to rule Italy could ignore the Five Stars any longer. Sicily was the only place where the movement was hanging fire—for the moment.

My Auntie Poldi had had something of a soft spot for Grillo the Grumbler ever since he proclaimed 8 September 2007 to be *Vaffanculo,* or "Eff-Off," Day. This was when the Italian people were to give their government the one-finger salute—a profoundly Bavarian attitude with which Poldi could readily empathise.

"Rob the rich, arm the poor, social justice means civil war!" chanted Poldi, brandishing her left fist, in the course of telling me about the vineyard episode the following evening.

"Yes, yes," I said dismissively. I'm rather unpolitical by nature, but my Auntie Poldi was just getting into her stride.

"No more justice, no more peace, it's the fault of the police!"

"*Forza* Poldi! One more for the road."

"One? You underestimate my repertoire. I never missed a demo in the old days."

I'd asked for it.

"Words not deeds is for the birds—Power to the people —Fascist might can ne'er be right—Moderation wrecks the nation—Spare the gun and spoil the fun!—When strikes the hour, we'll come to power!"

So much for my Auntie Poldi's political complexion. No wonder her uncompromising opposition to authority endeared the Five Star Movement to her.

"The only problem is," she qualified, "even the best movements always attract utter cretins and notorious troublemakers."

And the neurotic young man seemed to be one of the latter.

"Oh, so you're German?" he said thickly. "Italian politics has sold its soul to the German fiend! Merkel is the Devil in disguise."

Poldi drew a deep breath and prepared to deliver a cogent retort, but Avola forestalled her.

"Enzo," he snapped. "The signora is a guest!"

The young man promptly dried up, seeming to crumple like a lettuce leaf anointed with too much vinegar. He didn't utter a word thereafter. It was as if he needed to ponder the reprimand like a Zen pupil digesting a paradoxical instruction from his master.

"Enzo's quite a nice young man when he's sober," Avola said apologetically. "He's also one of our party's great white hopes."

"Good for you," Poldi said drily.

She turned her attention to the most eye-catching person present, who was seated immediately opposite her.

"May I introduce Giuliana, Madame Sahara?" said Avola, following the direction of her gaze. He topped up the glass of the woman concerned, a platinum blonde who promptly knocked it back.

Poldi found it hard to guess her age. She might have been forty. Or sixty, or seventy. Or a hundred and seventy? One of those ageless beauties whose stainless steel willpower is proof against transience and the passage of time, she was slim and wore black patent leather shoes, skin-tight black stretch pants and, in spite of the heat, a black roll-neck sweater. Suspended from a chain around her neck was a silver talisman which Poldi, who knew about such things, immediately identified as a phoenix.

Poldi might have taken the woman opposite for an architect, had she not worn a whole host of silver bangles and rings on every finger. The platinum blonde in black did not appear to sweat. She looked as though all the rigours of this life, all the noise, the loquacity, the spirit of the age, the banality and the Dorises of this world, were water off a duck's back to her. To Poldi she looked genteel in the best sense, despite her careless make-up and tired eyes and the way she splayed her fingers when talking, which looked a trifle vulgar. She was also—my auntie clocked this at a glance—wearing a wig. Poldi took to her on the spot.

"Giuliana is a celebrated clairvoyant and fortune-teller from Santa Venerina. I'm sure you'll have seen her posters—they're all over the place."

Poldi had indeed seen them. She was thrilled.

"No! *You* are Madame Sahara?"

The platinum blonde raised her glass. "Please call me Giuliana."

Poldi couldn't believe it. Madame Sahara . . . The name

seemed suddenly to hang in the air like the sweetish smoke of some forbidden resin. Madame Sahara . . . Even the lizards in the cracks in the walls whispered her name. Everyone was familiar with the posters in vivid cherry pink and dandelion yellow that adorned so many walls, junction boxes and bus shelters, for they promised amazing things.

MADAME SAHARA

Past, Present, Future

Palmistry
Astrology
Tarot
Life Counselling
Contacts with the Other Side
White Magic

Consultations by Arrangement

No telephone number, no address. Everyone knew where Madame Sahara was to be found: a detached house in Santa Venerina overgrown with woodbine and bougainvillea, relatively remote from the main road and prying eyes. The house stood empty between October and April, when only the police and foxes patrolled it. Come the warmth of April, however, it was animated once more by voices and laughter. Borne to Santa Venerina on vernal breezes or a broomstick —who could tell?—Madame Sahara returned every spring, and summer could not be far behind.

Notorious ill-wishers were routinely informed by the police that Madame Sahara's business did not contravene the law or decency in any way, nor did it endanger the environment or public order; furthermore, it was officially authorised and regularly inspected. Thank you for your call, send us a fax, *click*.

Madame Sahara . . . All who knew her applauded her charm and affability. She paid the appropriate compliments and never forgot a name. Madame Sahara was as much a part of the Etna area as gorse and lava fields, secondary craters and wine, the scent of pine resin, summer storms and the soupy mists of autumn, potted plants and death notices, fatalism and melancholy. She was a vessel for wishes and desires. A friendly springtime ghost. A summer night's fancy.

"Do you also do regressions?" asked Poldi.

"Past, present and future, my dear."

"Well, I'm damned! I mean, how wonderful."

"Please give me your hands."

Poldi hesitated. Then her hands shot out like children who know they must obey instructions. The celebrated clairvoyant squeezed and kneaded them, flexed the fingers and checked their shape and skin texture before concentrating on the palmar creases. Poldi was becoming apprehensive.

"You're very strong-willed and dislike being hampered by trifles. You're happy to take on responsibility. You're also inquisitive." Madame Sahara looked at Poldi. "Very inquisitive."

"*Mah!*" Poldi exclaimed in Italian, implying that she couldn't help it.

"You're a very old soul."

That was no news either.

"Which is why you also enjoy your own company." Madame Sahara's fingernail traced the creases in Poldi's palm like the needle of a record player. "You should take care of your liver and your heart—those are your weak points."

Still no news.

"Many changes of location, many farewells," Giuliana went on. "The most recent one about a year ago. In a far-distant place . . . in Africa. Someone cheated on you. It broke your heart, but you've reinvented yourself. I sense a great deal of phoenix-like energy in you. You're strong. You experience powerful emotions, not always pleasant ones, but you prefer to keep them to yourself rather than burdening other people with them."

Poldi wanted to leave it at that and tried to withdraw her hands, but the clairvoyant wasn't finished with her.

"You had a difficult childhood. You were often ill, on one occasion gravely so. You're a very spiritual person with a connection to the other side. Exalted ideals, but enough of a realist to know that life has many disappointments in store."

"You don't say!"

Madame Sahara ignored this dig. "You're like a pendulum with a wide trajectory between optimism and gloom. It almost cost you your life not long ago. No . . ." she amended, gazing into Poldi's eyes, "you tried to kill yourself."

Poldi was now feeling thoroughly uneasy. Tipsy Enzo, who was seated beside Madame Sahara, had broken off his introspective musings and was now listening intently to her analysis. Poldi saw that Doris had left her place and stolen up behind her so as not to miss anything.

By now, Poldi really did want to retrieve her hands, but Giuliana still wasn't finished.

"We want to take at least a little look into the future, don't we?"

Focusing her attention once more on Poldi's palms, the clairvoyant compared the left with the right and turned pale. Poldi distinctly saw this. A little start, a momentary widening of the eyes that suggested she'd opened a door and was unexpectedly looking at a crime scene.

"What is it?" Poldi asked in alarm.

Giuliana released her hands. She was already smiling again.

"A lot of good things. There are some major tasks ahead of you. Another change of location. You'll have a difficult decision to make, but happiness awaits you thereafter."

Poldi found this a bit too airy-fairy, but it was rather unnerving when a fortune-teller turned pale with fright.

"The thing is," she told me later, "fortune-tellers, clairvoyants and charlatans all subscribe to the same code of honour: never say anything negative when you look into the future. No one pays good money for bad news, or lousy novels."

Poldi nonetheless wanted to know the nature of the bad news affecting her immediate and longer-term future, but Madame Sahara's mobile phone rang.

Instinctively, as if she'd been expecting the call, she answered it. "*Pronto?*"

The magic of the moment was over and the spell broken, dispersed by the authoritative voice of a telephone call. Another look of alarm flitted across the clairvoyant's face — Poldi clearly detected it. Possibly a kind of professional tic, she surmised. Excusing herself with a smile, Madame Sahara rose and left the table. She spoke in a low, urgent voice, gesticulating as she did so. Clearly not a pleasant conversation. Maybe a business matter, thought Poldi.

"At our age we should beware of looking into the future," Doris whispered confidentially over her shoulder in a thick German accent.

"Thanks for the tip," Poldi grunted. She rinsed out the bad taste in her mouth with a swig of wine.

"Would you like to come with us? We're going to visit another winery now."

"Enjoy yourselves."

"It wouldn't cost you anything. Evelyn's got gastric flu, so there's a vacancy."

"Thanks all the same."

Poldi once more sensed the searching and ever-disapproving expression with which the Dorises of her life had always scrutinised and then discarded her.

"Suit yourself." Looking piqued, Doris turned away and marshalled the *deliziosi* and the tour guide around her.

Madame Sahara had meanwhile ended her phone call and returned to the table. She was looking somewhat paler than before, but she gave Poldi a broad smile and handed her a business card.

"Come to see me sometime, my dear, and we'll do a regression." Still standing, the clairvoyant picked up her half-empty glass and raised it to Poldi. "To love and life!"

"*Namaste,*" murmured Poldi, mopping her brow.

Madame Sahara was clearly pressed for time. A mwah-mwah for Avola, a quick wave to the rest of the table, and she hurried down the mountainside to her car.

As if in response to an abracadabra, the party now broke up. The harvesters picked up their baskets and their sticky secateurs and plodded off to garner the last grapes of the year, Doris and the *deliziosi* hurried off to their next wine-tasting, Enzo tottered into the house to throw up, and Russo took his leave of Avola. The two men exchanged chummy slaps on the back, but to Poldi it looked forced. Russo shot her a glance she was too far away to interpret, then whistled to his dogs and set off down the hill.

Avola received a phone call. He listened for a moment, and his face hardened like cooling lava.

"Okay, I'll deal with it."

"What must you deal with?" Poldi asked when he rang off.

"The mash pump is acting up and the men don't have the right spanner. I must nip into Trecastagni and get one."

"I could come with you."

Avola smiled at her. "I won't be long. Just wait here, if you don't mind. As soon as I'm back I'll have all the time in the world for you."

He touched her gently on the arm, far from perfunctorily or accidentally this time. Then he too walked off. Poldi felt depressed by all the comings and goings around her. She had been left alone and was sitting there as though glued to her plastic chair, as useless as an ill-fitting spanner, her heart overshadowed by memories and presentiments and a second glass of wine in her hand. Depression and thirst—always a dangerous combination for my Auntie Poldi, who was now reminded of her original life-ending plan, her private arrangement with death. She had once more reached a stage where things lost their colour and she herself lost her will to live.

"The rest of the world can kiss my ass!"

She knocked back her second glass and refilled it. A brief check revealed that all the bottles on the table were at least half full. Poldi drank a third glass and reached for them. First she assembled them around her in a semicircle, like an audience. That was too intimate, however, so she paraded them in front of her in single file. Parade all the bottles — a nice idea. She toasted it with another glass.

And another.

Eventually she stopped counting and ceased to savour the Polifemo's delicate scent of almonds. It became no more than a red wine in which shame and contrasts and memories and the shadows clouding her heart dissolved into something better. At length she rose and went back to her Vespa, meaning to end the day comfortably at home with the shutters closed, and get totally plastered.

But down beside the gate, where she'd left the Vespa, she saw Avola again. Avola, whose whole manner and every gesture reminded her so painfully of Peppe, and who smelt so good.

He was arguing fiercely with a man who looked like his spitting image — in fact, Poldi had to concentrate quite hard to tell them apart. Avola, who caught sight of her as she slowly approached them, said something to his clone and then dismissed him with a brusque gesture. Clearly annoyed, the second Avola got into an old Fiat Panda and slammed the door. When the Panda turned, Poldi sighted another man in the passenger seat: the peculiar dowser with the triskelion tattoo.

"So you have a twin brother," said Poldi, trying hard not to sway or slur her words.

"Er, yes." Avola seemed to have to pull himself together. "Surely you aren't going already, Poldi?"

"It's getting late."

"I won't hear of it. I'm all yours now."

In response to those words—who wouldn't have welcomed them!—Poldi allowed Avola to take her arm and escort her back up the hill. While he was busy making wine in the shed across the way, Poldi finished off last year's Polifemo in front of the house. And when evening descended on the flanks of Etna, gentle as a goodnight kiss, she found herself alone with Avola at last and also quite blotto. In other words, smashed, zonked, plastered. Avola told her how wine is made, and he still smelt so good, and he ended by refusing to let her ride home in her condition.

"There's a guest room here in the house. It's no problem."

"No problem!" whispered Poldi, and she kissed him.

"Whaaat?" I broke in when she told me this. "I don't believe it!"

"That's because you're such a tight-ass, such a control freak. Where was the harm?"

I struggled for words. "Where was the harm? I mean, it was totally unprofessional of you!"

Direct hit.

Poldi hummed and hawed. "I'm the emotional type, that's all, and I was feeling a bit weak. God Almighty, as if I need to justify myself to *you!*"

"So what happened then?"

"Well, 'it,' if you know what I mean."

"I've no idea. Can't you be more specific?"

"I'd only embarrass you again."

"It doesn't bother you as a rule. So what happened next?"

Poldi shuffled around uneasily on the sofa. "I don't remember."

"Surely not? A mental blackout, you mean?"

She nodded contritely. "It was most unprofessional, I know, but what can I say? It just happened. The next thing I remember is lying beside Achille with the dawn light in my eyes."

"Very nice. And then?"

"Then fate sent me a sign."

She handed me a small, curved fragment of pottery with an inscription on one side. A single word in Greek capitals, scratched long ago into the fresh clay of a fair-sized amphora: ΟΥΤΙΣ.

"Meaning?"

"*Outis*," she said, "means 'no one' in ancient Greek. Vito explained it to me. Homer made Odysseus use that cute bit of wordplay to trick Polyphemus. You know: when the giant asks him his name, Odysseus, being the cunning devil he is, replies 'No One.' In other words, *Outis*, get it? So later on, when the blinded Cyclops flips and is hunting for Odysseus and calling to his buddies to help, he yells, 'No One has blinded me, No One is escaping from my cave!' And so on."

"I understand," I lied. "But what does this piece of pottery have to do with your mental blackout?"

"You're always so impatient!"

My Auntie Poldi, it must be said, had experienced quite a shock on surfacing beside Achille's sleeping form, naked and unbewigged and without the faintest idea how it had come to this — if it had. At all events, she had to get out of there sharpish, before Avola woke up.

She slipped out of bed, hurriedly snatched up her wig and her belongings and crept out of the room like a cat that has smashed a vase and knows there'll soon be hell to pay. Avola was snoring softly. Having pulled on her clothes in the kitchen, she went outside. Below her in the distance, the sea resembled burnished metal; nothing around her but silence and cool, moist air. Poldi briefly debated what to do. She was still rather unsteady on her legs, but after a few deep breaths she felt strong enough to totter down the hill to her Vespa and ride it home. She was wearing her red-and-green dirndl and grape-adorned headscarf, so she virtually melted into her surroundings.

Still a trifle woozy, Poldi picked her way through the vines, whose golden ranks stood arrayed in the light of the rising sun — quite a beautiful sight, she thought. After a few metres she had to sit down and catch her breath. While hunkered down among the vines, she saw something glint amid the volcanic ash and picked it up. A fragment of pottery, it bore an inscription scratched in ancient Greek lettering: ΟΥΤΙΣ. It meant "no one" — not that she knew that at the time. She simply liked the look of it, so she picked it up. All that broke the silence among the vines was Etna, relatively near now, whose periodic rumbles made the morning air vibrate. Between the rumbles it was quiet enough for Poldi to hear her own shallow breathing and the thud of her big, sad heart, which, though lost so often, was still beating. The heart that was persevering like a gallant comrade who staunchly, and with only a grumble or two, fights on to the bitter end — the heart that was so inflammable. All alone among the vines with herself and Mother Nature, groaning because her knees ached and perspiring beneath her wig, my Auntie Poldi reflected on the strangeness of a life which, after washing her up like jetsam on many a distant shore, had finally landed her in the bed of a previously unknown wine grower.

Boom! Etna again. Half a million years old—exactly the age Poldi felt at that moment. Remembering what Doris had said to her and Madame Sahara's dismay on looking into the future, she realised that this strange life of hers might really be *finito* sometime soon, and was filled with dread. Which promptly reminded her that she could use a drink right now. Which in turn triggered another sensation —an inopportune one, she thought.

She needed to pee.

Quite badly, what was more.

"Oh dear," I said when she told me this later with the appropriate pauses for effect. "What happened then?"

She shrugged. "Then I hoisted my dirndl and did a little Isar. The only trouble was, I'd failed to notice I wasn't alone any longer."

"Not alone" being a relative term.

While a little Isar trickled from under Poldi's dirndl and threaded its way through the loose volcanic ash and she was once more feeling a little less mortal, she noticed that her glittering rivulet was blithely meandering downhill towards a shadowy figure just below her. It looked in the grey light of dawn like someone who was peacefully sleeping off a skinful among the vines.

Poldi froze, possibly because she was startled, possibly because of the awkwardness of her squatting position.

"Hello?" she called hesitantly. Then, a little louder in Italian, "Can you hear me?"

Evidently not. That was when Poldi, inoculated with the genes of her father, Detective Chief Inspector (ret.) Georg Oberreiter of the Augsburg Police, had a premonition that she was heading for trouble again—big trouble. That she would again drink less from now on. That she would make herself unpopular and put herself in danger's way. And also that she would not yield to her initial impulse, which was simply to turn a blind eye and walk away. Not my Auntie Poldi. So she quickly completed her morning toilette, regained her feet with the aid of a vine and adjusted her dirndl.

The figure lying curled up among the vines still didn't move as my apprehensive Auntie Poldi drew nearer. It was a woman in a platinum-blond wig beaded with dew. The wig was askew, and there was a great deal of coagulated blood beneath it. Poldi recognised the clairvoyant at once, despite the look of pain and horror that had convulsed her fine features. She couldn't help thinking of the pink-and-yellow posters that would soon become weather-worn and bleached by the sun, never to be replaced and soon to be pasted over. At that moment, strangely enough, this thought distressed my Auntie Poldi far more than the sight of Madame Sahara's dead body.

4

In which Poldi converses with nature in the raw and makes a promise. She launches a first-class "preliminary attack" on her own initiative and rather forcefully hits upon a preliminary clue, puzzling though it may be. Because of the understandable fuss that results, she suffers from another minor lapse in communication. This means that she has to explain her conduct to several official parties and take account of a continental drift.

My Auntie Poldi was jolted out of her benumbed state by a rattling sound. A buzzard that had landed on a vine just behind her was fluttering its wings and uttering plaintive cries—a youngster with brown-and-white plumage. Although Poldi could have reached out and touched the bird, it betrayed no sign of fear. On the contrary, it looked dignified and grave, like someone accustomed to assessing situations objectively. Clinging to the vine with its talons, the buzzard cocked its head and looked in turn at Poldi and the corpse as if trying to form a preliminary idea of the deceased and the prime suspect. Having evidently come to a conclusion, it stared at my Auntie Poldi and emitted a plaintive cry.

"It wasn't me," Poldi insisted in a low voice, unused to dealing with nature in the raw and overcome by a shyness to which she had seldom succumbed since childhood.

The buzzard didn't take its eyes off her and, although it was silent now, she felt it was trying to tell her something. For a while they simply gazed at each other, my Auntie Poldi and the buzzard, while the rosy light of dawn continued to creep over Madame Sahara's lifeless form. Then everything suddenly became clear to Poldi and the universe opened a crack, allowing her to catch a glimpse of how wonderful life is. Poldi was so overcome by this realisation that it shook her. She sobered up in a trice.

"I'll deal with this, I promise," she said softly.

The buzzard emitted another plaintive cry, then pushed off and propelled itself into the air with two powerful wing-beats.

"Bye, Papa!" she called after it.

"I'm sorry? Hello?" I queried, puzzled, when Poldi told me about this episode. "Why Papa?"

She was looking dead serious. "It's obvious: because I'd realised in a flash that the buzzard was the reincarnation of my father. He'd always been interested in birds of prey. I mean, it's clear what had happened, isn't it?"

"Kindly explain."

"You don't pay attention, that's your trouble. Too preoccupied."

"Too preoccupied with what, pray?"

"Why, with the fear that you won't land a woman and sort out your novel while you're still in the first flush of youth. Once the youth train has pulled out, you'll have no choice but to bury your dreams and complete that tragic teacher training course of yours. Hence your premature midlife crisis."

"I'm not suffering from a midlife crisis!"

"Yes you are, but don't panic, we're working on it."

I stared at her. Far from grinning, Poldi was looking entirely serious. She took a swig of whisky and puffed at her MS, the cigarette Italians have nicknamed *morte sicura*, or certain death.

I tried to revert to the case. "So the buzzard was your father," I said.

"Sure, that's why I sobered up so suddenly."

"And what did he tell you?"

"Why, that I had to solve the case. That I was to take a close look at the crime scene. And that he loved me, naturally. All the things people say when they've been reincarnated."

"Oh, of course."

Poldi ignored me. "At that moment a weight was lifted from my heart and all was well again. I'd seen the light of pure love, and I know a thing or two about love and broken hearts."

She would not have been my Auntie Poldi if a broken heart had deterred her from investigating a murder, for murder was clearly involved here—Poldi needed no autopsy report nor buzzard nor full daylight to convince her of that. Judging by the amount of blood that had seeped into the volcanic ash from beneath her wig, Madame Sahara must have died of a severe traumatic brain injury. Poldi could detect no gunshot wound, so a fall or a blow seemed the only possibility. However, she could not locate a single stone big enough to have caused death after an unfortunate stumble and an even more unfortunate impact. Moreover, the dead clairvoyant was lying curled up as though asleep, having been arranged in that position post-mortem. Almost gently, thought Poldi, touched by the murderer's solicitude. Yet he had not been able to efface the pain and terror from her features and mould them into a serene smile. The lips were parted as if in speechless horror. But the mouth was not the worst feature, for Poldi knew that the general relaxation of the muscles after death produces such rictuses. Worst of all was the horror in Madame Sahara's eyes, which had seen the past, present and future, and had looked into Poldi's future only a few hours before.

Poldi looked around for footprints, but the soft soil had been churned up by the grape pickers' shoes, not to mention her own as well. It dawned on her that she would very soon have to explain herself to a certain commissario.

"What a god-awful mess!"

Silence still reigned in the vineyard—midway between earth and sky, as it were. Etna was wafting a long plume of smoke across the sea; the sun had made it over the horizon and was portending another hot day. Poldi knew she had to be quick. In spite of her aching knees, she hunkered down again and examined the body with care, trying to memorise every detail. The dead woman's arms clasped her body as though trying to protect it. Her trousers and sweater bore a sprinkling of red volcanic soil. All her rings and bangles appeared to be there. Was anything missing? Poldi couldn't have said, nor could she detect any other injuries, grazes or bruises. Had there been a quarrel? Had the dead woman screamed? Could she have been heard? Poldi tried to esti-mate the distance to the house and wondered whether she ought to test this by calling for help, then decided not to because she needed more time. She was also aware that nothing is more dangerous during a preliminary investiga-tion than a premature hypothesis.

"In the first place," she told me once, "you think, that's it, it's cut and dried. That's because you want to wrap up the case in double-quick time—because you think you're a ge-nius. Yes, don't laugh, that goes for you too. From then on, your premature hypothesis hangs around your neck like a millstone, and you never get rid of it. It makes eyes at you —it waggles its plausibility at you. You fall madly in love with your premature hypothesis—you examine every clue, every piece of circumstantial evidence to see if it fits. If it doesn't, you bend it to fit without even noticing. Your lovely hypothesis has blinded you, and then—pow!—dead end. And I know a thing or two about falling in love and dead ends."

So Poldi strove to concentrate primarily on details that were, at first sight, less obviously suggestive of a quarrel and homicide. That was why she eventually spotted a hex-agonal silver ballpoint pen lying in the sand, a classy, very feminine object of French manufacture. The point was ex-tended. Had Madame Sahara tried to defend herself with it? Poldi didn't venture to touch the thing, but there were no traces of blood on it as far as she could tell.

The ballpoint nagged at her—its image became locked into the jigsaw puzzle of first impressions and could not be detached. Although Poldi knew it was high time to call Montana, she continued to hesitate, trying to make sense of the pen. It looked too small and fragile to be a weapon, but she focused all her still rather woozy senses on it. And then it struck her: the pen pointed towards the corpse.

I imagine that this was a revelation such as only a hangover can grant you in the limbo between nausea and a crash landing in reality, when the world reassumes its familiar shape and your brain still attaches importance to little things it usually ignores. A state of enlightenment, fundamentally. Or so I imagine, but I am, of course, far less experienced in these matters than my Auntie Poldi.

Be that as it may, Poldi found that the ballpoint's tip was pointing straight at the body. Now that this fact had occurred to her, she took it seriously, so she knelt down in the sand with a groan in order to check the pen's precise aiming point. Although her kneeling might obliterate potential evidence, it was, so to speak, collateral damage. Like love and public transport, criminology subsists on compromises. And although Poldi had never in her life had any truck with compromises, she was no stranger to the power of intuition.

The tip of the pen was pointing at the upper half of the body. Poldi now noticed that the dead clairvoyant's hands were clenched. This almost evoked a triumphant cry from her, but she was able to control herself. Cautiously, she tried to open the dead woman's fingers. The night had been very chilly, and rigor mortis had not yet stiffened her joints, so Poldi managed to open her fingers with little effort. She inferred from this that Madame Sahara must have been killed less than six hours earlier, or at a time when Poldi herself had just embarked on a voyage of erotic discovery with the wine grower. In other words, around the time of her mental blackout.

The right hand was empty, but the palm of the left hand bore an inscription in ballpoint. The capital letters were still quite legible.

"Well, what did it say?" I asked, because Poldi had inserted a long, pregnant pause.

"Give me your hand."

"Er, why?"

"Don't ask. And look away."

Sighing, I did as I was told. My aunt scrawled something on my palm—not a very pleasant sensation, I'm bound to say.

"Make a fist."

I complied.

"Now take a look."

I looked down at my fist.

"Well?" I said.

"Well, go on, open it."

That was when I saw what Poldi had scrawled on my palm, and what she had discovered on Giuliana's: ETNA-ROSSO.

I tried to wipe it off, but no luck. Poldi, with her taste for the dramatic, had used an indelible red marker. *Etna Rosso:* I knew it only as an indication of origin on Italian wine labels.

"So what does it mean?"

"Oh, you and your obsessive love of explanations. With you it's always chop-chop, wham-bang, rubber-stamp it and next, please. But things aren't like that in criminology—or in literature either, so bear that in mind. Well, at this stage only two things were clear to me: first, that the woman had left us a clue to her murderer on the verge of death; and second . . ." She cleared her throat in some embarrassment and swigged her whisky.

"And second . . ." I said, helping her back into the saddle.

"And second," she sighed, "that it was time to call Vito."

"Poldi? Is something the matter?" Montana had picked up after the first ring. He sounded worried.

Poldi was tempted to say no. There was nothing she would have liked better than to tell him, honestly and cheerfully, that all was well—that all she wanted was to hear his voice, which was warm and still husky prior to the first cigarette of the day. This was impossible, though.

"That's one way of putting it."

Instantly, his voice lost its hoarseness, becoming as calm and cool as a mountain lake. "What's happened?"

Poldi looked over at the body and shrugged apologetically. "A murder."

She heard him draw a deep breath.

"Are you sober?"

"Don't ask stupid questions! Of course I'm—"

"Who's been murdered?"

"Giuliana—I mean, Madame Sahara. She's . . . lying here in front of me."

"Are you alone?"

"Yes."

"Where?"

Poldi told him.

"What in God's name are you doing there?"

"Vito, please can we sort that out later? Can you come here? At once?"

"I'm on my way. Have you informed the police?"

"That's what I'm doing."

"Dial 113. At once. Dial 113, not 112, you hear?"

"I've only found a dead body, Vito, I haven't lost my mind."

"And leave your mobile on. I'll be with you in half an hour. Oh yes, and . . . Poldi?"

"Yes, Vito?"

"Don't touch anything!"

My Auntie Poldi felt tempted to utter a waspish retort, to tell him he could stuff his detective chief inspector's tone of voice, et cetera. It was an unruly impulse to which she had normally yielded since girlhood whenever some man gave her an order or forbade her to do something. In this case, however, it occurred to her that it might perhaps be advisable to hold her tongue. So an awkward silence ensued, and before she could thank him, Montana rang off.

Alone once more, she dialled 112.

The same mistake she had made when she found her handyman's body, but Poldi was no great shakes with figures, especially in her condition.

I should explain that Italians dial 112 to reach the Carabinieri in an emergency and 113 to get the Polizia di Stato, which doesn't make a great deal of difference when they want to report a murder or need assistance. Basically, the Carabinieri and the Polizia di Stato are competing organisations with the same function. Although this is traditionally intended to ensure that the Italian police forces act as a check on each other, in practice it leads to even more bureaucracy and wrangling over spheres of responsibility. As a commissario of the Polizia di Stato, Montana naturally wanted *his* boys to seal off the crime scene, not some morons from the Carabinieri. And this brings us back to the popular prejudice according to which all carabinieri are intellectual odds and sods with IQs of minus three potatoes. Hence carabinieri jokes like this one:

Two carabinieri are pounding their beat. One says to the other, "Look, Ciccio, there's a foot lying there!" "So there is," says Ciccio. They walk on, shaking their heads. "*Madonna*, Corrado," says Ciccio, "there's a torso lying there!" More head-shaking. They walk on. After twenty yards, Ciccio gives a yell. "Corrado, look. There's a head lying over there!" On examining the head more closely, they make a grisly discovery. "*Madonna*, Ciccio, it's Carabiniere Luciano!" Ciccio: "Yes, Corrado. Let's hope nothing's happened to him."

Or how about this one? What's the difference between a carabiniere and a bottle of beer? None. They're both empty from the neck up.

One more? A carabiniere to his superior officer: "Sir, we need some room on the shelf. May I burn the old files?" Officer: "Good idea, but photocopy them all first."

Very funny, but the truth is that Italian carabinieri are no whit inferior to hard-boiled New York cops.

Poldi didn't notice her mistake until a few minutes later, when she saw an Alfa come racing uphill to the gate. It disgorged two young officers in immaculate dark blue uniforms with smart red stripes down their pants, hands loosely fanning their holsters like a couple of pistoleros in a B feature. Resembling identical twins thanks to their military buzz cuts, they eyed Poldi and her dirndl with suspicion. Poldi, who knew a thing or two about policemen, was nonetheless delighted. They epitomised just the sort of bad-tempered, clean-shaven, uniformed masculinity which so appealed to her, and which had granted her so many memorable nights in the course of her life. It was no wonder she instinctively got out her mobile phone to take a photo of the carabinieri twins for her album of policemen.

"Was it you that called us, signora?"

"Oh, it's all right. I dialled the wrong number by mistake. Would you mind notifying your colleagues in the Polizia di Stato? Thanks, very nice of you."

The two policemen exchanged a look and approached Poldi from opposite sides, scanning their surroundings with a professional eye.

"Oh, and mind if I take a quick photo of you? You've no need to smile, even."

"Kindly put your phone away, signora."

"You reported a murder."

Poldi sighed. "She's lying up there in the vineyard. Her name was Giuliana. Or Madame Sahara."

On hearing the latter name, the two carabinieri started as if my Auntie Poldi had announced that the president or Donatella Versace were lying up there.

"What?"

"Who?"

It might have been an echo.

Poldi felt her crown start to throb again. She suspected that everything would soon become extremely complicated.

"She's lying up there among the vines. She was murdered —hit on the head."

She was already tapping 113 into her mobile when one of the policemen stepped forward and snatched it out of her hand.

"Your ID!"

No novice when it came to dealing with the authorities, Poldi preserved her cool and gave the twins a disarming smile. She now saw that one of them had green eyes and the other blue.

"It's in my Vespa's helmet compartment. May I?"

"Yes, but slowly."

"And I want to see your hands at all times." Green Eyes put his hand on his holster.

"Relax, boys. I'm an old biddy with a hell of a hangover, and I've just found a dead body. You're in no danger from me as long as I don't lay hands on some lipstick and a bit of rouge." Opening the helmet compartment nice and slowly, she handed Green Eyes her identity card.

He turned the piece of plastic this way and that, looking puzzled, then handed it to his colleague. "She's German."

Blue Eyes checked. "You're German?"

"From Munich, but I'm living in Torre Archirafi."

The card was submitted to a renewed check.

Poldi felt her knees go weak. She perched on the Vespa's seat and thought of the buzzard and her father. She thought of Madame Sahara and the way she'd looked yesterday evening, so alive and strong and beautiful, and various questions arose in her mind. Had she defended herself? Had she known her murderer, and how long had their argument lasted? Above all, why had she written something as cryptic

82

as "Etnarosso" on her palm, not simply the name of her murderer?

"Your theory?" Poldi asked me some weeks later, interrupting her narrative flow. Her tone was inquisitorial, and she prodded me in the chest with her forefinger.

Two things I detest, especially when combined.

"Er . . ."

"Go on, quite spontaneously. Spontaneity isn't your thing, I know, but just try."

"Well . . ." I began, playing for time, but she promptly broke in again.

"Never begin a sentence with 'Well . . .' Bear that in mind! Never. Never ever. It only shows people you're uptight and don't have a clue, and it's a reflection on your virility. Saying 'Well . . .' makes as stupid an impression as fiddling with your glasses or fervently tasting wine for minutes on end. Get it?"

I nodded meekly before replying. "Job conditioning."

"Meaning?"

"She was a clairvoyant, and clairvoyants always express themselves in an oracular, mysterious way. In the end, they can't help it."

Poldi nodded as if this was, at least, not the stupidest answer in the world.

"That's what I thought at first, but someone in their death throes would be more direct, wouldn't they? So it occurred to me that Etnarosso could be something quite specific, like the murderer's name."

"A pretty silly name," I said dubiously. "Who ever heard of anyone called that?"

"One's entitled to expect a bit more imagination from a novelist—all right, would-be novelist. The Sicilians are knee deep in daffy surnames. You only have to think of Ficarotta, Fregapane, Sederino, Mastronzo, Dalla Palle, Ammazzalamorte, Passalacqua, Zizzadoro or Licenziato. With a name like that, you might as well lie in bed every day of your miserable life and get drunk, so why shouldn't there be someone called Pippo Etnarosso?"

"Well?"

She pulled a face. "No, damn it. I couldn't find one, not even on the Internet—and you can stick that look of triumph where the sun doesn't shine!"

But, Bavarian bloody-mindedness being proof against drizzle, troublesome neighbours and the rigours of daily life, my Auntie Poldi refused to be discouraged by such a minor setback and was already pursuing another hypothesis. She would not, however, reveal it to me that evening.

"For purely dramatic reasons, understand? Get this straight: you have to toy with your audience. They don't want you to give away all your secrets at once. They want to be wooed and enchanted. It's like a ballet. It's what you might call literary precision engineering."

I forbore to comment.

Meanwhile, the two carabinieri were muttering requests for instructions from headquarters into their car radio and keeping a sharp eye on my aunt the whole time.

"Boys," she said, "I don't mean to nag, but there's a dead body up there. You need to notify forensics. Above all, you need to notify the Polizia di Stato. Commissario Montana is already on his way from Acireale."

"Who?"

"Why the Polizia di Stato?"

"After all, we're here."

The two carabinieri exchanged a puzzled glance, as if to reassure themselves that they really were there, then reverted to the business at hand.

"Where exactly is this body?"

Poldi got off the Vespa with a sigh. *Madonna,* how old she was feeling! And tired, very tired.

"I'll lead the way, okay?"

She didn't get far, for just then she heard a siren. A navy-blue Alfa Romeo came roaring up the hill and skidded to a stop right beside the gate, closely followed by a Polizia di Stato patrol car with blue lights flashing. The carabinieri flinched like gazelles that have just spotted a pride of lions in the grassy savanna.

Out of the blue Alfa stepped a worried and grumpy commissario, every square inch of whose no longer youthful body my Auntie Poldi had spent recent weeks exploring with a positively Humboldtian taste for adventure. The patrol car behind him proved to contain two old acquaintances: Pippo Zannotta, a pot-bellied, mustachioed inspector, and Marco Console, a very young, baby-faced constable. It was they who had interrogated Poldi on the beach at Praiola some weeks earlier, when she had found Valentino with his face blown away with a sawn-off shotgun. No matter. Pippo and Marco eyed their colleagues from the competition in a way that instantly chilled the air several degrees, and the carabinieri stiffened. Like elementary particles with a different polarity, all four guardians of the law were spoiling for a fight.

Pippo and Marco recognised my aunt immediately, Poldi having since become a kind of local celebrity. They nodded to her as to a colleague, and drew themselves up behind Montana like bodyguards. Montana himself did not at first deign to glance at his Bavarian companion on so many stormy nocturnal voyages.

As ever when on duty, he was wearing his crumpled grey suit and a white shirt, and on this occasion the Indian necktie with decorative Lurex motifs from the *Ramayana,* which Poldi had recently bought him at a fair-trade shop. She thought it went well with his olive-wood complexion, his greying beard and moustache and his scowling green eyes, which at certain nocturnal moments could open wide and regard her with astonishment, as if they had just witnessed a revelation of some kind. It has to be said that my aunt always liked those moments when she herself was surfing back to the shores of reality on a billow of bliss. She liked everything about Montana: his perspicacity, his sarcasm, his way of mashing out half-smoked cigarettes in the ashtray like criminals under arrest, and the reverent delicacy with which he devoured marzipan cherries. Whenever Montana looked at her, my Auntie Poldi promptly experienced a painful itch all over her body, as if she were being enveloped in a tickly web of yearning and desire that Montana alone could tear asunder with his shapely, purposeful hands. Her words, I should point out, not mine. But her pleasure at seeing Montana became mingled at once with something else: uneasiness at being in hot water.

He looked tired, she thought. Tired, pale, dishevelled and irate—not a good sign. He looked like a man who, after a hard day's work exacerbated by incompetent idiots, has had

to spend the entire night hammering out personal relationship problems with the aid of too little wine and too many
cigarettes.

The image of the gazelles and the lions may have been a
bit laboured, I grant you, but—as my Auntie Poldi always
says—"restraint is a sign of weakness" in the first place,
and second, Montana made an undeniable impression on
the uniformed duo despite his less than gigantic stature.

"Who are you?" Blue Eyes snapped bravely, but that was
as far as it went.

Montana held his ID under the carabinieri's noses. "I ask
the questions. What are *you* doing here?"

Montana's ID plus the don't-mess-with-me look in his
eyes did not fail in their effect.

"We were here first," Green Eyes said defiantly. He
pointed to Poldi. "She called us. She's . . . German."

He spoke as if that explained everything, including climate change, the euro crisis and the tribulations of the Sicilian soul.

Montana turned his lovely green eyes on Poldi for the first
time. But the colour of a person's eyes is not the colour of
the expression in them, and Montana's expression wasn't
green, it was thunderstorm grey. My aunt raised her hands
in submission.

He shook his head in bewilderment, then readdressed
himself to the carabinieri. "All right, you can piss off now."

"But we were here first."

"Where's the body?"

"Somewhere up in the vineyard. So she says."

"So why are you dingbats still standing here?"

"Uh . . . because we had to question the suspect?"

"Have I got this straight? Someone informs you that there's a dead body in the vicinity, and you promptly arrest her for murder?"

"We're only going by the book."

Poldi could tell that Montana's bile was about to overflow — or his magma, to remain in Sicily's volcanic world of imagery — and that an eruption of Pompeian dimensions, complete with pyroclastic flow and all the trimmings, was imminent. Pippo and Marco, smirking in the background, were also waiting for their boss to tear the carabinieri to pieces, devour them and regurgitate a few pellets of dark blue uniform. Poldi didn't want it to come to that. She was sick of the performance anyway, so she got off her Vespa. She felt like greeting Montana with a kiss, but she restrained herself. Thin ice. The man was on duty, after all, and could not be allowed to look foolish in front of those Carabinieri muppets, so she simply walked over to the gate.

"Stop squabbling, boys. I'll take you there."

Poldi half expected that Madame Sahara had recovered from, say, a fainting fit, got dazedly to her feet and left the vineyard, suffering from a slight residual headache. She couldn't resist the idea, because the truth is, we all think of ourselves and our nearest and dearest as immortal until the time comes, and even then we wrangle with fate and hope that dead doesn't mean dead — that there's such a thing as half dead, almost dead, more or less dead. Scope for negotiation, in other words.

The fact was, however, that Madame Sahara was still lying amid the Nerello Mascalese vines just as Poldi had found her. Except that she wasn't alone any more. When

Poldi trudged up the hill with her retinue of uniformed na-
ivety and chief inspectorial grouchiness, Achille Avola was
standing beside the body wearing jeans and a well-worn
T-shirt, his hair as ruffled as if he had received an electric
shock. On catching sight of my aunt and the policemen, he
stepped back quickly.

Montana flashed his ID. "And who are you?"

"This is my vineyard," Avola replied, as if the dead
woman had been trying to dispossess him of it. "I just got
out of bed . . . My God, what happened?"

Montana signed to Pippo to check Avola's personal par-
ticulars and instructed the carabinieri to go up to the house,
seal off the immediate vicinity of the crime scene and wait
for forensics. This struck the carabinieri as acceptable, although they disliked taking orders from the competition.
The sight of the dead clairvoyant appeared to have upset the
two young men, however. They looked positively relieved to
be able to toddle off up the hill like two puppies no longer
compelled to "Sit!" Montana concentrated on the corpse.
He pulled on latex gloves, knelt down and examined the
dead woman from every angle. He spotted the exposed
palm and the inscription on it. He felt the head wound and
scanned the footprints round about. Rising with a grunt, he
made a brief call to headquarters and then turned to my
aunt.

"When did you find her?"

"Just over an hour ago. I called you right away."

"Somebody opened her fingers post-mortem. Was it
you?"

Lying was pointless.

"Er, yes."

Montana growled a Sicilian oath that associated the Virgin Mary with something unsavoury.

"What were you doing here, anyway?"

"Last night . . . well, I wasn't really fit to drive, so Signor Avola was kind enough to offer me a bed at his house. And earlier on, when I was catching a breath of fresh air, that's when I found her."

"I see. And you recognised Madame Sahara at once."

"Her name was Giuliana. I only met her yesterday. We were introduced by Achille—Signor Avola, I mean."

Montana skirted the corpse and came over to my aunt. He got so close he needed to do little more than whisper— so close that Poldi could smell the cologne she had often smelt on herself in the mornings.

"Pin your ears back, Poldi. I don't want to have to worm everything out of you. You're now going to tell me exactly what's been going on. Why you were here yesterday, what you noticed and how you came to find the body. I want to know everything, every last little detail, is that clear?"

That was what Poldi was afraid of.

"But what if a few, er, details escape me?" she replied meekly.

"Details of what magnitude?"

"Well . . . like the whole of last night?"

There was nothing to be done, though. Montana insisted on a complete report, so Poldi gave him as detailed an account as she could. He didn't interrupt her once, just smoked, but she saw the furrow between his eyebrows grow steadily deeper. It might have been a continental divide reshaping the globe.

"Give my colleagues a description of the dowser," he growled when Poldi had ended her account. "You can make a formal deposition at headquarters. We'll discuss the other matter later." He heeled his cigarette and turned without further comment to Avola, who had been fidgeting nervously a few feet away. "Show me the winery. We'll talk up there."

"Do you still need me?" Poldi called after him.

"Do as you please" was Montana's sole response.

5

Tells of jealousy, remorse and wine. Poldi gains some new recruits and receives help from still, deep waters, but she also grasps that the shit has hit the fan and doesn't want to lose Montana because of "it." Although he has no wish to discuss their relationship, he comes out with a surprise that gives Poldi a great deal to think about.

Montana's jealousy affected my Auntie Poldi even more than the heat, her thirst, showers of ash and her throbbing tooth. Although she generally ploughed her way through life regardless and cared little whose nose she put out of joint, she was a fundamentally sensitive person. Furthermore, she was—believe it or not—a faithful soul. When she gave her heart, she did so unreservedly, without a money-back guarantee or insurance cover. She accepted the fact that this could abruptly end in tears, as witness what had happened in Tanzania. Poldi was just not made for compromises, for the grey areas of life, for rear-view mirrors, loopholes or get-out clauses. In affairs of the heart she gave herself and everything she possessed—absolutely. The only trouble was, she could sometimes be derailed by a weakness for dashing traffic cops, pregnant Adam's apples, well-toned forearms and an occasional glass too many. She castigated herself on the way back to Torre Archirafi for that and for her one-night stand with Avola. There was zero possibility that she had ended up in his bed without having it off with him, and Montana seemed to have sensed this right away.

"I mean," Poldi told me some weeks later, "the man's a detective chief inspector and a Sicilian to boot. That means he has an inbuilt radar for lies and concealment. And for women. That's because jealousy, like everything else, was invented in Sicily — invented in 1538 by a certain Principe Ignazio di Uzeda."

"Eh?" I interjected.

"Just checking to see if you were listening. Okay, back to Vito. However much of an animal he is in bed — and he is, I must say — he can naturally sniff out rival alpha males. He simply sensed that I'd, well, done it with Achille."

"*It?*" I said, a trifle stung by her little attention check. "Why so coy all of a sudden? It isn't like you. Why not say you had great sex together? Why not say you tore off each other's clothes, licked each other from head to foot and screwed each other with such abandon that Etna choked on its own magma in awe?"

Poldi stared at me, her expression conveying anger, surprise and pity in quick succession. "I can tell you're hurting and uptight deep inside, and my down-to-earth ways have been too much for you. I'm sorry, okay? You don't have to say anything, I can sense it. I used the word 'it' because it's a wild card, so to speak. Because there's still a big black hole in my memory, understand? I wasn't myself at all, that's why I said 'it.' Wait a while. You'll understand when you hear what I found out later. You'd sooner say 'it' yourself if you were in my place. An unresolved variable in the equation, you follow?"

"I'm sorry, Poldi."

"Okay, let's forget it."

"Tell me something: when are you going to introduce me to your friend Valérie?"

"Oh sure, you'd like that, wouldn't you?"

"I mean, hey, what's the objection?"

Poldi gave me that "Oh yeah?" look which girls since the Stone Age have mastered by the time they're eleven. "Well, do you or don't you want to know how the case progressed?"

What had happened to Poldi in the preceding twenty hours would be called by an airline press officer "a fatal combination of circumstances," and by the man in the street "a can of worms." In Poldi's case, it would usually have provided the ingredients for a right royal fit of depression followed by a plunge into the arms of Signor Bacardi. She hadn't even the strength to fill the empty jerrycan at the public taps or sweep up the inches-thick layer of ash in front of her house or on the roof terrace. She simply wanted to get drunk and fall asleep in the hope that total inebriation would put an end to the heartache and the thousand natural shocks that flesh is heir to. Poldi was in full Hamlet mode. But then she remembered her magical encounter with the buzzard and her promise.

To take her mind off her impending tête-à-tête with Montana and concentrate on essentials, Poldi began by playing a Zucchero hit at full volume and on repeat. It was just what she needed to fortify her morale. Then she rinsed off the ashes and her hangover under the shower, scented herself liberally, put on a comfortable caftan and treated herself to a wheat beer. According to my Auntie Poldi, nothing perks you up better after a solid night's boozing than a decent wheat beer, if only because it regulates the pH level in your blood.

In a recent issue of *La Sicilia,* which Poldi fished out of the waste paper, she found a photograph of Elisa Puglisi, the murdered district attorney. She carefully soaked the Polifemo label off a bottle and printed a pixellated photo of Madame Sahara from the Internet. Then she pinned the two photos on either side of the wine label to the corkboard on her bedroom wall, which she used during investigations. A photograph of poisoned Lady, already there, she moved down a little, and a print of Russo's topographic map joined it. Last came an index card inscribed *Etnarosso* and a bold question mark—and *ecco là!* All in all, an informative picture, Poldi thought. A picture that allowed of no conclusion other than that the murders of Elisa Puglisi and Madame Sahara were connected, and connected via Achille Avola's vineyard. And Russo was behind it all somehow.

Satisfied with herself and her investigative progress, fortified by Zucchero and splendidly refreshed by a wheat beer, she pursued various inquiries into Etnarosso on the Internet, consumed a slice of Thursday's cold roast pork, watered the plants in the courtyard with what was left in the jerrycan, and then did what had recently become a favourite habit of hers: she went to Sunday Mass.

"I've never been devout," she explained later, before I could query this in surprise, because I knew that Poldi harboured a fundamental aversion to the Church. "I'm spiritual but not devout, know what I mean? I've never had much time for the Church. The mere thought of it infuriates me. The males-only organisations, the pope, the original-sin malarkey, the inhibited cult of the Virgin Mary, the false promises of redemption, the proselytism, the misogyny, the daft words of the psalms and hymns. Mind you, I've always liked the tunes. I always enjoyed chanting in the ashram, you know. I screwed every hippie in the temple of that Kali sect in Nevada, I've meditated in Buddhist monasteries, and I believe in reincarnation and karma and all that, likewise in people's essential goodness. I don't know if there's a god and if he's got something against sex and unbelievers, but I can't help it, I'm Catholic. It's like malaria: once you've got it you never get rid of it, and sooner or later you go and make peace with it."

But this was only half the explanation for her regular churchgoing of late. In the first place, she had become friendly with Padre Paolo, who chain-smoked and cheated at gin rummy, and second, for all her dislike of the institution itself, Poldi liked churches. And she had a particularly soft spot for the little church of Santa Maria del Rosario in Torre Archirafi.

Outwardly, it was an altogether unremarkable chunk of a building right beside the sea, with narrow windows and two squat towers. In order to summon people to Mass, Padre Paolo, never hostile to modernity, had supplemented the two out-of-tune bells with loudspeakers installed in the towers, which blared out apocalyptic Bach cantatas, operatic arias and pop songs several times a day, at full blast and completely distorted.

In other words, it was a typical Italian fishermen's church, originally designed more as a multifunctional sea defence and unworthy of a pit stop on a sightseeing tour. Or so one might think. In reality, however, its stout volcanic rock walls housed a unique baroque jewel. Another rule to be observed in Sicily: never be fooled by an unprepossessing exterior or superficial blemishes. What applies to fruit applies equally to churches: outward dilapidation and discoloration always give promise of inner splendour, delicacy and sweetness, though only to the observant.

This went for the church of Santa Maria del Rosario as well. As soon as you escaped from the heat through one of the side doors or the bronze west door, with its reliefs of sea monsters and saints, and entered the chill of the little nave, the density of the air seemed to change, becoming lighter. In fact everything seemed suddenly lighter, as if it were about to take off and hover. Everything in the church was directed upwards and heavenwards, every gilded plaster curlicue, every little cherub with his toy harpoon, every hand of the Madonna, every eye of every saint in the massive oil paintings on the walls. Even the gilded octopods, sea serpents and swordfish on the organ loft were fervently striving to leap out of their plaster waves and soar to heaven as though summoned by a mighty voice and exempted from the laws of gravity. Such is the impression you gain on entering Santa Maria del Rosario in Torre Archirafi in the parish of Riposto in the district of Catania in the region of Sicily in Italy: that it is relieving your shoulders of a burden you may not have known you were carrying around. Your breathing becomes easier, your fingertips tingle and, drawn there by the architecture as a whole, your gaze rises to the vaulted ceiling and lingers there in awe.

For up there, life sings and shouts and exults and laments. Up there rages a battle between angels and demons, colourfulness and baroque kitsch. Like a *carretto siciliano,* the ceiling is parcelled into separate pictorial panels that fast-forward biblical scenes from the Creation to the War in Heaven to the Temptation of Saint Anthony. They are opulent scenes replete with Sicilian knights, buxom village belles, walrus-mustachioed footpads, muscular fishermen, lecherous putti, shy mermaids, volcanoes and sea monsters. In the seventeenth century, some Principe Uzeda or Barone di Longarini must have taken it into his head to plant the little church on the foundations of a fishermen's chapel like a marzipan mandarin on a dead branch. Possibly for his mistress, possibly to impress his kinsfolk, possibly from sheer boredom or plain, honest piety. Not, at all events, out of a desire for understatement.

Poldi had a thing for places that exuded power, and understood them. She always sensed at once whether they were good or not, whether they drained you of vitality or infused you with an abundance of it, whether they set you back on your feet and made you vibrant. And Santa Maria del Rosario, with its sensual baroque kitsch, which celebrated the miracle and adventure of life, was one of the most power-infused places Poldi had ever set foot in.

"They're usually churches," Uncle Martino told me once as he gently dunked a gigantic octopus in simmering water, ash from the fag in the corner of his mouth dribbling down his vest. "Why, you ask? *Beh,* it's quite simple. Because people have always found places where goodness issues from the ground like sulphuric gas from a fumarole on Etna. Humanity's very earliest cult sites were erected in such places.

In the Bronze Age a shrine for an earth spirit would have been built there, later perhaps a Roman temple of Minerva, and at some stage the first church. Whatever you do or don't believe in, these places are a reality, anyone can sense that. And there are more of these power-filled places in Sicily than anywhere else on earth. Nothing can change that, not us Sicilians, nor our ignorance and fatalism, nor climate change, environmental pollution, the euro crisis, the CIA or the Mafia."

Which brought Uncle Martino back to his favourite subject: the links between the CIA and the Sicilian Mafia. But more on that another time.

By the time Poldi entered the small but well-filled church that Sunday morning, bobbed and crossed herself, the service was in full swing. Or rather, Padre Paolo was. He had just embarked on his sermon, the highlight of all his Masses. Poldi located her friend Signora Cocuzza and sat down beside her.

The invariably sad and taciturn signora, who ran the only café bar in Torre with her sons, frowned disapprovingly. "You're late, Donna Poldina."

"I was detained."

A meaningful look.

Signora Cocuzza raised her eyebrows and leant forward. "Don't tell me . . ."

Poldi put two fingers to her lips and kissed them in the traditional Sicilian sign language signifying "dead as a doornail."

Signora Cocuzza crossed herself, torn between horror and delight. "Santa Maria! Who?"

"Later. I may need your help."

"You can count on me, Donna Poldina."

Just then: "I am the vine and my Father is the wine grower!" Padre Paolo thundered at his awe-struck fan base, aiming a Judgement Day glare at Poldi and the sad signora.

The two ladies stopped whispering, and Poldi was unsurprised that Padre Paolo should be speaking, today of all days, about wine. To my Auntie Poldi there were no chance occurrences in life, only the infinitely complicated system of the universe, which we shall never understand, and which deluges us with bucketloads of good fortune and disaster in turn.

"Jesus spoke thus to his disciples," the priest went on, satisfied with the undivided attention he was now receiving. "'Every branch in me that beareth not fruit he taketh away.' What is that meant to tell us, dear brothers and sisters?" Pause for effect. "That there are Christians who, no matter how pious and devout, remain infertile and are ultimately severed altogether from the vine of Christ. Pruned! Cut off! Cast aside forever!" He gave Poldi another meaningful glance before continuing. "On the other hand, the Lord purifies and tends every vine that bears fruit. The divine wine grower is merciful. He dissolves the crusts of idiotic egoism and dull-witted sensual pleasure. He prunes away uncontrolled growth and lascivious desire. He pulls up the weeds of sloth. For only in that way, dear brothers and sisters, does he enable healthy shoots to sprout, to thrive, to yield knowledge and understanding and a harvest of sweet, ripe grapes —the fruits of the Lord."

"A fine sermon," Poldi told the priest when the three of them were sitting together outside the café, their invariable habit after Mass every Sunday.

She had just brought her new friends up to date, which was why a momentary hush had descended on their little table. The sad signora was sipping her coffee, Padre Paolo spooning up his mulberry *granita* and puffing at his cigarette between mouthfuls. It could have been said that smoking was a sure sign that Padre Paolo was still alive.

"But there's something I don't understand," Poldi went on, when the silence began to irk her. "If the Almighty is a wine grower himself, how can he have anything against getting drunk?"

In default of an immediate answer, Padre Paolo stirred his sorbet into a mush. "When Noah emerges from the fuggy, cramped interior of the Ark after forty days," he said eventually, "and his rheumaticky legs tread terra firma once more, what's the first thing he plants? A vine! Yes indeed, making wine is the first thing that occurs to him, and the wine he makes isn't half bad. It's drinkable, so one day the inevitable happens: Noah has one over the eight, and the next morning he finds himself lying in his tent, not only naked but with no recollection of how he got there. Imagine, a man of his age!"

"I get you," said Poldi, stung by the priest's less than subtle innuendo. "The Almighty is hopping mad, of course, because his best man has let him down."

"Wait, Donna Poldina, not so fast. The Almighty doesn't punish Noah for getting drunk, he punishes someone else. Noah's sons are naturally shocked to see their father so plastered."

"Naturally."

"*Beh*. So Shem and Japheth cover the old man up, but

Ham finds nothing better to do than to publicise the embarrassing episode."

"These days he'd have taken a selfie with the poor man and posted it on all the social media," said Signora Cocuzza. "Disgraceful!"

"Brava, signora. And that's why Ham and his descendants were accursed of God."

"Am *I* supposed to infer something from all this?" Poldi demanded suspiciously.

Padre Paolo sighed. "You must have a care, Donna Poldina. There are evil people who exploit weakness unmercifully. You're a public figure now. You have responsibilities."

Signora Cocuzza gave a vigorous nod.

"Can't you be a bit more specific, Padre?" Poldi said plaintively.

The priest threw up his hands. "*Madonna,* what if Avola got you drunk and seduced you merely to provide himself with an alibi?"

Poldi considered this.

"No," she said, shaking her head, "it doesn't make sense."

"So how are we going to proceed?" asked Signora Cocuzza.

Poldi stared at her. "*We?*"

"What else, Donna Poldina! A hand or two of gin rummy once a week and you making our mouths water? You'd like that, wouldn't you. No, no, we're a team now. Go on, Padre, say something."

Padre Paolo nodded, and it was the nod of a man who has already looked into every pit of abomination—a man who knows he's embarking on a distasteful mission, but someone has to do it. He folded his hands on the table. "You're the boss, Donna Poldina, but on one condition . . ."

A meaningful gaze. Signora Cocuzza nodded sternly. Poldi already knew what this signified. No more blackouts. No falls from grace, no Signor Bacardi, nothing to drink before four, nothing after nine.

"So be it." She sighed.

"*Et Spiritus Sancti,*" said the padre.

"*Namaste,*" said the sad signora.

"All right, you comedians," said Poldi. She thought for a moment. "We must discover the connection between this murder and Elisa Puglisi's. Padre, as a respected figure, please sound out my neighbour Dottore Carbonaro. He's a district attorney in Catania himself, so he's bound to have known Elisa Puglisi. Also, Etnarosso may mean something to him. Can you manage that in an unobtrusive way?"

The padre rubbed his hands. "I'm only a shrivelled little grape on the Lord's vine, but I'll be damned if I don't squeeze something out of Carbonaro. He gets up my nose in any case, with all those girlfriends he picks up on dating sites and brings here for weekends, leaving his wife back in Catania with the children."

"Padre!" said Poldi, wagging her finger at him with a mixture of reproof and satisfaction. If he had worn a police uniform instead of a cassock, he would have fitted perfectly into her scheme of things.

"I might have some ideas on the Etnarosso front," Signora Cocuzza broke in, framing her words in the conditional—not an unusual practice for an Italian. Whenever emotions, suppositions or vague or ticklish subjects are concerned, the Italian language tends to shift down a gear.

It's all connected with the *bella figura* principle, the glue that holds Italian social life together in everyday matters, business and road traffic: "Make sure you never look foolish yourself and never make other people do so."

Poldi was amazed. Scarcely had she been compelled to accept the existence of a team than the investigative machine had begun to function like clockwork.

"I'm all ears, my dear."

"Love doesn't exist, only evidences of love." Thus Picasso, and he should have known. Poldi thought so too, because she knew a thing or two about love. Not that this made things any easier. Whenever she surrendered herself and her heart, she yearned for evidences of love—not for gold or bling, though she always gladly accepted them, but for the small gestures, words and surprises men can sometimes think of bestowing when they're genuinely in love. Above all, there were two words that bore clearer witness to love than any other, and which never, ever became hackneyed: thank you.

Not that Poldi had expected any thanks from Montana for her fall from grace, certainly not, but she hoped for at least a sign of clemency. So she tensely awaited her commissario's arrival and valiantly resisted the urge to have a little drink.

The doorbell rang at about half past eleven. Montana was even greyer and more crumpled than his suit, if that were possible, but Poldi did not delude herself. It was not a sign of weakness, for the man outside her door looked about as exhausted and innocuous as a Russian nuclear reactor on the verge of a meltdown. Sure enough, when Poldi leant forward to kiss him in the doorway, he brusquely raised his hand.

"May I come in?"

With a sigh, Poldi stepped aside, and Montana, having marched into the inner courtyard, lit an MS. Poldi thrust a cold beer into his hand, and the commissario took it without a word.

"Do sit down."

"No need, I'm not staying." He surveyed the courtyard, on which a thick layer of volcanic ash had already settled. "Don't you have anyone to help you with that? You need to get rid of that stuff. One shower of rain and it'll block up all your drains. Sets like concrete."

Poldi, construing this as a good omen, said nothing. With the utmost self-control, she left the next move to Montana. And he made it. He drew in his breath in preparation for meltdown.

"How could you do it, Poldi? You're simply shameless."

"Do *what?*"

Montana began to pace up and down the courtyard, kicking up such clouds of volcanic ash at every step that it looked as if he were rising from Hades. "Oh, don't give me that!" he yelled. "You know exactly what I'm talking about. I've hardly left your bed before you're screwing the first wine grower that comes along. *Madonna,* I just don't get it! Well, was he good? Wasn't I enough for you?"

My Auntie Poldi became quite calm, as she did whenever a man began to make demands of her, shout at her, turn nasty or be aggressively jealous. Not that Poldi wouldn't have felt flattered by male jealousy, especially as she herself suffered from that emotion because of the handsome commissario's continuing failure to end his affair with that woman Alessia. She set great store by her independence, however, and on principle refused to be dictated to. Cool as Mrs. Robinson in *The Graduate,* she gracefully crossed her legs and regarded Montana with the Anne Bancroft expression she had mastered so well. It could dissect a man like a cute little laboratory animal.

"In the first place, my dear Vito, I had a mental blackout and have no idea what I did or didn't do. Secondly, I'm no more accountable to you for whom I screw than you are to me. And thirdly . . . oh, *vaffanculo,* forget it. Was that all?"

"No, not by a long chalk! Still, maybe it's all over between us. Is that what you want, Poldi? To call it a day, *finito, basta?*"

"No, Vito. I want you to calm down, and it would be nice if you put out your cigarette in the ashtray. The courtyard may look like one, but it isn't."

Montana stared first at Poldi, then at the butt between his fingers. With a grunt, he stubbed it out in the ashtray on the table.

"And now, please sit down."

Montana did as he was bidden, still tense but reasonably approachable.

"Another beer, *tesoro?*"

"*Dai!*"

Poldi brought him one at once. She would have liked to join him but controlled herself.

"Thanks," he said grudgingly.

And, *ecco là,* there it was, the magic word that portended hope and a silver lining, somewhat perfunctory but uttered nonetheless. Poldi breathed a sigh of relief.

"Just as a matter of interest," she said warily, "what did Avola say? I mean, did we do 'it' or not?"

"He says you did."

Poldi sighed. "I'd have been surprised if we hadn't. But you know what? I've had more than one mental blackout in my life. I'm not particularly proud of that, but it happens now and then. I meant to, I admit. Not because you've stopped being enough for me — that's far from the truth, you know that perfectly well — but I was just . . . well, feeling bad about the way you treated me the last time we were together. I don't mean that as an excuse, to be clear, only as a backstory."

She waited to see whether Montana would comment on this, but he merely glared at her and sipped his beer, so she added rather venomously, "So what else is new? How's your beloved Alessia?"

Montana brushed the question aside like an annoying insect. "We've arrested your wine grower."

"You're joking. Just because we —"

"No, of course not," he growled. "Because he confessed to the murder. It's as simple as that."

Even my Auntie Poldi was momentarily speechless.

"I'll get straight to the point," Montana went on, seemingly relishing her consternation. "I always begin by asking, 'Did you commit this murder?' Well, Avola nodded and made a thorough confession."

"I don't believe it," Poldi whispered in dismay. "Anyway, when could he have done it? He was with me."

Montana shrugged his shoulders. "*Beh*. We have his confession on record."

"And his motive?"

"We're working on that. Right now he refuses to say anything more. I'm awaiting the results of the DNA analysis. So, now I want to know why you were at Avola's place at the time of the murder."

Without more ado, Poldi told him all about the wine bottle and the label.

"You're incredible, Poldi!" he said. "It was pure coincidence."

"Oh yeah? And the fact that Madame Sahara was murdered in that very vineyard the next day — that was one too? Let me tell you something, Vito: I've discovered something that escaped you and hit the bull's-eye. Russo's involved — you should concentrate on him. And on Etnarosso.— Any idea what that means? And don't go telling me it's a designation of origin."

Montana shook his head.

"Did you check out that American?"

"We did. He's clean. A tourist."

"He was . . . I don't know, weird somehow. You ought to—"

"I want you to keep out of this, Poldi. I genuinely mean that. It's been hard enough hanging on to the case and getting rid of those dickheads in the Carabinieri. They were all for interrogating you as a suspect, and I should really do the same. After all, on the night of the murder, you and the probable killer were . . ."

"Engaged in 'it,'" Poldi put in helpfully.

Montana bit his lip. "If you can't remember a thing, Avola's confession stands."

Poldi nodded sadly. "But it wasn't him. He's just not the

murderous type. I know what I'm talking about, and I can tell that you don't believe it either."

Montana clicked his tongue indignantly. "A confession's a confession. Just stay out of it, okay? If you don't, I may not be able to help you."

"Am I in trouble, then?" Poldi asked softly, leaning forward a little.

It was something of an ambiguous question and something of a request for forgiveness, for it must be said that Poldi was pierced to the core by the very sight of Montana looking so dishevelled and moody and unjustifiably jealous. It was a long time since any man had set her aflame the way he did. He expanded her heart, his touch scorched her skin and made her vibrate, made her feel lighter than she had for a long time. She wanted to kiss and embrace, caress and fondle him all at once. She wanted to hold his hand, lay her head on his nice hairy chest, sleep at his side, simply look at and admire him, sit on a bench beside him in the sun, watch him smoking and eating, hear his voice and know everything about him. And that was why losing him was what she did *not* want at any price, even if it meant she had to become a good girl at her age. Well, let's say, try at least to do so.

"No, you aren't in trouble, not where the investigation is concerned," said Montana. "Not so far, anyway. Come to headquarters tomorrow and give a statement, and that'll be that." He rubbed his hands together as though ridding them of dirt of some kind, the traditional Italian gesture meaning "Done, finished, sorted, let's not talk about it any more." He drew a deep breath. "As for me personally, I'm not going to stipulate what you can or can't do, nor do I expect an apology. Although . . . yes, come to think of it, perhaps I do. Yes, I certainly do expect an apology, because I didn't like 'it' at all, you hear? Not one little bit, I didn't. I feel tempted to make a scene you'll never forget. I feel tempted to smash the place up, but I can control myself. I'm not the stereotypical Sicilian male who bristles at every last little thing and insists on seeking satisfaction with a sawn-off shotgun. I'm a paragon of self-control, that's why. I spend the whole day dealing with idiots and liars, I'm utterly overworked and short of sleep, but do I blow my top? No, I control myself. I'm supercool. Be damned to my Sicilian blood. You'll do as you please in any case, whether I go berserk or knuckle under. *Madonna*, I'd like to go berserk sometime, I really would, but I keep a grip on myself, understand? I behave like a civilised central European, but only because I'm sick to death of discussing personal relationships for nights on end. Know something? You can get stuffed!"

"Who can?" Poldi retorted amiably. "Women in general or just Alessia and me?"

Another mean little dig, true, but it simply tripped off her tongue.

Montana stared at her aghast, as if it had struck him only now that he had long been engaged in a losing battle and his back was to the wall. He sighed. "*Vaffanculo*, Poldi! *Vaffanculo!*" He got to his feet with a grunt. "Don't bother, I know the way out."

He had gone before Poldi could bring herself to apologise, and she had a nasty feeling that she might have overdone things a bit.

"A bit risky, wasn't it?" I remarked when she told me about it later. "I mean, competing directly with the younger woman like that?"

"I couldn't help it. I live in the here and now. And besides, I sensed things weren't going too well between Vito and Alessia. I could well imagine her putting him through the wringer all night, because she naturally had a woman's intuition like me and sensed there were times when Vito wasn't up to the job."

"'It,' you mean?"

"The man had utterly worn himself out with me, and even the most active volcano needs a break between eruptions. With Alessia, I suspect that 'it' may have been more of a damp squib than a firework display."

Her expression as she told me this was smug and self-assured.

"Besides, I had a murder to solve, didn't I? One's private life has to take a back seat on such occasions, unlike what you see on TV. Even though the right of way through my noddle had been temporarily suspended, I strove to concentrate on essentials. For instance, on what in the world could have prompted Achille to confess to the murder."

"It didn't occur to you that he might actually have committed it?"

Poldi regarded me pityingly. "Ever heard of the word 'intuition'? Does it mean anything to you?"

"Honestly, Poldi, give me a break!"

6

*Tells of the fruits of the Lord, messages sent us by
life, and the Sicilian notion of "under normal circumstances." Uncle Martino comes up with a theory
that posits a link between the Cyclopes and the CIA.
Poldi becomes concerned and goes full speed ahead,
only to be detained by an elderly gentleman and
Saint Venera. Soon afterwards, she makes a shocking
discovery in an accursed place.*

The fruits of the Lord . . . Poldi couldn't get the phrase
out of her head. It got caught up in her thoughts like
an autumn leaf under a windscreen wiper, and it was beginning to get on her nerves.

But things that annoy us, Poldi once told me, are simply
messages sent us by life and ought to draw our attention to
something. And my aunt knew a thing or two about life's
messages.

The only question was, what was life—in its peculiar,
inarticulate way—trying to convey to her this time? Poldi
sometimes imagined herself to be a plump, sweet grape on a
vine, waiting in sun, wind and weather for the wine grower
to pick her and transform her into something delicious.
Sometimes she thought of Padre Paolo's admonitory para-

ble about Noah's drunken stupor. Sometimes she thought of Avola, who was a wine grower and possibly a murderer. And sometimes the whole of life, which could end so swiftly and abruptly, seemed to her like a vine that could be killed off by a single hailstorm. And the way in which the Almighty treated his noblest fruit sent my Auntie Poldi into a towering Bavarian rage that made her forget all about her heartache and hangover, swept away her doubts and cleared her head. In short, my auntie was back in the zone. She was a ruthless investigative machine, a criminaloid, a deduction queen, a born huntress. Or so I imagine.

"*Namaste*, life!" she said, grateful for this purifying rage, clasping her hands together on her bosom. "The rest of the world can kiss my ass!"

But where to begin her investigation? Padre Paolo had been unleashed on Dottore Carbonaro, and Signora "Still Waters Run Deep" Cocuzza had undertaken a "special mission."

Poldi was touched. "It seems," she told herself, "that having a team isn't *such* a bad thing."

It felt good to have friends and not suffer from cosmic loneliness.

But she still had to decide what her own next step should be, and that made her head spin a little. She could have done with a beer, but no way. Poldi's self-control was positively superhuman by this time. She felt like Odysseus, lashed to the mast and listening to the song of the Sirens.

So she could now have launched her investigation with supercharged energy. But only "could have," because at that precise moment she was visited by my Aunts Teresa, Caterina and Luisa and my Uncle Martino, plus Totti the dog and my cousins Ciro, Marco and Laura. It was Sunday lunchtime, after all, and with us that always means *pranzo* with the family.

Sicilian relations are no different from relations elsewhere in the world. They can be annoying. You love and respect them, you enjoy seeing them on high days and holidays and at weddings, children's birthdays and funerals, you tolerate their quirks and laugh at their old chestnuts. Yes, but only in small doses, please. And that's the problem with Sicily: small doses don't exist. It's the works or nothing. The up-side of Sicilian relations: they bring mountains of food with them.

My own family members are no exception in that respect; they're perpetually annoying. At the same time, those Sundays devoted to overeating, listening to good advice from the aunts and horsing around with my cousins have been the happiest times imaginable ever since my childhood. Moreover, our family possesses a secret weapon in terms of wit and eccentricity: Uncle Martino.

Just as he had every day since retiring, Uncle Martino had spent the whole morning roaming Catania's fish market with the utmost concentration, a dog-end eternally lodged in the corner of his mouth. The fact is, buying fish in Sicily is serious business, a quest for maximal freshness and minimal prices, and thus a largely male-dominated affair.

"You must think of it as a stock exchange," Uncle Martino told me once, "ruled by supply, demand and greed. Every customer is an expert and, consequently, your direct competitor. From the moment you walk through the Porta Uzeda and plunge into the turmoil of the market, you have no friends any more. All that matters is your mission: to snap up the best fish in the world at the very best price. For example, you want to buy some tuna, and you only want the best cut. And what's the best cut? *Beh!* The belly meat, of course. You see that Alfio has three tuna left in his tub, but a queue has formed in front of his stall, so it's unlikely there'll be any belly meat left by the time it's your turn. You could try to worm your way to the front, but you know you won't catch your competitors napping. Turi, in the stall next door, hasn't any tuna at all, and his neighbour Tano has only two, but they're too measly for you. Tuna are in great demand, so prices are high. It's a tense situation. Everyone's on edge, time is going by, midday is approaching. But now comes your chance. Enzo's stall is still bare. He has probably gone far out to fish and will return within the next hour. Even if he has caught some tuna, your competitors will already have met their requirements. That means demand will fall, likewise prices, and you'll get a nice, cheap cut of belly meat. But what if Enzo doesn't return in time or fails to catch anything? Then you'll go away empty-handed. So the question is, queue up or wait? To be or not to be? All or nothing? You need nerves of steel, instinct, years of experience and the agility of a panther to elbow your way to the front and strike."

Which was what Uncle Martino had clearly done that Sunday.

Needless to say, Sunday lunches in Torre Archirafi involved covert inspection tours by the aunts, who discreetly gauged Poldi's alcohol intake and frame of mind. She said she'd only deferred her plan to drink herself to death beside the sea, so the aunts were still at the Code Yellow level of vigilance.

They came wafting in like a wonderful gust of high spirits, loquacity and affection. Laden with three cooler bags filled with fish, seafood, bread, vegetables, oyster mushrooms, tomato sauce, parsley, peaches and fresh parmigiana, they commandeered the kitchen, poured Poldi's Scotch down the drain and fired up the barbecue in the courtyard. Totti went racing around the house barking excitedly, Ciro changed some defunct light bulbs, Marco filled Poldi's jerrycan at the old mineral water plant, Laura sprawled on the sofa with Totti and chatted to girlfriends on her mobile phone, and Uncle Martino scaled some sea bream. All at once, No. 29 Via Baronessa was pervaded by the scent of cheese, grilled fish and fresh tomato sauce, by laughter, barking, the blare of the television, pop music, charcoal smoke, midday heat, appetite, stolidity, fatalism and joie de vivre. In short, by *sicilianità*.

My Aunts Teresa, Caterina and Luisa were Taureans — in other words, good-natured, cheerful, sensual creatures, and not easily ruffled by anything. They were also inveterate fans of police procedurals, so their reaction to Poldi's account of the last twenty-four hours was rather blasé, not least because she could always be expected to dramatise to the nth degree. Or perhaps because they had been in Catania during the eighties, when someone was gunned down nearly every day in the course of the last big Mafia war and the first decisive anti-Mafia operations. The aunts were far more worried by Poldi's fall from grace and her mental blackout than by Madame Sahara's murder.

Luisa, the youngest, displayed an undisguised interest in

the case. "Does this mean you're investigating already?" she asked.

"What do *you* think? Vito is far from happy about it, but I owe it to Giuliana."

"Do you already have a suspect?"

"Yes, of course. Russo must be behind it, for whatever reason, but I don't think he did his own dirty work. He's probably got some kind of hold over Achille."

Before Poldi could pursue this, lunch intervened.

It was only a brief interruption, though, because leisurely meals partaken of by extended Sicilian families seated beneath orange or olive trees are as much of a modern myth as uproarious Italian weddings celebrated to the strains of massed mandolins. They really take the following course: hours-long preparations entailing the utmost care and the largest possible quantities of the finest raw materials available, then everything onto the table at the same time, then some ten minutes' lip-smacking carnage and dissection worthy of a school of sharks running riot in a shoal of tuna, then a brief, contented "*Che buono!*," a friendly, knowledgeable debate as to whether the *spigola* could have been a trifle fresher, the vinegar for the *agrodolce* a trifle sourer, the onions a trifle sweeter, and whether it is permissible to tenderise octopus. (Absolutely not!) To end with, perhaps a ripe peach or a mocha gelato. Cigarettes and coffee, then quickly back in front of the TV to watch Formula One or take a little nap. Whoever coined the phrase "Keep calm and carry on," it certainly wasn't a Sicilian. There's more enjoyment and appreciation to be had from this headlong dive into the trough than from many a celebrated six-course dinner complete with the chef's compliments, palate-cleansing sorbets and matching wines.

At my aunts' table, everyone knows full well that what they're eating is the freshest and most delicious food a person can cook, and they do it justice by bolting it in silence, immersing themselves in its divinity, becoming one with the universe, and gaining enlightenment from *pasta al nero, spigola in agrodolce, pepata di cozze, lumache in salsa di pomodoro, calamaretti fritti, insalata di arance e finocchio selvatico, caponata siciliana* and *parmigiana alla Teresa.* The duration of the collision is as unimportant as it is in love and in particle physics, because enjoyment—as we all know—bends space-time. If I could ask a good fairy to grant me a wish, it would be to spend the remaining Sundays of my life exactly as outlined above.

Uncle Martino had a theory about Etnarosso. He had a theory about everything, and all his theories reposed on three bedrocks: Cyclopes, Frederick II and the CIA.

Martino believed the Cyclopes to be the mythical indigenous inhabitants of Sicily, a race of tall aborigines with close-set eyes that provide the missing link between Neanderthals and modern *Homo sapiens.* He regularly and nonchalantly quashed my objection that there was no evolutionary evidence for anything of the kind.

"In Sicily," he declared, "reality is so closely entwined with myth that certain truths cannot be perceived and measured with the blunt instruments of conventional science. The Cyclopes have left behind no written records, after all, and they're also—alas!—extinct. They were probably exterminated in ancient times by some Greek pirate with herpes, but before that they interbred with the earliest conquerors of the island. All of us are a bit Cyclopean, even you."

At all events, according to Martino, the Cyclopes invented the Pyramids, colonised Atlantis, were taught by the earliest extraterrestrial visitors how to alchemise lead into gold, and much more besides.

The brilliant Holy Roman Emperor Frederick II recognised this during the twelfth century. He made Sicily the centre of his empire and gathered the world's most celebrated scholars around him with the aim of exploiting the Cyclopes' store of arcane knowledge for the benefit of humankind.

As ill luck would have it, the Knights Templar robbed Frederick II of these arcana shortly before he could put his grand scheme into effect. After their order was disbanded, the Templars just managed to get the secrets to safety aboard a caravel bound for the as yet officially undiscovered New World, where they were guarded for centuries by their various successor organisations at a location corresponding to modern downtown Manhattan. Yes, and guess what the Templars' present successor organisation is. Exactly, the CIA. It's the CIA that forms a clandestine world government, manipulates the price of gold, is poisoning us with chemtrails, denies the existence of UFOs, and was responsible for reinstalling Lucky Luciano and the Mafia in Sicily after the Second World War.

That's the point at which Uncle Martino gets so carried away that he sideslips from Italian into Sicilian, digresses into current politics, and then, with astronomical precision, locks horns with his son, my cousin Marco, until Aunt Teresa ends their altercation with a furious cry of *"Basta!"* — and we all go outside for a smoke.

Uncle Martino's theory about Etnarosso was that it was the Sicilian offshoot of a successor organisation of Propaganda Due, a secret Masonic lodge of higher-ups from politics, industry, the military, the secret services and the Mafia, their aim being to infiltrate and dismantle the Italian government and the Vatican. This conspiracy had been discovered by a certain Tindaro Martorana from Agrigento, who had been smuggled into the lodge by the MoVimento 5 Stelle, had paid for this heroic feat with his life, and was unofficially revered as a hero by the Five Star Movement. Since Propaganda Due, or P2, was known to have been an instrument of the CIA, Etnarosso was another. It was, therefore, a successor of the Knights Templar, who had meant to deploy the extraterrestrial knowledge of the Cyclopes and Frederick II against the whole of humanity. Because organisations of this calibre are excellent at disguising themselves, it had taken the gifts of a clairvoyant to perceive all this, so Madame Sahara had probably unearthed one of the most perfidious global conspiracies and been killed in consequence. But not without leaving behind a final clue: according to my uncle, the American with the divining rod was very probably a CIA killer. Case solved.

Silence fell. Everyone stared at Uncle Martino, who, satisfied with himself and his theory, was sucking a fish bone. If there's another word for mischief, it can only be Martino.

"What nonsense!" said Aunt Caterina, always the voice of reason. "This is a murder—it's no laughing matter."

Aunt Teresa reproved her husband with a sidelong glance;

Marco, Ciro and Laura smirked; and Aunt Luisa sighed because she loved conspiracy theories and Martino's theory had really appealed to her. Poldi still said nothing.

"*Beh!*" said Uncle Martino, shrugging his shoulders. "That's my theory, and I'm sticking to it."

Aunt Teresa started to say something, but Poldi got there first.

"There may even be something in it — basically, I mean."

"Why?"

"Because Signora Cocuzza told me something of the kind," Poldi went on. "The thing is, she recently consulted Madame Sahara about . . . well, a private matter, and she saw something. An envelope. A perfectly normal C4 envelope — you know, buff-coloured, with something inside and 'Etnarosso' written on it in capitals. It was lying on Madame Sahara's desk, Signora Cocuzza says, and she wondered what it meant, whether it was a name and whether Madame Sahara was into wine — you know, the sort of thing that goes through your mind when you're nervous because it's the first time you've consulted a fortune-teller. Well, when Madame Sahara noticed Signora Cocuzza staring at the envelope, she hurriedly put it away in a drawer. And that's why the signora remembered it."

"And what do you deduce from that?" asked Aunt Caterina.

"Madame Sahara was on to something, that's what I deduce, and I also deduce that the key to Etnarosso and her murder is still at her home in that envelope."

The aunts smelt a rat.

"You're not to, Poldi," Teresa said sharply. "Absolutely not!"

"Not to what?" Poldi protested, innocence personified.

"You're not going to break into Madame Sahara's house and look for that envelope!"

"What do you take me for? Of course I won't. It'd be stupid, considering what a splendid piece of bait that envelope makes."

"What do you mean?" Aunt Caterina asked suspiciously.

"I'm going to keep the house under surveillance. It's quite obvious the murderer will sooner or later turn up in the hope of destroying any clues to his identity."

"And you'll keep it under surveillance? How?"

"I've now got a team, didn't I tell you? A couple of angels, so to speak. Anyone feel like a martini?"

"Don't change the subject, Poldi," said Caterina. "What sort of team? Who'll be keeping watch on the house, for heaven's sake?"

"Why, Signora Cocuzza in her old Cinquecento, of course. Special Ops."

"But if you're right and the murderer comes looking for the envelope, it could be really dangerous. What if he spots the signora?"

Poldi brushed this aside. "If anyone can be totally invisible, it's the sad signora. She's perfect for the job. Besides, she suggested it herself, and anyway, all she has to do is take photos of any suspicious activity from the other side of the street."

"But you can't keep her watching the house for days and nights on end, not on her own. Who knows, maybe no one will ever turn up."

"I'll relieve her from time to time. We must act! Signor X could put in an appearance at any moment."

Poldi sounded a trifle defensive. She now realised that she'd been carried away by the sad signora's thrill of the chase.

"What else could I do, she was so keen on the idea." Poldi picked up her mobile. "All right, I'll call her off."

She glanced at the other aunts to see whether there were any further objections. There weren't. With a sigh, she waited for Signora Cocuzza to respond from her observation post.

Which she didn't. The phone rang twice, thrice, four times. The fifth time, her voicemail cut in.

"She's not answering," Poldi told the aunts rather helplessly.

"She isn't?"

"Just her voicemail."

"Try her again."

Poldi called again—with the same result. The sad signora didn't answer. Poldi was becoming uneasy.

"Dear Signora Cocuzza, where are you? Poldi here. Please call me back soonest. I'm cancelling the operation, you hear? So get out of there. Where are you, for God's sake?"

Poldi stared irresolutely at her phone as if it could enforce Signora Cocuzza's recall, but no dice. With every second that passed, she was becoming more convinced that something had gone badly wrong up in Santa Venerina, that her melancholy friend might be in mortal danger—that it might already be too late.

"I'm going to Santa Venerina," she announced. "Hell and damnation, why on earth did I let her do it?" She slipped her sandals on and dashed into the house.

"Wait!" called Aunt Teresa. "We'll come too!"

"You most certainly won't."

"No arguments, Poldi!"

A few moments later, like two Special Forces teams, four aunts, an uncle and a dog erupted from the front door of No. 29 Via Baronessa, piled into Poldi's old but overpowered Alfa and Uncle Martino's battered, asthmatic Fiat, and sped off towards Etna. Poldi made several vain attempts to get through to her friend en route, which only heightened the general sense of panic.

The route from Torre Archirafi to Santa Venerina is circuitous and winding and takes in potholed secondary roads, a motorway, two level crossings and several straggling little towns. The latter, which basically consist of a main street, a bar and a small piazza in front of the church, are boring in the extreme. Under normal circumstances the trip takes barely twenty minutes, but "under normal circumstances" isn't a Sicilian concept. In Sicily, it always means a bizarre concatenation of mundane factors. This time only two were involved: senile overconfidence and Saint Venera.

"I should explain," said Poldi, interrupting her account at this point, "that Venera is the patron saint of Santa Venerina."

"Really, Poldi," I protested. "Fancy going off at a tangent about some saint just when it's getting exciting."

"Pull yourself together, boy, it's all a way of building up the suspense—make a note of that for your novel. You have to take your foot off the gas occasionally."

"But not now, surely?"

Poldi serenely sipped her Scotch. "I can also stop right there."

"*Forza* Poldi," I said with a sigh.

"Well, during the second century Venera was a beautiful Gaulish girl who came to do missionary work in Sicily, where she lived in caves and healed the sick. Everyone loved her, she was such a dear, and she left a scent of roses behind whenever she preached. Naturally enough, the authorities persecuted her for this. She was arrested and taken to Acireale, where the Roman governor tortured her good and proper. She had boiling olive oil poured over her, the poor thing. But lo and behold, Venera emerged from every bout of torture even lovelier than before. In view of this miracle, the sadistic Roman governor repented—he burst into tears and became a convert. Lovely Venera was a phoenix type like me—I feel a certain affinity with her—but it did her no good in the end because they beheaded her. My, what dark days they were . . ."

I stared at her. "Is that it?"

"Yes, sure. Nice story, isn't it? Whenever you tell a story, it has to have a moral—make a note of that. Well, now we've got that out of the way, on with the motley!"

Just before Santa Venerina, Poldi had let Uncle Martino overtake her on a bend because he knew the way to Madame Sahara's house the way he knew every last corner of Sicily. He raced into the town with his foot hard down, closely followed by Poldi's Alfa, missed the turning at a roundabout and headed straight for the town centre. There, having realised his mistake, he performed a James Bond skid-turn down a no-entry side street with cars parked on both sides, leaving just room enough to pass.

As bad luck would have it, factor number one supervened

in the shape of a cussed old man who had just pulled out in his rattletrap of a Fiat 500. Since he also preferred to drive down the one-way street and knew the dimensions of his fifty-year-old treasure to a tee, he had decided to turn round and—guess what—miscalculated. The little Cinquecento was stuck sideways-on. It could neither advance nor retreat. There was nothing doing.

Uncle Martino screeched to a stop so abruptly that Poldi almost ran into him from behind. Thumbing his horn and gesticulating feverishly, Martino indicated that the signore in the Cinquecento should clear the road as soon as possible, but the elderly gentleman didn't even glance at him, just doggedly continued to inch backwards and forwards. Realising the situation was hopeless, Poldi didn't hesitate; she slammed her gear lever into reverse.

Which was when factor number two came into play. At that moment, a procession in honour of Venera debouched into the street behind her. In the lead came a priest swinging a censer, followed by four ministrants with a huge figure of the saint on their shoulders and, devoutly singing in their wake, half the inhabitants of Santa Venerina in their Sunday best. Before Poldi could reverse so much as a metre, the procession had reached the bottleneck and come to a halt. Now there was really nothing doing.

At such moments in Sicily, mythical, elemental forces take hold: subterranean telluric currents that shape people's destinies, create chaos and disentangle it. Uncle Martino had already got out in order to resolve the elderly gentleman's predicament in some way, but to no avail. Totti bounded around the little car, barking happily. Aunt Luisa got out to clear a space for Poldi to reverse out of the street, but more and more people were pouring down it. There was no hope of extricating themselves.

"What appears to be the problem, signora?" the priest politely inquired of Aunt Luisa. He passed the word to his ministrants, who promptly put the heavy saint down and crowded around the Cinquecento, where their pieces of good advice only exacerbated the chaos.

Poldi, at the end of her tether by now, pounded the steering wheel with her fist. "Hell's bells and buckets of blood! God give me strength! Get out of the way, you knuckleheads, this is a matter of life or death!"

But not even Poldi's mastery of Bavarian invective could dissolve the blockage. On the contrary, her piercing cries only attracted more curiosity.

"What's going on up ahead?"

"No idea. Sounds like someone's slaughtering a goat."

"On a Sunday?"

"It's a flash mob."

"A what?"

"Like on the Internet, Mamma. I showed you. Just wait, next thing you know, someone'll sing the 'Ode to Joy.'"

"Really? How nice."

"It's an epileptic fit, sure as eggs. I know that from seeing my neighbour's husband."

"When are we going to move on?"

"Ask that signora in the wig, the one in the car, shouting."

"Isn't that the padre shouting?"

"Have you heard? The padre's having an epileptic fit. The Devil is speaking through him."

"Is he spitting nails?"

"No, but the crazy signora in the wig is."

"It's only a goat, folks."

"I'm a member of the Salvation Army. Can you give me her number?"

Poldi eventually blew her top. Getting out of her Alfa like the Devil incarnate emerging from Pandora's box, she grabbed every able-bodied young man she could lay hands on. "You and you and you and you, come with me. *Avanti! Forza!*"

Impressed by the furious apparition in the black wig, the young men obeyed without demur and followed Poldi up the street to the sideways-on old-timer, where she stationed one beside each mudguard. Cries of "Bravo!" began to make themselves heard.

"Would you mind getting out for a moment?" Poldi asked the elderly signore, every inch the courteous professional, even in this extreme situation.

"Why?"

"Because then we can lift your car and turn it round, that's why."

"No."

"What do you mean, no?"

"Don't bother, I'll manage."

Poldi forced herself to take two deep breaths before she replied.

"No you won't. You're sweating like a pig and your heart can't take much more. Kindly get out."

"This is my car. I refuse to be evicted from it."

By this stage, Poldi would gladly have hauled the old man out of his car and high-handedly thrashed him in the presence of Saint Venera, notwithstanding the respect due to age. He looked so gaunt and decrepit, my aunt could have torn him to shreds, but she didn't. She had a better idea. Bending down, she put her head through the window and whispered something in his ear, so softly that no one else could hear, whereupon the elderly signore abruptly turned pale, stared at Poldi and struggled out of his car.

Naturally I asked Poldi what she had whispered to the old man. I made every effort to squeeze it out of her, but she flatly refused to tell me. "That'll remain my little secret" she said coquettishly. "Where the stronger sex is concerned, I simply know which button to press."

However, knowing my aunt as I do by now, I suspect she put her faith in the traditional effect on Sicilian men of a mildly whispered threat, something like, "I made him an offer he couldn't refuse." That, combined with the sound of the German language, never fails to send them to panic stations and trigger Code Red. The actual wording is immaterial. I could even imagine Poldi reciting Hölderlin.

To the accompaniment of cries of "Bravo!," laughter and applause, the youths made a concerted effort to heft the Cinquecento in the desired direction, and in a few moments the traffic jam dissolved, the scared old gentleman was able to drive off, Saint Venera was hoisted into the air, and Uncle Martino and Poldi could step on the gas again.

They got to Madame Sahara's house a minute later. It was like something out of a fairy tale. Behind a high, lava stone wall loomed a four-square, pistachio-green old villa with basalt window arches and a wraparound terrace. Bougainvillea climbed up its walls like all-enveloping violet foam, strelitzias and bananas reached to the first floor, palms and cypresses seemed to be standing guard on every side. A huge hibiscus aimed its fat, yellow, trumpet-shaped blossoms at the house as if their principal function was to awaken it from its dreams every hundred years; tubs of cactuses and rubber plants paraded on the terrace. The shade-dispensing greenery all around made the house look like a forgotten island jutting from a slumbering ocean of flowers and foliage.

An inconspicuous brass plate beside the entrance to the garden read *Villa Sahara*. Next to it was an iron bell pull. The first-floor windows stood open to reveal silk curtains billowing lazily, invitingly, in the warm late-afternoon breeze. No other form of movement could be detected, nor was there anything to be heard but the omnipresent hum of honeybees and bumblebees.

Poldi spotted Signora Cocuzza's small Japanese car parked across the road beside a wall overgrown with bougainvillea. The little silver runabout was almost invisible amid such a sea of blossom. More importantly, it was empty.

Poldi dialled the sad signora's number for the umpteenth time, yet again without success. There was no answering beep from inside the car, either. It was locked and displayed no signs of violence.

"Where on earth can she be?" asked Aunt Luisa.

"She's been gone too long for a trip to the loo," Poldi mused aloud. "So there's only one possibility." She pointed to Madame Sahara's house.

"Why would she have gone inside?" demanded Aunt Caterina.

"It was a spontaneous decision," Poldi concluded. "Something must have happened. She's inside there, I tell you. Stay here." And she made straight for the house.

"You'd like that, wouldn't you!" Aunt Teresa called after her. "We're coming with you."

"Oh no you aren't."

"Oh yes we are."

"It could be dangerous."

"That's just why we're coming. *Basta!*"

Did I already mention that it's quite pointless to argue with Aunt Teresa? All three aunts are as soft and gentle as a breeze in springtime, but they were born under the sign of Taurus, which means they're stubborn too. Once in motion, they're unstoppable.

It was dawning on Poldi that membership of a team had its disadvantages, and that she would have to address the subject of joint decision-making at her next team meeting. At present, however, there was nothing to be done.

So they all passed through the unlocked wrought-iron gate, under a basalt arch and into Madame Sahara's enchanted garden. Poldi led the way, followed by Totti, Aunt Teresa, Aunt Luisa, Aunt Caterina and, bringing up the rear, Uncle Martino, who kept looking in all directions with total professionalism.

Beyond the gate, a narrow path meandered towards the house, flanked by waist-high grass and luxuriant flowering shrubs. Poldi gave a little start when a snake crossed her path, then pressed boldly on with aunts, uncle and dog at her heels.

The front door had been jimmied open. The interior was cool and hushed, the thick walls being proof against the heat of the day. An old refrigerator hummed somewhere. No one ventured to say anything or breathe too loudly. Poldi and her team crept around the house as if loath to awaken evil incarnate enjoying a postprandial siesta. They realised that they might at any moment come upon Signora Cocuzza lying in a pool of blood, if not something even worse.

But all they encountered at first was devastation and disorder. Someone had made a thorough search of the house. Every cupboard, drawer and chest had been opened and its contents strewn across the floor. It looked as if a storm or demon had rampaged through the building, unnoticed by the world outside. In the kitchen Poldi waded through smashed crockery and spilt milk mingled with the contents of the open refrigerator and packets of pasta and instant coffee.

In obedience to a sort of inspiration and her criminological instinct, Poldi quickly took some photographs with her mobile phone as she picked her way cautiously through the mess like a skater on thin ice.

"I did so," she told me, "because the same thing applies to criminology as to sex: a bird in the hand—"

"Is worth two in the bush," I said.

She gave me a look. "Bear that in mind."

The old upholstered furniture and Moroccan pouffes in the living room had been slit open, and great wads of stuffing covered the flagstoned floor and the rugs like foam on a beach, mixed up with the remains of smashed vases and lamps. Next door to the living room was a studio in which Madame Sahara had received her clients. Obviously the villa's former private chapel, it was a semicircular room facing the garden, with a vaulted ceiling and a library of old books, most of which lay scattered across the floor, together with papers and documents. Occupying the centre of the room was a heavy, circular oak table and four massive chairs, and in one corner stood a dainty rococo chaise longue. Clients may sometimes have reclined on it when pouring out their hearts to Madame Sahara. Or perhaps she had used it herself when recovering from an exhausting séance.

Whatever the truth, that same chaise longue was now occupied by the motionless form of Signora Cocuzza.

She looked even paler and greyer than she did in her most melancholy moments. Her eyes stared into space, and a thread of drying saliva was visible in the corner of her mouth. No sign of any blood.

Poldi dashed over and felt the inert woman's pulse, then put her ear to the parted lips. "She's alive!"

"*Dio mio!*"

Poldi patted her friend's cheeks. "Signora! Signora, can you hear me?"

Patting proved ineffective, so Poldi resorted to firmer measures and slapped her hard on both cheeks. That did the trick.

The signora gave a start. "*Porca Madonna!*" she said, alarmed by the sight of Poldi's face only inches from hers.

"Don't worry, signora, it's only me. Don't be frightened, all is well."

The sad signora took a few moments to recover her senses. Her eyes roamed the ravaged room as if she couldn't recall how she came to be there. It wasn't until she had sipped a glass of water that she got her bearings and recovered her memory.

"I . . . I took a photo," she whispered. "With my phone."

But the phone wasn't there any more. The aunts combed the whole room and Totti eagerly sniffed the chaos, but the mobile phone did not come to light.

"He took it off you, of course," said Poldi, "after he knocked you out."

What had happened? The sad signora had only a fragmentary recollection.

"I'd taken up my observation post," she began, "but there wasn't much to be seen. Nothing at all, actually. It was rather boring—sorry, Donna Poldina, but it was. But then! Then I spotted a movement at one of the upstairs windows. Just for a moment, more a kind of shadow, I'd say. Well, I wasn't sure. Maybe it had been a reflection or the curtain moving, I really wasn't sure, but I couldn't take my eyes off that window from then on, know what I mean?"

Poldi sighed. "Didn't we agree that you'd call headquarters at once if you spotted anything?"

"I know," Signora Cocuzza admitted contritely.

But she hadn't, and she was loath to say what on earth had come over her. The thrill of the chase, I suspect. At all events, after a brief few minutes of uncertainty and hesitation she had got out of her car.

"Well," she confessed, "all I meant to do was cross the road for a closer view of the window, you understand, but . . ."

"But then you went inside," Poldi amplified, "seeing as how the gate was already open and the front door likewise."

"I'm feeling really poorly, Donna Poldina."

"Think yourself lucky, my dear. You could have ended up dead. Never mind, though. What happened then?"

In a nutshell, what happened was as follows: Signora Cocuzza crept into the house. Step by silent step she toured the rooms and used her mobile phone to photograph the universal devastation. She kept her ears pricked for the smallest sound, but heard nothing, and in the end became convinced that she had only imagined the movement at the window, the way one sometimes does. Anyway, she eventually discovered something in the studio that captured her attention to such an extent that she promptly took a photo of it. She was so preoccupied that she failed to hear someone coming up behind her. All she was aware of was a sharp pain in her neck, and then she'd felt as if someone had pushed her off a cliff into a big, dark chasm.

Poldi heaved another sigh.

"He gave you an injection. It's a miracle he didn't kill you."

Signora Cocuzza made no comment on this—after all, it wasn't her job to theorise. Feeling simply happy to be alive, she even managed a faint smile.

"What was this exciting thing you discovered?" Poldi asked eventually.

"Names," said the signora, and a look of triumph came into her eyes.

"Names?"

"Yes, at least I think so. Names on a kind of list."

"What sort of names?" Poldi asked. "Try to remember!"

But the signora just shook her head. "I'm sorry, I've forgotten."

"It doesn't matter," Poldi lied.

"Is that bad?"

"No, my dear, of course not."

"You may be right," Signora Cocuzza said archly, "because it's lucky I've still got this." So saying, she triumphantly produced a small piece of folded paper from a pocket in her skirt and handed it to Poldi. "The whole table was littered with these pieces of paper, all bearing names. I pocketed one of them before photographing the rest, and then, well . . . pow!"

Poldi almost wrenched the paper from her hand. She was about to unfold it when . . .

"What the devil's going on here?"

A familiar voice. A smoky voice filled with *sicilianità,* ill temper and suppressed passion.

Poldi swiftly palmed the folded scrap of paper. Turning, she saw Montana standing in the doorway, and behind him, as if permanently stapled to his heels, Detectives Zannotta and Console.

Montana's question was understandable in a way, coming from a homicide chief who enters the home of a murder victim and finds the place completely trashed, and in the midst of it his own lady friend, whom he has recently and quite reasonably told to keep out of things. But no, she blithely tramples all over the clues and evidence with the help of her three sisters-in-law, her brother-in-law, a dog and a neighbour on a chaise longue, all of whom look guilty, even the dog, with the sole exception of his lady friend. All she says is "I know what you're thinking, Vito, but I can explain everything."

7

Tells of the truth in the corner of a person's eye, and of lists. Poldi makes away with something else and philosophises about optical illusions. An old acquaintance visits her, bringing unwelcome news from the management of fate. This boosts the forces of the subconscious and points Poldi in the direction of a suspect who had yet to appear on anyone's radar. And this, in turn, leads her back to Santa Venerina and a renewed recognition of the age-old Sicilian relationship between actuality and appearance.

Wow!" I said, highly impressed, when Poldi described the whole episode to me later. "And then?"

"Well, you can imagine. A volcanic eruption is a warm breeze by comparison. I mean, the man is a detective chief inspector and a Sicilian, which means that every emotion, from love to rage, is multiplied by two. Men like him aren't to be measured by normal human standards. They're human volcanoes, and I know what I'm talking about. Only very special people can cope with them."

"Let me guess. People like you, for instance?"

"You can keep your sarcasm. Even a man like Vito Montana wants to be loved, but most women crack up because they can't endure such passion, such fire. You need to have a strong, sensual personality like mine, because I know a thing or two about pain and passion and volcanoes."

"Of course, Poldi. Well, how did he react? Did he go berserk, smash the place up and drag you through the house by your hair, singing arias from *Otello*?"

"Get away with you!" Poldi sighed. "Mind you, it's a nice idea—I might have enjoyed it. No, the first thing he did was send Teresa, Caterina, Luisa, Martino and the dog out of the room. They were only too pleased, as you can imagine. Totti especially, because an animal like that can sense the dark forces of violence that linger at a crime scene like the smell of frying fat in a burger bar. Next, Vito got rid of his two stupid sidekicks and shut the door on them. And then . . . well, the balloon went up."

"Meaning?"

"I won't go into detail now. Suffice it to say, he made such a din, the curtains fluttered and I was afraid he'd blow Signora Cocuzza out of the window. She's tougher than she looks, though, I noticed that. Well, when he'd calmed down, he pulled up a chair and sat down, but all he said when I made to sit down too was 'No, not you.' Signora Cocuzza promptly jumped to her feet, but he growled at her to stay put. 'What difference does that make, pray?' I said. He didn't answer, just demanded to know what had happened in every detail. So I told him."

"Truthfully?"

"Of course, what else? But first I asked him why he hadn't turned up before. It was getting on for evening and the murder had occurred early that morning, which meant that Madame Sahara's house had stood empty for nearly twelve hours."

"How did he react to that?"

"He didn't like it, I could tell. Of course, I realised he'd been investigating nonstop in the interim, and he may have treated himself to a little well-earned siesta between times. 'But,' I said, 'you must admit, Vito, that if you'd been quicker to seal off the house and put it under guard, Signora Cocuzza wouldn't have risked her life and we wouldn't have had to come here, the whole bunch of us, and all the nice clues to the murderer would still be here.' Pow! That hit home. He almost blew a fuse again, did the signor commissario, but he couldn't fault my reasoning."

"And then you were a good girl and handed over that list of names?"

Poldi cleared her throat and took a sip of whisky.

"Well, Poldi?"

"Well . . . somehow I forgot about it in all the excitement. That was quite understandable."

I sighed. "Honestly, Poldi, you're . . ."

"I'm what? Feel free!"

I grinned at her. "You're a cool cat."

My Auntie Poldi thought so too. She tweaked her wig straight with a satisfied air and topped up my glass. Then she slid a small piece of folded paper across the table.

"Is this it?"

"Open it."

I unfolded the piece of paper. It bore a short, handwritten list of names. A very peculiar list of names.

Easton Ros
Rena Sotos
Stan Roose
Astor Enos
Santos Roe
Rosa Stone

"What sort of names are they? I mean, who would be called that?"

Poldi shook her head. "It's obvious you've no talent for criminology. So, what's the first thing that strikes you?"

I stared at the list. "They're English names. Or American."

"Very good. What else?"

"Well, as I say, they look odd."

"All right, but you're German too, so that doesn't necessarily mean anything. Go on, what else do you notice?"

"Two women, four men."

"*Cento punti.* What else? What's the most striking thing about the list—the thing that turns it into a genuine lead?"

I stared at the list in perplexity, devoid of ideas. "Phew . . . Give me a clue."

My Auntie Poldi did not, of course, do me that favour. She retrieved the piece of paper.

"Don't worry, I didn't catch on right away either, I admit. But once you do, it's like these picture puzzles in the newspapers, where you look at them for long enough and wind up seeing a naked woman. They're optical illusions."

"Optical illusions? Naked women?"

She sighed. "The same rule applies whether you're talking about love or criminology: if you really want to see your object of desire, stop staring at it, you'll only blind yourself. You must aim off a little. Why? Because the truth reposes in the corner of your eye. Bear that in mind."

If anyone knew this, it was my Auntie Poldi.

When Poldi got back to the Via Baronessa after that long, unpleasant and eventful day, tired and groggy and vaguely suspecting that she'd finally overstepped the mark with Montana, all she wanted was to flop down on the sofa and get wasted. However, when she walked into her *salotto*, having fetched a bottle of grappa and a glass from the kitchen, the sofa was already occupied by Death, the apparition that haunted her from time to time, who eyed her disapprovingly.

"Well? At it again, Poldi?"

He hadn't changed a bit since their last meeting. Still looking ill and overworked and on the verge of a burn-out, he was wearing shabby grey tracksuit bottoms and a grimy grey hoodie bearing the logo of an American university, with the hood, as was only to be expected, pulled down low over his face. Poldi, who found this get-up unprofessional, assumed it was a kind of leisure-time look. Death also smelt a trifle sweaty, which Poldi hadn't noticed during their first encounter. It suggested a neglect of personal hygiene. Or a glandular problem. Did she really want to be escorted into the hereafter by such an individual? If Death looked so scruffy, what would the aftermath be like? Still, leisure-time look or no, it had not escaped Poldi that he'd come equipped with the clipboard holding his to-do list, so he seemed to be still on duty. And that was enough to put the wind up anyone.

"I mean," Death went on in his nasal voice, "not that it's any concern of mine, but I'm surprised you feel like hitting the bottle so soon after your fall from grace last night."

"What business is it of yours, pray? You sound like my nephew from Germany, and that's not meant as a compliment." Poldi deposited the grappa bottle on the coffee table and sat down beside Death, taking care to do so gently, for fear of catapulting him into the air.

"Thanks for being so considerate," he said through his nose.

"Got a cold?"

He made a dismissive gesture. "Don't ask. In this job you catch your death." He chuckled hoarsely, promptly choked and had a coughing fit.

Poldi rolled her eyes. "All right, so it's time, is it? Where do I sign?" She wrenched the clipboard from the hand with which he'd been nervously tapping his list the whole time.

"Hey!" he cried in dismay, trying to snatch it back.

No easy matter with an opponent like my Auntie Poldi. She wasn't the type to let things go.

"This is against the rules!"

"I don't give a shit about the rules, my lad. If I'm already as good as dead, I've nothing left to lose."

"But you may have."

"Oh?" Poldi let go of the clipboard in surprise. "What does that mean?"

"It's *not* your turn yet!" Death cried irritably, and he clasped the clipboard to his pigeon-chested bosom as if it were the love of his life. "How often do I have to say it?"

"So what? I mean, in that case, what are you doing here?"

"Might I have a glass of water? Just tap water, please."

Poldi looked at him searchingly to see whether he was messing her about, but he made a thoroughly calm and serious impression, so she rose with a sigh and went into the kitchen.

"Let it run, please," Death called after her.

"There's only water from the jerrycan, but it's fresh. Acqua di Torre, finest-quality mineral water."

"Don't go to too much trouble on my account."

Poldi handed her pallid guest his glass of water and waited. Death drank it in precise little sips, and it dawned on her that the universe had chosen its greatest pedant to wield the scythe and snuff out the candles.

"Better?"

Death shrugged. "It tasted awful, but never mind." He put the glass down carefully and readopted an official tone of voice. "My reason for being here . . ." He cleared his throat and started again. "The truth is, I'm far exceeding my authorised remit—in fact, I wouldn't be surprised if it cost me my job. Still, nobody else is eager to take it on, so I'd probably wind up with everything back on my plate."

"Stick to the subject," Poldi admonished him. She was becoming rather nervous.

"Well," he said reluctantly, "since we've recently built up what I might describe as a rapport, I thought I ought to put you in the picture about certain, er, changes in the structure of fate."

"Changes?"

"Well, the board of directors is currently engaged in submitting the whole of fate to an activity analysis aimed at an increase in the effectiveness of risk management while simultaneously achieving a reduction in staff. Overmanning and structural problems have arisen, and these are now to be rectified in the course of a transformative process."

"What the hell does all that mean?"

Death tapped the death list on his clipboard. "There have been one or two, er . . . lifespan adjustments. The bottom line is that these will lead, staff-wise, to greater productivity and, in terms of the balance sheet, to a significant increase in operational results."

Poldi's blood ran cold. "So what you're telling me is . . ."

"That you've less time than originally specified. Yes, sorry."

She gasped for breath. "How much less are we talking about?"

"Afraid I'm not allowed to divulge any information on that score, you know that, Poldi. Just this: the clock is ticking." Death was now looking positively disconsolate. "Hey, it wasn't my decision. I'm only responsible for the transfer, but I thought it would be fair to drop you a little hint. A little tip from me to you: *Carpe diem*, if you know what I mean."

Poldi knew. "So the Almighty feels like pruning his vines a bit, is that it?"

"Well, you'd be surprised what the Almighty feels like, or you will be sooner or later. In your case sooner, as I said." Death got up off the sofa. "Anyway, I must be going. Thanks for the water."

"Wait!" Poldi caught him by the arm.

"No, Poldi, I can't give you a precise date of death. I got into a lot of hot water the last time."

"I don't mean that. I mean . . . well, perhaps you could let me know who killed Madame Sahara, then I wouldn't have to leave any loose ends behind. *Carpe diem*, you know."

Death was clearly of two minds.

"I think you already owe me that little favour," Poldi added.

"Very well, since it's you," Death said with a sigh. "But it won't be more than a pointer in the right direction. Do you have a pen and paper?"

Hurriedly, Poldi fetched him a ballpoint and a tear-off pad from the kitchen. He splayed his fingers like a concert pianist and feigned profound concentration, then bent over and jotted something down. Quite what, Poldi couldn't make out. All she saw was that Death was writing slowly. Painfully slowly. He wrote and wrote and wrote . . .

When Poldi awoke from wild dreams the next morning, she was almost surprised to find she hadn't been reincarnated as a bug of some kind. Instead, she was wearing her red silk pyjamas and lying in her bed, beside which her wig was neatly perched on the head of an old shop-window dummy. The Sicilian morning was blinking at her between the slats of the shutters, laden with the scent of jasmine and the nagging voice of Signora Anzalone from next door, which was probably what had woken her.

She remained lying there like that, totally compos and somewhat surprised to be still alive. It worried her that she was once again unable to remember how the night had ended, or what Death had written down for her, or how she had got to bed. The next sensation she experienced, however, was one of relief that it had all been no more than an unpleasant dream.

So my aunt was feeling perky—perkier than she had felt for a long time. Even her crown had stopped throbbing. In the highest of spirits, she got up and attended to her toilette. She sprayed herself liberally with scent, slipped into a billowy caftan, and combed and teased her big black wig before clapping it on her head.

The bedroom was the only place where my aunt ever removed her wig. No one apart from my late Uncle Peppe and Vito Montana had ever been privileged to see what lay hidden beneath it. Needless to say, everyone in the family had a theory about what her thunderstorm of a wig concealed and what her natural hair colour was, but Poldi firmly rejected any such questions. Not even Aunt Teresa, her favourite sister-in-law, had ever been granted a glimpse of what lay beneath the holy of holies. Even old beach photos depicted young Poldi in a skimpy bikini—and a wig.

Then, magnificently resurrected like the phoenix tattoo on her left breast, freshly titivated and ready for the next stage in her investigation, she cast a preliminary glance at the corkboard to which she had pinned all her clues and leads and connected them with woollen thread. Two things at once caught her eye: (a) the piece of paper the sad signora had secured in Madame Sahara's house, and (b) a sheet from her tear-off pad.

It bore another list of names.

But an entirely different one.

Poldi was thrown for several moments because she couldn't recall when she had made this list and pinned it to the wall. I mean, who would want to believe that her little chat with Death had not been just a drunken hallucination?

It reassured her to find no half-full tumbler in the living room, but the tear-off pad and the ballpoint were still there. Poldi removed the piece of paper from her corkboard and scrutinised it.

I should mention that my Auntie Poldi had a thing about lists. To her, lists had always possessed a magical quality. Lists were a lever with which to prise open the workings of the subconscious. Lists were beacons in the mists of meditation. Lists mitigated chaos, instilled order and harmony. With the help of lists, one could surf on one's memory to the shores of knowledge. Lists could fill the pit of despair with consolation and dissuade my aunt from drinking. They were also just fun. Poldi kept a lot of lists. Long lists, short lists, shopping lists, playlists, ratings lists, lists of names, odd and mysterious lists. Depending on their age and importance, these were clamped to the refrigerator with magnets of many colours and in various physical conditions, fluttered on the washing line with the laundry like Tibetan prayer flags, or hung framed above Poldi's bed. One type of list came into being as follows: Poldi would relax, try to let go of all disruptive and negative thoughts, close her eyes, breathe steadily, open her eyes again and simply write down whatever was going through her head. It might be a list of her lovers, lists of the handsomest policemen in the world, to-do lists, bucket lists, lists of magical places, lists of hitherto unnoticed things, lists of unloved animals, ratings lists of her favourite songs, favourite restaurants, favourite demons, favourite saints, favourite names and all the countless things my aunt simply liked. Or lists of suspects in a murder case. This was just such a list:

RUSSO
MR. X (HIT MAN EMPLOYED BY RUSSO)
THE AMERICAN WITH THE DIVINING ROD
DORIS AND THE DELIZIOSI
THAT ODD YOUNG MAN ENZO
AVOLA'S (TWIN?) BROTHER
SOMEONE WANTING TO COVER FOR AVOLA
AVOLA HIMSELF
ME

Poldi thought it quite plausible that she would find herself on the list. After all, she couldn't remember a thing. Madame Sahara's prognostications had dismayed her, not to say jinxed her a little, so she couldn't be altogether ruled out as a suspect. She thought it a good list, generally speaking, though she crossed out Doris and the *deliziosi* right away. She would have liked to do the same for Avola, but there was that confession. She considered it mendacious but surmised that Avola intended it—for whatever reason—to cover for the real murderer.

Anyway, it was a list she could work her way down, step by step, in a thoroughly professional manner.

Nevertheless, something pricked her subconscious like a laundry tag in a new cashmere sweater. There was something wrong with the list. It looked incomplete somehow. Poldi strove to remember that afternoon in the vineyard and all the people who had been seated at the long table. The grape pickers were also suspects, theoretically, but Poldi presumed that Montana had already questioned and checked them all forensically. She realised that this also went for the persons on the list, of course, but it wasn't about the list; it was about gaining access to her subconscious and giving her intuition a leg up.

There was someone missing.

She closed her eyes and breathed deeply.

It was someone who didn't have to have been seated at the table that afternoon.

Poldi emptied her psyche like a Zen master.

And then it came to her.

She went back into the living room, where the tear-off pad lay on the glass-topped coffee table. The ballpoint had left indentations on the next sheet. This was only natural, except that the sheet bore a ghostly, barely discernible name that did not appear on the original list. Poldi found this spooky, but, spooky or not, she wasn't an ungrateful person, so she put her hands together and said, "*Namaste, Death.* In other respects, get stuffed."

She shaded the indentations with a pencil and the additional name took shape: MAGO RAMPULLA.

A new player, so to speak, but not an entirely unfamiliar one. *Mago* Rampulla, a clairvoyant and fortune-teller by trade, proclaimed his comprehensive services—palmistry, tarot, crystal ball, numerology, regression, aura analysis, life counselling, lottery number predictions—on posters all over the place, usually right beside those of Madame Sahara. He not only advertised himself, with scant originality, as "The Incomparable," but went one better by including a picture of himself. Ill-advisedly, one is bound to say, because the black-and-white photo of a corpulent, balding, mustachioed man in an ill-fitting suit conveyed the crafty truculence of an utter charlatan or sleazy estate agent—or worse. He was probably less than five feet tall, and thus, according to Uncle Martino's Mafia gauge ("The shorter the man, the likelier a Mafioso"), practically self-revealed as a small-time crook.

Prize question: What do Sicily and remote Carpathian villages have in common? Answer: The extent of their superstitions. There are few places in the world where centuries-old superstitions have persisted as stubbornly and are still celebrated as in Sicily. The multiplicity of clairvoyants and fortune-tellers speaks for itself. It may be down to the Sicilians' primordial angst, for they have been plagued by successive conquerors for thousands of years. All Sicilian superstition revolves around one thing alone: *malocchio,* the evil eye. One either has *malocchio* or one hasn't; it can be neither rejected nor deliberately acquired. The *gettatori,* who possess it, can jinx, sicken, sterilise, bankrupt, disfigure or even kill their fellow mortals. All human activities are threatened by *malocchio.*

What to do? The best thing, of course, is never to catch a *gettatore's* eye, or to make a *fica* by sticking your thumb between the index and middle fingers — an obscene gesture, but unavoidable in this instance, as is the *mano cornuta,* the horned hand, which is also widespread in the heavy-metal scene, but for different reasons. Another popular defence against the evil eye is a red *corno,* or devil's horn, worn as a talisman round your neck. *Toccaferro,* or touching a piece of iron, is also reputed to help, and never goes amiss because it's supposed to bring good luck in general.

The list of Sicilian superstitions is endless. You never deposit your hat on a bed. You don't spill salt on the table; if you do, you throw a pinch of it over your left shoulder. You never open an umbrella inside the house, never cross your knife and fork on the plate, never wear lilac in a theatre, never give anyone a knife, and never, ever wish someone success. Instead, you say, *In bocca al lupo,* or "Into the wolf's mouth." You never sit down thirteen at a table, because that was the number of those present at the Last Supper. In any other context, thirteen is a lucky number—unlike seventeen, because that numeral symbolises a hanged man on a gallows.

Things become even more complicated when it comes to oneiromancy and numerology. To dream of a butterfly brings good luck, a black hen signifies a wedding, a balloon indicates a lie, and an egg stands for bad news. White grapes mean tears, the loss of teeth portends a death. Numbers are allotted to each of the ten million things a person can dream of in a long night. These must be entered on your lottery ticket. Or not, as the case may be.

But who has the power of discernment? One person alone, of course: a *mago,* the magician or clairvoyant in whom you have faith. A Sicilian *mago* combines naturopathy with superstition and ancient magical rites, supplies voodoo dolls, prophylactic amulets and love potions, or simply listens to you. He brings back your unfaithful husband, helps you out of a predicament and embroils your enemies in one. Above all, though, he protects you from the evil eye.

The nearest *mago* will usually be practising not far away, so your best plan is to consult the Yellow Pages. In case of doubt, however, drive up to Santa Venerina, because that unremarkable town on Etna has three claims to fame: the Pasticceria Russo, where you can buy the best marzipan fruits in all Sicily, the Distilleria Russo, which makes the very best limoncello, and—last but not least—its fortune-tellers. Nowhere else in the world will you find so many fortune-tellers, shamans, clairvoyants, palmists, astrologers and charlatans in one place.

And one of them was *Mago* Rampulla.

From a brief search of the Internet, Poldi discovered that *Mago* Rampulla had posted the vilest remarks about Madame Sahara on a social network and accused her of being a charlatan. In short, the sleazy *mago* had been Madame Sahara's prime competitor and therefore had a motive for murdering her.

Poldi reasoned that Montana would in any case check on all the other candidates on the list, so she could wait to coax his preliminary results out of him—a process for which she had ways and means. This being so, her most logical course of action was to concentrate on the only suspect that had yet to occur to the handsome commissario. Undercover, of course.

The phone rang only twice before "The Incomparable" answered.

"*Pronto?*"

Strong Sicilian accent, voice as oleaginous as yesterday's caponata, dripping with mistrust, an inferiority complex and avarice. Or so it seemed to Poldi.

"My name is Isolde," she trilled into the receiver as demurely as she knew how. "I'm German, Maestro, so you must forgive me if I don't speak your language too well. The thing is, I saw your wonderful posters, and they awakened something deep within me. Tell me, do you also do, er . . . regressions?"

Did he! As luck would have it, he'd had a last-minute cancellation, so . . .

Poldi appeared *tutto in nero,* all in black. Her voluminous chiffon gown had a fringed skirt, a lacy décolletage and understated appliqués of little gold chains on the sleeves. She thought the latter beautifully symbolised her imprisoned soul, which was craving release. Instead of stilettos, she had opted for flamenco shoes with broad heels. She wanted to look respectable—meek and demure too, so she had draped a veil over her wig, which transported her face to a dreamy borderland midway between erotic promise and graceful timidity. That, at least, was what she believed.

I can picture her in this outfit as she drove her old Alfa with the roll bar back up the winding road to Santa Venerina, past Madame Sahara's house, now sealed off by the police, then a little way out of the town and farther up the mountainside to a run-down housing estate opposite the Distilleria Russo. The road consisted almost entirely of potholes, and right outside the house, garbage overflowed from two rusty bins, which even the feral cats and wild dogs steered clear of. There were the usual sagging sun blinds in every window, and cheap underwear was hung out to dry on the balconies. A small path redolent of cat piss and dead mice led up to the clairvoyant's front door.

Mago Rampulla received Poldi in a shabby dark suit and bedroom slippers. He was a very short man indeed. His face was unshaven and filmed with sweat, and the shadows beneath his eyes suggested that he had slept badly, though less from drink, Poldi's expert eye told her, than from brooding about some disaster. His handshake was about as firm as fresh dough.

"I am . . ."

"I know, signora. Please come in."

His voice was surprisingly soft and pleasant—far less oily than it had sounded on the phone. Poldi was almost disappointed.

With a ceremonious gesture, Rampulla ushered her into the house, which smelt of stale cigarette smoke, cleaning fluid and desperation. He led her past some closed doors beyond which a television was burbling and through a kitchen in which an old woman continued to chop onions without deigning to glance at my aunt.

The Incomparable's studio lay at the end of a passage. It was claustrophobically small and very different from Madame Sahara's. Its only furnishings were a little, old round table with ball-and-claw feet and a lace cloth and three rickety chairs. Hanging on the walls were prints of alchemistic formulae and treatises, astrological tables, kitschy pictures of angels and framed photos of the *mago* with minor Italian celebs in better days.

Rampulla closed the door as softly and silently as he moved in general. To Poldi, it was as if he didn't want to wake an evil spirit that was sleeping off its bloodlust somewhere nearby.

"Please, signora." He gestured to my aunt to sit down at the table, seated himself opposite and regarded her with rheumy eyes. He said nothing for a while. Then, "I charge a hundred euros for the first hour and fifty for each additional hour or part thereof. You can pay cash or with a credit card. Forgive me for being so blunt, but you didn't inquire about my scale of charges on the phone, so I thought it better to make it clear right away. Is that all right?"

"Perfectly all right, Maestro," Poldi said huskily. She was beginning to feel a bit uneasy under the *mago*'s unwavering gaze.

"So what can I do for you, Donna Poldina?"

Poldi gave a start. "How . . ."

Rampulla sighed. "I could tell you I have second sight, but the truth is, I also read the papers. I know who you are, Donna Poldina, and I fear I also know your real reason for being here."

This took the last of the wind out of Poldi's sails. She had meant to employ the ultra-psychological tactic of playing on the *mago*'s vanity with spurious awe and flattery and skilfully drawing him out with some outrageous horror story from her past. And now this. For some reason, her investigation was not going to plan. But then, she reflected, nothing in her life had ever gone to plan. Life didn't give a fig for plans of any kind, but despite its unpredictability, it had always behaved magnanimously.

"*Namaste,* life," she said softly. "Poldi *contra mundum.*"

"I beg your pardon?"

"So why am I here, in your opinion?"

The *mago* heaved another sigh, as he did before every re-mark he uttered. His sighs resembled the minor eruptions of a spent volcano shortly before its total extinction.

"I didn't kill Giuliana."

"Who did, then?"

"Who would know better than a clairvoyant, is that what you mean?"

"Well, yes."

Mago Rampulla clasped his soft, hirsute hands together on the table. "I don't know. I could tell you if the murderer were sitting here in this room, but that's all."

"You could? How would you recognise him?"

"By his aura. Nothing damages and darkens a person's aura more than murder."

"You expect me to believe that?"

"Although my gifts are limited, Donna Poldina, Giuliana's were far more so. She was a charlatan, fundamentally, but the boundaries in our profession are fluid in any case. The fact that I didn't always say nice things about her makes me a suspect, but I never had anything against her personally; it was merely business. Yes, I admit I was envious of her. The fact is, though, Giuliana had plenty of glamour and sensitivity but no gift for clairvoyance. People simply liked her. Me, on the other hand, they dislike, and do you know why? Because I'm a *gettatore:* I have the evil eye. It's true, I attract evil and pass it on to other people willy-nilly, like a curse. The evil eye can't see into the future, but it can see auras. I sometimes wish I couldn't, because it can often be unpleasant, believe me. I do the whole hocus-pocus with cards, numbers and palmistry just to pass the time and because people expect it, but I always see at once what's wrong when a person is in front of me. Then the mischief takes its course."

This sounded familiar to Poldi in some way.

"Why are you telling me all this?"

Another sigh.

"Because your kind never gives up, Donna Poldina. If only you could see what I see . . . Your aura is like a red-and-yellow conflagration above your head. You're someone who sets everything ablaze, yourself first and foremost. You came here to convict me of murder and atone for something to your lover, your father and Giuliana. That's to your credit, and I'm prepared to assist you in any way I can. Because, as I said, it wasn't me. I have no alibi for the time of the murder, alas, but I do have a motive. This means that if you turn your commissario loose on me, I'll have a problem. Being investigated by the police is bad for business, and my business isn't doing too well, as you can see, so I suggest you simply ask your questions and I'll answer them to the best of my ability."

The *mago* was looking depressed, as if bowed down beneath an existential burden, and his eyes were suddenly bloodshot. He mopped his brow with a handkerchief, clearly struggling to maintain his composure. And Poldi believed him, because she knew a thing or two about the difference between hypocrisy and true humanity. So she felt ashamed of her own hypocrisy and rush to judgement and was once more reminded of the traditional Sicilian principle governing true beauty: perfect sweetness and genuine quality always lie hidden beneath the most unattractive exterior. Outside, ugh! Inside, wow! It might be called an oriental concept: all splendour is private and must be protected from the envious and rapacious.

"Please excuse my cheap charade, Maestro," said Poldi. "You're absolutely right, but I can't help myself."

"I know, Donna Poldina."

"This conversation will remain between us, I assure you. Commissario Montana will not learn of it. It's just that I feel I owe it to Giuliana to find her murderer. I notice you also call her by her first name. Were you on close terms?"

The *mago* looked Poldi in the eye. "She was my sister, Donna Poldina."

8

*Tells of traditions, patriotism and algae. Poldi learns
something about Madame Sahara's career plans and
feels she's being manipulated. She gets an idea for a
short cut, meets an unexpected admirer, is forced to
abandon a pet theory and feels she's being manipulated again. And then, fanned by the first cool breeze
for weeks, she encounters an alga and makes a disturbing discovery.*

O ur parents and grandparents were fortune-tellers
too," the *mago* began. "The profession was passed
on down the generations. To us it was a profession like any
other. You'd be surprised how much training it requires.
Giuliana wasn't as gifted as me, but she had other talents.
She was good at business. She was also glamorous. People
liked her, felt attracted, appreciated and loved by her. The
natural warmth and strength she radiated were infectious,
so it didn't matter when her predictions went astray. Many
people can discern the past and present, you know. It's seeing the future that's the challenge, but people paid to enjoy
Giuliana's company for a while—to recharge their batter-
ies. Can you understand that?"

"I think I understand perfectly, Maestro."

Rampulla sighed. "Politicians, businessmen, sportsmen, Mafiosi—they all flocked to Giuliana. She loved the influence she wielded, but she wanted more. She wanted to get right to the top."

"Meaning?"

"Television. Her own show, that was her dream. She wanted to become known all over Italy."

Poldi pricked up her ears. "Did she receive any firm offers?"

"I don't know. She didn't discuss it with me, and she wanted to produce the whole thing herself. Knowing her as I do—did, I mean—I'm sure it would have been a success. Financing was the only problem."

"What do you mean?"

"Well, Italian banks have been very reluctant to extend credit ever since the euro crisis, especially for a TV show. Even Giuliana got nowhere, so she had to pre-finance it all herself."

"Did she have the money?"

The *mago* regarded her sadly. "I can't answer that, Donna Poldina. I only know she was afraid of something. Very afraid."

Poldi frowned. "It's easy to say that after the event, Maestro. I suspect this is the part of the conversation where the witness tries to lure the brilliant female detective in a particular direction, don't you?"

He shrugged his shoulders. "I'm only telling you what I saw, and I saw the grey specks in her aura. Giuliana was scared, I know it. I wanted to ask her about it, but a petty-minded feeling of schadenfreude held me back. The thought torments me now. I might have been able to help her. She might still be alive." The *mago* took a used tissue from his jacket and clamped it to his eyes.

Poldi wondered whether to interpret this as crocodile tears, but the clairvoyant's distress seemed genuine, and she knew a thing or two about distress and crocodile tears.

"So you really believe you would recognise Giuliana's murderer by his aura?"

"I didn't say that. I can recognise a murderer by his aura, but I couldn't tell if he'd killed Giuliana."

Poldi gave him a broad smile. "Would you excuse me for a moment? I'll be back in no time."

Taking her mobile from her pocket, she went out onto the veranda and made a phone call.

I can picture her from Rampulla's viewpoint as she murmured something into her phone, sweet as sugar, while her aura blazed in all the colours of the rainbow. The *mago* should have been warned—he should have suspected what Poldi had in mind.

For, dogged Bavarian that she was, she wanted to work her way down her list in double-quick time and pursue her favourite suspect. She was also partly motivated, of course, by a wish to impress Montana with a sure-fire solution to the case, and although she still couldn't be absolutely sure the *mago* wasn't taking her for one hell of a ride, the aura business seemed at least worth a try. After all, my Auntie Poldi knew a thing or two about unconventional ways of solving problems.

"Would you care to come and have a coffee with me?" she asked Rampulla after finishing her phone call.

The *mago* hesitated, possibly uncertain of my aunt's intentions—and no wonder.

"I'll happily stand you a gelato as well," she added. "Or two. Oh, don't look so scared, I'm not going to eat you! I simply want your help in identifying a murderer."

And who could have said no to that?

Half an hour later she was with *Mago* Rampulla at the Cipriani, her favourite café bar in Acireale. Not only did it sell the best pistachio ice cream in the world, but it was situated immediately opposite the church of San Sebastiano, patron saint of gays and my aunt's favourite too, because he agonised so fetchingly under a shower of arrows fired at him by Diocletian's Numidian archers. Poldi had always considered it a virtue to preserve one's charm—indeed, to look even more seductive—when suffering.

She was not, in fact, sharing a table with Rampulla but sitting outside on her own, clearly visible, while the *mago* had been instructed to twiddle his thumbs inside the café, where he would have a good view of the auras of my Auntie Poldi and her date.

Her date turned up punctually, wearing jeans and the sort of salmon-pink polo shirt that looks good only on well-tanned Sicilians. The rest of his outfit consisted of white sneakers without socks and the trendy sunglasses without which no Italian male in his right mind would ever sally forth, and which he didn't remove until he spotted my aunt. Poldi noticed for the first time quite how good-looking Russo was. Firm little tum-tum, and obviously gym-toned everywhere else as well. Bright, watchful eyes, full lips. Unhurried and unsuspecting, he nodded graciously to various people as he approached on his own, unaccompanied by

Hans and Franz. He was a man afraid of nothing and no one, not even my Auntie Poldi.

A king mingling with his subjects.

A boss.

Without more ado, he sat down at Poldi's table and plonked his sunglasses down between them like Hernán Cortés planting the Spanish flag in Mexican soil — or so I imagine.

"What a surprise, Donna Poldina."

"Nice of you to spare me some time at such short notice, Signor Russo," said Poldi, looking him in the eye. "I know you're a very busy man."

"But a man above all else," Russo replied without taking his eyes off her for an instant. "An inquisitive man. A man who could never deny a beautiful woman."

Poldi scraped the last of the sugar from her espresso cup and licked the spoon. "Now you're embarrassing me."

Which was true in a way, because she hadn't expected him to switch to flirtation mode so quickly, though his glances at the vineyard that afternoon had already conveyed something of the kind.

Russo ordered a coffee and a *granita di limone,* then gazed at Poldi intently.

She felt herself blush and had to pull herself together. She wasn't there to flirt, after all. Far from it.

"Where did you get my mobile number?"

"Valérie was kind enough to give it to me."

Russo nodded. He was looking totally relaxed.

"And how can I help you?"

"Perhaps by telling me who killed Madame Sahara."

Russo didn't turn a hair. "Come now, Donna Poldina, you can do better than that. Let's start again. How can I help you?"

Touché.

Poldi composed herself. "That afternoon at the vineyard," she began again, "Madame Sahara read my hand. But I was less impressed by what she told me about my future than by her aura. I took to her at once, and I can't understand why such a wonderful person had to die. I want to find her murderer."

The coffee and the *granita* came.

Russo sugared his espresso, taking his time over it. "That's better," he said. "Giuliana was a wonderful woman. I don't know why she had to die—I don't have the slightest idea, but I think it's the job of the police to find that out, not yours or mine."

"Is that a threat? If I don't back off, will you have me torn limb from limb by those dogs of yours?"

"You've got the wrong idea, Donna Poldina. Hans and Franz love you! Their behaviour is a way of expressing pure affection. Stay out of it, I really mean that. Whoever killed Giuliana will kill you too if you happen to pick up his trail."

"That sounds as if you know who the murderer is," Poldi said softly, leaning forward to display a little more cleavage. "Don't you think?"

Russo pursed his lips and took a spoonful of *granita*. Very symbolic, thought Poldi. It looked as if he needed to cool down. Deciding to go in for the kill, she took her coffee spoon and helped herself to some of Russo's sorbet. He raised no objection.

"I'm worried about you, Poldi, that's all. I may call you Poldi, mayn't I?"

"If you think I'm in danger, then you don't think Achille Avola killed Giuliana?"

Russo drew a deep breath. "I went to school with Achille. We . . . oh, never mind. No, it certainly wasn't Achille."

"So why has he confessed?"

"Ask him that, not me."

"But I'm asking you now."

"Perhaps you should ask his brother."

"Why? What would he tell me?"

Russo spread his hands as if what he was about to say was common knowledge. "Perhaps he'd tell you about the kidney he donated to his twin brother."

Poldi caught on. "Are you implying that his brother killed Giuliana, and Achille covered for him out of gratitude for the kidney that saved his life?"

"I'm not implying anything. I only know that Achille would never commit murder. I know him. Besides, he had no motive."

"But his brother did?"

"As I said, ask him yourself."

These vague allusions were beginning to get on Poldi's nerves, and she wondered what Russo was playing at. Then it occurred to her that she herself was playing a game with him, because the *mago* was still sitting inside, consuming one gelato after another and examining Russo's aura.

"If you'll excuse me for a moment," Poldi said hurriedly, and she swept off into the café.

As instructed, Rampulla was seated at a small bistro table near the entrance, busy with his third gelato. He wasn't looking particularly happy.

"I don't have much time," Poldi told him. "How's it looking?"

The *mago* shook his head. "His aura has a few grey specks, it's true, but in other respects it's green on the inside and a fiery red on the outside. It's the aura of a man who doesn't balk at getting his hands dirty if he has to. But a murderer? No, that he isn't."

Poldi couldn't disguise a certain feeling of disappointment. "Are you quite sure? I mean—"

"Donna Poldina, you asked me to do you this favour, and I've done it. If you've no objection, I'd like to go home now and grieve for my sister." The *mago* rose and handed Poldi his chits. "Take good care of yourself, Donna Poldina."

"No hard feelings," Poldi said with a sigh, "and thanks all the same."

Rampulla hesitated. Evidently there was something on his mind.

"May I ask you something, Donna Poldina?"

"Of course."

"Find Giuliana's murderer. Sensing a murderer's aura is extremely taxing, but I'll gladly help you if I can. Giuliana and I had a difficult relationship, even as children. I was always the fat little brother everyone was ashamed of. But she was my sister, wasn't she? I . . . well, there it is."

Poldi felt touched. "I'll do my best, Maestro," she promised, "and I shall take you up on your kind offer. Many thanks."

Mago Rampulla smiled sadly. Before he finally took his leave, a figure in a suit as grubby as his own aura may have been, he turned once more. "Incidentally, Russo's aura becomes more intense in your vicinity, Donna Poldina. It becomes positively incandescent, which usually means—"

"Yes, yes, thank you," my aunt said hastily. "I can imagine, but my life is more than complicated enough already."

Having waited for him to leave the café, she paid his bill, ordered herself a Prosecco and knocked it back. Then, composed and refreshed, she rejoined Russo, who was just tapping out a text message on his phone.

"You're looking discontented," he said. "Everything all right?"

"Everything's fine," Poldi warbled. She sat down again, but this time took care to display less cleavage. "Okay, so you don't want to tell me anything more about the Avola brothers, I get that, but I'd still like the answer to one question." She paused for effect. Russo looked attentive but not apprehensive. "Why are you interested in the vineyard?"

"Am I?"

"Come off it, Signor Russo, I—"

"Italo. Call me Italo, Donna Poldina."

"Oh sure, you'd like that, wouldn't you? I have dinner with you tonight and we wind up in the sack, is that what you're thinking?"

My Auntie Poldi was never one to beat about the bush, but Russo did not seem at all disconcerted.

"Stop grinning!" she told him. "Okay, why are you interested in the property?"

Russo turned serious. Her rebuff seemed to bounce off him. "Because I want to buy it. We were supposed to sign the contract that evening, but Achille backed out at the last moment."

"Why?"

"He didn't tell me."

"Why would you want to buy a vineyard, anyway? It must be less than ten hectares and it's miles away from your tree nursery."

"It's not about the wine. Achille could go on making his wine there. I'm interested in something far more valuable —something that lies beneath that extinct crater."

He looked at Poldi as if the answer were obvious, but she was stumped.

"Er, what would that be?"

"Water, Donna Poldina. It so happens that that old secondary crater sits on top of one of the biggest natural reservoirs in the whole region."

"I see," said my aunt. "And of course, you need water for growing your palm trees. A lot of water."

Russo brushed this aside. "I've enough water already. People always behave as if Sicily is a desert, but look around you. Does this look like a desert? Everything remains green and luxuriant, even in summer. In the ancient world we were Europe's granary. Sicily abounds in lakes and springs. Distribution and access are the problem. The Arabs had a sophisticated irrigation system, but their know-how got lost like so many other things."

"Don't make me weep," Poldi said sarcastically. "Why should you need to buy a mountain full of water if you don't need it?"

"Ah, now we're coming to the crux of the matter. I've been waiting for you to ask me about Etnarosso all this time, Donna Poldina."

She stared at him with her mouth open. "Well, blow me down with a feather. How did you . . . ?"

Russo relished her surprise. "It doesn't matter. You see, for me the purchase would have been just another write-off. I could have helped my old school friend Achille out of a financial fix when he invested in the new winery, and I wanted to prevent someone else from buying the vineyard. Someone who wouldn't treat a vital resource as responsibly as I, who was born here and loves his native land. Someone descending on Sicily like a biblical plague of locusts."

"The Mafia."

Russo burst out laughing. "Donna Poldina! The Cosa Nostra is a Sicilian infection we'll never manage to cure, but which will never be the end of us. Ours is a symbiotic relationship between host and parasite. No, the people I'm talking about are vampires. If we let them, they'll suck this country dry and leave behind a withered husk."

"Could you be a little less airy-fairy, Signor Russo? What does all this have to do with Etnarosso?"

Russo glanced at his watch.

"Damn it all, don't tell me you've got to go," Poldi snapped. "Come on, give!"

Russo beckoned the waiter.

"Etnarosso is the name of a water development programme which an international food company named Oceanica is planning to set up in Sicily. Mainly here in the east, which abounds in water. Oceanica trades in mineral water throughout the world." Starting to gesticulate, Rosso put his thumb and fingertips together and shook his hand in the universal Italian gesture that underlines the importance of some statement. He clasped his hands together and shook them, raised his forefinger, clenched his fist and reopened it in front of Poldi's eyes like a big, delicate bud. "They're drilling wells in India, Pakistan, the States, everywhere. They're stealing the inhabitants' water, bottling it in plastic bottles and selling it to them. The same water that used to gush from hydrants free of charge. They're draining whole tracts of land in this way. Bottled water has become a status symbol in the Third World, and they're planning to create the same situation here. They're criminals who'll stop at nothing."

Poldi remained quite calm. Although she could well have done with another Prosecco, she restrained herself from calling the waiter.

"And why are you telling me all this?"

"Because I want to gain your trust, Poldi. I'm not your enemy. I'm not even Valérie's enemy."

"Oh really?"

"I have a high regard for Valérie, and I'll do my best to help her keep Femminamorta, but it's no use if she goes bankrupt and loses the whole estate."

"To you, I suppose."

Russo rose. "Now I really must go. It's been a pleasure, Donna Poldina."

Poldi remained seated. On impulse, she put out her hand. He took it and, as if it was the most natural thing in the world, brushed it with his lips.

"I'll be in touch."

As she watched him put on his sunglasses and saunter confidently down the Corso Umberto, Poldi wondered, not for the first time, what the devil life had in store for her.

What was its plan? Why did it always have to take the most complicated routes? These considerations usually led her to brood in a melancholy way, so she ordered herself another Prosecco after all and quickly made a few notes of what Russo had told her. None of it made much sense to her.

"Mind you," my aunt told me later, "life has never promised to make much sense, so you've always got two options."

A brief pause for me to ask what they were.

"I'm listening."

"Either you develop worry lines and ruin your teeth by grinding them, or you say *namaste* and go with the flow."

"I never grind my teeth!"

"Yes you do. You don't notice, that's all. All right, do as I do."

She put her hands together.

"This is utterly daft, Poldi."

"Just do it."

I complied.

"Now breathe."

"I *am* breathing."

"Now make a bow."

"You're joking."

"Do it!"

I bowed.

"And now, say after me: *Namaste,* life."

"*Namaste,* life."

"Thank you, life, for helping me with my lousy novel."

"Oh? Is that what it's doing?"

"Go on. *Dai!*"

"Thank you, life, for helping me with my lousy novel."

And on impulse I added, "The rest of the world can kiss my ass."

Poldi nodded happily, and I must admit that everything immediately felt a trifle easier. Rather as if I weren't barking up completely the wrong tree, and as if something far away on the horizon were waiting patiently for me to catch up. And then, as I sat there on the sofa with Poldi, who scratched herself under her wig and topped up our glasses with red wine, there in the midst of all her knick-knacks, the china poodles, the photos of my Uncle Peppe and the collection of antique weapons on the walls, with a mild Sicilian November night and the distant roar of the surf outside— there at that moment I felt something else. Something I'd been missing for a long time, and which was coming back to me like a stray cat that has been busy elsewhere for a while but now leaps onto your lap, purring, as if it had never been away.

I took my Auntie Poldi's hand and squeezed it hard. "*Namaste,* Poldi."

"No problem."

Poldi felt irritated by Russo's blatant come-on. That was all she needed. As if she didn't have enough trouble *amore*-wise. Besides, she couldn't shake off the suspicion that everyone she questioned was shooting her one line after another. But, as she always said, "Nothing attracts an investigator more than a mixture of half-truths and subtle eroticism." So she knocked back another Prosecco and set off for Femminamorta to see Valérie, collect her thoughts in the shade of a palm tree and plan the next steps in her investigation.

As so often, the delightful property looked deserted when Poldi dismounted from her Vespa. The only living creature to greet her was Oscar, companion of the late, poisoned Lady, and he was far less effusive than usual. No jumping up, no hoarse barking, no rolling around on the ground. Looking years older, the little mongrel with the underbite came trotting out of the house—cautiously, as if nothing there was safe any more—and sniffed Poldi's hand in a less than excited way. Poldi picked him up and made her way round the house into the garden. She forbore to call her friend because it was siesta time. Valérie hardly slept at night (which, in my novel, only intensified my overheated description of the myth of a voluptuous nymph in an enchanted garden), so she needed her nap in the afternoons.

On entering the garden, Poldi was met by two sights that could not have been more grotesquely different from each other.

The first: the motionless figures of Doris and her German *deliziosi* in skimpy bikinis, lying in a row on plastic loungers on the lawn, duly anointed with factor 50 sun cream and braising in the afternoon heat.

The second: a peculiar creature on the other side of the garden. Outwardly, it appeared to be a human being. A naked human being, but Poldi couldn't tell whether it was a man or a woman, nor had she ever seen a figure so beautiful, dainty and translucent, so sexless and slender, pale and graceful. And so different from herself that it almost broke her heart. The creature wasn't much taller than a child—a tall child, perhaps. Its skin was paler than any pigmentation Poldi had ever seen: almost completely white, as if it had never been brushed by a single ray of sunlight. It resembled moonlight, thought Poldi, who could not stop looking in turn at the creature and the frying tourists.

The pale-skinned creature was crouching almost motionless under a big palm tree. Poldi now saw that it was moving, albeit infinitely slowly. Fluidly, and as if in extreme slow motion, it straightened up and, without a tremor, unfolded like a white blossom. Poldi, whose knees gave her trouble, wondered where it found the strength. Once the creature had unfurled sufficiently for her to glimpse its primary sexual characteristics, Poldi discerned that it was anatomically a man, although his little best friend was really very small —almost invisible, in fact. She also saw that the man was Japanese, and this, in turn, put her in mind of Butoh, a Japanese type of expressive free-style dancing.

"*Mon dieu,* one simply can't take one's eyes off him, can one?"

Valérie, who had suddenly materialised beside her, dared only whisper.

"Who or what is he?"

"My new guest. An alga."

"Come again?"

"That's what he calls himself."

"Like that slimy green stuff in the sea, you mean?"

"His name is Haru Higashi. He's a performance artist, though I'm not sure he really is a man. What do you think? Not that it matters. He's . . . he's so incredibly beautiful. Like moonlight."

Poldi thought so too.

Quite undisturbed by the two women's presence, the "alga" proceeded to embrace the trunk of the palm tree and slide down it to the ground as if becoming fused with both tree and ground.

Valérie took Poldi's arm and led her over to a table in front of the house, where another Japanese, seated in the shade, was munching Valérie's stodgy homemade biscuits and playing a game of skill one-handed on his smartphone. He was a chubby man in his late twenties, Poldi estimated. His hair hung down over his face, and he wore a big pair of glasses and a T-shirt printed with tour dates and the logo of a Korean crossover indie band. A stereotypical nerd, in other words.

When Valérie and Poldi sat down, he looked up from his phone and beamed at them. "Good afternoon," he said in excellent Italian. "These biscuits are delicious."

He introduced himself to Poldi as Aki, a student of vulcanology at the University of Catania and part-time guide for Japanese tourists.

"Higashi-san has engaged me to act as his interpreter and personal assistant for three months, to enable him to present his performance with an easy mind. He is a very shy person."

"You don't say."

Still munching a biscuit, Aki beamed at Poldi as though she had just paid him a compliment and went on talking with his mouth full. "Higashi-san will begin his performance beside the main crater of Etna, at over three thousand metres, and then descend by degrees to the sea. That is what he has told me. Then he will glide slowly into the sea and become an alga."

"And then?"

"Then nothing. That's it. Don't ask me, I haven't a clue about such performances. It's pretty cool, though, don't you agree?"

"And you'll record the whole thing on video, so Signor Higashi can screen it later?"

Poldi had to wait for Aki to gulp down the biscuit mush in his mouth.

"No, Higashi-san wants no record of it. He also wants no audience. I'm not even allowed to take selfies with him. I have, but I'm afraid I can't post them, or . . ." He drew a finger across his throat and grinned. "He just does his thing without making waves. He told me he's devoted four solid years of work to rehearsing this performance. Dead cool of him!"

Poldi didn't think so at all. On the contrary, she thought it was pretty loopy. On the other hand, she had a soft spot for crackpots and fantasists of every stripe as long as they behaved in a friendly manner, and pale, dainty Higashi-san seemed about as unfriendly as a baby Angora rabbit. My aunt was moved by the sight of this fairy-like creature, who had no wish to kill anyone—no mongrel, no fortune-teller and no district attorney—and who had come to Sicily with the sole intention of dancing from Etna into the sea, silently and unobserved, and becoming an alga. This mute self-sufficiency and total devotion to beauty briefly restored Poldi's faith in goodness. In a world where beings like Higashi-san existed, there was still some hope, and possibly even some justice.

"Higashi-san is a superstar in Japan," Aki nattered on. "He appears only rarely and leads a very reclusive existence, but people idolise him. A hundred thousand euros has been offered on the Internet for a single sample of Higashi-san's procreative semen. The whole planning of this Sicilian performance had to be carried out in the strictest secrecy. Higashi-san's management flew me to Kyoto and made me sign a mass of confidentiality agreements. If a single screaming fan turns up here, I'll be scuppered for the rest of my life."

"If he's so famous, where are his management and security people?"

"Back in Japan. Higashi-san wants only me to be present, no one else. Heaven knows why, because *I* don't. He's . . . well, a very special person, you see. But he's doing fine. He likes it here. Working for him is a great honour."

"*Mon dieu*, he's absolutely charming," sighed Valérie. "So are you, Aki. I'm delighted to have you both here."

A gentle breeze sprang up for the first time in weeks. Just a puff of wind, a hint of a breeze, it might have followed Higashi-san from Japan like a tenacious admirer — or so Poldi fancied. The breeze was laden with salty air and a promise that the heat would soon subside and Madame Sahara's murder be solved. It cooled Poldi's brow and briefly stirred her wig before wafting on and fluttering around Higashi-san. Cooler now by a couple of degrees, Poldi noticed a feature of the scene that had escaped her hitherto: Oscar.

The dog was sitting under one of Valérie's two avocado trees, where he formed a skewed rectangle with the sunbathing Germans, the "alga" and Poldi herself. And little Oscar was doing something very unusual. Something he had probably never done before in the whole of his friendly, canine existence. Something that disturbed the order of things in a disquieting way. Poldi noticed it only because at that moment everything was hushed and still in Valérie's paradisal garden—perfectly still except for a low, primeval sound which seemed to issue from the very depths of that shaggy body.

Poldi pointed to the dog. "Listen to him, Valérie."

That was when Valérie noticed Oscar sitting in the shade. "*Mon dieu!*"

"Does he do that often?"

"Never. I didn't think he was capable of it. What's the matter with him?"

"Never, eh? Well, well," said Poldi. "Interesting."

9

Tells of existential issues, of disappearance and discovery, of inspiration, grammar and gold coins. Poldi gives her subconscious a leg up, learns how to make a lake vanish and enlightens her nephew on the connection between the passato remoto *and Sicilian eroticism. Padre Paolo has some small but useful secrets, and Signora Cocuzza has to keep watch again, and because everything, but everything, in life is connected, Poldi has every reason to be grateful to her father.*

I had in the meantime gone back to Germany to spend a joyless month slaving away at my novel and my job at the call centre, filled with nostalgia for *granitas, involtini di pesce spada, pasta al nero,* Cyclopean dreams and the machine-gun chatter of Sicilian dialect, not to mention evenings on the sofa with my Auntie Poldi. Whenever I had to help customers reset their mobile phones or listen to their angry tirades, I pictured Poldi putting a suspect through the mill or sitting in the garden with Valérie. Discounting a few fun nights with my cousins in the newsgroup, I heard nothing from Sicily for four long weeks. Poldi was naturally too busy, and my other aunts still regard phoning Germany as a "long-distance" call, to be made only when someone is dying, war has broken out, or at Christmas. I knew it all too well. Sicily lives so much in the here and now that it forgets you as soon as your plane takes off. However, it remembers you just as quickly when you emerge from the airport, to be told to pick up your cousin's daughter from nursery school and deliver her to Aunt Caterina. This family silence annoyed me, I must admit. However, since I don't like to impose and was, alas, too broke to book myself a flight, I waited eagerly for an invitation. It came in the middle of November, by way of a call from Aunt Luisa.

"Can you come, *tesoro*? It's urgent."

Her voice sounded tense.

"No problem," I said as coolly as I could manage. "Has something happened?"

"You'll see," Aunt Luisa prevaricated. "She's been . . . a bit unstable, and she asked for you. Could you come tomorrow?"

I certainly could. I didn't even need to pack a bag, because I'd left all the essentials in my stuffy Sicilian attic in the Via Baronessa, which had by now become a second home. Exultantly, I ditched my part-time job at the call centre.

But when Poldi came to the door I was appalled. Her left arm was in plaster, and I made out a bandage under her wig. She was also wearing sunglasses to hide the bruise under her right eye, and she limped a little.

"Good Lord!"

"I'm all right," she said dismissively. "It looks worse than it is."

"You look like you were involved in a showdown worthy of Scorsese."

"That's not far from the truth, but all in good time."

In fact, Poldi stubbornly refused to tell me what had happened and bullied the aunts and cousins into maintaining the strictest secrecy about it. At least this accounted for her weeks-long silence, which I even found a trifle flattering.

So I forced myself to be patient, spent the days tinkering with my novel as usual and heard the latest results of the investigation on the sofa in the evening.

"I suppose you aren't going to tell me what Oscar was doing," I grumbled when she got to the episode with the "alga" at Valérie's.

"I'd be daft, wouldn't I? I mean, if this were a novel. If you ever write a thriller, which would be quite a challenge in view of your butterfly brain, I'll remind you of it."

"What do you mean, butterfly brain?"

"Why, you think I haven't noticed you can't focus on one particular thing for love nor money? You're always jumping up and running around, looking this way and that. Your novel will never come to anything like that."

"Come off it, Poldi. These are just cheap tricks designed to heighten dramatic tension. I learnt it all at the last writers' workshop I attended: the reader and the investigator must always be at the same stage of enlightenment. Information must be disseminated nice and evenly, so conclusions can be drawn."

"Really? Don't you think the reader wants to be surprised occasionally?"

"Yes, but that's where the skill lies," I argued. "Anyway, I already know what Oscar did."

Poldi didn't pursue the subject. "Skill doesn't come into it. Writing a thriller is no more of an art than investigating a murder. You concentrate on your work as hard as you can and hope you don't get bogged down or go astray. To a pro like me it's rather like maths. You only get the result and are supposed to derive an equation with twenty-five unknowns from it. And that takes the sort of concentration you lack."

"Drop it, Poldi." I sighed. "I'll never write a thriller anyway."

My Auntie Poldi looked at me, and her face took on an expression midway between mischievous and melancholic.

"Never say never."

Anyway, I imagine that Oscar's behaviour rang a discordant bell that jangled annoyingly somewhere in my aunt's super-brain.

But whatever may have caused the dog to emit that deep, heartfelt growl, it evaporated as soon as he was called by one of Valérie's workers from the palm plantation. Filled with curiosity and scenting the possibility of food, the dog jumped up and scampered off.

The occupants of the sun loungers suddenly stirred. As if in obedience to an unseen choreographer, the Germans rose with a grunt, hauled their loungers back into the shade and continued to stew. Doris caught sight of my aunt and waved to her. Poldi instantly felt her nagging crown again: a slight pain on the right-hand side of her upper jaw, like a distant thunderstorm irresistibly bearing down on her. She returned the wave half-heartedly, hoping that this wouldn't be construed as an invitation to chat. Luckily, it wasn't. Doris had more important things to do at present. Having purposefully creamed herself some more, she eyed the Japanese disapprovingly and rolled over onto her stomach.

The "alga," who had meanwhile concluded his dance with the tree, straightened up in a single, fluid movement and looked over at the house. Poldi could detect no form of emotion on the man's face, which was not unfriendly but mask-like. It was as if the celebrated Butoh dancer had just bestowed all his emotions on the palm tree and the ground.

Plump Aki, by contrast, sprang to life. Picking up a silk kimono that was lying ready to hand, he hurried over to his charge and helped him into it.

Seemingly weightless and without bending so much as a blade of grass, the pallid "alga" came over to Poldi. He bowed and said something very softly in Japanese.

Now, at close quarters, it struck Poldi how small and translucent-looking Higashi-san was. He resembled a teenage girl who had not yet decided if she would ever become a woman. Everything about him was dainty and delicate and reminded my aunt of a masterpiece by an old porcelain artist. He wore his black hair gathered into a neat bun, and nothing but his really tiny pecker, which Poldi had briefly glimpsed, betrayed his gender, yet—pecker or no—he seemed to have none. The very question was nullified by his face and body as if it were wholly unimportant. Poldi began to sense why, apart from his talent as a dancer, Higashi-san was a star in his native land: he was, quite simply, unique.

"Higashi-san is delighted to make the acquaintance of the estimable Signora Poldi," Aki translated. "He wishes you much success with your investigations."

"How . . . ?" Poldi started to say, looking astonished.

"*Moi,*" said Valérie. "Higashi-san is very interested in criminology."

"Well, well, is he really?"

Still perturbed by Oscar's uncharacteristic behaviour, Poldi looked at the Butoh dancer more closely, like someone examining a rare orchid and wondering why nature indulges in such a complex form of beauty. Wondering too, perhaps, what abyss lies hidden behind it. She noticed that the "alga" was regarding her with similar curiosity.

Higashi-san said something else in Japanese, speaking as softly as before, and Aki translated.

"Higashi-san would be delighted if the estimable Signora Poldi could sometime tell him more about her investigations, but only if it's not too much trouble."

"Tell Signor Higashi I'm flattered. I'm most impressed by his art and would like to learn more about it."

The "alga" waited for the translation. Then he bowed, said something and watched Poldi intently while Aki translated.

"Higashi-san looks forward to an exchange of information, even though his contribution to it will be very modest."

Having bowed several times, the dancer allowed Aki to shepherd him off to his room, and Poldi momentarily felt as if he were taking a little of the world's beauty with him — as if the air in the garden had suddenly become a trifle staler.

"What a man," said Poldi. "One's immediate thought is that he must be a very unhappy person."

"*Mon dieu,* how true," Valérie said with a sigh, turning to face her friend. "*Alors?*"

"*Alors* what?"

"A report, of course! I want to know everything, every last little detail. I won't let you go until I do!"

So Poldi spent the next two hours updating her friend on the current state of affairs. Valérie listened attentively, punctuating my aunt's remarks with an occasional "*Mon dieu!*" and drinking one cup of coffee after another.

"So what do you think?" Poldi asked when she had concluded her account with a description of her meeting with Russo.

"You've got a problem," said Valérie. "You've got a whole heap of problems, of course. Your jealous commissario, that wine grower, this surprising new admirer . . . *Mon dieu*, how on earth do you manage it? But you've got one problem above all: you're running out of time."

Poldi gave a start. She couldn't help thinking of her dream about Death in a hoodie—if it really had been a dream.

"How do you mean?"

"Well, Montana will be too quick for you. He's more experienced and he's got a laboratory and so on. He can do things you can't: search premises, arrest and interrogate people, shoot them or whatever. His, um, forensics people —isn't that what they're called?—have probably found something long ago, some DNA or something, and when they've evaluated it, *voilà!*"

"*Voilà?*"

"Time is against you, Poldi. You've gone astray, if you ask me. You're doggedly going through your list of suspects and questioning them, but they lie through their teeth to you. Your *mago*-and-murderer's-aura idea was just a feeble attempt to take a short cut. How many suspects do you propose to canvass before you find Madame Sahara's murderer? And it isn't a sure-fire procedure, either. Even if you're lucky enough to find the murderer before Montana, he won't be pleased, and that will complicate your relationship even more. Men don't like it when women are smarter and more successful than they are. No man does. Believe me, I know a bit about such things."

So did Poldi. She pondered Valérie's words like someone reflecting on a long-recognised but not yet accepted truth. Her old crown passed a vitriolic comment on these thoughts in the form of a throbbing pain. She had to admit that things were going far from smoothly.

"By the way," Valérie said, "how's that nephew of yours?"

"Eh?"

"Well, your nephew from Germany, the writer you're always talking about. Will he be paying you another visit soon? Bring him with you sometime. I think he'd like it here, if he's really as full of phoenix-like energy as you always say."

"I don't believe it!" I broke in, gobsmacked. "She said *that*? 'Bring him with you sometime'?"

"I can't remember her exact words. In fact, she may not have said it at all."

I ignored that. "So you talk about me to other people?"

"Well, only the way you talk about your relations when you've run out of conversation."

"What was all that about 'phoenix-like energy'?"

Poldi dodged the question. "You're starting to get on my nerves, you know that, don't you?" she said. "Valérie must have misremembered something I said, that's all. *Basta!*"

"You've been boasting about me, Poldi. That's it! You can't bear me being such a loser in my jeans-and-navy-blue-polo-shirt look, so you tell the same sort of lies about me as you do about the celeb friends you invent."

"Balls! I don't tell people anything about you, and certainly not lies. The truth, the whole truth and nothing but the truth, that's my motto. What I said before, I was simply improvising for the benefit of my audience, i.e., you. Of course it didn't happen, but make a note of this for your novel: it's never wrong to flatter the reader a bit now and then."

"So why has your face gone all red?"

"Because I'm getting angry—really angry, I tell you. All right, do you plan to go on bugging me, or do you want to hear how, investigation-wise, I hauled myself out of a morass by my wig?"

My Auntie Poldi isn't the type to harbour many illusions about herself and the world in general; she tends to mould the world the way she wants it. But if the substance of the world proves rock-hard and resistant instead of yielding and malleable, my Auntie Poldi will take that in her stride. And attempt to blow up the obstruction.

"Any suggestions?" she asked Valérie. "The thing is, I don't know what to do next. I'm stuck."

"Remember your strong points."

"And they would be?"

"Think around corners. You're a person who doesn't make it easy for herself or other people. You may even be slightly dotty, but that means you see quite different things from some commissario who doggedly proceeds by the book and experience. Take a route no one else sees. Obey your intuition. Don't search, find."

That sounded nice and flattering, but it was easier said than done. Poldi had to admit she didn't have a clue how to proceed. And, as ever when she didn't have a clue—when something obstructed the flux of her intuition and had to be blown away, when nothing made sense any more and there was no signpost anywhere in sight—Poldi drew on her subconscious.

And made a list.

With a flourish, she opened the notebook Uncle Martino had given her, picked up her pencil and shut her eyes. This time, without thinking for long, she wrote down a series of questions that either occurred to her spontaneously or had been going through her head for quite some time:

WHY DID RUSSO TELL ME ALL THAT?
WHAT DOES AN AURA LOOK LIKE?
WHAT DOES AN ALGA THINK?
HAS EVERYBODY BEEN LYING TO ME THE WHOLE
   TIME?
SHOULD I TELL VITO I'M SORRY?
CAN MEN HAVE MULTIPLE ORGASMS?
DO I NEED A CLIPBOARD?
WHY WAS MADAME SAHARA'S HOUSE TRASHED
   LIKE THAT?
WHY DO PEOPLE LIKE DORIS ALWAYS MAKE ME
   FEEL SO SMALL?
WAS PAPA EVER PROUD OF ME?
HAVE I EVER BEEN PROUD OF MYSELF?
SHOULD I KEEP MY TRAP SHUT MORE OFTEN?

SHOULD I REVERT TO DRINKING MORE?
WHAT DID DAVID BOWIE WRITE ON MY HAND
   THAT TIME?
WHAT'S JOHN DOING AT THIS MOMENT?
DID I TURN THE STOVE OFF?

My Auntie Poldi treated her lists as Paul Klee treated his
pictures. She had read once that the painter continued to
work on a picture until it "looked at" him. Well, the list was
now "looking at" her.

"*Voilà.*"

"Will you read it to me?" asked Valérie, who had seen
that the list was written in German. She listened intently as
Poldi read it out. "Not bad. If you ever find out about the
multiple orgasms, I'd be interested. But why the clipboard?"

"No idea. It merely occurred to me when I thought of
death."

"No, it's *not* all pointless, Poldi. On the contrary! And by
the way, I'm very proud of you, just so you know. I'm sure
your papa was too, and we're certainly not the only ones.
You could keep your trap shut occasionally, of course, but
it's no big deal if you don't. You must explain that bit about
the Dorises to me sometime. Hey, did David Bowie really
write something on your hand?"

"A prophecy, he said it was. With his fingernail, back in
the day in Berlin. He was absolutely shitfaced, but always so
polite and kind. A dear fellow. We wrote to each other for
years."

"*Mon dieu.* And who's John?"

"No one. I don't know why I wrote that."

Poldi stared peevishly at her subconscious laid out in

black and white, and Valérie asked no more questions. Silence reigned until, all at once, the penny dropped. "Well, tickle my ass with a feather!" Poldi said.

"What is it?"

Poldi tapped the question halfway down the list. "Why was Madame Sahara's house trashed like that?"

"Well, because the murderer was looking for something that would either have nailed him at once or that he was hell-bent on getting hold of."

"Exactly. He must have been quite certain it was somewhere in the house. But why did he trash the place so completely?"

"I don't understand . . ."

In high excitement, Poldi produced her phone from her pocket and showed Valérie the photos she'd taken when searching for the sad signora. "Look, everything was upside down—it was total chaos. Maybe there was more than one of them. Every drawer was pulled out, every wardrobe emptied of clothes, even the cushions were slit open. How long would that have taken? Hours, you bet, and there was always a risk of being spotted by someone who would call the police, but not a room in the house was left untouched."

"Why does that puzzle you so?"

Poldi stared at her friend, cheeks flushed with the thrill of the chase. "Because it can only mean one thing, my dear: the murderer didn't find what he was looking for, or at some stage he'd have been able to stop his orgy of destruction and disappear. But Signora Cocuzza caught him unawares, so he had to do so prematurely. And what does that mean?"

"*Mon dieu!*"

"Exactly. Whatever he was looking for, he didn't find it.

Nor did the police, so it's probably still somewhere in the house. And you know what, Valérie?"

"No, don't tell me, Poldi!"

"Oh yes. I reckon it's waiting for me."

At Padre Paolo's express request, the team discussion took place in the sacristy of Santa Maria del Rosario.

"Because it's the only bug-proof place in the entire world," he said grimly, fag in the corner of his mouth, as he slammed a grotty aluminium *caffettiera* down on a camping hotplate and made an espresso. "The Mother of God and these thick walls will protect us from any eavesdroppers. Even the NSA and the CIA would find it a hard nut to crack."

Signora Cocuzza had brought some homemade almond biscuits from her establishment, and over *caffè* and *biscotti* the padre insisted on kicking off by reporting the results of his investigation of District Attorney Carbonaro, Poldi's neighbour. Which he promptly did with much gesticulation and in every detail, from the traffic jam on the main road to Catania to the colour of Dottore Carbonaro's tie (green paisley, very dapper).

Poldi's initial reaction to the padre's hogging of the agenda was a bit sniffy, given her own eagerness to inform the team of her flash of inspiration, but she retained her composure and made allowances for the tendency of Italian males to deliver grandiloquent speeches. Her late husband Peppe had been no exception in that respect, but Poldi had always loved his long and detailed effusions on irrelevancies of all kinds, because my Uncle Peppe, like every Italian male, had naturally succeeded in stripping the mundane of all its mundanity and transforming it into something radiantly wonderful. What's more, this genetically programmed urge to spout polished rhetoric leads its practitioners to enunciate perfectly. Anyone wanting to hear proper Italian would do well to listen to Italian parliamentary speeches. The content is total crap, of course, but the delivery is crystal clear.

Poldi enjoyed listening to the padre too, but his remarks boiled down to only one sexy piece of information. Not very subtly, he had asked the district attorney whether Etnarosso meant anything to him, or whether his murdered colleague Elisa Puglisi had ever mentioned it. And lo, she had actually done so in the canteen one day (the *plat du jour* was *pasta alla norma*). At this point, as expected, Padre Paolo inserted a dramatic pause and drank a glass of water as if this information had shaken him to the depths of his faith.

Poldi, who was getting tired of this, thought it time to make clear which of them was the master detective. "Etnarosso," she said, getting in first, "is the code name of a water development project being undertaken in Sicily by a Swiss firm named Oceanica." She relished seeing the padre's jaw drop as if the Mother of God herself had farted in his presence.

The sad signora gazed at my aunt in admiration.

"Where the devil . . . ?" the padre gasped, stubbing out his cigarette.

Poldi nonchalantly brushed the question aside. "I haven't been idle myself. But please go on, Padre."

The priest's face preserved its flush of disappointment

until he had recovered himself sufficiently to light another cigarette.

"It's true, Donna Poldina," he growled. "But according to that adulterer Carbonaro, Elisa Puglisi was in the process of investigating Oceanica because there was a well-founded suspicion that the firm was cooperating with the Mafia."

There it was again, the M-word, indispensable to any features-section article, any travelogue, any conversation between friends about Sicily, and which indissolubly adheres to the island like an old hazardous-goods label that nobody takes seriously any more.

"Context, please, Padre," Poldi said in a businesslike tone, helping herself to another almond biscuit.

Back in more self-satisfied waters, Padre Paolo briskly deposited a stack of photocopies of articles from *La Sicilia* on the table. Poldi, every inch the pro, began by glancing at the dates on each.

"They're all from last spring!"

"Quite so," said the padre. "I had them copied in the newspaper's archive. One call from me, you know, and they jump to it. But read them yourself, Donna Poldina."

Poldi skimmed the articles and was amazed to find that they all dealt with an incredible discovery: a big stretch of water near Caltagirone, a whole lake no longer marked on any modern map and seemingly forgotten by everyone. It had allegedly dried up thirty years earlier and then disappeared, but it actually still existed, well filled and largely fenced in.

"I don't understand," said Poldi. "How in the world can a whole lake simply disappear like this?"

"Yes, it's strange, isn't it? Everyone, even us Sicilians, think we live in an arid region, but it's bullshit. Distribution of the water is the problem. Many lakes and drinking water reservoirs are privately owned, and the Mafia realised decades ago what a good business water could be. So they and their corrupt henchmen in the communities and district administrations allowed a few publicly owned bodies of water to "dry up" and then disappear. It amounted to enforced privatisation of a vital public resource, with the aim of selling previously free water back to the communities for a lot of money."

"You mean there are several such cases?"

"You can bet on it, Donna Poldina. This particular scandal came out only because one or two journalists asked awkward questions and took some aerial photographs."

"But I still don't understand . . . Surely a whole lake can't disappear from the memory of the local inhabitants, just like that?"

"This is Sicily, Donna Poldina. We invented fatalism. Of course they remember the lake. They still have a clear recollection of the days when they didn't have to pay anything for the water they drink and use for showering and cooking and irrigating their fields. But they shrug their shoulders, they're scared, and there's some cousin, brother-in-law or acquaintance in the local administration who may not belong there because he's an unqualified moron, but who does one the occasional favour. Everybody knows how the system works. We Sicilians breathe an age-old aerosol of fear and nepotism. It poisons us and keeps us alive at the same time."

"*Omertà*," said Poldi.

"No comment, Donna Poldina. I've already said too much."

"And how do the Sicilians put up with it all?" my Auntie Poldi asked me suddenly, halfway through her report.

She caught me completely on the wrong foot again.

"Er . . ."

I'm not too good at tests. It isn't that I suffer from examinitis or anything like that, but I'd sooner do a job in which one is never tested or criticised in any way. Like writing novels or something of the kind.

But as usual, my Auntie Poldi didn't expect me to answer anyway.

"By using the *passato remoto*," she explained. "If you ever want to really understand Sicily, you must supplement that miserable Italian of yours with the *passato remoto*."

"My Italian is quite adequate for everyday purposes," I objected.

"Nonsense. In Milan, maybe, but not here in the south. Without the *passato remoto* you'll never understand a thing about *sicilianità*."

I think I already mentioned that the Italian *passato remoto* is the historic perfect, a past tense separate from the normal *passato prossimo,* which luckily doesn't exist in German. The *passato remoto* is used to express actions that are far in the past and, above all, finished and done with, and it's an utter swine of a tense for language students to learn because of its irregular formation. The verb is scarcely recognisable, it harks back so far — to the Bronze Age at least. In other words, for Sicilians, yesterday.

One generally comes across the *passato remoto* in literary texts, which is bad enough. It almost never occurs in everyday parlance—as long as one remains north of Naples. The farther south one goes, however, the more stubbornly it obtrudes into everyday speech, above all in Sicily. Even the humblest mandarin picker expresses past actions exclusively by means of the *passato remoto*. This, my Uncle Martino told me once, is because of Sicily's centuries-long occupation by conquerors of all kinds. Phoenicians, Romans, Greeks, Arabs, Normans, Hohenstaufens, Spaniards, Bourbons, English, Americans, German *deliziosi*—the list is a long one. In a country being constantly plundered by someone or other, the past is better regarded as over and done with, even the day after.

"By using the *passato remoto*," Poldi explained, "Sicilians convey that they live in the here and now, just like me. There's also a connection between the *passato remoto* and baroque Sicilian sexuality. The *passato remoto* is the grammar of Sicilian eroticism, so to speak. Forget about kundalini yoga and tantric sex."

"You can't be serious, Poldi."

"I most certainly am. People who live in the here and now, like the Sicilians, are better equipped to let go and focus all their energy on a single moment of ecstasy—switch off their brains, know what I mean? A bit of *passato remoto* would benefit your own love life. Then you wouldn't keep quarrelling with Sicily."

"Just a minute. When do I do that?"

"Why, all the time. Even when you order a coffee, you spend five minutes beforehand thinking how to say it, for fear of making a *brutta figura* of yourself. You're always complaining of the chaos and the dirt, not to mention your stress level when driving a car or your tantrums when you've lost your way again, thanks to your lousy sense of direction."

"In the first place, my sense of direction is fine, and second, the road signs are an absolute disaster."

"Wrong. Your lousy bump of direction is a family failing — Peppe always confused left and right. You're all deficient in that respect. Now . . . where did we get to?"

"*Omertà*, fatalism, disappearing lakes," I prompted.

"And you think, Padre, that this lake has some connection with Etnarosso?" asked Signora Cocuzza.

"It's obvious, signora. Elisa Puglisi of the district attorney's office in Catania was investigating the water Mafia and dealt with this case. And that concern Oceanica appeared on the scene at almost the same time. You really think that could be purely coincidental, Donna Poldina?"

Poldi wasn't sure.

"We shall see. Perhaps everything will turn out to be far simpler than we imagine. Many thanks, Padre."

Every inch the boss.

Padre Paolo reacted with a mixture of bewilderment and pique — this was still his sacristy, after all — but when Poldi went on to describe her meeting with Russo, her acquaintanceship with a Butoh dancer and her subsequent flash of inspiration, he was all ears.

"*Madonna*," whispered Signora Cocuzza. "What interesting experiences you always have, Donna Poldina. How on earth do you manage it?"

Poldi said nothing, just waited.

The silent sacristy was pervaded by the mingled scents of

cigarette smoke, coffee and incense. Padre Paolo puffed away. Signora Cocuzza nibbled an almond biscuit.

"What if the murderer himself has gone back in the meantime and found what he was looking for?" she asked between nibbles.

"That'd be plain bad luck."

"Well, well," said the padre. And again, just in case he hadn't been heard the first time, "Well, well."

"I shall go back to Madame Sahara's house on my own," Poldi said firmly. "I can't drag you two into it."

"That would be very unfair of you," said the sad signora.

"More than that," added the padre, "it would be rather foolish and doomed to failure. A thing like this calls for teamwork, planning, know-how. All the cogs must mesh." He demonstrated with the fingers of both hands. "Or don't you agree, signora?"

"I'm with you a hundred per cent, Padre," replied the sad signora, and her usually pale, sorrowful face flushed a little. "Unless you want to keep the whole adventure to yourself, Donna Poldina?"

Poldi sighed. She was surprised that neither of them had suggested calling in Montana, and that could mean only one thing: they'd been carried away by the thrill of the chase.

"Do you two comedians realise that we could all wind up in jail? And you, Padre, would be excommunicated into the bargain."

"He'd get a suspended sentence at most," said Signora Cocuzza.

The padre made a dismissive gesture. "The route to excommunication is longer than purgatory. Besides, this operation would surely meet with divine approval."

He did not, however, explain what made him so certain of this. Poldi could have used a beer at this stage. As if he had read her thoughts, Padre Paolo fetched an opened bottle of altar wine from a refrigerator under the wash-basin and filled three tumblers.

"To the truth, ladies, and the fruit of the Lord!"

The padre and Poldi drained their glasses. Signora Cocuzza only sipped hers.

"Very well," Poldi said a little more firmly. "But there's a problem."

"No, there isn't," said the padre, as if he had once more read her thoughts, and he rummaged in a drawer. "I've everything we need."

They sat outside Madame Sahara's house in the Alfa and waited until it was completely dark. Poldi decreed that Signora Cocuzza should again keep watch, which led to a minor altercation. Poldi ended it with a resolute "*Basta!* Risking your life once is enough!" Which led in turn to a brief drop in temperature inside the car.

Under cover of darkness, Poldi and the padre stole up to the front door. The priest's professional attire acted as camouflage in any case, but Poldi had squeezed into a pair of black stretch pants and a black roll-neck sweater. Although this outfit looked pretty cool and reminiscent of a sixties film noir, the prevailing temperature brought on one bout of sweating after another. Poldi was on the verge of heatstroke, but she gritted her teeth. Listening intently for any sounds inside the house, she gave Signora Cocuzza a whispered situation report on her mobile.

"Right outside the door. All quiet."

"Roger." The signora pronounced it with a rolling Italian *r*. "Same here."

"Please could you not say 'Roger'? This isn't *Mission Impossible*."

"But I've always wanted an opportunity to say 'Roger,' Donna Poldina. If I can't go inside with you, I can at least say what I want."

"Okay, suit yourself."

"Roger. Stand by."

"No, not 'Stand by,' my dear. 'Roger' if you must, but not 'Stand by,' can we agree on that?"

"Roger. Copy that."

It dawned on Poldi that Signora Cocuzza was only just getting into her stride.

The police seal on the front door was undamaged. A strip of adhesive tape, it was stuck over the lock and the door frame. A good sign on the one hand, but a problem on the other, because Poldi wanted to leave no traces behind. She had originally planned to break into the house via the first-floor windows, but the padre had a better solution. With a flourish, he produced a small, battery-driven hair dryer from his shoulder bag and directed a jet of warm air at the adhesive tape.

"Can't you be a bit quieter?" Poldi hissed nervously.

"It won't take long."

Sure enough, after a few moments' exposure to warm air the adhesive tape could be removed intact.

"Phase two," said the padre. He reached into his bag and produced a set of skeleton keys he'd removed from a drawer in the sacristy a few hours earlier. These, he'd nonchalantly explained, had been left behind by the thieves who burgled his church last year.

Poldi had refrained from pressing him on the subject, because she respected the fact that everyone had their own little secrets. The padre certainly had his, because he knew not only how to remove a crime scene tape undamaged, but also how to pick a lock with a skeleton key in a matter of seconds.

"*Ecco!*" He happily stole into the house like a cat.

Poldi followed him inside, closed the door and turned on her flashlight.

"Where shall we start?" the padre whispered.

"You upstairs, me down here."

"Roger."

"I'm warning you, Padre!"

With the beam of her flashlight directed at the floor and absolutely no idea where to look, my Auntie Poldi picked her way through the chaotic clutter, which looked even worse and more depressing than it had in daylight. Doubtful that she would really find anything there, she strove to concentrate on untouched, somehow forgotten places.

Inconspicuous places.

Places that weren't immediately noticeable.

Places where she herself might have hidden something of value.

Which was why she found it. It wasn't difficult; she spotted it as soon as they entered Madame Sahara's studio, the room containing the rococo chaise longue. Moonlight illuminated its hiding place, so it positively sprang to the eye. The main reason, however, was that at that moment Poldi heard the hoarse cry of a bird of prey and then had a bright idea in the form of a chain association: bird of prey–buzzard–papa–coin collection. It should be explained that Detective Chief Inspector (ret.) Georg Oberreiter of the Augsburg homicide division had since the 1950s collected not only antique weapons but also gold coins from all over the world, initially as a crisis-proof investment but later because it became a passion of his. Poldi had always detested this coin collection, as she had everything to do with Augsburg and her parents' suburban way of life. After their deaths, she had inherited the hateful little terrace house, together with the coin and weapon collections.

And she had had to find the coin collection before she could sell the house and all the trimmings. She had spent three days turning the whole place upside down in an attempt to find the damned coins, had rummaged through every drawer, upended every vase, shaken out every sock. Nothing. Not until she had eventually found the hiding place by pure chance.

"*Namaste,* Papa," Poldi whispered, profoundly moved, when she grasped how everything was interrelated.

Resolutely and confidently, she went over to Madame Sahara's old séance table and tugged the lace cloth off it, and she wasn't surprised to find that it was a pull-out table that could be extended in both directions. It creaked a little, as though in relief, as Poldi slid the leaves apart to reveal something secreted in the central cavity.

"The operation is over," she whispered into her mobile phone, overcome with emotion. "I've found it."

"What is it?" Signora Cocuzza croaked excitedly.

"It looks like a murder motive. We're coming out."

"Roger, copy that. Mission completed. Roger, over and out."

10

Tells of inspiration, the Cyclopean legacy, solidarity, and sicilianità. *Poldi pays her nephew an unexpected compliment and feels she's being followed. Examined in the sacristy, a motive for murder gives rise to some extravagant theories. Poldi suffers from withdrawal symptoms and again feels she's being followed. She plans to pay Montana a nocturnal visit, but is prevented from doing so by an old acquaintance.*

No one will be surprised to hear that I made great strides with my family saga while staying at my Auntie Poldi's. Energised by her stories, an abundance of Polifemo, Aunt Teresa's seafood lunches, salt air, mild November weather, *caffè*, pistachio ice cream, the sound of bells, stoically smoking Etna, my daydreams about Valérie and Femminamorta—in short, by the whole Sicily package —I felt more inspired and fulfilled than I had in a long time. Forgotten were all my cavilling and vacillation, gone were my self-doubt, inferiority complex and romantic heartache (the latter wisely concealed from Poldi and the other aunts). I felt good. In tune with Sicily. I could write. I was the future of the European novel.

At night I dreamt of nymphs and sirens, and of gigantic Cyclopes descending from Etna with measured tread and wading into the sea, where they turned into kelp. They strode over me—I could hear their breathing and their murmurous singsong voices, which sometimes seemed to utter my name. Yes, they were calling me, and I rose and followed them. I followed the call of my blood. I was a Cyclops. I was halfway through Chapter Three.

Great-grandfather Barnaba had by now arrived in Munich and was living with his Aunt Pasqualina, the illusionist and spy, in Westermühlstrasse. A magical new world of wonders and horrors opened up before him: Germany, the raucous German language, German food, discipline, traffic, blond girls. For weeks he could think of nothing other than his beloved Eleonora, whom he had left behind in the blazing heat of his distant homeland, where (all this seemed suddenly to write itself) she gave birth to the fruit of their volcanic passion—a boy, of course—and naturally had to conceal this from her tyrannical father (*or possibly ran away?* I left a tag at this point). Meantime, Barnaba was wasting away from nostalgia, frustration and an allergy to red cabbage. But young Italian males are like Etna: too much pent-up magma leads to massive eruptions. That is the only reason why the geologically youthful Mongibello is regarded as a good-natured volcano: it regularly lets off steam, does little damage and is very fertile. Like a young Sicilian, in other words. It was unsurprising, therefore, that athletic Barnaba with his olive complexion and sorrowful eyes soon gained a certain reputation among the young ladies of Munich's Glockenbach quarter. Whenever they spoke of him among themselves, they giggled dreamily and referred to him by various risqué code words.

Very few of them remembered his name.

Pasqualina, whose experience of life and love was wide, at first took an indulgent view of Barnaba's success with the young ladies of Munich. She also took a certain pride in it, but after he had spent several weeks in athletic idleness, she visualised the whole of the Glockenbach quarter teeming with little Barnabas and could imagine a host of angry claims for child support, none of which would be conducive to her secret double life. Although she sensed that the magic talisman given him by the preternaturally beautiful siren Ilaria would temporarily protect her eruptive and overly fertile nephew from unwanted fatherhood, it was time he did some work. Consequently, she found him a job with Calogero Vizzini, an occasional lover of hers from Ragusa, who ran a greengrocer's stall in Munich's central market. From now on, happy to be among his own kind and surrounded by the familiar cooing of his native dialect, Barnaba toted around crates and pallets filled with oranges, lemons, artichokes and aubergines from midnight until well into the day. He unloaded wagons and loaded horse-drawn carts, swept the stall, carried out all kinds of repairs and, protected by the preternaturally beautiful siren Ilaria's talisman, fought with Vizzini's neighbouring stallholders and customers whenever questions arose over the exact boundaries of Vizzini's stall or the current price of mandarins.

A thoroughly agreeable phase in his life.

At this point, satisfied with my progress, I inserted another tag (*Research!!!*) with the intention of opulently colouring in Barnaba's tough years of apprenticeship at a later stage, painting a rich and vibrant picture of Munich in the 1920s and acquainting the reader with Barnaba's inner pain and the harsh, unvarnished reality of a Sicilian migrant's life in that period. A stark, savage, sensually baroque novel was taking shape. Passion, poverty, fatalism, hope, violence — it had everything, plenty of mandarins included. The quintessence of Sicily, in fact. I visualised my hero, who had yet to reach the age of twenty, as an unpolished lump of obsidian filled with Cyclopean strength and savagery. He spoke not a word of German and would never learn the language, he worked stripped to the waist all year round, and his muscular body was covered with scars, both inward and outward. Needs and desires, poise and purpose, contradictions and development — my hero possessed all that I'd learnt in various seminars and from books about how to create unforgettable characters. I felt I was at the zenith of my narrative potency. I loved my hero. I discovered an immense number of subconscious parallels with myself. I *was* Barnaba.

Calogero Vizzini, whom I visualised as the archetypal old-school Mafioso with a heart of gold, soon realised that wild, melancholy, taciturn Barnaba possessed a special talent: he was very adept at mental arithmetic. He could work out the most complicated sums in his head, and the answers were always correct. So Vizzini took his protégé out of the day-to-day business and taught him figures. From then on, he made him check invoices, work out prices, protection-money percentages and bribes, and double-enter deliveries that had never taken place. In other words, he soon left Barnaba in sole charge of his accounts. The young man now knew almost all there was to know about Vizzini's business affairs, and this, among the more criminal members of the Sicilian population, always presented the following instinctive dilemma: kill or adopt?

Vizzini opted for the latter alternative and made Barnaba a partner. Shortly afterwards, Vizzini died under unexplained circumstances or disappeared without trace. His body was never found, nor could it have been, because Barnaba had seen to that with Pasqualina's assistance. Just twenty-one years old, he was now the respected sole proprietor of a flourishing fruit and special goods import business, wore nothing but bespoke white suits and employed a private secretary who could speak German. Meantime, the hard-working talisman given him by the preternaturally beautiful siren Ilaria finally gave up the ghost and failed to prevent a buxom young waitress named Rosi, who could carry twelve steins of beer at once and possessed a certain acrobatic skill, from becoming pregnant by him. And since Barnaba was a man of honour and also besotted with Rosi and her nocturnal acrobatics, he acknowledged the child as his son, moved out of Pasqualina's house, rented a seven-room apartment three doors away, and moved into it with Rosi and the discreet private secretary. In short, Barnaba was now a made man and ready to go on holiday to his old home for the first time since leaving it. A great cliffhanger, I thought. End of Chapter Three.

Thoroughly satisfied, replete with *sicilianità* and feeling rather cool, I bought a butter-yellow shirt at the HiperSimply supermarket and, since Poldi was still out, sat on the roof terrace at sunset with a dry martini, toasted distant Etna like an old friend, waited for nightfall and the resump-

tion of Poldi's narrative—and smoked my first-ever cigarette.

"What?" Poldi said, aghast, when I told her that evening.
"What put that daft idea into your head?"

"A packet of yours was lying around," I said evasively.

"And you took that as an invitation to screw up your life,
did you? Fancy starting smoking at your age. Couldn't you
at least have waited till your midlife crisis?"

"I'm thirty-four, Poldi, and I'm not starting smoking," I
said defensively. "We only smoked a cigarette together.
Okay, two."

"We?"

"Yes, Etna and me."

She stared at me in disbelief, and I sensed that the more I
said, the sillier I'd look. But, as my Auntie Poldi always says,
"Faint heart never won fair lady." And anyway, I was a
grown-up. I didn't have to defer to anyone.

"The thing is," I said, "I enjoy sitting on your terrace. I
enjoy drinking my breakfast cappuccino there, I enjoy eating a lunchtime *arancino* from the café there, and I enjoy
drinking a beer there in the evenings. Those are times when
I'm all mine and my own master, know what I mean? I like
your terrace with that mountain brooding in the distance all
the time. When the sun goes down behind the main crater,
it looks like a dark angel unfurling its wings. And it smokes.
It smokes all day and all night. It smokes without a break.
It's been smoking for half a million years or more."

"So you thought you'd smoke too."

"I know it sounds completely daft."

"It *is* completely daft."

What could I say? When she was right, she was right.

My Auntie Poldi gave me a searching look and topped up our glasses.

"Nice shirt. New?"

"Mm."

"Suits you. You're the Mediterranean type. You can wear strong colours."

"Thanks."

"A little tip: undo one more button and you'd make an almost casual impression."

With a sigh, I undid one more button. "That better?"

Poldi nodded and drank and continued to eye me intently. "What's next, now that you've sniffed the flower of coolness? Going to get a tat or a piercing?"

"Listen, Poldi, I . . ."

She silenced me with a gesture. "How did it make you feel, smoking?"

"How did it make me feel?"

"Go on, be quite spontaneous."

"Connected," I said. "Somehow connected with the volcano and everything else here. Sicily suddenly became far less annoying. On the contrary, it feels . . ." I hesitated.

Poldi nudged me with her elbow. "Come on, just say it."

"Like home."

She nodded as if I'd answered a question correctly for the first time in my life, then took another sip of her drink. "It is and remains totally daft. On the other hand, people who never do anything totally daft are highly suspect, so welcome to the club."

We clinked glasses.

And I realised that I was really very fond of my Auntie Poldi.

"You now have a new friend," she told me. "Etna. I predict you'll smoke many another cigarette together in the future, but that only goes to show that even a stuffy slowpoke like you has a few Cyclopean genes. Right, now tell me about your new chapter."

"No, leave it, Poldi. First I want to know what was in that pull-out table."

The padre had managed to reattach the undamaged police seal to the front-door lock. He and Signora Cocuzza were eager to know at once what Poldi had found, but my aunt was in too much of a hurry.

"Quick, into the car, Padre! We must get out of here."

Back behind the wheel of her Alfa, she sped through deserted villages and along dark, winding roads, ignoring every red light and continually checking her rear-view mirror for potential pursuers. This, coupled with her style of driving, filled the car with a certain tension and the sound of quick, muttered prayers, but they got back to Torre without further incident. Poldi parked outside the church and hustled her team into its bug-proof interior.

It was quiet inside the sacristy. Not a sound penetrated its thick walls, but there was nothing to be heard outside in any case, other than the murmur of the sea, an occasional bark or the putt-putt of a moped. The inhabitants of Torre Archirafi were sleeping, eating, arguing, procreating or watching the Champions League, but either within their own four walls or in their cars.

It was quiet inside the sacristy, yes, but particularly because Poldi, Padre Paolo and Signora Cocuzza were staring silently at the old refectory table as if loath to wake what was lying on it because it might bite. But books don't bite, and the book on the refectory table didn't look as if it was about to start. It looked wholly unremarkable. A small black pocket diary for the current year, complete with ribbon page marker and leather cover, it offered a page a day, and almost every page listed appointments neatly entered in Madame Sahara's legible handwriting. Poldi had already seen this much back at the house.

"Well," she said, breaking the silence. She pulled on a pair of latex gloves and sat down at the table. "Let's take a look."

She began by holding up the diary and riffling the pages to see whether there was anything lodged between them. Discounting a few crumbs of tobacco, there wasn't. With the padre and the sad signora on either side of her, Poldi eventually opened the diary and went through it page by page.

"What are we looking for?" asked the padre.

"We aren't looking, we're finding," Poldi told him. "No overhasty theories, though. We must form a general picture first."

And that was what they got. Each entry consisted of a surname and an abbreviated forename, the fee to be charged, usually ticked (120 euros an hour), and sporadic marginal notes such as "Very nervous," "Extremely worried," "Debts," "Depressive," "Narcissistic," "Cocaine problem?" and "No charge!" Madame Sahara had supplemented some of these remarks with cryptic little signs whose meaning Poldi had yet to elucidate. Madame Sahara had also entered other figures against many of the names, some of them in four digits. Although the euro sign was never inserted, Poldi had no doubt that they were sums of money.

"Do these names mean anything to you?" she asked after the first few pages.

"They certainly do," growled Padre Paolo. "They include every local politician of any repute."

"I also noticed two actors," Signora Cocuzza added, "and a footballer."

"I see," said Poldi, annoyed that they hadn't imparted this information sooner. She turned back to January and got them to brief her on every name of any prominence.

A pattern emerged, because the more prominent names were the ones with the bulk of the four-figure sums and cryptic signs against them. Poldi did some rough mental arithmetic and arrived at a total of approximately 120,000 euros for the period up to June. To her, there was only one logical explanation.

"She must have blackmailed these people, don't you think?"

"Without a doubt," said the padre.

"It seems so," said Signora Cocuzza, her habitual caution kicking in. "But they could also have been donations or loans. What's the word . . . crowdfunding?"

The padre groaned. "Really, signora!"

Poldi checked him with a gesture and looked at her friend admiringly. "Not bad, my dear. That sounds far more plausible. To finance the production of her own TV show."

For the first time in ages, the merest hint of a smile flitted across the sad signora's face.

"Thank you, Donna Poldina."

"Because," said Poldi, pursuing the idea, "if she'd black-mailed all these different people, one is bound to wonder what she used. Where would Giuliana have got all the relevant information?"

The padre was piqued. "Well," he growled, "she was a fortune-teller, after all."

That presented the sad signora with an easy lob.

"Really, Padre Paolo!"

"Either that or she was laundering dirty money."

"How, Padre? A fortune-teller isn't a pizzeria."

"Nor is it a café bar like yours!"

"No bickering, my friends," Poldi said sternly. "According to her brother, Giuliana's fortune-telling abilities weren't great in any case." And, because nothing is harder than abandoning one's own theories, she added, "But we shouldn't completely discount blackmail, not yet. It's just too good a motive for murder to be ditched altogether. And we'll also continue to bear your money-laundering theory in mind, Padre."

That smoothed everyone's ruffled feathers.

Poldi went on leafing through the months, and the names her team reeled off included almost the entire who's who of the Catania-Messina region. Politicians, actors, footballers, businessmen—they had all consulted Madame Sahara and sometimes donated a handsome sum—or gritted their teeth as they forked it out, who could tell? Not all were prominent figures. More than half the names meant nothing to the sad signora and the padre. They were ordinary local folk with fears for the future or broken hearts, Poldi supposed: childless women, unemployed men, artisans, petrol pump attendants, seamstresses, lemon pickers, bank clerks, pensioners and charwomen who wanted to invest their hard-earned money profitably or boost their chances of winning the lottery. "Possibly," Poldi thought as she turned the pages, "the sort of clients Giuliana sometimes wrote 'No charge' against."

Among the March appointments, Poldi eventually came across the first name that was familiar to her as well: *E. Puglisi.*

"Ah!" she said triumphantly. "I said it. The two murders are connected! You were wrong, Vito. You were *so* wrong."

It turned out that the murdered district attorney had consulted her clairvoyant at least once a month from March onwards. On two occasions a smallish four-figure sum was jotted down beside her name.

Satisfied, Poldi continued to turn the pages—until her good mood was abruptly dispelled by the sight of another name.

"I don't believe it. I just don't believe it."

She stared aghast at the name, which might have preferred to sneak out of the diary and avoid her gaze: *V. Montana.*

Silence in the sacristy. The sad signora and the padre shuffled uneasily in their chairs. Poldi saw that the consultations had begun shortly after she and Montana got to know each other.

"A common enough name," the sad signora whispered.

The padre nodded vigorously. "A common name. Fills whole pages in the phone book. My grandmother was a Montana."

"It's him, I just know it is," Poldi groaned. "How could you do this to me, Vito?"

"You mean they were . . ."

"No, of course not. Far worse. He went running to Madame Sahara after we met. Why did he never tell me about it? Besides, it means he's mixed up in this case."

"Perhaps Madame Sahara was an undercover detective," the padre hazarded.

"Or he may have needed advice about some . . . well, affair of the heart."

Poldi stared at her friend for the second time that night.

Signora Cocuzza shrugged her shoulders. "Perhaps you'd better not mention it to him, Donna Poldina. It would go against the grain, but you'd be doing yourself a favour, believe me. Know what you ought to do now?"

"What?" Poldi said between her teeth.

"Take some deep breaths and then we'll carry on, eh? We're pros, after all."

"*Et Spiritus Sancti*, amen."

"*Namaste*, you comedians," Poldi said, sighing. She was unsurprised by the next familiar names she came to.

A. Avola and *C. Avola*, for example, or a certain *S. Torso* on a Wednesday in September. She shivered when she recalled the dowser in the baseball cap. The very name induced a feeling of trepidation, as if it robbed her of the strength to breathe. It turned out that Sean Torso had paid only one visit to Madame Sahara, and he was the sole client she'd made no marginal note against. No fee, no remarks, no cryptic symbol, nothing.

"Perhaps he had an appointment but simply failed to turn up," the padre suggested.

"It's possible," said Poldi. "Or maybe their conversation was about something quite different."

She confessed to me later that she'd counted on finding some unusual entries in the weeks preceding Giuliana's death. Eye-catching names, horrendous sums, smudged handwriting, tear stains, names blacked out—something like that. After all, *Mago* Rampulla had claimed that his sister had been very frightened recently.

Nothing of the kind, though. Madame Sahara's handwriting looked as neat and assured as ever, even in the very last entry, made on the day before she died. By then, according to Poldi's rough estimate, she had taken in nearly 250,000 euros. Not bad for a fortune-teller, she thought.

There was, however, one puzzling entry after Elisa Puglisi's last visit, the day before her death. It was obviously a quotation, because Madame Sahara had put it in inverted commas: "The Hedgehog has the money!"

Neither the sad signora nor the padre could figure out who the Hedgehog was, but Poldi, certain that the murderer and his motive were down there in black and white, right before her eyes, felt queasy despite herself.

Although the meaning of the cryptic symbols in the margins still escaped her, Poldi surmised that they were mnemonic aids for Madame Sahara's fortune-telling service. She shut the little book but rested both hands on it. She was perspiring, she noticed. Her hands were moist and sweat trickled down beneath her wig.

"Are you feeling all right, Donna Poldina?"

"I'm fine," she said. Then, "This diary is clearly a motive for murder, and it contains the name of a double murderer. It was the Hedgehog. We must proceed on that basis."

An extravagant theory, but the team nodded gravely.

The sad signora handed Poldi a handkerchief. "What do you propose to do now, Donna Poldina?"

Poldi mopped her brow. "I'm loath to say so, but we'll have to hand this diary over to the police."

"Whaaat?" the padre and the sad signora exclaimed in unison.

Poldi raised a conciliatory hand. "But first Montana will have to pay a price for it, and second, we'll have to evaluate it first. Do you have a scanner, Padre?"

"Er, only a multifunction printer. Will that do?"

"Admirably." Poldi handed him the diary. "We need a copy of every page. Thanks." She turned to Signora Cocuzza. "I'd like you to make a list of all the names, entries, dates, symbols and so on."

"An Excel table, you mean?"

"Not necessarily."

"Yes, nothing else will do. That way, we can filter and sort the entries by name, date and sum of money."

"And you can handle that?"

"I sit behind a cash desk, Donna Poldina, remember? I may only run a little café bar in a boring seaside town, and I may not have many talents, but I'm not a complete nincompoop."

"Of course not, my dear," said Poldi, touched. "You certainly aren't."

And she put her arms round her sad, frail, brave friend, clasped her to her ample bosom and planted a smacking kiss on her cheek.

"What if the padre sees us, Donna Poldina?"

"Let him. Maybe he'd like to join in."

Signora Cocuzza giggled softly.

"How long will the Excel table take you?"

"I won't be able to sleep. You'll have it by tomorrow morning. Go to bed, Donna Poldina. You're not looking too good."

"Later. There's something I have to do first."

"*Madonna,* what do you propose to do now?"

"Go to the police, of course. What else?"

"But it's the middle of the night."

"And that, my dear, is always the best time to call on a policeman."

Padre Paolo had scarcely finished photocopying the last page of the diary when Poldi snatched the little book from his hand and took her leave. A strange uneasiness, a kind of foreboding, urged her to hurry. It was the sort of feeling one sometimes gets when a storm is brewing. However, it might simply have been her old crown. The throbbing had now transmuted itself into a stabbing pain, and she sensed she wouldn't be able to avoid a visit to the dentist.

"Tomorrow," she told herself. "I'll go tomorrow. Faint heart never won fair lady."

There was no one to be seen on the promenade in front of the church. Waves broke sluggishly against the volcanic rocks, the Alfa was parked beneath a street light, a cat flitted along the sea wall. Before she emerged from the church into the glow of the street lights, Poldi lingered in the shadowy side entrance for a moment and looked in both directions. Earlier on in Santa Venerina she had felt sure she was being watched and followed.

Which wasn't a surprising sensation in a burglar.

But which probably hadn't been the case.

And which might well have been due to her overtaxed and alcohol-starved nerves.

Poldi could detect nothing suspicious, no sign of movement, no glowing cigarette end, no shadowy figures. Torre Archirafi was asleep, and Poldi herself would have preferred to go to bed with a little nightcap, but Madame Sahara's diary was an incentive to haste and abstinence.

"Tomorrow," she thought, "tomorrow I'll go to the dentist, and that'll be a good excuse for a drink."

Discounting a small glass of wine in the sacristy, she hadn't had a drink since that morning, and she had barely eaten. This resulted in a special form of tremulous paranoia associated with fits of sweating, accelerated heartbeat, stomach-ache, dry lips and a furry mouth, which precluded any other idea.

For the word "drink" had hardly crossed Poldi's mind when her whole body started whimpering uncontrollably, "*Drinkdrinkdrinkdrinkdrink! Nownownownownow!*"

Aware that she was suffering from withdrawal symptoms, Poldi planned to have a grappa with Montana rather than lapse into delirium the way she had the last time, in Tanzania.

"*Drinkdrinkdrinkdrink! Nownownownow!*"

"Don't panic, Isolde," she told herself. "Get into the car, call Montana and drive there. He'll give you a grappa."

"*Nonotlaternow! Drinkdrinkdrinkdrink! Nownownow now!*"

And the nerve under the old crown joined in.

It has to be said that Poldi was in no fit state to drive, but her withdrawal paranoia had now reached the point of no return.

Pulling herself together, she tottered over to her car, tossed the diary onto the passenger seat, started the Alfa and somehow piloted it through the narrow one-way streets and out of town. Then she called Montana, not wanting to turn up outside his door in the middle of the night if Alessia was with him.

The commissario picked up after the third ring.

He sounded as irritable as ever, but not as if she had woken him. Poldi even imagined she detected a hint of pleasure in his voice. He spared her the d'you-know-what-time-it-is routine.

"I'm on my way to you, Vito. Are you alone?"

At once, all the irritability and fatigue quit Montana's voice, and all that was left was the sharp, ever-wary tone of a detective chief inspector on duty.

"What's up?"

"I've got something for you."

"Can't it wait till tomorrow?"

"It's the murder motive and the murderer."

She heard him take a deep breath.

"Poldi, how often have I—"

"Are you alone, Vito?"

"Yes, damn it!"

"I'll be with you in twenty minutes. And I'll need a grappa."

She hung up and took care not to drive too fast. Turning onto the dark Provinciale, she concentrated on the narrow, winding stretch to Acireale and was just driving past the main entrance to Piante Russo when she noticed she was no longer alone in the car.

"Evening, Poldi."

Death was occupying the passenger seat.

This time dressed once more in a sombre suit that hung loose off his scrawny frame. In other words, official attire. Holding his clipboard in his left hand, he used the right to toss the pocket diary onto the rear seat, as if it were no longer needed, and clutched the grab handle above the door.

"I detest travelling by car, I really do."

Poldi was so startled, she almost drove off the road.

"Hell's bells and buckets of blood!" she exclaimed. "What the devil d'you mean by putting the wind up me like that, you bag of bones? I might have had a stroke!"

Death glanced at his clipboard.

"That'll happen in due course. I already hinted as much."

"Oh," said Poldi, taken aback. "You mean . . ."

Death nodded. "Yes, this time it's quite official, all stamped and notarised. Like to see it?"

"No, I wouldn't." Poldi took her foot off the gas, and with the last lucid thought of which she was still capable, she said, "You're just a hallucination. Now beat it, you Grim bloody Reaper!"

Death sighed. "That's what I hate about this job. Not the strange way people cling to life, which consists of nothing but failure and unhappiness, but their needless hostility when faced with the moment of truth. I honestly thought we'd built up something of a rapport by now, Poldi, but never mind, I'm used to it. People can beef at me to their heart's content. 'Go on,' they tell themselves, 'lay it on thick. It's only poor old Death, who cares?'"

Poldi was now concentrating fully on the road and doing her best to ignore Death's yammering.

"I'm still here," Death whined beside her. And, a moment or two later, "I still am."

"A stroke, did you say? What kind of stroke? Heart attack? Apoplexy?"

"You'll soon see." Death glanced at his cheap wristwatch. "Four, three, two, one . . ."

BANG!

Something heavy rammed the Alfa from behind. Poldi uttered a cry, was thrown around and started swerving. She saw that Death was still clinging to the grab handle, seemingly unconcerned. Regaining control of the car somehow, she looked at the other vehicle in her rear-view mirror. A big SUV with its headlights turned off, it was speeding along close behind her again. Then it rammed her a second time, more violently than before.

BAAANG!!!

"The Hedgehog" was Poldi's only thought.

The Alfa was now hurled diagonally across the Provinciale and, with a hideous metallic clang, cannoned into the lava stone wall that flanked it. Whoever was driving the SUV put his foot down and bulldozed Poldi along, complete with car and Death, straight for a sharp right-hand bend. Poldi tried desperately to regain control of the Alfa so as not to crash into the wall ahead. When braking did no good, she had the presence of mind to accelerate in the hope of getting away.

"Not yet!" she shouted to Death. "You hear? It isn't my time yet! I still have to—"

BAAANG!

Another impact from behind. Poldi was thrown forward, the steering wheel escaped from her grasp, and the Alfa raced unchecked towards the wall at the extremity of the bend. And that was that.

Poldi's penultimate thought was of Montana's hairy chest, and her very last thought before everything around her went black was of her beloved Peppe's muscular forearms.

11

Tells of Poldi's resurrection, needless to say, but also of her grand entrance, the sympathy she receives, and holding hands. She learns that even fate is only a kind of officialdom, does what a regular jailbird does, and is able to offer Montana a deal. Then she hears of a private security firm in Milan—and would have preferred not to.

And you think I'm buying that?" I asked, sounding wholly unimpressed when Poldi finally came out with the cause of her injuries.

"You winced, I saw you."

"No I didn't. Seriously, though, if you'd really had an accident like that, you wouldn't have got away with a black eye and a bruised arm."

"And that's your expert opinion, is it, Doctor?"

"You invented this accident, Poldi, admit it. Besides, I'd probably have heard about it from someone else."

"To be honest, nobody thought of you in the immediate aftermath."

"I see."

"Now don't take offence again, just be glad I'm still alive. As soon as I recovered consciousness, I imposed a news blackout on the family, because if anyone's going to tell you the whole story, it's me. Everything must be accurate, you hear? It must all be accurate for the benefit of posterity."

"How does posterity come into it?" I asked suspiciously.

Poldi looked at me with a touch of surprise and pity. "You mean you haven't caught on yet?"

"Er, what do you mean?"

She heaved a sigh of resignation. "I'll put it this way: I solve cases, you write them up. It's our ticket to international success."

I stared at her. "You're joking, aren't you?"

"Do I look like I've got any time to spare for silly jokes? Well, what do you say? I can see the dust jacket now, right before my eyes: *The Leopardess*. Great title, no? It'll go ballistic, I tell you. And our names up top in bold caps. Well, my name in bold caps, yours lower down and a bit more discreet."

"Tell me something, Poldi. Did they also examine your head after the accident?"

"Very funny, Mr. Author."

She really was in earnest—her face was utterly devoid of self-doubt. I began to have serious misgivings about her mental state and decided to have a word with Aunt Teresa the next day. For the time being I could only try to change the subject in a cool, firm, friendly way.

"You're crazy, Poldi. Forget it. Just put it out of your head."

"You realise you're throwing away the chance of a lifetime."

"Just forget it, Poldi. I shall never write a thriller, least of all about you."

230

"Is that your last word?"

"You want to hear my last word, Poldi?"

"I insist on it."

"Kiss my ass."

She stared at me for a moment, then burst out laughing. A dark laugh originating in the depths of her body, it erupted from her like a kind of volcanic joie de vivre that shook her to the core and made the whole sofa quake. It was a laugh that took me by storm and would have defeated the most inveterate misanthrope. And that was how we spent the rest of the evening: laughing, gasping for breath and drinking.

As for me, I was delighted to have skirted the subject safely. I had salvaged the situation and buried the subject once and for all.

So . . . Bang, penultimate thought, last thought, lights out. Just darkness and silence. The end. Nothingness. And, associated with it, the dread question: Was that it, or does purgatory or reincarnation have some basis in fact? Poldi certainly asked herself that question, anyway, because despite the darkness and silence, she still felt somehow *present;* somewhere in this endless, dark, silent limbo there hovered a rather grumpy residue of Poldi. She was naked and felt as light and fluffy as a snowflake. She was also holding something in her left hand. When she opened her fingers, she saw that it was the little shard of clay inscribed with the word ΟΥΤΙΣ, the one she'd found in the vineyard.

Outis. Nobody. That's what she was now: nobody. Over and forgotten.

My Auntie Poldi had wanted to be a lot of things in life, but never a nobody.

"I'm not nobody," she whispered despondently. "I'm Poldi. Isolde Oberreiter. Donna Poldina." Then, more vigorously, "I'm *not* nobody!" Finally, she really filled her lungs and let rip: "Hello! Hellooo! Anyone hear me? Hey! Hellooooo!!!"

No reply, not even an echo. The words simply drifted off into a void.

Poldi could no longer feel her body, which she presumed was scrunched up inside the wrecked Alfa. This thought infuriated her.

"Damn it all, what *is* this? Anyone mind telling me what the hell happens next? Hello? Am I going to float around here for all eternity, or what? This is a total snafu! Where's the divine light, or at least some decent fire and brimstone? Hey! Someone send Death to me soonest, I badly need to hold a post-mortem with him."

And so on. Poldi wouldn't leave it alone. She continued to work herself up into a rage, on the old Bavarian principle that throwing a tantrum can pay off.

As may be imagined, the main thing one loses in limbo is one's sense of time. Poldi had no idea whether she'd been fulminating for a few minutes or half an eternity when, at long last, there was a development. She heard a door slam in the distance, then shuffling footsteps drawing nearer in no great hurry, then an irritable sigh, and then she felt movement close beside her. A light came on at last, not the kind of divine radiance in pastel rainbow hues to be found in books in an esoteric bookshop, but a common or garden table lamp.

Poldi was sitting on her sofa in the midst of an infinite void. On her right, the occasional table with the lamp on it;

on her left, or where I normally sit, Death. He was once more wearing his scruffy leisurewear outfit and holding his clipboard. Looking extraordinarily cross, he was in the process of inserting a handwritten note beside one of the entries. Then he turned to Poldi. She saw, in the subdued light of the table lamp, that he was looking—by his standards—quite agitated.

"How are you feeling, Poldi?"

The question surprised her, if only because of its unusually personal nature. There was a cutting retort on the tip of her tongue, but she restrained herself.

"Oh, you know, the way you do when you're dead and you feel like a parcel delivered to the wrong address—one that nobody collects and it's obvious nobody wants."

Death appeared to understand the allusion, because he sighed. "Look, Poldi, I'm only doing my job. I'm just the operational infrastructure without which the whole system would collapse. I'm an Indian, not a chief. God knows we've got enough chiefs here. Everyone always wants to be boss, or at least team leader, but nobody wants to do the actual work. I didn't pick this job—that's not the way it works here. You'd be surprised how many things don't work. A whole heap of them. Our internal communication is beneath contempt. Separation of the factual from the emotional? Wrong! At board level they keep dreaming up new strategies to suit themselves. We at the lower end of the hierarchy are the last to hear, but it's we who have to put them into practice successfully. What's more, we have to do everything with the same number of staff as we had during the start-up phase. Co-determination? Flat hierarchies? Change management? Time off in lieu? Forget it. Someone like me, who's down among the grass roots day after day, would have plenty of ideas for improving matters. If only they'd take us along with them and make their messages clear, everything could work like a dream — I helped to construct the system, after all. But no, everything functions strictly top-down. The board are only interested in results. Growth, growth, growth — I can't bear to hear the word. At my last annual review I laid it on the line: the agreed targets, I told them, are totally unrealistic. I refuse, I said, to allow myself to be demotivated any further in this way. Pow! That shut them up. But does anyone really listen to someone like me? No, nobody. There isn't even a works council, can you imagine? But do I complain? No, I don't, I just do my job, though I don't know how much longer I can stick to it. I've done a thousand years' overtime. The board would look pretty silly if I packed it in. There have always been stressful phases, of course. The dinosaurs, Atlantis, the medieval plague epidemics, Spanish flu, the world wars. But those were *phases*. These days I can scarcely keep up with my workload — I'm at the end of my tether. And now something like this happens."

Poldi sensed that she was now under discussion. "Something like what?"

Death pulled a rueful face. "A couple of digits got transposed, but nobody spotted it because the board abolished quality control a long time ago — rationalising, they called it. I used to handle that as well, once upon a time, but I haven't been able to manage it for ages."

"So what does that mean in words of one syllable?"

Death drew a deep breath. "It wasn't your turn yet, Poldi. Because you kicked up such a fuss, the mistake came to light in the entry registration office. There was a hell of a stink, I can tell you. It wouldn't surprise me if someone there got the sack. Of course, they tried to sweep everything under the carpet as usual and did their best to pin it on me. 'Leave me out of it,' I told them. 'You messed it up, you sort it.' I always get stuck with it in the end, though."

Poldi felt her hackles rise again, but she controlled herself. "Okay, my lad, so I'm not dead at all."

"No. Sorry about the circumstances, but you can forget about receiving an apology from this organisation, any more than Job and his family did back when. However, I did persuade them to credit at least a little something to your lifespan account as a goodwill gesture."

Poldi pricked up her ears. "How much time are we talking about?"

Death grimaced with embarrassment. "I'm not at liberty to—"

"Yes, yes, I get it," Poldi broke in irritably. She gave him a searching stare.

He was looking tired and drained, as if he, too, could use a drink. Poldi had really got to know him recently, and she almost felt a trifle sorry for him.

"Your organisation stinks to high heaven. If you think I'm so relieved I'm going to say thanks, *namaste*, let's forget all about it, you've got another think coming, you hear? You can give your board a message from Isolde Oberreiter: they're welcome to kiss my ass!"

Death positively quailed under Poldi's tirade. He seemed unable to endure friction and emotional outbursts. Poldi wondered what actually qualified him for his job. "But," she thought, "perhaps it was just that, there too, someone wanted to do a favour for the brother-in-law of a cousin of a good friend and find an addled member of his family a cushy job where he couldn't harm anyone." She chuckled to herself.

"Can I send you back now?" Death asked. "Are you through?"

Poldi was bracing herself in readiness to utter a curt "Like hell I am!" when she thought of something else—something that ought to occur to any dissatisfied customer.

"Just a minute, not so fast, my lad. What about compensation?"

This seemed to catch Death on the wrong foot. "Uh, what?"

"Com . . . pen . . . sation! You know, for the shock, the emotional upset, the post-traumatic stress. I'm not budging an inch without compensation. You can thrash it out later with your accounts department. I mean, read your Job. He didn't get an apology either, but he did get some compensation in the end. So don't go telling me it's unusual."

Death sighed. "What sort of com . . . pen . . . sation did you have in mind, Poldi?"

She put her face close to his.

"Don't be so cheeky, my lad. A really juicy clue, that's what I'm asking for. A really solid lead. Who is the Hedgehog?"

Death just rolled his eyes.

Hey presto, Poldi was in her bedroom. Or rather, a replica of her bedroom, floating in the darkness complete with all its appurtenances. She was standing in front of her corkboard and looking at all the results of her investigations. Death was standing beside her.

"Well, so what? Am I supposed to work it out for myself again?"

"It's all there, Poldi. Just look closely."

Poldi scrutinised the corkboard until her eye lighted on the mysterious slip of paper Signora Cocuzza had purloined from Madame Sahara's house.

Easton Ros
Rena Sotos
Stan Roose
Astor Enos
Santos Roe
Rosa Stone

And at that moment everything became clear to her.

Two days after her accident, therefore, Poldi regained consciousness in a foul temper but feeling thoroughly relieved at her return to life. Life, to which she was so attached despite melancholia and advancing years, heartache and minor ailments. The darkness around my aunt lifted, and she was soaring over a misty landscape that turned out, when the mist finally dispersed, to be a sickroom. A sickroom, however, that resembled a greenhouse, because the windowsill and every other flat surface were covered with vases holding luxuriant flower arrangements, each more splendid than the next.

Poldi made out Aunt Caterina and Aunt Luisa seated on two plastic chairs beside the bed and talking together with Totti lying at their feet. Seated on the other side of the bed, likewise deep in animated conversation, were Uncle Martino and Vito Montana. My aunt was particularly touched and pleased by the sight of Montana, who kept glancing anxiously at an ECG machine.

The bed, of course, was occupied by none other than herself, eyes closed and hooked up to a drip and the ECG machine. Poldi saw that her head was bandaged, her right eye bruised and swollen, and her left arm in plaster. Some sympathetic soul had not only perched her wig on top of her bandaged head but had even backcombed it a little. For all that, thought Poldi as she floated overhead, she didn't look good. Not good at all, but at least not dead. It was time to demonstrate this.

"Right, let's get cracking," she told herself firmly, returning to her less than youthful but familiar and stout-hearted body, which had experienced so much joy and sorrow and was eager to experience more.

Since Poldi knew how to make an entrance, she kept her eyes shut for a little longer and listened to what was being said all around her.

Caterina and Luisa were quietly discussing their sons and their sons' current girlfriends. The gist: too skinny, too temperamental, too needy, too Scandinavian.

Martino, mounted on his hobby horse, was telling Montana how, after Sicily had been liberated in the Second World War with the aid of Lucky Luciano, who was serving a life sentence in the United States, the CIA had permanently reinstalled the Mafia there. Changing the subject at breakneck speed, he expounded another pet theory of his: that after the Battle of Trafalgar, Lord Nelson had been gifted the small *castello* at Bronte, where he joined the Templars in planning a new world order (the origin of the founding of the CIA), and where Nelson's nieces, Charlotte, Branwell, Emily and Anne, often spent their summer holidays and subsequently adopted the place name Bronte as their nom de plume. This was strongly disputed by Montana, who unexpectedly turned out to be a Bronte expert and insisted that the sisters had never set foot in Sicily.

"But they *might* have!" Martino brazenly retorted, unashamed at being caught out in a minor historical distortion.

Poldi could easily have joined in the dialogues to left and right of her and repeated them in unison, they were so familiar to her, and she rather resented them, considering that she had just returned from the realm of the dead. She would have welcomed a bit more concern and anxiety. High time for a reprimand. She opened her eyes with a jerk, like Bela Lugosi as Count Dracula.

"God Almighty, am I hungry! I could also use a beer."

My Auntie Poldi certainly knew a thing or two about dramatic entrances and resurrections.

She discovered after the initial brouhaha—the tears, hugs and cries of joy—that one of Russo's lorry drivers had found her in her Alfa half an hour after the crash. The car was upside down and practically a write-off. The roll bar on the big-engined old hot rod was all that had saved her life. She had been unconscious for two whole days. For two whole days, her sisters-in-law, Martino, Totti, Signora Cocuzza, the padre and Montana had kept vigil beside her bed and feared for her life, had straightened her wig and washed her, had prayed and talked to her. When Poldi heard that, she herself had to fight back the tears.

"Thank you," she said quietly. "I love you all."

"I had a look at the car," Montana said sombrely. "It's a goddam miracle you survived."

Poldi endeavoured to sit up a little, but she felt so giddy, she promptly abandoned the idea.

"It was the Hedgehog," she whispered.

"No, there was no hedgehog on the road, Poldi."

"I don't mean that. Elisa Puglisi knew who her murderer was, and she called him the Hedgehog. He had all the money. It was the Hedgehog! It's all in the diary."

"I think you're still confused, Poldi. We'd better leave you to sleep."

"Shut up and listen to me, Vito. Where's the Alfa now?"

"At a police pound for confiscated vehicles."

"Is it secure?"

"Of course. Fenced in and supervised. Why?"

"That's good. You must go and get the book from it, Vito. Right away, preferably."

"What book?"

"Madame Sahara's appointments diary. That's why I was coming to see you. It's all in there. The diary must still be inside the car."

"What the devil . . . ?"

"I'll explain everything later, Vito, but please go and look for it. Please! Then you'll understand."

Seeing that she really meant it, Montana rose and turned to the aunts. "I'll be back in an hour. Make sure she stays in bed. If necessary, knock her out again."

"You can rely on us," Caterina assured him.

The handsome commissario had scarcely left the room

before Aunt Luisa bent over Poldi. "He was sick with worry. You should have seen him. He even held your hand."

"He *what?*"

Poldi was quite touched by this notion. Being a child of the hippie generation, she found sex a natural and indispensable form of self-expression. Whatever was involved—a one-night stand, a quickie on the beach, a fleeting affair or a regular gentleman visitor—Poldi made little of it and had left nothing untried. Sex was fun and as much a part of life as good wine and the first sunburn of summer. Sex could be pleasurably taken and given, after which the man could be casually dismissed. Wham, bang, thank you and goodbye.

Holding hands, by contrast, was an altogether different matter. Holding hands was the most intimate form of contact my Auntie Poldi could permit. Holding hands was reserved for love affairs. Poldi had often held hands with my Uncle Peppe, and had felt truly loved. The same had applied, not so long ago, to John. With Montana, on the other hand, it had so far been a line she was unwilling to cross for fear of heartbreak. And now Montana had sat beside her bed and held her hand as if it were the most natural thing in the world. At the moment, though, she didn't have time to decide whether she ought to emit a blissful sigh or snort with indignation.

Why not? Because first she had to consume two huge, ragout-filled *arancini di riso* provided by Aunt Luisa. She could have killed for a beer as well, but Luisa and Caterina refused to bring her one.

Soon the ward doctor came toddling in after his lunch break. He examined Poldi briefly and told her what she already knew: that she had got off with a black eye. Her arm had sustained only a hairline fracture and would, like the laceration on her head and the shiner, be healed within a few weeks. Her giddiness, too, would soon subside. However, said the young medic, who smelt of cigarettes and whose affected little goatee Poldi considered less than confidence-inspiring, he wanted to keep the signora under observation for another few days and carry out tests for possible neurological damage. Despite her giddiness, Poldi promptly construed this as a form of cold turkey.

"Out of the question," she snapped. "If I can go, I'll go. *Basta!* I've a murder to solve."

That was when the faces of Aunt Caterina and Aunt Luisa hardened like concrete.

"No, Poldi," Caterina said firmly. "You'll undergo these tests. If not, we'll put you on the next flight back to Munich. That's enough. You're ill, and now you're going to get better."

"I'm not spending another day in this hellhole!"

Hospitals were one of the few things my Auntie Poldi genuinely detested—especially Italian hospitals, because, as a young woman, she had almost died of undiagnosed blood poisoning in a hospital in Rome. To her, Italian hospitals were the last stop before purgatory. Giddy or not, she sat up in bed and would have plucked the cannula from her arm if the doctor hadn't restrained her just in time.

"Please, signora. Calm down!"

But his plea was redundant, because vertigo had already laid my Auntie Poldi low once more. Whimpering and nauseous, she lay back on her bed like Kafka's Gregor Samsa and wished that the cosmic accounts department had never noticed the error in her date of death.

"Do what you like to me, but take me home," she gasped.

Caterina and Luisa glanced at each other. Their answer was brief and to the point: "No."

By the time Montana returned, Poldi was feeling a little better, bar her raging thirst. She felt like begging him to bring her a beer or a grappa, but she just managed to summon up enough self-respect not to.

"Did you find it?"

"No. There wasn't any diary."

Poldi groaned. "Did you look everywhere?"

"Several times. Believe me, Poldi, there was no sign of it. It's time you told me what you're talking about."

Poldi shut her eyes and thought.

"That's why the Hedgehog rammed me. He was after the diary."

"Who is this hedgehog you keep talking about?"

"The murderer of Madame Sahara and Elisa Puglisi, it's obvious. He found out that I . . . I mean, that I happened to get hold of Giuliana's appointments diary. Two people had to die because of it, and I escaped death by a hair's-breadth."

"What are you driving at, Poldi?"

"He rammed me! Several times, that's why I went off the road. He wanted to kill me and get his hands on the diary."

Montana shook his head. "Listen, Poldi. Nobody rammed you. You simply crashed into the wall head-on and overturned. We examined your car."

Poldi felt too weak to argue. Her memory had often played tricks on her recently, and she could hardly expect Montana to believe that Death had been sitting beside her just before the accident. Realistically, she had to admit that she might well have caused the accident herself.

Yes, if it weren't for the missing appointments diary.

Poldi opened her eyes, feeling suddenly quite lucid and in command of herself again. Death might have been a hallucination, but the big SUV had been thoroughly real.

She looked at Montana. "It doesn't matter, Vito, I have photocopies of the diary you must look at. You must find out who the Hedgehog is."

"Let me have them, then."

She feebly shook her head. "Oh no, my dear Vito. You aren't getting away as cheaply as that."

My Auntie Poldi had to spend a full week in hospital. No matter how much she cursed and swore, the other aunts weren't having any. They made an agreement with the doctors and nurses: Signora Oberreiter was to be chained to her bed if need be. She was also to be strictly denied any alcohol, because opportunities for an official ban were few and far between.

Although Poldi accused her sisters-in-law of deprivation of liberty and torture, she eventually gave up — especially as, like all good jailbirds, she soon found a loophole in the system through which an occasional drop of something could be smuggled.

The loophole went by the name of Ciccio Pappalardo and was an unkempt old hospital orderly the size of a stunted hobbit, who spent all day mopping the floors in his scruffy blue overalls. This he did with a provocatively anti-capitalistic indolence that Poldi found thoroughly appealing.

Having made the acquaintance of Ciccio Pappalardo on her first trip to the showers, she had naturally got the picture right away.

Since then, Ciccio had passed by twice a day during those rare spells when Poldi had no visitors, smuggled a small bottle of beer into her room, scented the air with his miasma of stale sweat and ill-digested garlic, accepted his baksheesh with a mixture of obsequious cunning and dog-like subservience, and stood guard in the doorway until Poldi had slaked her thirst.

He addressed Poldi as *Voscenza,* the Sicilian abbreviation for *Vostra Eccellenza,* "Your Excellency" being the obsolete form of address reserved by common folk for persons of high rank and Mafiosi. He also offered her, in his broad Sicilian dialect, a positively boundless range of services.

"If you need anything else, *Voscenza,* don't hesitate to call on me. Always at your service, *Voscenza.* No matter what it is, Ciccio Pappalardo can get it. Ciccio Pappalardo has the best contacts."

"Thank you, Ciccio," Poldi always told him graciously, well aware of how to say no in Sicily without offending someone and making a *figuraccia* of them. "Rest assured, I shall bear you in mind when the time comes."

Whereupon Ciccio would kiss my Auntie Poldi's hand, dispose of the empty bottle and disappear like a puff of wind.

Poldi seldom got a chance to think that week. The visitors and bunches of flowers kept coming. Italo Russo sent two parlour palms and a strelitzia with "heartfelt" wishes for her speedy recovery. Valérie, Signora Cocuzza, Padre Paolo and the aunts came and went, always laden with fresh lasagne or a parmigiana, potted vegetables, seafood salads, *arancini,* sweet *cannoli alla ricotta, pasta di mandorla, babà al rum,* marzipan fruits, pistachio ice cream, and whole gâteaux from the café in Torre Archirafi. Half of Torre filed past my aunt to wish her well, bring her the latest gossip and make *un selfie con Poldi.* Doris and the German *deliziosi* had sent her a get-well card, and even *Mago* Rampulla put in an appearance. He seemed infinitely relieved to find Poldi alive and in good spirits, and he assured her that her aura would soon be shining in all the colours of the rainbow—a clumsy bit of lyricism on the fortune-teller's part, thought Poldi. The *mago* declined to answer her suspicious inquiry as to whether he'd foreseen the accident, just repeated several times how glad he was to find her still alive.

Her sickroom soon resembled a baroque genre painter's idea of the Land of Cockaigne: a jungle of flower arrangements, ornamental palms, scented orchids and other delights, and, holding court in a nest of white sheets at its midpoint, a high priestess of joie de vivre. Although Poldi felt, alcohol-wise, like an unwatered office plant, she was so touched and overwhelmed by the solicitude lavished on her from all sides that it almost compensated for her deprivation.

She had only a very vague recollection of her near-death experience. She could remember Death and his talk of an error in the accounts department. She could also remember holding the little shard of clay in her hand and standing in front of the corkboard in her bedroom. She could not, however, recall why. She merely sensed that she had discovered something important, only to forget it again when coming back to life.

Something important.

About the Hedgehog.

On that slip of paper.

But trying to remember made her feel dizzy again, so at some stage she gave up.

Vito Montana turned up punctually at five every afternoon, bearing flowers and marzipan. As soon as he entered the sickroom, all the other visitors present respectfully withdrew, exchanging meaningful winks. Montana would then pull a chair up to the bed and, if he was a bit less ill-humoured than usual, hold Poldi's hand.

To her mingled relief and dismay, he had still made no progress with the two murder cases.

"I could spit," he told her on the fourth day after her resurrection. "We released your wine grower today."

Poldi pricked up her ears but said nothing.

"I grilled him a bit and the contradictions came tumbling out. He cracked, of course, and withdrew his confession."

"Because he'd thought it was his brother, and he owed him on account of the donated kidney."

Montana promptly looked suspicious again.

"How . . . ?"

Poldi gestured dismissively. "But it wasn't his brother either?"

Montana sighed. "He has an alibi for the time in question. And no discernible motive."

Poldi thought for a moment.

"Any news of the Puglisi case? Have you found out who the Hedgehog is?"

He shook his head, and the frown line between his eyebrows divided his forehead into two continents.

"That's because you still don't believe the two cases are connected, Vito. It's probable that the individual who tried to kill me has Madame Sahara and Elisa Puglisi on his conscience as well."

"No one tried to kill you, Poldi!" snapped Montana. "There's absolutely no evidence of that. You were hallucinating, that's why you failed to make it round the bend."

"The fact that a person is paranoid doesn't preclude them from being chased," Poldi told him calmly. "Yes, I was hallucinating, but someone tried to kill me." So saying, she opened the drawer of her bedside table and took out the big buff envelope Padre Paolo had recently brought her in his secret agent's guise. She deposited it on her lap and rested both hands protectively on top. "I'm convinced of it, because it's all in here. Why else should the appointments diary have vanished?"

Montana said nothing, but he put out his hand.

Poldi didn't budge.

"Incidentally, Vito, your name's in here too."

She saw him blush. Whether with shame or anger, his poker face made it impossible to tell, but she knew she now had him over a barrel.

"What are you implying, Poldi?"

"I'm not implying anything. I'd simply like to know why. The bottom line is this: if you officially accept this appointments diary as a piece of evidence, you're out of the running because it shows you're involved—because you visited her regularly. On the other hand, these are only photocopies, so they can't be used as evidence because I might have doctored them. Unfortunately, the murderer now has the original diary. I could, of course, relinquish these legally invalid photocopies to you unofficially. On a purely private basis."

Montana was breathing heavily to stop himself yelling. "Why would you do that, Poldi?"

"Oh, because friends do each other favours. Or because friends don't always have to ask questions." She gave him a look of lamb-like innocence.

Montana was a model of self-control.

"Like what?"

"Like why did you go and see Madame Sahara, Vito. Or how did I come to lay hands on this appointments diary."

"You realise you're trying to blackmail me, Poldi."

Poldi's eyes widened like those of a silent film star reacting to the entrance of a heartless villain. "Vito! The very idea!" Then, in quick succession, "Do you *feel* I'm blackmailing you?"

"You're on thin ice, Poldi," he growled indignantly. "Very, very thin ice, believe me."

"In that case, let's get off it quickly." She replaced the envelope in the drawer.

"*Madonna,* give it here," he snarled.

"Between friends?"

"Yes, between friends, damn it. From one nosy, foolhardy, blackmailing, exasperating, criminally inclined friend to another."

Montana tried to take the envelope at last, but Poldi continued to hang on to it.

"It's really a question of *two* favours."

"Enough, Poldi. Stop playing games."

"All I want to know is what you've found out about Elisa Puglisi. Bring me up to date, that's all. Where's the harm? Look at me. Do I look like I could prejudice your investigation? An old biddy suffering from withdrawal symptoms after an attempt on her life? I'm out of the running, Vito. You'll solve these cases by yourself. I'm curious, that's all. Come on, do me a favour."

Montana didn't believe a word of it, naturally. He drew another deep breath and at last relieved her of the envelope.

"All right, fair enough."

He swiftly leafed through the photocopies, grunting occasionally but evincing no indication of whether the entries struck him as relevant in some way. When he'd finished, he replaced the photocopies in the envelope.

"Hm, not uninteresting."

"Oh, come on," said Poldi. "What do you think those big sums of money represent? Extortion, money laundering, crowdfunding?"

Montana eyed her with a mixture of sorrow and dejection, like someone with something serious on his mind, but something he can't avoid unloading onto someone else. Poldi, who recognised that expression, felt her blood run cold.

"Vito?"

"There's something I have to tell you, Poldi," Montana began with an audible lump in his throat. He took possession of her hand again.

"Please don't," she said softly.

Montana grimaced. He stroked her hand for a while before answering.

"Alessia and I . . . we're getting married. And . . . we'll be moving to Milan. I applied to a private security service, and they're taking me on."

12

*Tells of heartbreak, Prometheus and consolation
prizes. Poldi chucks the case, contemplates another
move and is offered a cultural programme. With the
friendly assistance of Inspector Chance she encounters some old acquaintances, first in Syracuse and
then in Taormina. That kind of thing revives a person's spirits and arouses the hunting instinct. Poldi
immediately experiences one and a half enlighten-
ments, becomes briefly invisible and is then impaled
on the horns of a dilemma.*

I don't believe it!" I said when Poldi dropped this bomb.
"Tell me it isn't true!"

"Afraid it is," she replied calmly and took a big swig of
her drink.

"I just don't believe it. What's got into him?"

Poldi smiled faintly, like someone who has been cut to the
quick and is waiting for the wound to heal. Like an *outis*, a
nobody who welcomes a little sympathy but has no wish to
be a burden to anyone. Like someone out of sight of land
who simply swims on and on.

"The night I was on my way to him," she went on, "that
was when he proposed. I could tell they'd been chewing the

fat for nights on end lately. Well, Alessia guessed that Vito was having an affair with me, and she insisted on a decision. Who can blame her?"

"But Auntie," I said, "it's obvious who he should have plumped for: the jackpot, not the consolation prize."

Poldi stroked my cheek. "Sweet of you, my boy, but I'm the consolation prize."

"Nonsense. You're the jackpot, Poldi. You're smart, you're funny, you still look great, and you're an absolute humdinger in bed."

"Get on with you! You're right, of course, but you aren't qualified to judge."

"I most certainly am. Those unvarnished descriptions you keep giving me of your nights of passion—they're enough to scorch my ears. Anyone who can talk about sex like that knows their onions."

"It's what it is."

"And what's all this shit about a private security service in Milan? He must have been considering it for weeks."

Poldi sighed. "And that's what hurt me most, that he discussed it with Madame Sahara and not with me. In Germany you consult a life coach, in Sicily a fortune-teller."

"It all sounds like utter bullshit," I said, still gobsmacked by the news. Then I had an idea, a suicidal but extremely chivalrous idea. I jumped up off the sofa. "Listen, Poldi, I'll have a word with him—I'll go and see him right away. I mean, okay, so he's a detective chief inspector, he's probably three times as strong as me, he's bound to know karate and he'll be armed into the bargain, but hey, who cares, I'll tear him off a strip. I've got Cyclopean genes too, don't forget."

I was Barnaba, after all, and somehow it felt pretty good

to speak out for once. I was feeling rather dizzy but in full vendetta mode.

"I'll give him a piece of my mind, demand an explanation for Alessia and Milan and everything. I'll give him a roasting, even if he tears me to pieces and drops them out the window. I don't care, I'm Sicilian enough. He's trampled on *my* honour as well as yours. Nobody treats my Auntie Poldi like this and gets away with it."

Poldi quickly moved my wine glass out of reach. "Stop talking nonsense, and sit down before you fall down. You can't afford to stand in your condition."

"What condition, and why have you taken my glass away?"

She yanked me back onto the sofa. "Just sit down. Nobody's ever had to suffer for the sake of my honour, but thanks for the gesture, my boy, even if it was a pretty daft idea born of the bottle. Besides, the story's far from finished. Everything became a bit more complicated in the end."

"Okay" was all I said, because the rapid up-and-down movements were affecting the speech centre of my brain. I reached for my wine glass in order to lubricate my synapses.

But Poldi moved the glass even farther out of reach. "That's enough Polifemo for today. Teresa hauled me over the coals about your smoking recently. If you start boozing as well, your aunts will kill me, all three of them. It isn't that I'd be a loss to humanity, but you'd never get a first-hand account of how I eventually solved the case."

Montana's confession broke Poldi's heart. That's the plain truth, and it has to be said: it simply broke her heart—the big heart that had been broken so many times, then healed and cicatrized. And now Montana. His words seemed suddenly to come from very far away, as though not intended for her at all. But then they penetrated the skin, bored steadily deeper, found their target and broke my Auntie Poldi's heart.

It surprised her how calm she remained, lying there in her sickbed in the midst of her miniature jungle, while a sad and contrite Montana came out with all the terrible, hackneyed sentences that rendered her heartbreak almost unbearable. *It was obvious from the start. You know it yourself. It would never have worked. We were always so good together. You're very important to me. I've been considering it for quite a while. I need a change of scene. I love you. Let's still be friends. Say something, won't you?*

"Would you please go now, Vito?" was all Poldi said in a whisper.

And it wasn't until he had left the room that she finally allowed herself to weep.

Strangely enough, she didn't this time feel an urge to get totally blotto. Later, when Ciccio Pappalardo brought her her nightly Moretti, she silently drained the bottle of beer as if it were a kind of medicine she took because she had to. There was nothing left that could alleviate her pain. Nothing but time.

Or, of course, some crucial progress in a murder inquiry.

And that she once again owed to the friendly assistance of Inspector Chance. You know, the scruffy colleague in the cubbyhole at the far end of the corridor, the one who prefers to do less work than more. Unsackable, unpunctual and unpredictable. The colleague who never says hello and never plays Santa at the Christmas office party. The colleague no one ever invites to join them for lunch. The eternally suspect colleague who can be an absolute disaster in the field but sometimes contributes the vital lead in an inquiry. An unpopular colleague, albeit one in constant demand. But I'm getting ahead of myself.

Aunts Teresa, Caterina and Luisa never tired of dissing Vito Montana as the most heartless, perfidious and despicable man who ever lived. Even Totti, out of character for the amiable mongrel he was, took to sneezing disgustedly at the sound of Montana's name. It was as if he'd developed a kind of commissario allergy, but it might also have stemmed from the fact that Uncle Martino secretly rewarded him for his displays of sympathy with morsels of mortadella.

Not altogether without reason, the aunts were afraid that Poldi might anaesthetise her broken heart by getting blind drunk. Accordingly, they concocted a master plan designed to keep her permanently busy and under supervision after her discharge from hospital, and they recruited Valérie, Padre Paolo and sad Signora Cocuzza for the purpose.

Poldi apathetically submitted to everything they dreamed up: excursions to the Nebrodi Mountains to look for mushrooms, hours-long gin rummy sessions, visits to Valérie's gloomy Bourbon relations, uninspired exhibitions at the Zo cultural centre in Catania, innumerable boat rides, car rides, walks and shopping trips to the fish market. She simply didn't care. Yes, there were times when she really did yearn to get well and truly plastered, but she had herself under control. Of course she drank — the gods couldn't have prevented that — but she didn't get wasted. Some faint voice of reason in the farthest back room of her brain must have whispered that she would soon need to have her wits about her.

In her mailbox one morning she found a letter from Montana, which she tossed unopened into the dustbin. She blocked his number on her contacts list, and then, because that still didn't hurt enough, deleted it altogether. At the same time, she received emails and phone calls from Russo, who asked after her and invited her to dinner. Poldi deleted all his emails. She was through with men. She occasionally thought in a rather disgruntled fashion of Achille Avola, who had sent neither flowers nor a get-well card and never phoned. She wondered briefly whether to call him, but pride and melancholy forbade it.

She had also dropped the case. Yes, of course she had made a promise to her papa in buzzard guise, but she just couldn't fulfil it. She had lost the urge. She was through with investigations of any kind; she didn't have the energy. She even considered abandoning her pet project—a drunkard's death beside the Mediterranean—and returning to Munich to finish herself off quietly, without a view of the sea.

In short, she was in a really bad way.

But the inevitable happened: whenever you think you've reached rock bottom, fate disabuses you with another shitload of misfortune.

In order to take Poldi's mind off her troubles, Uncle Martino had devised a little cultural programme. Cleverly, he had obtained three tickets for a Tuesday afternoon performance of Aeschylus's *Prometheus Bound* at the Greek theatre in Syracuse—in other words, the story of a very inquisitive man whom the gods punish by chaining him to a rock, where an eagle regularly pecks at his liver.

When the Greeks drove the Sicanians out of Sicily in the fifth century BC, what were the first things they built? Temples? No, theatres! And the theatre at Syracuse had fifteen thousand seats, which made it the biggest in the ancient world. During the summer months it is still in use today. Uncle Martino insists that the plays of Euripides and Aeschylus were first performed there. Aeschylus, who visited Sicily more than once, also died there. (The cause of his death was remarkable: clobbered on the head by a falling tortoise.) He knew how to charm his audiences with sophisticated stage effects, and this tradition continues to inspire Sicilian directors to this day.

Just as they were in antiquity, performances are staged in daylight, in the afternoon. This means it is still hot, so Uncle Martino had paid a couple of euros extra for seats in the shade. Whenever you go anywhere with Martino, you get there too late or just before closing time. At the very last moment, just when you should be leaving for your destination, he will nip off to buy cigarettes or a newspaper, fish or bread, take the dog for a walk or look for his glasses. That presents you with a choice: either blow a gasket or make another booking, because Uncle won't be back within the next hour. It's simply that Uncle knows one has to make regular sacrifices to the gods of happiness by wasting time, and his own happy life bears this out.

Not so Aunt Teresa. Like any other sensible person waiting on tenterhooks with bags packed or three tickets for shady seats in the Greek theatre, she goes ballistic and bombards her husband with imprecations when he finally reappears. It's all water off a duck's back to Uncle Martino. Never at a loss for some dubious explanation, he calmly insists that there's still plenty of time. Amazingly enough, this often proves to be the case.

Syracuse is just under an hour's drive from Catania, but afternoon traffic is always backed up. It's little use trying to overtake everyone on the hard shoulder, because you aren't the only one to do so.

Syracuse is a bright, cheerful place built of pale sandstone. In Catania, that dark old baroque and art nouveau city built of volcanic basalt, the soul dives down into mythical depths; in Syracuse it returns to the light and breathes anew in its Renaissance squares or beside the Fountain of Arethusa. If Catania is the Cyclops, Syracuse is the nymph. No wonder the Greeks erected their largest theatre there.

Needless to say, the performance had been long under way by the time Uncle Martino, Aunt Teresa and Poldi finally got there, perspiring and irritable after their drive with one eye on the clock. Grouped on the semicircular stage was an ancient chorus attired in tunics, and a less than youthful Prometheus was solemnly addressing the gods in Italian. Poldi couldn't understand a word. What she likewise failed to understand was the presence of a yellow crane on the right side of the stage. And of course—how could it be otherwise?—their expensive seats in the shade were already occupied. The usher pointed to the spot where three elderly ladies in black were gazing doggedly at the chorus and Prometheus with stony faces. Poldi watched Uncle Martino thread his way through the tiers of spectators and accost the three ladies in a friendly manner. However, they displayed no sign of allowing themselves to be evicted from their nice seats, even when he showed them his tickets. From the way they grimly ignored him, he might have been thin air.

Meanwhile, Aunt Teresa and Poldi waited up top in the sweltering sun. Aunt Teresa fanned herself, and even Poldi, who liked hot weather, found the heat a trial. As sweat trickled down beneath her wig, she began to lose her temper, a sign that her animal spirits were gradually reviving. When she saw that Martino was too much of a gentleman to simply shoo the three witches away, she went striding down to join him.

"Ladies, these are our seats, so would you mind?"

No reaction. The three old scarecrows merely looked more obdurate than ever. They seemed to neither see Poldi nor hear her.

And then, as ever in Sicily, everything—sweet and sour, salty and bitter—combined to form a whole. My Auntie Poldi regained her Sicilian attitude to life.

Members of the audience began to complain, urging her to shut up and stop obstructing their view of the stage.

"Please, signori, there are still plenty of seats," an usher said soothingly, indicating the last unoccupied seats, which were in full sunlight.

"No way, you goddam piece of shit!" Poldi swore at him in Bavarian. "I insist on having a seat in the shade or there'll be hell to pay, understand? Fix it, you cretin, and make it snappy!"

Yet again, the brutish German language demonstrated its drastic effect on a simple Sicilian soul.

The usher flinched, then pointed panic-stricken to some vacant seats in dappled shade. "Those are still free, signori. Please sit down, the performance is in progress."

Just then they heard a bang. Down on the stage an explosive charge was detonated behind some artificial rocks, setting off a minor firework display, which the audience greeted with delighted oohs and aahs. While Poldi sullenly made her way towards the vacant seats, she caught sight of a stagehand busy behind the scenes. With a fag in the corner of his mouth and wearing a yellow high-vis vest, he hauled a cable from one side of the stage to the other while Prometheus, out front, was stealing fire from the gods. This explained the significance of the crane, because Prometheus was now hoisted into the air (away from the gods), where he continued to declaim. But the winding gear evidently jammed, causing Prometheus to dangle helplessly midway between heaven and earth. Overcome with panic, the actor gesticulated wildly at the ground. Another bang, a second explosive charge. Prometheus uttered a scream. The afternoon air suddenly smelt of burning, and Poldi saw little specks of ash swirling overhead. And this typically Sicilian mélange of drama, misadventure, amateurishness, showmanship and chaos was enough to make her laugh for the first time in many days.

Her shoulders shook as the laughter burst from her like a cork from a champagne bottle. Mirthfully shaking her head, she watched Prometheus being lowered to the ground. And when she, Aunt Teresa and Uncle Martino had finally taken their new seats and the remainder of the day was promising to be quite enjoyable, Poldi spotted a familiar figure sitting four rows in front of her.

Achille Avola.

And he wasn't alone.

He was nuzzling Alessia.

Poldi had met Alessia only twice, once with Montana at the Lido Galatea and again in the corridor of police head-quarters in Acireale, but she recognised her right away, just as she recognised the wine grower. Of course, it might have been his twin brother Carmelo, but somehow Poldi had no doubt that the man was Achille. And he was canoodling in public with the woman Montana planned to marry.

"What do you say to that?" Poldi asked me at this point.

"Disgusting, I call it. What did you do?"

"You mean, did I wait till the end of the performance and then catch them in flagrante? Did I make a big scene? No, that's not my style. I told Teresa I wasn't feeling well and the three of us just drove home."

I thought for a moment. "How did it make you feel, see-ing them canoodling like that?"

"Sad."

"Not even a little triumphant? I mean . . ."

"That only goes to show, yet again, that you don't have a clue how complicated love can be. Why should anyone feel triumphant, having to watch someone making a cuckold of the person they love? I didn't want to get Vito back that way —as a broken man, so to speak. I would never have let on to him about Achille and Alessia."

"And they were sitting three rows in front of you, purely by chance?"

"Four, but that's just the way it was."

"And you really kept it to yourself?"

"You always ask the wrong questions."

"Oh?"

"Doesn't it surprise you that Achille was with Alessia, of all people?"

"Yes, it does rather."

"Then you must ask yourself what their connection was. It's always about the same thing in love and criminology: connections. Remember that."

"And what was the connection in this case?"

"Patience. Then came the Wednesday."

On Wednesdays my Auntie Poldi always drove to Taormina, to the Babilonia Language School run by Michele, a friend of my cousin Ciro's. I don't know why; Poldi spoke fluent Italian. It was so good, in fact, that her Bavarian accent misled Sicilians into thinking she came from Milan, which to them was almost in Sweden. But Poldi was a woman full of contradictions. Casual and negligent though she was in many spheres of life, and however chaotic and easy-going she could be, where languages were concerned she strove for perfection.

On the other hand, it might have been because of Michele's attractive teaching staff. Gianfranco, for example, had been a 400-metre freestyle national champion and possessed a Michelangelesque face as well as a perfect body, and Poldi once told me that no woman in her right mind had ever dropped out of a one-to-one course with Gianfranco.

Quite apart from that, however, the Babilonia is one of the best language schools in Italy. It occupies an excellent site beyond the Porta Messina and beside the Greek theatre. The teachers are competent, the classrooms welcoming and air-conditioned, and for intermissions there's a wonderful, shady inner courtyard, great for improving one's vocabulary and flirting. What more could anyone want?

Anyway, it was in the said courtyard at lunchtime on the said Wednesday that Poldi, after her one-to-one lesson with Gianfranco, encountered an old friend from her Munich days.

"No, don't tell me!" I broke in when she drew a deep breath in readiness to unveil her big surprise. I already sensed what sort of "old friend" Poldi was going to come up with, and I wasn't going to let her get away with it this time.

"Stop behaving as if I'm an open book. If you never let a girl have her say, you can kiss goodbye any nookie later on, so bear that in mind. No matter how good you are with your tongue, the preliminary phase of foreplay depends on three things: listening, listening, listening. A few convincing nods and interested questions don't do any harm either, understand?"

"Drop it, Poldi. I just don't believe you."

"Why, what have I said?"

"Just skip it, okay? Skip it and get on with the story of your investigation. We've reached the third act. It's heading for a brilliant dénouement."

"Oh, so now you're a playwright, are you? Don't be such a bighead, Mr. Would-be Novelist. Listen to your aunt. As my nephew, you owe me some respect, you hear?"

"*Forza* Poldi!" I said with a sigh. "Let me guess: Madonna was sitting in the courtyard, swotting up on her *passato remoto*."

"Stuff your sarcasm, laddie. Of course it wasn't Madonna—Madonna knows Italian from her background. No, it was Cher." A pause for effect, to allow the name to sink in.

"I know who Cher is, but I don't believe you. Not in the courtyard of the Babilonia."

Poldi was unmoved. "She's a very dear friend of mine," she went on. "Such a nice person. After her concert in Munich she had a nervous breakdown in the P1 Club, so Peppe and I put her up at Westermühlstrasse. She stayed with us for a week, did Cher. Hardly ever left the house, just wept. We chewed the fat all day long, the two of us. She loved Bavarian sausage, and we spent the time boozing and having a laugh. Happy days! Needless to say, the paparazzi found out and were lurking outside the door, but I got hold of Georgie, who was the chief gossip columnist of the *Abendzeitung*. 'Georgie,' I told him, 'give Cher a break or there'll be trouble.' Well, Georgie knew where to draw the line. He'd always been keen on me, and he didn't want me to think less of him. Smart guy, Georgie. Good in bed but dead now, worse luck. Drugs."

Poldi was once more wearing the faraway expression she always adopted when indulging in sentimental memories of happier days. It was reminiscent of the sky above the Ammersee on a November afternoon, just before the first snowfall.

"Where did I get to?"

"Babilonia, courtyard, Cher."

"Exactly! Cher was waiting for her new lover, my teacher Gianfranco. As soon as she saw me she jumped to her feet. "Darling!" she cried and flung her arms round me. Thanks to her, like it or not, I was back on the case again soon afterwards."

"Listen, *darling*," I said, "this really is a bit too much like Inspector Chance. Ding-dong, hello, hokum alert! Who's going to believe all this?"

"Nobody has to believe *me*, just you. It all depends if you're talented enough to put it across believably."

"Not for the first time, Poldi, forget it. You're not going to make me the chronicler of your Münchhausen stories. My aim is to write proper literature, not pulp fiction, *capisci?*"

All right, I'll put it down on paper the way my Auntie Poldi told it to me, disclaiming liability for any pulp-fiction allergies. On the other hand, Poldi wasn't a person who lied at the drop of a hat. She wore her heart on her tongue and usually found lying far too stressful, because she could never remember what she'd told to whom. I've never checked whether all those celebs genuinely were friends of hers, nor do I care in the least. There simply are people who can stretch time, space and the truth to suit themselves. People with the talent to open up vistas for you. People who make you feel light and airy in their presence, and you can only be grateful for it. Angelic people. *Namaste*, Poldi! *Forza* Poldi!

Besides, Taormina is a magical place in which the most unusual encounters can occur. Picturesquely perched on the flanks of Monte Tauro, the little town overlooks the Bay of Naxos and the Gulf of Catania, and has thus been strategically valuable to conquerors since ancient times.

Taormina is famous for its Teatro Greco, which is really

a Roman building erected on the foundations of a Greek theatre. A gap in the middle of the stage affords a splendid view of Etna, whose impressive eruptions occasionally up-stage the actors and steal the show.

The town enjoyed a brief heyday in the Middle Ages, af-ter which it gradually went downhill until, in the eighteenth century, it was just a poverty-stricken fishing village. Taor-mina was visited by Goethe, who described how enchanting he found it in his *Italian Journey*, which became the most important generator of modern Italian tourism. Several decades later, English aristocrats discovered the town, made it their winter quarters and developed it into the jewel it is today. At the end of the nineteenth century, attracted by its mild climate, the tubercular photographer Wilhelm von Gloeden settled in Taormina, where he photographed half-naked young fishermen in suggestive poses. This, in turn, attracted painters and writers like Oscar Wilde, Thomas Mann and D. H. Lawrence, who needed a respite from the wintry weather and prudery of their native lands and may also have . . . well, consorted with Gloeden's young fisher-men. At all events, Taormina is still a favourite destination of the international gay community, which always makes such places blossom into miniature paradises. Anyone who needs convincing of this should visit the Bar dei Cazzi up in Castelmola.

Taormina also holds a film festival that has been attract-ing international stars since the 1950s, so it's quite possible that Cher, wearing a black tunic, hat and big sunglasses, really was waiting for her young lover in the Babilonia's in-ner courtyard.

· · ·

She was simply sitting there—no bodyguard—in a basket chair in the shade of an almond tree, reading a screenplay given her by Gianfranco, who wanted more out of life than being a teacher and an object of desire. Cher had already posed for some selfies and was enjoying the peace and quiet, but that went out the window once she sighted Poldi. The star leapt to her feet, dashed over to my aunt and hugged her as if she'd just saved her life—which Poldi and Peppe may actually have done thirty years earlier.

There ensued a whirlwind of hugs, kisses and reciprocal compliments on each other's fit and youthful appearance. Dismay at the news of charming Peppe's death almost ten years before, sentimental memories of that magical week in Munich, pleasure at the news of Poldi's new life as a detective in Sicily, and swift updates on their current love lives.

"What do you think of Gianfranco?"

"Hot," Poldi said. "A simple soul, but definitely hot."

"I know, he's too young. And a lousy screenwriter. On the other hand, he does have . . . well, you know, certain other talents. Do you still have a thing for traffic cops?"

"I also go for detective chief inspectors these days."

"Omigod, that sounds great! What are Sicilian detective chief inspectors like?"

"In a word, volcanic."

"Omigod, introduce me to one, Poldi. I could use a Sicilian policeman!" In high delight, Cher took my Auntie Poldi by the arm and towed her out of the courtyard. "I *must* introduce you to someone. A real cop, the hard-bitten kind, you'll like him. I met him yesterday in the hotel bar. He's just what you need right now."

Brooking no dissent, and without waiting any longer for the talented Gianfranco, Cher led my aunt out into the Via Teatro Greco and set off in the direction of the ancient theatre. Seemingly untroubled by the fact that the tourists and strollers on the Corso gawped at her and instinctively whipped out their mobile phones, she shepherded Poldi to the entrance of the Grand Hotel Timeo, where the rich and beautiful sojourned, where the waiters were snooty and the prices exorbitant, and where Poldi used to sip the occasional limoncello.

Just as they reached the handsome wrought-iron gateway leading to the hotel garden, Poldi saw a familiar face outside on the terrace. The man was sitting by himself in the shade of a sun umbrella, but she recognised him at once. He looked just as he had the last time she saw him: jeans, polo shirt, baseball cap, buzz cut.

Sean Torso.

Poldi stopped dead and yanked her friend back into a space between the gate and the wall of the hotel, hoping that Torso hadn't spotted her. The shock of seeing him was mingled with something else — something that came back to her from far away and filled her with renewed oomph: the thrill of the chase.

And something else came back to her as well: a recollection of what she had grasped when looking at her corkboard during her near-death experience.

That the curious names on the slip of paper were all anagrams.

Anagrams of "Etnarosso."

Just like Sean Torso.

Sean Torso, the Hedgehog.

"What was it? What did you see?" demanded Cher, who, according to my Auntie Poldi, had believed in paranormal phenomena ever since her nervous breakdown in Munich.

"That man in the baseball cap—is he the cop you wanted to introduce me to?"

"Yes, his name is—"

"Sean Torso, I know."

"Oh."

"And you're sure he's a cop?"

"Darling, I know a cop when I see one, and that guy's a hundred and twenty per cent cop. He plays the oddball dowser, but he wears a graduation ring from the FBI Academy in Quantico."

"Oh." Poldi hadn't noticed that the last time. "Not bad."

Cher smiled at her. "What now, darling? Are we going to stand here whispering till the last tourist has finished snapping us?"

She wasn't far from the mark. A small knot of people had already gathered, and Poldi saw another problem approaching from the other side of the Corso: Italo Russo and *Mago* Rampulla.

They were heading straight for the hotel, deep in animated conversation like two men discussing some important business venture. Poldi had no time even to fulminate about Rampulla's audacity; they would spot her in a few moments. She had to act.

"Go in and speak to Torso," she told Cher quickly. "Mwah-mwah, small talk, then go up to your room. I'll call you later."

"Okay, chief. Great, some action at last. What'll you be doing meanwhile?"

"Watching, darling."

Poldi now tried to keep an eye on two things at once: her pal Cher plus Russo and Rampulla, who were coming steadily nearer and would undoubtedly blow her cover in the next few seconds. She urgently needed some camouflage.

As soon as that word whizzed through her mind she realised what she had to do. She reached in her handbag and produced the oldest of all detective's camouflage: a new, still unread edition of *La Sicilia*. Open it in one swift movement (*crack!*), hold it in front of her face (*ecco là!*), and Poldi was virtually invisible.

"Oh yeah?" was my only comment when she told me about it.

"Sex and criminology, the same rule applies: when in doubt, always fall back on tried and tested tricks. Then you can't go wrong and you'll stay the course."

And my Auntie Poldi knew a thing or two about staying the course.

Her camouflage appeared to be working. Like the Doppler effect of a police siren, she heard from behind her newspaper how the voices of Russo and Rampulla, who were talking animatedly in Sicilian, first approached in the lower-frequency range and then receded in the higher-frequency range. No sign that she'd been spotted.

For safety's sake, Poldi continued to hold *La Sicilia* in front of her face for a few more moments, not least because her eye had just lighted on an interesting article about the recently discovered reservoir at Caltagirone. It seemed that a number of suspects had been arrested, but the men behind the scenes were still on the wanted list. Poldi was surprised to see a photo of the nervous young drunk from the vineyard. The caption beneath it read: "Dott. Enzo Rapisarda, press officer of M5S, Catania Province."

Well, well, so neurotic . . . a *dottore,* thought Poldi. However, that means as little in Italy as it does in Austria, where everyone is either a *Herr Doktor* or a *Herr Baron.* Any Italian who has graduated from high school is often addressed as *dottore,* or at least as *ragioniere,* which really means "accountant" but always passes for a polite form of address.

Dottore or not, Enzo looked quite as cracked and fanatical in the photo as Poldi remembered. In his capacity as spokesman of the Five Star Movement, he commented on the affair as follows: "This business is a disgrace to the whole of Sicily. The Mafia and our decadent political elite have robbed us Sicilians of our water. It is clear that we must seek out the persons behind this in government, judiciary and civil service, but I strongly doubt we shall ever see anyone arrested. This country is going to the dogs and needs radical reform, but as long as corrupt officials connive at devouring our beloved Sicily like a Christmas panettone in company with the Mafia, the multinationals, the EU and, above all, Germany, this should not surprise us."

Typical Italian bombast, thought Poldi, who was all too familiar with such effusions. Even so, Enzo's statement stirred something within her—something in the dust that had settled on her depression. It was a little something too easily overlooked. At once, as if this alarming little something had just grazed the nerve beneath it, her old crown started throbbing again.

Poldi's attention had strayed. The return of her toothache jolted her back to reality. Startled, she peered over the newspaper at the hotel terrace, where Sean Torso was sitting.

Or rather, where he had been sitting.

The American's disappearance unleashed a string of Bavarian expletives.

Poldi's pal Cher was nowhere to be seen either, nor were Russo and Rampulla. Still cursing her unprofessional aberration, she broke cover and stole into the hotel garden for a better view of the terrace, but there was no sign of Torso, Russo or Rampulla, either outside or in. Poldi stood there for a moment, amazed that she had—let's be honest—fucked things up.

Uttering another barrage of imprecations, she returned to the street, where she might well have worked herself up into a towering rage if someone hadn't caught her by the arm.

"Well, well, what a nice surprise!"

It was Doris and the German *deliziosi,* who were obviously on their way back from the nearby Teatro Greco. Poldi was virtually corralled.

"What are you doing here? Why are you swearing like that? Are you in need of help?"

There was no escape. Poldi was treated to a concentrated dose of solicitude and Dorisness. Long time no see, how was she, their educational tour was nearly over, they'd seen so many (very tatty) Greek and Roman temples, what was she doing here, wouldn't she like to come and have a nice salad with them, meals at the hotel were so terribly expensive.

As usual when she encountered a Doris or Doris's ilk, Poldi was at a loss for words. Dorises simply knocked the stuffing out of her. What was more, she could say goodbye to her camouflage.

"No time," she blurted out. "Things to do."

She tried to escape, but a Doris is not to be eluded so easily.

"There's always time," Doris said firmly. "First we'll have a nice Mediterranean salad, and then we'll give you a detailed description of our tour. It'll interest you."

She took Poldi's arm and towed her back towards the Corso Umberto. Flanked by the other retired schoolteachers, Poldi felt as if she was under arrest.

"God help me," she muttered under her breath.

And her prayer was promptly answered.

"Excuse me, ladies!"

A powerful voice from behind them. A voice that could have parted the waves or carved a roast. A calm, sonorous voice that silenced any objection and promptly sent cold shivers down Poldi's spine. A male hand grabbed her other arm and spun her round. Sean Torso smiled at her, but without a hint of warmth.

"There you are. I thought we'd lost each other."

Torso spoke in English, but Doris immediately let go of Poldi as if she'd scalded herself — to Poldi's regret. She even tried to take Doris's hand, but the woman had already stepped back out of reach.

Sean Torso, or whatever his real name was, continued to hang on to Poldi's arm. He bared his teeth at Doris and the *deliziosi*.

"Ladies," he said in English, "I'm really sorry, but I must deprive you of this charming lady's company."

"No," Poldi croaked in German, "he musn't!"

Doris had recovered her composure by now. "No problem," she told Poldi hurriedly, "we're bound to see each other at Valérie's. We don't leave till the day after tomorrow."

Poldi went weak at the knees. "Please don't go!" she squeaked, but the *deliziosi* seemed overawed by Sean Torso's sheer presence or the triskelion tattoo on his forearm.

A subdued chorus of bye-byes, and Poldi was obliged to watch Doris and her tour party beat a hasty retreat.

Sean Torso continued to hold her tight.

"Come along," he said sharply in English. "Keep your trap shut and don't try to run. I'll find you anyway."

"What do you want?"

"We need to talk."

"No, you're the Hedgehog! You want to kill me the way you tried to with the car—kill me like Elisa Puglisi and Madame Sahara. Heeel—"

Poldi's cry died in her throat, stifled by Torso's vise-like grip.

"Stop that! If I'd wanted to kill you, I've had plenty better opportunities."

Without further explanation, he switched his smile back on and dragged my Auntie Poldi across the piazza to a side street leading off the Corso Umberto.

Poldi reacted at last, or rather, her body took over. Not so young any more and the worse for boozing, arthritis and toothache, it tripped the main switch, flooded itself with adrenaline, engaged autopilot and activated an age-old genetic programme that always works in case of doubt: flight!

With the agility and strength of a pouncing leopardess, Poldi twisted free of Torso's grip, hit the disconcerted man in the face with her bulging handbag and ran for her life.

"*Aiiiuuutooo!!!*" she yelled across the Corso. "Muuurder!!! Heeelp!!!"

13

*Tells of hares and hedgehogs, of the flight reflex,
scent sprays and dirty deals. Poldi turns into a gazelle and runs into a trap. She feeds Montana with
the choicest part of a* pauro *and realises that rivalry
sometimes blinds one to details. A "bighead" makes
her an offer she really can't refuse, but since she prefers to play by her own rules, soon afterwards she
herself makes another "bighead" an offer he can't
refuse.*

Wow," I said, interrupting the dramatic pause for effect that Poldi had inserted at this point in her story.
"Is that all you can say?"

"Am I supposed to get gooseflesh?"

"Meaning what?"

"Oh, you know, Poldi, it's all a bit obvious. You keep hitting me with these cliffhangers, but we're sitting here on the
sofa, all nice and comfy, so I know everything turned out all
right in the end. I mean, it really is a bit—"

"Go ahead."

I squirmed. "Don't take offence, but hey . . . *leopardess?*
Seriously?"

"Don't you want to hear any more? Shall I stop? Okay, I'll stop. Let's just go on drinking in silence. I'm good at keeping mum when I have to. Back in the ashram I kept mum for days on end, even when I was having sex."

"Listen, Poldi, I didn't mean it like—"

"Maybe it's just that you can't stand the suspense. Is it too much for your nerves? Like to take a break and go for a smoke upstairs with your friend Etna? You're looking tired. Maybe you'd sooner lie down. Nobody's forcing you to listen night after night to your daft old auntie's adventures, which an anal, uptight type like you would never have. And why not? Because you don't have the guts to try. Because you're scared of failure."

"Really?"

"That's what I told Quentin when we were both living in that commune on Sunset Boulevard. He was still a youngster in those days, Quentin was, and so shy. He did nothing all day but read paperbacks—you know, pulp fiction. 'Quentin,' I told him, 'only mistakes make good stories.' Without mistakes you've nothing to tell. Mistakes prove you've tried, at least. Ultimately, success is merely the end product of a series of failures 'from dusk till dawn,' I told him. And Quentin took that on board."

"Okay, okay." I sighed. "So what happened next?"

Poldi drained her glass with a serene expression.

"Please, Poldi," I begged her contritely.

She emitted an ungracious snort. "Yes, well, I ran for my life. But then . . . all I'll say is, it was like the Grimm Brothers' hare-and-hedgehog story."

. . .

Poldi practically flew across the Corso Umberto in the direction of Porta Catania. She resembled a gazelle in flight mode, an unstoppable projectile—or so I imagine. She felt neither her age nor her weight nor her painful knee. Anaesthetised from wig to foot by adrenaline and mortal fear, she zigzagged through the crowds of tourists in search of the nearest mustachioed policeman, at whose uniformed breast she could hurl herself.

"Muuurder!!! Heeelp!!!"

In her agitation, alas, she shouted it in German. The cosmopolitan strollers and even the German families shrank away, grabbed their children and handbags, and stared after her, shaking their heads. They probably thought she was a lunatic or mistook her for a street artist who would soon go round with her hat, and both alternatives were better avoided. Nobody stopped my Auntie Poldi, but nobody offered her help or protection, possibly because she made such an intimidating sight as she sprinted along, yelling at the top of her voice. Still, she seemed to have given Sean Torso the slip.

She had made it all the way along the Corso by the time she ran out of breath and adrenaline.

And saw Vito Montana coming towards her.

Her first thought was that he was a hallucination, but he was thoroughly real. He put out his arms and caught hold of her. And yes, it really was him, her commissario, with his muscular arms and his familiar smell. A haven in distress and the essence of Sicily, all in one. Vito Montana, the man she loved.

"Vito! The murderer . . . he's here. He's trying to . . ."

"It's all right, Poldi. Calm down."

Yes, everything was fine. She felt safe at last.

Until she heard the voice behind her.

"Hot damn, she was fast!"

Turning, Poldi saw Sean Torso standing there.

"Just in time, Montana," he went on breathlessly, in Italian. "I almost lost her."

"Well, how d'you like that?" Poldi broke off triumphantly.

I was genuinely thrown.

"Wow, go on, Poldi. No messing!"

"It was hare versus hedgehogs. That's exactly how I felt, like the hare and the hedgehogs—"

"Yes, yes, get on with it!"

"You've no idea what I was feeling at that moment. Mortal terror, total exhaustion, knee-ache, betrayal, suspicion, thirst—the works. A sort of emotional *pizza capricciosa,* know what I mean? It was an emotional extreme, and I know a thing or two about emotions and extremes."

"Poldi!"

"All I knew was, the moment of truth had struck."

"Your last moment, you mean."

"No, Dottore, I don't mean that, because I gathered this much: those hedgehogs weren't going to bump me off in the middle of the Corso."

Poldi would still have preferred to make a run for it, but her last reserves of strength had dissipated in Montana's arms. She simply didn't have enough left to emulate a leopardess, gazelle or projectile, especially as the commissario was continuing to hold her in an iron grip. The hedgehogs had tricked the hare.

"Don't believe a word he says, Vito," Poldi managed to gasp. "He murdered Elisa Puglisi and Madame Sahara."

"Take it easy, Poldi," said Montana. And, to Sean Torso, "What about Russo?"

"Gone, of course, what else? Your lady friend really screwed things up again."

Montana uttered a monosyllabic oath. Then he did something very Sicilian, something that upset my aunt more than anything else: he glanced at his watch and said, "I don't know about you two, but I'm famished."

"Vito, believe me, he's the killer!"

Montana looked at her. "Look at me, Poldi. Do you trust me?"

"No."

He sighed. "What about some food, though? A beer, maybe?"

Poldi was going to say no, but her body, which knew better, reluctantly acquiesced.

"That's more like it." Montana took Poldi's unresisting arm and headed for a small trattoria in a side street off the Corso, where he shepherded her to a table in the farthest corner.

The pretty proprietress greeted Montana with a kiss on both cheeks and an expression that aroused a flicker of jealousy in Poldi, but the three ice-cold beers she deposited on the table aroused a flicker of vitality in her.

After Poldi had downed Montana's beer as well as her own and felt her animal spirits revive a little, she eyed the men sitting silently across the table from her. Sean Torso made no secret of his dislike. He looked about as good-natured as King Kong deprived of Fay Wray.

"I—" Montana began, but Poldi cut him short.

"No, let's not start with you." She looked at Torso. "Who are you?"

"This is—" Montana started to introduce the American, but Torso broke in.

"I'm Sean Torso. Let's leave it at that."

"That's just an anagram of 'Etnarosso,'" said Poldi. "In other words, the last and only clue to her murderer Madame Sahara was able to give. She unmasked you, mister, and so have I. *You* killed her, and Elisa Puglisi too, probably. D'you hear, Vito? I don't care what this man has told you, he's a murderer. Got your handcuffs with you?"

"Bullshit," Torso growled. "Sure, the name's an anagram. It seemed relevant to this operation. I like anagrams, but to be absolutely clear: I didn't kill Madame Sahara."

"Bill—I mean, er . . . Sean and I have known each other since my time in Rome with the special anti-Mafia unit," Montana put in. "Sean belongs to an FBI team covering organised crime in Italy."

"And that'll have to be enough for you," said Torso.

"Oh yeah?" Poldi picked up his untouched glass and knocked that back as well. This third beer dispelled the last of her fear and made room for something that suited my Auntie Poldi much better. "I'll tell you something, *buddy,*" she snarled at the American, "that certainly won't do me. I want some explanations. From both of you!"

"Let's eat something first," Montana said with deliberate

bonhomie, beckoning the proprietress. "After all, we're in Sicily."

Poldi had never seen her commissario so nervous. Without glancing at the menu, he ordered a few starters, two more beers and a Coke. Meanwhile, Poldi and Torso continued their ocular duel. They eyeballed each other, but without exploding.

"You've been nothing but trouble," Torso began angrily. "You keep sticking your oar in. Operation Etnarosso would have been over long ago if it wasn't for you. Now everything's in the balance. I could puke!"

"What Sean means to say is—" Montana began, but that was as far as he got.

Torso ignored him. "I should have put you out of circulation right at the start," he went on, his jaw muscles working rhythmically. "But you know what really makes me sick?"

Poldi could hardly wait to hear.

"The fact that we need you."

"Let's discuss it after the starters," Montana put in.

But Poldi wasn't finished yet.

"I want to know one thing first, Vito. Do you really intend to marry Alessia and move to Milan?"

"Well . . ." Montana cleared his throat sheepishly. "Well, um . . . no. We did discuss it, yes, but I . . . well, no. I don't know if it would have been a good idea, because . . . oh, it doesn't matter. And as for Milan . . ."

"Well, Vito?"

"I made that up."

"Why?" Poldi demanded in her iciest tone of voice.

"*Madonna*, to eliminate you from the game!" he blurted out. "I tried everything, but you're like a dog with a bone, so I had to bring up some bigger guns to blight your interest in the case. Your life was in danger, after all."

"So now you do believe that someone tried to kill me?"

"I realised that all along, Poldi. Believe me, it was only for your own g—"

He got no further. Poldi had slapped his face—hard.

"Good" was all she said. "That settles that."

And then the antipasti came.

Montana's left cheek was on fire, but he bore the slap with composure. Having swallowed the last morsel, he dabbed his lips with his napkin.

"Sean's team investigates Cosa Nostra activities extending from Sicily to the United States. He has spent the last three months undercover, shadowing Cosa Nostra bosses who are making money out of water here in Sicily. A great deal of money."

"I heard about it. The lake at Caltagirone."

"And that's just the tip of the iceberg," said Torso. "Etna-rosso was a criminal enterprise that hadn't shown up on many people's radar. We knew Cosa Nostra and Oceanica were in cahoots, but we still hadn't found an evidential link. Until I fingered Elisa Puglisi."

"And the poor thing had to die before she could give you the name of the missing link?" said Poldi.

"Wrong. She *was* the missing link. Elisa Puglisi worked for the water Mafia. She camouflaged and coordinated the whole business. We can prove that."

"Oh? So why was she murdered?"

"That we don't know."

"And Madame Sahara?"

"We suspect she was one of Puglisi's sources of information and laundered money for the Mafia."

"That's only a working hypothesis," Montana said. "We still haven't found the money, and all the 'donors' in her appointments diary flatly deny paying her more than the usual fee."

"Doesn't sound too convincing."

"We'd have made a lot more progress if you hadn't kept getting in our way," Torso growled.

"Know what you sound like, Mr. Torso, or whatever you like to call yourself? Like a loud-mouthed schoolboy who goes boo-hoo as soon as a girl slaps his face." She said that in English. The next word was in Bavarian: "Bighead!"

Torso went pale with anger.

Poldi smiled broadly at him and Montana in turn. "Why did Madame Sahara write 'Etnarosso' on her hand?"

"She didn't," said Montana. "According to forensics, the word was scrawled on her hand post-mortem. We haven't been entirely idle either, Poldi."

Poldi ignored this. It simply didn't make sense.

"You mean the murderer laid a false trail, but why? I mean, if I've understood you correctly, Etnarosso is at the bottom of all this. Why should the murderer lay a false trail that isn't a false trail at all? Hello?"

Montana sighed. "As I said—"

"The missing link is missing, I know."

As though on cue, they were brought their fish. The missing link between starters and sweets, so to speak, it was a *pauro,* a magnificent sea bream grilled and served simply with olive oil, lemon juice and parsley—the usual thing in

Sicily, where a really good fish isn't spoiled with sauces and overly pungent spices or garnishes.

The proprietress prepared to fillet the *pauro* herself, but Poldi forestalled her. Taking her knife, she carefully removed a juicy cheek from just in front of the gills, then balanced it on her fork and proffered it to Montana.

Montana got the message. With a smile, he opened his mouth and obediently allowed my aunt to pop the choice morsel into his mouth. It should be explained that in Sicily the cheek, being the tenderest and sweetest part of the entire fish, is always given to one's lover. Feeding someone a fish cheek was on a par with holding hands, according to my Auntie Poldi's scale of intimacy, which had no upper limit.

Torso grunted disapprovingly and shovelled half the *pauro* onto his plate, hacked it up with his fork and proceeded to devour it with his left hand in his lap, American fashion.

"I hate this country," he growled between mouthfuls. "My parents were immigrants from Ragusa, and I was assigned to this team because I speak passable Italian. I love my job, but I really hate Sicily. Always fish, fish, fish. Everyone talks about food, but they can't produce a decent burger. Know what they call a hamburger here?"

"A *panino*," Poldi said with a grin.

"Yeah, a *panino*. A bread roll. Jesus, doesn't that say it all? Shitty country!"

Poldi wouldn't leave it at that. There were more important matters at stake.

"Let's assume what you've told me makes some sense. Where do the Avola brothers come into it?"

"They don't," said Montana. "Their only concern is the reservoir below the vineyard."

"But why did Achille say he'd killed Madame Sahara?"

"He honestly thought it was his brother Carmelo, and that he owed him because of the donated kidney."

"And what motive would Carmelo have had?"

"The evil eye," Montana said coolly. "Carmelo Avola owns a small reproduction-furniture factory in Trecastagni. You know, hulking great pieces for the sitting room with ball-and-claw feet and thick brocade upholstery. The business did well for years, but it's been going downhill ever since the euro crisis. It's expensive handmade furniture, produced solely for the Sicilian market. Nobody wants stuff like that abroad. Like many other people, Carmelo went to Madame Sahara to ask for advice—maybe a little witchcraft as well—but things went from bad to worse. After that, Carmelo spread the word that Madame Sahara had put the evil eye on him—that she was intent on ruining him. He evidently became obsessed with the idea."

"You can't be serious."

"I certainly am. Anyway, it seems Achille took the matter seriously, because the day before her death Madame Sahara had a violent row with Carmelo. He really threatened her, apparently."

Sean Torso looked at his watch and gestured impatiently to Montana to get to the point at last.

Poldi was relieved to sense that, despite their years of cooperation, the two men were not bosom pals. Montana was looking increasingly annoyed with his American colleague and seemed to find him a nuisance, and Poldi was beginning to understand why. "He's feeling small," she thought in surprise. "My strong, handsome Vito is feeling small, and he hates it. Sean Torso is Vito's Doris."

Rivalry between men can have a motivating and stimulating effect, as Poldi knew from pleasurable experience, especially with policemen, but it could also be poison to a successful murder inquiry. So what was the best antidote? Logically, an entirely impartial, utterly objective, thoroughly incorruptible and single-minded female detective who still had her wits about her.

"Anyway," Montana went on irritably, "it wasn't either of them. Achille was seen in a bar in Trecastagni at the time in question, and this chimes with the location info from his mobile phone server. Yes, Poldi, no need to look like that. He left you and went off to have a nightcap, and Carmelo was in bed with his wife at his home in Trecastagni."

"Maybe she's lying. Women who love their husbands sometimes do."

"Listen, Poldi. If the two murders are connected, the brothers had no motive for killing Elisa Puglisi. That case has a totally different dimension."

"And we could have cleared up both of them if you hadn't kept getting in our way," Torso began again, polishing his plate with a piece of bread. "Carmelo Avola was my door to Etnarosso's back room. Three goddam months of undercover work as a hydrologist. I was *that* close!" He pinched his thumb and forefinger together. "To my target, I mean. And then you came along. My target got jumpy and drew in his horns."

He was starting to get on Poldi's nerves, but she had sunk her fifth beer by now and eaten well, so she was once more in command of herself.

"Which brings us back to point number one," she said in an altogether calm and professional tone. "Namely, why you need me in spite of everything."

Torso and Montana glanced at each other.

"And then you blew my cover with your hysterics," Torso went on. "That rules me out permanently. Game over. But —and I really don't like to say this—you're still in it."

The identity of Torso's principal target was beginning to dawn on Poldi, but she wanted to hear it from Montana.

"Well, Vito, why do you need me?"

Montana hesitated. Looking at him, Poldi could see that the whole subject stuck in his craw.

"To get at Russo," he said with a sigh. "Russo is the boss behind Etnarosso."

"No!" Signora Cocuzza said.

"No!" Padre Paolo chimed in.

Poldi just nodded.

Torre Archirafi's little café bar was closed on Thursdays, so they had the place to themselves.

It was nearly noon, my Auntie Poldi's favourite time of day. Outside, families were setting out on their *passeggiata*. The weather was still warm, and Etna was still huffing at regular intervals in the distance. For the first time, however, a light breeze blowing over from the mainland was ruffling waves and hairdos, soothing frayed tempers and lightening hearts a little. Through the window Poldi could see work-men dismantling the boardwalks, cabins and shacks on the promenade. It meant that the vacation season was officially over.

Poldi, the padre and the sad signora were sitting in air-conditioned gloom at a table beside the cash register. The long counter and the display cabinets, cool and empty and highly polished, were dreaming of the *gelati, granitas,* almond milk, *cassatas, cornetti, babàs al rum,* almond pastries, *millefeuilles* and strawberry tartlets that would once more, from tomorrow, waft their scent of vanilla and promise of paradise as far as the piazza.

"Because the world keeps on turning," Poldi reflected a trifle sadly, and briefly became engrossed in the question of whether it might have been a special fragrance that had lured so many invaders and immigrants to Sicily. Like a great, big, sticky, captivating, irresistible orchid, Sicily emits a scent that whispers, "Come! I'm your Eden, your Atlantis, your Eldorado, your heart's desire. Come and melt into me."

Poldi realised at that moment that she would never again go back to Munich, because she had reached her fragrant Eden long ago. She would dissolve there and become part of Sicily — indeed, she was well on the way to doing so.

"Donna Poldina?"

The padre and sad Signora Cocuzza were waiting impatiently for her to go on.

"Sorry, my dears." She paused for a moment. "I always knew it, but now it's rubber-stamped by the FBI and official: Russo is a *capo mafioso,* and he turned off my water. Sean Torso made an undercover attempt to get close to him, posing as a hydrologist. He tried initially to gain an entrée to Russo through the Avola brothers, hoping to become a kind of confidant of his and gather more evidence."

"It all sounds very complicated," the padre said sceptically.

"And was doomed to fail from the outset, of course.

Russo is a fox who can scent a cop from three miles away with the wind blowing in the wrong direction—just like me, by the way—especially when the cop is conceited and stupid enough not to remove his FBI graduation ring. What a *figuraccia!* Me, I've got a sixth sense where policemen and lies are concerned. Russo and the *mago* managed to fool me with their cock-and-bull stories, but Sean Torso never stood an earthly chance."

"And now they propose to use you as their secret weapon," Signora Cocuzza said, half horrified, half admiring.

"As a Trojan horse, more like. Torso expects me to flirt with Russo and gain his trust, hoping that over time I'll be able to supply him with evidence."

"So you and Russo are to . . ."

"No, that was never suggested, but I can go as far as I think fit."

"And Montana expects this of you?"

"He doesn't like it one bit, naturally, but his hands seem to be tied. It's Torso's plan."

"Then Montana is a damned coward!" the padre said. "You surely can't lend yourself to such a sordid scheme, Donna Poldina."

Poldi shrugged her shoulders a trifle coquettishly. "Oh, I admit it's not without a certain appeal."

"You can't be serious, Donna Poldina!" whispered Signora Cocuzza.

Poldi gave the other two a searching stare and kept them waiting for a reply.

"No, of course not, what do you think! I don't say I'm not attracted by such an undercover mission—my talents lie in that direction, of course—but do I look as if I would let myself be used by the first bighead that comes along, even if he is from the FBI? Torso has messed up, and now I'm supposed to save his ass. I can't even be certain he won't drop me like a hot potato if a better opportunity presents itself. Besides, I don't believe we'll solve Madame Sahara's murder this way. No, my dears, I've other plans. If I play the game, I'll play it according to *my* rules."

Rules which she promptly explained to her team. At her request, Signora Cocuzza handed over her evaluation of the appointments diary, which Poldi had still not forwarded to Montana.

"I knew we could count on you, Signora Cocuzza!"

It turned out that the sad signora had not only laid out a well-arranged Excel table but produced a regular dossier on most of Madame Sahara's clients, complete with contact dates, connections and cross-references. Poldi realised at once that it disclosed some patterns that had certainly escaped Montana's notice so far.

"You're a genius, my dear," Poldi said when she saw, for example, that many names had one thing in common: the Avola brothers, neurotic Dottore Enzo, Elisa Puglisi and Madame Sahara herself—all were, or had been, members of the Five Star Movement, but other clients not numbered among the suspects, or dead, also belonged to that party of protest.

"Then there are these sums of money. Undisclosed Five Star party donations, all of them," Poldi surmised. "No wonder the cash has never come to light anywhere."

The signora nodded. "I thought that too."

She had discovered, with the aid of a few mouse clicks, that Elisa Puglisi and Carmelo Avola had stood for the Five

Star chairmanship in Catania Province. Puglisi had ultimately won the election.

"That was like putting a fox in charge of the henhouse," said Poldi. "A corrupt district attorney employed by the water Mafia became chair of a party dedicated to the protection of water resources."

"Maybe that's why she met her death," Padre Paolo put in, every inch the Sicilian Sherlock Holmes.

"Or maybe not. There could have been some quite different reason," Poldi muttered, refocusing her attention on the signora's dossier.

An unmistakable signal: genius at work. A breathless hush, tense expectancy, nerves on edge. Even the café's air conditioning seemed to hum a little more softly so as not to disturb my aunt. All she said from time to time were things like, "My, look at that!" or "Who'd have thought it!" in German.

"What do 'Cyclops' and 'Maxlove' mean?" she asked the signora when she came across those words, which appeared on their own at the foot of the table.

"Heaven knows," Padre Paolo put in. "They were handwritten on the diary's inside cover. I noticed them while I was photocopying the contents."

"They sound like racehorse names," hazarded the sad signora.

Although Poldi thought this rather far-fetched, she was puzzled by the two mysterious words, which she had originally overlooked. They might be wholly insignificant, but she fed them into the Internet as search items and was surprised when they yielded an immediate and definitive result.

"Oh!" the sad signora exclaimed.

"I'll be damned," said the padre.

"Not horse names, maybe," Poldi said with a grin, "but something to do with stallions."

"Cyclops" and "Maxlove" turned out to be pheromone sprays for men obtainable in various strengths online. Although their actual effect on women was not clinically proven, they were advertised as being guaranteed to render any man irresistible.

"Who would use such stuff?" Signora Cocuzza whispered, sounding not entirely uninterested.

"Adulterers like Dottore Carbonaro, of course," growled Padre Paolo. "In order to hook young girls."

"No," Poldi said. "He's well heeled, he needs no pheromones. Sprays like these are used by only one type of man."

She produced the little shard of clay with the Greek inscription, the one she'd found in the vineyard, and put it on the table. *Outis,* it read. No one.

"Stuff like this is only used by a nobody who'd like to be a Cyclops," said Poldi. "A narcissist with a mind like a sewer and the willy of a hedgehog."

She closed her laptop, took out her mobile and dialled a number.

"Poldi!" Russo's delighted voice answered after the second ring. "You called at last!"

"I'll be at your office an hour from now" was all Poldi said. "And you can keep your pants on." She rang off.

"Nothing beats straight talking," she told her team contentedly. "Sex or skulduggery, the same applies."

Just under an hour later, my Auntie Poldi entered the lobby of Piante Russo, Russo's palm and potted plant empire, and gave her name to the receptionist.

This time she wasn't shown out by security or chased away by Hans and Franz. On the contrary, Russo came to fetch her in person. He kissed her on both cheeks like an old friend and escorted her at once to his office, whose small size and spartan decor she found surprising.

An old desk with a PC and stacks of papers and folders. Some filing cabinets and pictures on the wall, photos of his children, a Madonna, and a big map of Sicily bristling with pins of various colours. Facing the desk a shabby leather sofa and a coffee table already set with two espresso cups, a coffee pot, sugar and a plate of biscuits. The room's only decorative feature was a floor vase filled with white camellias. And that's what it smelt of: coffee, dusty files and white blossoms. In spite of the surprisingly unpretentious and puritanical atmosphere, it was also redolent of something else —power. One thing was quite clear: this man had no ego problems; he needed no pheromone sprays.

"No phone calls, no interruptions," Russo told his secretary. Closing the door, he watched Poldi sit down at one end of the sofa, cross her legs and unceremoniously pour herself some coffee.

"Where are those dogs of yours, Signor Russo? I almost miss being savaged." She injected a touch of ambiguity into her voice and held his gaze.

"Hans and Franz are out on the grounds somewhere, playing. Shall I call them? I'm sure they'd love to see you again."

Poldi made a dismissive gesture. "I don't miss them as much as all that."

Russo looked irresolute. Obviously trying to assess the situation, he sat down behind his desk instead of joining Poldi on the sofa.

"Well, what can I do for you, Donna Poldina?"

Poldi refused to be hurried. She calmly continued to stir sugar into her espresso, then drank it in little, dainty sips before replying.

"We Germans have an awful habit. We always skip long preambles and come straight to the point. It's almost inevitable that intercultural problems will arise."

Russo said nothing.

"I'll offer you a deal, Signor Russo. A dirty deal from my angle, but I have my reasons."

She paused and waited until Russo silently nodded to her to continue. He made a calm, almost sleepy impression, but Poldi saw that his eyes were wide awake and alert.

"I know all about you and Etnarosso," she went on. "I could even prove it to a certain extent, but I don't have to, as you'll see in a minute. I'm sick of being lied to by you and your informant Rampulla, so let's not beat about the bush."

"By all means. Let's talk turkey, Donna Poldina."

Poldi put her coffee cup down and squared her shoulders. "Did you have Elisa Puglisi and Madame Sahara murdered?"

"No."

She nodded. "No, I don't believe you did. If someone like you employs a hit man, you can be sure the bodies are never found. What's more, murders like that have to pay off in some way, whereas the deaths of Elisa Puglisi and Madame Sahara have brought you nothing but headaches, right?"

"Please go on, Donna Poldina."

"I can see to it that these headaches stop. For a while, at least."

Russo reacted for the first time. He raised his eyebrows.

"But there are conditions."

"Assuming that what you say makes some sense, Donna Poldina, and that I'm the person you take me for, what—if anything—would you have to offer?"

"You'll see that in a minute. First, my conditions: one, I want to know who killed Madame Sahara; two, I want my water turned back on; and three, hands off Femmina-morta."

"And four?"

"That's it."

Russo sat back in his chair. "Believe me, I don't know who killed Giuliana. That's the honest truth."

Poldi shook her head. "Let's give poor old truth a break for once, it could use a rest. I want a lead I can use."

Russo considered this, then picked up the phone and pressed a quick-dial key.

"Giovanna and Arianna to my office."

Two uniformed women appeared moments later. Russo got to his feet.

"I must ask you to submit to a brief body search, Donna Poldina. I'm sure you'll understand."

So saying, he left the room.

With a sigh, my Auntie Poldi removed her clothes and jewellery. A trifle embarrassed by her ample nudity, she watched the security guards search her handbag and clothing for bugging devices. But the phoenix tattooed on her left breast spread its wings with every breath she drew, filling her with strength and courage. And then it was over. She calmly got dressed again and waited for Russo to reappear.

He came in bearing two glasses of white wine and joined Poldi on the sofa, but he didn't drink.

"All right, ask your questions."

"Who is the Hedgehog?"

He stared at her. "What are you talking about?"

"Madame Sahara made a note after speaking with Elisa Puglisi: 'The Hedgehog has the money.' I'm convinced that the Hedgehog killed both women."

"No, that can't be."

"Then you know who the Hedgehog is?"

Russo sighed. "Not the Hedgehog, the Hedgehogs."

"Oh."

Poldi started to speak, but he cut her short.

"Before I say anything more, I want to know what you have to offer."

Poldi took the mobile phone from her handbag and showed Russo a photo she'd secretly taken that afternoon, when returning from the restaurant toilets.

"Ever seen these men?"

"One of them is your friend the commissario. The other is the American who's looking for water, the eccentric Californian who was staying with Achille."

"His name is Sean Torso. That's not his real name, it's an anagram of 'Etnarosso.'"

Russo's jaw muscles tightened. "FBI?"

"He's been dogging your footsteps for the last three months."

"What has he found out so far?"

Poldi shrugged. "Not enough."

"What about Montana?"

"He'd be glad to get rid of the guy, and he wouldn't be responsible as long as no one got murdered."

Russo looked at my aunt, shook his head a trifle wonderingly and raised his glass.

"*Benvenuto in Sicilia,* Donna Poldina. I think this is the beginning of a wonderful friendship."

14

Tells again of hare and hedgehogs, ice caves, ninjas and body signals. Poldi gets her running water back, thinks things over and finally understands which way the hare went. She gets pricked and gets her cheek stroked, is treated impolitely and then, with the friendly assistance of the Fortschau Armoury, obeys her hunting instinct. The trouble is, she ends by overlooking an important detail and has to improvise. A few tears are shed.

Okay, shoot. Where did you hide the mic?" I demanded when Poldi inserted a pause for me to express my admiration. "In your ear? In your mouth? Between your . . . er, never mind. Come on, where was it?"

"Nowhere! I was completely clean. You think I'd run such a risk when there was so much at stake?"

"Oh, so you really were in earnest?"

"Of course, what d'you think? In the long run, it was the only way to put a stop to that *capo mafioso*'s activities, I realised that at once. The end justifies the means, and you can't afford to be squeamish in a murder inquiry. You have to get your hands dirty occasionally. And besides"—Poldi chuckled to herself—"I got rid of that idiot Torso. Everyone knew who he was inside two days, and the FBI called him off. Actually, I did him a favour, don't you agree? Vito as well."

"Have you told Montana about your deal with Russo?"

"Are you crazy? That remains my dear little secret, and I'm counting on your own discretion as well, you hear? But sooner or later, when I've gathered enough evidence, I'll light the fuse."

"You're on thin ice, Poldi."

A dismissive gesture. "Get on with you! Think I'd shit on my own doorstep?"

"What if Russo wants . . . well, more? *It,* I mean."

"The rule that always applies in operations like this is, keep the ball in play but never shoot. It would be child's play for me to make Russo sexually dependent on me, of course, but I'm a pro. I'm on the side of justice—I still know where to draw the line."

That's just what I was doubtful about. At the same time, I knew I was the last person to talk my aunt out of something, for despite her sixty years and wide experience of life, I was beginning to realise that Poldi had remained a child. One of those children who occasionally, when things are going too well and they're feeling their oats, can't resist looking over the edge of a precipice, only to give themselves a little shake and scamper home in relief. When that dawned on me, I vaguely sensed that I might not be so helpless after all.

That life might have had a particular reason for depositing me on Poldi's sofa.

It was so that I might look after her.

Because I might be not only the last but also the only person who could save Poldi from falling into the abyss. It was the sort of task you could neither put off nor delegate to someone else. You simply took it on, said "*Namaste*" and hoped you wouldn't blow it.

"Hey, what's the matter, sonny boy? Why are you trembling like that?"

"I'm not trembling, everything's fine." I drew a deep breath. "Did Russo meet your conditions?"

"Don't be so quick off the mark. Say, d'you have that problem with *it* as well? If so, no wonder you don't have a girlfriend. Still, there are ways of curing it — you know that, don't you? A bit of yoga can work wonders."

More deep breathing. "Well, who are the Hedgehogs, and how do pheromone sprays come into it?"

She laughed. "Damned if I'm giving that away at this stage!"

"Come on, Poldi, thrillers always invite the reader to guess, so give me something to work on and then surprise me. Or, if I guess the murderer's identity correctly, do me the favour of a spectacular showdown."

Poldi looked at me intently. "My, my, so now we're an expert on thrillers, are we?"

I remained adamant. "You've got to deliver, Poldi. So who were the Hedgehogs?"

"Hare versus hedgehogs, that's all I'm saying. It kept going through my head when Vito and Torso nabbed me. Subconsciously, I'd already caught on. You know the story of the two identical hedgehogs that win every race because one of them is always at the winning post before the hare takes off? They're in cahoots, that's the secret, and the hoax can't be proved as long as they don't slip up. Mind you, everyone does in the end."

When Poldi tried the kitchen tap the next morning, it spat out some rust-brown liquid. Soon afterwards, clear water once more flowed from every tap in the Via Baronessa. Its residents breathed a sigh of relief.

Satisfied with herself and reconciled with the world, Poldi had her first proper shower in weeks and brewed herself some coffee. Then, for the first time in ages, she braved her aching knees and climbed the steep stairs to her roof terrace, where she sat in the basket chair I'd recently put there for my cigarette breaks. It was still early, and Etna was being gilded by the rising sun. Poldi thought of her Peppe and softly asked him to watch over her.

"*Namaste*, Smoky," she said, raising her coffee cup to the volcano. "Poldi *contra mundum!*"

Then she shut her eyes and deliberated. She knew who the Hedgehogs were, and she knew how much money had been involved. A lot of money. A very great deal of money. My Auntie Poldi knew quite a lot by now, but she still couldn't prove it. She briefly considered calling Montana and telling him what Russo had said about the Hedgehogs. Then she remembered that she'd deleted his number, and besides, first she wanted to understand how Madame Sahara's murder had occurred.

But no matter which way she looked at it, everything seemed quite cut and dried until she recalled what Montana had said about the results of his inquiries, and her neat little house of cards collapsed. Things simply didn't add up. And then, like a derisive comment on the international situation, the nerve beneath her old crown started throbbing again. Poldi swore beneath her breath. A toothache was the last thing she needed for solving a murder.

Rising from my basket chair with a groan, she went downstairs and shuffled back into the kitchen. She considered aiding her concentration with a small bottle of beer, but she decided to take an ibuprofen instead and waited for it to work. This took time.

The tooth continued to throb away like a radio beacon pulsating for navigational purposes. Throb, throb, throb . . . And again: throb, throb, throb . . . So as not to be entirely idle, Poldi opened her laptop and re-examined the sad signora's dossier, filtering the list of names according to various criteria. She clicked around purely for something to do. Throb, throb, throb . . .

And then she saw it.

The connection.

The hedgehog trick.

Throb, throb, throb . . . Two names with the same address. She hadn't noticed it before, but that's life. Fate has some odd ways of nudging us in the right direction. A toothache, for one.

"*Namaste,* tooth," Poldi said softly, surprised to have suddenly grasped how everything fitted together.

She also grasped that a visit to the dentist was inescapable.

After a brief phone call to Russo, Poldi bravely set out.

She was scared, naturally. Who wouldn't have been? I mean, dentist and murder inquiry—who but my Auntie

Poldi would have had the nerve to venture into such a lion's den?

She would never have believed that a drunk, neurotic young spouter of crude political slogans could be a dentist, but Dottore Enzo Rapisarda did in fact own a remarkably chic practice in Trecastagni. He also restricted himself to private patients, so she didn't have long to wait. Moreover, in contrast to her memory of him at the vineyard that afternoon, Rapisarda made a thoroughly calm, composed and —above all—sober impression in his snow-white smock when Poldi's turn eventually came. There was no trace of the fanaticism he'd displayed on that previous occasion.

"Oh, you're German?" he said delightedly in German when Poldi introduced herself. "I love Germany. I studied in Bochum."

"But Merkel is the Devil in disguise, wasn't that it?"

Rapisarda frowned. "I'm sorry?"

"Don't you remember me, Dottore?"

He stared at her for a moment, then blushed. "Oh yes, of course I do, signora. It was . . ." He stammered in embarrassment. "That's to say, I was rather . . ."

"Loaded, but never mind, so was I. Let's forget it." Poldi sat down in the dentist's chair. "After all," she said with a broad smile, "we're both professionals."

Rapisarda smiled back shyly. He proved to be a remarkably sensitive and sympathetic practitioner. His injections were administered so skilfully that Poldi hardly felt a thing, and he stroked her cheek with his finger as if she were a child. It was a new experience for her.

"The crown will have to be replaced," he told her. "For the time being, all I can do is treat the underlying inflammation. That will at least relieve the pain. We can begin the treatment proper in a week's time, if you're prepared to place yourself in my hands."

Poldi mumbled an assent with her mouth open and surrendered. She had no choice in any case.

It was all over within half an hour. Poldi's mouth was numb, but Rapisarda assured her that she would feel no pain when the anaesthetic wore off. He shook my aunt's hand and prepared to show her out, but her fingers tightened on his.

"Thank you, Dottore, but I'm afraid we aren't through yet."

Rapisarda looked startled.

"Eh, what more can I do? All your other crowns look fine."

"I want a word with you about your neighbours, the Hedgehogs. And about Madame Sahara and the money she collected for your party. Above all, though, about the way the Hedgehogs killed her and Elisa Puglisi."

Rapisarda went red in the face. He prepared to say something, perhaps even to shout something, but Poldi, who was still gripping his hand, drew him a little closer and used her other hand to put a finger gently to his lips.

"Hear me out before you blow a fuse, Dottore. I can imagine you owe your neighbours a great deal. The interest-free loan for your smart practice, for instance. No, Dottore, don't deny it. Signor Russo told me, and he got it from your neighbours themselves. In view of their generosity, you naturally made no great effort to discover how a furniture manufacturer on the verge of bankruptcy and a wine grower who had just renovated his entire winery managed to produce so much liquid cash. You were aware that Madame Sahara was collecting donations for your Five Star party, and you somehow discovered that the money never reached it, didn't you? You should really have put two and two together, Dottore, but you didn't. You're a good dentist and you campaign for a just cause, but I'm afraid you've got your paws dirty. Gratitude is one thing, but what does your conscience tell you?"

She released Rapisarda's hand at last. The young man was trembling. He collapsed onto his treatment stool like a punctured balloon.

"What do you propose to do now?" he asked in a whisper.

"It's quite simple. I propose to ask you two questions, Dottore, and if your answers are satisfactory there's just a chance you may get off cheaply. I don't want to lose such a good dentist, and with a bit of luck some of the party donations may yet come to light. So what do you say?"

Rapisarda nodded.

"Chin up, Dottore. Look at me."

The young dentist raised his head and looked at her.

"Ask your questions, signora."

"Very well. First, what was the usual route Five Star party donations were supposed to take? Second, on the day after the grape harvest—in other words, the day after Madame Sahara was murdered and you woke up late with a god-awful hangover—did you by any chance find yourself in possession of something that didn't belong to you?"

Rapisarda stared at my aunt as if she had second sight. "How did you know?"

"What was it?" Poldi asked, although she already knew.

The Hedgehogs had lost their last race.

"Carmelo Avola's mobile phone," said Rapisarda. "I took it to him at once, of course. I was so plastered, I must have pocketed it by mistake."

"Believe me, Dottore," Poldi said quietly, "you didn't."

"Whoa, whoa, whoa!" I took a paper napkin from the table and waved it in the air in a token of surrender. "I may be a complete knucklehead, Poldi, but I just don't get it. Mobile phone? Hedgehogs? Party donations?"

"Well, it is a bit complicated, and I didn't get it myself, not right away. The thing is, anyone who commits two such murders must suffer from a grossly overinflated opinion of himself, don't you agree?"

"Sure."

"And pheromones are thoroughly consistent with the image Achille adopted in order to seduce women. He was a nobody who wanted to be a Cyclops and wasn't one. He was just a wine grower who robbed his political party of a tidy sum of money in order to finance his new winery, because Italian banks have become so stingy with their loans since the euro crisis. The same went for his brother Carmelo, who was on the verge of bankruptcy. The two of them needed money, lots of money, so they helped themselves."

"So the Avola brothers were the Hedgehogs."

"Exactly. That's what they called each other as children, because, being identical twins, they enjoyed fooling their schoolmates. Hare and hedgehogs was a game they were good at, and a nickname like that can stick to you for life."

"Why Elisa Puglisi?"

"Well, she was supposed to launder the cash donations

Madame Sahara collected for the Five Star party. Also, she had an affair with Achille, who had used the pheromones on her. He somehow grasped that she was playing a double game with the water Mafia and blackmailed her. In other words, he pocketed the party donations in return for her silence."

"And at some stage Puglisi had had enough and refused to play any more."

"She was still a district attorney, that's why. She felt safe enough to threaten to bust him, so he applied the emergency brake and hit her over the head with a bottle of Polifemo. Overinflated self-esteem, as I said."

I was beginning to understand. "But she'd told Madame Sahara first, and since the fortune-teller knew who had murdered her friend, she had to die too."

"Now you've got it. *Cento punti!*"

"But how could Achille get away with it?"

"The brothers simply played hare and hedgehogs—it was the only way. A bit risky, of course, but they virtually had their backs to the wall. And what was the other factor involved?"

"Overinflated self-esteem?"

"Spot on. Plus an ego problem. Well now, I knew from Montana that Achille had been seen in a bar in Trecastagni at the material time, and that was consistent with his mobile phone's location data. Except that it was Carmelo in the bar, not Achille. Carmelo had Achille's mobile on him, thereby providing his brother, who must just have killed Madame Sahara, with an alibi."

"Ah!" I exclaimed. "So Carmelo foisted his mobile phone on Enzo, who was drunk and lives in the same building, so his mobile, too, registered an unsuspicious location for the time of the murder."

"And Carmelo's wife claimed her husband had been at home all night."

"Pretty risky."

"I'll say so. Overinflated self-esteem again. Play hare and hedgehogs all your life and you automatically think you'll win every race. It's a routine you never get out of."

"But why did Achille Avola confess?"

"Because it was a clever move. Because his DNA, fingerprints and so on were all over the body, and he knew that he and his brother had alibis. After the murder he even laid a false trail by writing 'Etnarosso' on Giuliana's palm. Very risky again, but highly successful in the end. The touching story of the brother and the donated kidney, remember? In Vito's defence it must also be said that Sean Torso was breathing down his neck at that time, and Torso didn't give two hoots about the murder. It took a pro like me to grasp the tie-ups in their full complexity. The Avolas knew that Madame Sahara must have left a lead in her appointments diary, but they didn't find it. Then, when they made a second attempt to do so, I got to her house before them. They didn't dare do anything then because the padre was there. They waited till I was alone and on my way to Montana with the diary, and then they rammed me."

"Wow!"

"Got it now? Ready for the showdown?"

"*Forza* Poldi!"

My Auntie Poldi was loath to waste any more time. However, she didn't delude herself that her evidence was really water-tight. It wasn't at all. What she needed was a genuine confession, and for that, her experience of a narcissist like Achille Avola indicated there was only one way: brutal provocation.

Poldi was back on dangerously thin ice. It might easily go wrong—lethally wrong. She realised that she couldn't entirely dispense with assistance.

When it came down to it, she needed Montana.

Since she'd deleted his phone number and didn't know it by heart, she called police headquarters. A snooty telephone operator informed her that Commissario Montana was out somewhere, and refused to give her his mobile number. Although Poldi stated that it was a matter of life or death, the operator sounded as if she heard this every day of the week. She did, however, condescend to say she would leave a message for Montana.

Poldi hung up, cursing, and waited for an hour. And another hour. She waited until evening, but Montana never called back, and at nightfall the thrill of the chase triumphed over common sense. It's like that when you're overcome by the thrill of the chase: postponing things is out, as everyone knows.

Poldi decided to call someone else.

Alessia.

Yes, exactly, how did she come to have Alessia's number? The fact was, she'd had it for some weeks, ever since yielding to a base instinct and secretly going through Montana's messages while he was asleep. One doesn't do things like that. Never. Ugh! Especially as what Poldi saw didn't appeal to her in the least and robbed her of sleep. Nevertheless, she now had Alessia's mobile number.

Unfortunately, only her voicemail replied.

"Per favore lasciate un messaggio dopo il beep. Vi richia-merò non appena possibile."

A warm, friendly voice, not snooty at all, not a bit suggestive of airs and graces. A voice that could give good advice, dispense consolation, emit full-throated laughter. The voice of a woman who might under other circumstances have been a friend. A voice that made my Auntie Poldi feel sheepish. She rang off and had to rally herself for a moment before trying again.

"Alessia, it's Poldi. I'm . . . well, yes, you know who I am, of course. I'm afraid I can't reach Vito, and it's important. It's about the case, I mean. I'm just off to see Achille Avola at his vineyard and force him to confess. Achille Avola killed Elisa Puglisi and Madame Sahara. Please could you let Vito know. And . . . thank you."

That evening, when Achille Avola walked into his cottage on the slope above the vineyard, after checking his steel tanks, tasting the young wine as he did every day and gently correcting the pubescent Polifemo with copper finings, he found a visitor waiting for him.

My Auntie Poldi was wearing full combat gear—tight black stretch pants under some tension, together with black sneakers and a tight black T-shirt—and had made herself at home in an old easy chair. Strapped to her tummy with sticking plaster beneath the T-shirt was a small recording machine, and loosely held across her lap was her father's ancient muzzle-loader from the Fortschau factory, a 19 mm rifle with a walnut stock and a worn barrel. Deactivated, admittedly, but pretty impressive if you didn't know that.

"Good evening, Achille."

"Poldi!" The wine grower stared at my aunt and her antiquated firearm.

He didn't look particularly surprised, she thought. That should have made her smell a rat, but it's always the same: once the play has begun, all you can think of is remembering your lines.

"How did you get in?"

"Oh, Padre Paolo showed me a trick, and your lock is old."

Avola shut the door behind him and came a step closer. "Listen, Poldi, it was only one night. I don't know what you were expecting, but for me that was it, so put that gun away."

Poldi burst out laughing. "Oh, Achille! Don't worry, I didn't come here to insist on a shotgun wedding. Sit down, then we can talk."

"What about?"

Poldi pointed the gun at him. "Siddown!"

This time the wine grower complied. He sat in the nearest chair at a due distance from my aunt.

Scrutinising the man under the dim ceiling light, she found it strange that he should ever have had such an effect on her. He bore no real resemblance to her Peppe despite his lanky build, Adam's apple and muscular forearms. "Hey," she thought to herself, "maybe there's something in these pheromones after all." In a way, she thought that wasn't such a bad thing.

She held up a small plastic aerosol can. "Look what I found in your bathroom: Cyclops, and there's a little can of Maxlove as well. What do you use Cyclops for, you loser — really tough young nuts or old bags like me?"

"I can explain everything if you put that gun away."

"Oh yes, you're going to explain a few things. What it feels like to be a nobody, for instance. A failure in bed. A loser who can't get it up any more. I may have passed out, but I know this much: you flunked it that night."

This more or less summarised Poldi's interrogation tactics — provocation and sarcasm directed at the subject's *amour propre*. It always scored a direct hit.

Avola reacted according to plan. He sprang to his feet, but Poldi raised the rifle again.

"Sit down! You used me purely as an unconscious alibi, but you must explain how you managed to seduce Elisa Puglisi. I mean, how could a classy woman like Elisa bear to do it with a failure like you? The pheromones must have flowed in torrents. Do you spike your wine with them sometimes? And what about Madame Sahara? Did you already know you were going to kill her when we met that afternoon? Had you planned it long ago, you and your brother?"

Achille Avola had himself under control. He sat back in his chair.

"I don't know what you're talking about, Poldi."

"I can prove it, Achille."

"Really? So why are you sitting here all on your own? Why aren't the police here?"

"They're on their way — be here in a minute. I didn't want to be deprived of the pleasure of hearing it from the horse's mouth, that's all. So, how did you plan it, you losers?"

And at that point everything went wrong. The interrogation crashed and the play took an unscheduled turn. Poldi should really have known better. Cue: hare and hedgehogs.

Unfortunately, she didn't notice her mistake until it was too late.

Achille sprang to his feet and hurled himself at her — not exactly what a nobody would do, but appropriate to someone with a full-blown personality disorder. Poldi pointed the useless muzzle-loader at him but didn't even have time to shout "Bang!" Simultaneously, she sensed a movement behind her and, before she could call out, Carmelo Avola jabbed a hypo into the back of her neck, just as he'd done to Signora Cocuzza at Madame Sahara's house. Poldi hadn't considered that possibility.

All she had time for, before lapsing into unconsciousness, was resentment that the hedgehogs had tricked the hare once again.

The first thing she felt when she came round was pain in her wrists and ankles. No wonder, because they were tightly bound with zip ties. The Avola brothers had also gagged her with duct tape and were toting her across the vineyard by her hands and feet.

Not really the outcome Poldi had been planning.

"I underestimated the dose. She's coming to."

"Let her, who cares? It'll all be over soon."

That didn't sound good, thought Poldi. Far from promising, in fact. She made desperate attempts to kick and struggle, but the brothers held her too tightly.

"*Madonna*, what a weight she is!"

"We're almost there."

Not being in the first flush of youth, they grunted and panted at every step.

From her position Poldi could see little more than shadowy rows of vines and a cloudless Sicilian night sky with a waning moon at the zenith. All was silent because nearby Etna had stopped erupting, as if it were breathlessly following the course of Poldi's destiny.

After a while, Poldi saw where the brothers were taking her. It was a narrow shaft leading down into the mountainside, probably a bubble in a solidified stream of lava formed thousands of years ago. The Avolas dumped her on the ground in front of it and cut the zip ties. Needless to say, she instantly tried to stand up and make a run for it, but Carmelo put a knife to her throat.

"Keep still!"

Achille ripped the duct tape off her mouth.

Poldi now saw that he had the muzzle-loader slung over his shoulder.

"Scream as much as you like, no one'll hear you up here."

Poldi needed no further prodding.

"HEEELP!!! HEEELP!!!"

Unperturbed, Achille shone a flashlight down the shaft. "This is a natural refrigerator," he said. "It's pretty deep. Our grandparents and great-grandparents used to store Etna snow down there so they had something to cool their drinks with in August."

It was chilly at an altitude of nearly a thousand metres. Poldi was trembling, but not because of that alone.

"Now the shaft is just a hazard for the grape pickers," Carmelo added. "People fall in and end up in hospital. It's high time we filled it in before someone else gets hurt."

Poldi got the message. "Please don't do this," she said as bravely as she could manage.

But she realised there was no point in arguing or pleading with them. Resolute action was the only answer.

"Kneel down!" Achille told her, forcing her to the ground. "That's right."

"I'm not *outis,* not no one," thought Poldi as she knelt on the edge of the shaft. She guessed what his plan was and knew this was her last chance.

Achille wiped the muzzle-loader with a cloth and pulled on gloves. "Open your mouth."

Poldi complied. Achille thrust the muzzle of the old gun into her mouth. His finger curled round the trigger. Poldi saw Carmelo step back. Then Achille pulled the trigger.

Click.

That was the moment.

Taking advantage of Achille's surprise, my Auntie Poldi grabbed the barrel with both hands and pushed him away from her with every ounce of strength she possessed. That, however, had been the full extent of her plan. How she was going to extricate herself from this unenviable predicament and get the better of two grown men, she didn't know. So she improvised, because my Auntie Poldi knew a thing or two about men and improvisation.

I picture her wrenching the gun from Achille's grasp and trying to roll sideways, ninja fashion. She didn't get far, because (a) she was no ninja, and (b) Carmelo hurled himself at her, and he still had his knife. She swung the rifle and cracked him across the shins, causing him to yelp and stumble. She raised the gun again, but Achille tore it from her hands. She did her best to scramble up and away from the mouth of the shaft, but the brothers pinned her down.

I can picture my Auntie Poldi fighting for her life in that vineyard, advancing years and bad knees notwithstanding. She didn't present a particularly dignified sight, spread-eagled on the ground in a clinch with the Avola brothers, but all that counts at such moments is sheer survival. It's clear that my Auntie Poldi fought like a tigress. It's also clear that a person's strength multiplies tenfold in such a situation, and that Poldi might well have dealt with the two men single-handed.

Maybe not, though.

In any case, this is all idle speculation. The fact is that each brother uttered a yell in quick succession, twitched violently and then went limp.

Poldi was too nonplussed at first to grasp what had happened. She merely saw Alessia standing in front of her with a flashlight in one hand and a police stun gun in the other.

"Are you okay?"

"Uh, yes, I think so."

"Quick, give me a hand, they're coming round already." Alessia produced a bunch of zip ties from her pocket and handed them to Poldi. "I'd never have found you if you hadn't called for help," she said as she swiftly pinioned Carmelo's wrists and ankles.

Poldi did the same for Achille, who was surfacing with a groan.

"Where's Vito?"

"You must call him. I came on my own, and I'm going to make myself scarce in a minute."

"But why?" Poldi asked in surprise.

Both the Avola brothers were now lying safely immobilised on the ground.

Alessia straightened up, drew Poldi aside and pointed to Achille. "Because I don't want Vito to find out about *him*. I don't know what possessed me. He was so persistent, and I was angry with Vito and jealous of you, and there was something irresistible about the man. I didn't go to bed with him, I'm happy to say."

Poldi looked at Alessia, her face bathed in moonlight.

"Achille uses pheromones," Poldi said. "He'd already outsmarted Vito. He was only interested in cuckolding him as well."

"Yes, I thought as much. The worst thing is, he's a murderer. I feel so . . . so dirty."

She trembled and started to cry. Poldi put her arms round the policewoman and held her tight.

"Shh, it's all right. You saved my life, Alessia. I'd be dead but for you."

But Alessia couldn't stop crying, and my Auntie Poldi, who also wept easily, cried too. She had reason enough to, after all.

So Alessia and Poldi held each other and wept together. Meanwhile, the Hedgehogs writhed around on the ground, panting and clearly mystified by the turn of events. At length the two women drew apart—carefully, as if at pains not to hurt one another's feelings.

"He loves you far more than me," Alessia said in a low voice, smiling bravely.

"Oh, I don't know . . ."

"Yes, he does. Besides, it would never have worked with

us. I'm going back to Milan, and Vito hates Milan. He's a Sicilian through and through. All the best." With a laugh, Alessia handed Poldi the Taser. "Here, take it. You managed this all by yourself, okay? Not a word about me to Vito."

"I promise," said Poldi, touched. She put her hands together and bowed to Alessia. "And . . . *namaste*."

15

Tells of surprising developments, of letting go and arriving. Poldi is obliged to pull a fast one on her nephew, discovers how to deal with a slug plague and rids herself of her shadow. She picnics with Valérie in a lava field, holds Montana's hand and, soon afterwards, other parts of the commissario's body. Finally, right at the end, she receives an unexpected visitor.

Another week at my Auntie Poldi's was over, and I was feeling proud of myself. That needs saying occasionally. I was in full flow. I was the adjective ace, the metaphor magician, the sorcerer of the subordinate clause, the expresser of emotions, the master of a host of startling but entirely plausible turns of events. The whole of my fourth chapter had been completed within a week. I was a paragon of self-discipline and inspiration, the perfect symbiosis of Germany and Italy. I was a Cyclops of the keyboard. I was Barnaba. All I lacked was a nymph, but my new Sicilian styling would soon change that.

In the fourth chapter, Barnaba had fathered another son with his beloved Eleonora during his first trip home in years. His firstborn, little Federico, subsequently my grandfather, was a rather sickly, tearful child who coughed a lot and didn't like pasta. This tended to arouse Barnaba's suspicions, but Federico's great big paws and the characteristic kink in his little finger left no doubt as to Barnaba's paternity. Although this ultimately saved Federico from a tragic accident while bathing, Barnaba's relationship with his eldest son would never be an affectionate one. But I'm anticipating.

Barnaba had succeeded by making shrewd investments and pulling the right strings in conning half his property out of Eleonora's father, the hard-hearted landowner Grasso, for next to nothing, thereby developing his Munich market stall into a miniature fruit importer's empire. For, native land and *sicilianità* notwithstanding, Barnaba's thoughts were forever turning to Germany—to his business in Munich, acrobatic Rosi in Westermühlstrasse and tea dances in smart Munich restaurants.

Of course, he still loved Eleonora with all the passion of a mythical centaur, but he also began to detect a typical Sicilian lassitude and somnolence in her. Eleonora often complained of the heat, preferred to spend the whole day in bed in her darkened bedroom, guzzled marzipan cherries, cocked her little finger when speaking and yearned for the evenings. Barnaba's innate Cyclopean virility demanded sexual gratification every hour, but Eleonora allowed him access to her only after nightfall and always fell into an exhausted sleep after the third coupling.

So no one will be surprised to learn that Barnaba moved back in with Ilaria, the preternaturally beautiful Cyclopean siren, who not only initiated him into the most intimate mysteries of the female body and taught him certain amatory refinements, but supported his business endeavours with age-old earth magic. In consequence, a number of Barnaba's envious rivals and competitors disappeared from the face of the earth, Eleonora's father among them.

Having purchased a thirty-room house for Eleonora and his future dynasty on the Corso Italia, in the centre of Catania, Barnaba returned to Munich, where the 1920s were just getting under way. It was the perfect time for a handsome young man with a fierce thirst for life to stake his all on the wheel of fortune.

Everything might have gone swimmingly — and this was the next brilliant twist in my plot — had not Calogero Vizzini's corpse been discovered in a cave on the banks of the Isar, and had not a dogged, grumpy, ultra-Bavarian police inspector named Vitus Tanner been doubtful that Vizzini had died of natural causes because of the strangulation marks on his neck.

"You can't be serious," my Auntie Poldi said with a sigh after I had read her my fourth chapter the night before my departure.

We were sitting together on the roof terrace, wrapped in blankets because a touch of autumn had found its way to Sicily at last. The nights were cool again, with a chill clammily creeping up from the sea.

"What do you mean?"

"Vitus Tanner. I won't even start on the rest of your Cyclopean tripe and your descriptions of 'it,' but Vitus Tanner . . . That was when I finally flipped."

"But Tanner supplies a sort of thriller element I wanted to introduce so as to keep the conflict simmering over a low flame until—"

"A low flame—yes, that describes it perfectly. Can't you see what a load of codswallop you're concocting? For God's sake, it's time you made up your mind what you're writing: a family saga, a fantasy, a thriller, a police procedural or what? Combining them all into one doesn't work. This Vitus Tanner of yours—get rid of him, he's unbelievable. I won't let you put my cases through the mincer and blend them with the sausage meat of your pubescent fantasies. It's all or nothing, understand?"

"But what about artistic licence?"

"There's got to be some art to make free with in the first place."

My Auntie Poldi knew a thing or two about art and freedom and objective criticism.

Shaking her head, she picked up her glass of wine and glugged it.

"Vitus Tanner! I ask you!" She looked at me and grinned. "Vitus Tanner, eh?"

"Restraint is a sign of weakness," I said with a shrug.

And then we both burst out laughing.

When our mirth had subsided, my aunt abruptly turned serious. Something seemed to be preying on her mind.

"We may not be seeing each other for a while, my boy."

"Oh?"

"Don't look like that. It's nothing to do with you."

"All right, I'll call my Bavarian police inspector something else."

"Nonsense. Leave everything the way it is. Art needs to be free."

"But I thought I might have—"

"It's just that I'll be needing the attic for a few weeks, understand? For a . . . well, for a guest."

The recordings on the machine Poldi had strapped to her tummy with sticking plaster put the Avola brothers' guilt beyond doubt. Achille Avola's SUV bore any number of scratches and traces of paint from Poldi's Alfa Romeo. The brothers confessed to the murders of Elisa Puglisi and Madame Sahara the same night. They claimed to have been overpowered by *two* women, but for one thing, this couldn't be proved, and for another, Montana put their assertion down to wounded pride. He didn't even ask how Poldi had come into possession of a Taser with an inventory number identifying its source as police headquarters in Acireale. He didn't ask many questions in general, just listened attentively as Poldi told him how she had finally nailed the Avola brothers. His brow looked much more furrowed than usual, she thought, but she also thought it might be wiser to curb her activities for a while.

Not altogether, though, because she still had one more thing to do.

The next morning, my Auntie Poldi had a brief telephone conversation with the vet who had carried out the postmortem on little Lady. Then she rode her Vespa to Femminamorta, where the travel agency's minibus was parked in the courtyard.

Poldi did not go straight into the garden as usual, but

went to see Mario, one of the workmen on Valérie's palm plantation, who had created an *orto*, or kitchen garden, and fenced it in neatly with chicken wire to keep the hares away from the vegetables. "Grapes aren't the only fruit of the Lord," thought Poldi, rather touched to see the carefully tended little allotment. "Man doesn't live by wine alone."

Half an hour later, she appeared in Valérie's enchanted garden, where Doris and the *deliziosi* were having a farewell breakfast with Valérie before flying home. All were packed and ready to go in their sensible clothing, and all were yearning to get back to their provincial German towns.

Doris was unsparing in her criticism of Sicily. "Take that place Noto," she was saying, "that so-called baroque town. It's nice and tidy, yes, but nothing compared to Ottobeuren Abbey. Back home in Upper Swabia you can see baroque buildings worthy of the name." She broke off on catching sight of Poldi. "Oh, look who's coming!"

Without saying hello to Doris and her tour party, Poldi sat down at the table and asked Valérie for a few moments alone with the *deliziosi*.

"Why did you send her away?" Doris demanded when Valérie had left them to themselves.

"Because she's such a wonderful person," Poldi told her. "Because she never thinks her guests are anything but charming, and I don't want to disillusion her just because one of them was a lousy dog murderer."

Doris started to say something, but Poldi raised her hand and put something on the table. A small cardboard tube adorned with a photo of a slug eating a lettuce leaf and the inscription *Lumachicida*, it was half full of blue pellets.

"This is slug bait," Poldi went on quietly. "You use it for

ridding your garden of slugs. It contains metaldehyde, really nasty stuff capable of killing babies or dogs. Lady died of it, anyway."

"How awful!" Doris said. "Where did you get it?"

"From Mario."

"Poor Lady. You think he . . ."

"No. Mario and Turi were fond of Lady. Mario bought the stuff in case he had an infestation of slugs in his vegetable garden. He's never had one, so he never opened it. Even if he had, he's fenced in his allotment so well that the dogs couldn't have come into contact with the filth. Just now, when I asked him about it, the tube was open and half empty. Strange, no? Mario simply couldn't account for it." Poldi looked Doris in the eye. "Can you, perhaps?"

"What are you implying?"

Poldi sighed. "It wouldn't have crossed my mind if Oscar hadn't growled at you the other day. I always suspected Russo, which shows one shouldn't jump to conclusions. Mario remembered your coming to see him and asking how he got rid of vermin, and he showed you the tube."

"So what?" Doris demanded coldly.

"Well, the door to his shed is always open, and he's out working all day. Anyway, he didn't notice until just now that someone had helped themselves to his slug bait."

Doris rose abruptly. "I'm afraid we must be going. Our flight leaves soon."

"Sit down!" snapped Poldi. "One call from me and a certain commissario who owes me a favour would be only too happy to detain you here for a day or two. In full compliance with Italian law, of course. No fun, though, I can promise you."

Doris sat down, but her companions and the tour guide shrank away as if she had the plague.

"You can't prove this."

"I don't have to. I can't bring poor Lady back to life, either. I imagine she had to die because she annoyed you by yapping at night."

"So what do you propose to do?"

"Why, I propose to tell you I despise you from the bottom of my heart. I despise you for your heartlessness and self-righteousness. No, that's wrong. If the truth be told, I'm plain sorry for you—and, of course, even sorrier for your former pupils. But it's like Job, isn't it? Although he didn't get his late wife back, he did get some decent compensation. And that, Doris, is why we're going to the nearest bank, where you'll make a very generous bank transfer to the account of Acireale's animal shelter. And if I consider that bank transfer really, really generous, you may yet catch your flight home."

And at that moment, because everything had somehow conspired to become too much for her—because Lady and Madame Sahara and Elisa Puglisi were dead, and all for the sake of lousy money or a lousy night's rest—tears sprang to my Auntie Poldi's eyes. At the same time, she realised that the spell had been broken. She was finally rid of the shadow that had pursued her all her life. None of the Dorises of this world would ever succeed in making her feel awkward or inferior again.

My Auntie Poldi heard nothing from Vito Montana in the days that followed. She hadn't seen him since making her formal statement at police headquarters. Having wondered for the first few days whether this was a good or bad sign, she simply waited and decided to accept whatever life would bestow on her or deprive her of.

The following Sunday, she and Valérie went for a picnic to an old lava field high up on Etna, a lunar landscape composed of rugged volcanic tuff extending as far as the eye could see.

Parked not far away was a car in which Aki was playing a game of skill on his smartphone, and in the midst of the lava field, naked and slug-like, the "alga" was gliding over the rocks. For once, Higashi-san had permitted Valérie and Poldi to watch his performance. In return, Poldi had had to describe her investigation in every detail.

The pallid Japanese dancer appeared almost to melt into the rocks. It looked at times as if the lava would entirely absorb him like the first rain after a long summer, only for Higashi-san to detach himself from it like a sulphurous cloud and seem to float away on the wind. Poldi thought she had never seen anything more peaceful and dignified, and this reconciled her a little to a life that gave and took away as it pleased. Or to the accounts department of the universe. Or to Padre Paolo's Lord God, who tended or pruned his vines as he thought fit, not that Poldi could discern any plan underlying his activities.

She sighed.

If she turned her head a bit, she could see Death. He was stretched out on a rock with his hoodie off and his pale, weedy chest exposed to the late autumn sunlight. His clipboard lay unheeded beside him.

As if that were not enough of an indication that all was well for the moment, Poldi heard a hoarse cry overhead and saw a buzzard circling above the lava field.

"*Namaste,* life," she murmured softly in German. And then, as ever, "The rest of the world can kiss my ass!"

"*Pardon?*" said Valérie. The German language always made her feel uneasy.

"Nothing." Poldi pointed to the naked Japanese. "Doesn't he feel the cold?"

"*Mon dieu,* let's hope he doesn't catch pneumonia!"

"How long did Aki say he would take to reach the sea?"

"Two months."

"It'll certainly be cold by *then.*"

For a while they reverted to watching the "alga" in silence, nibbling their *panini* from time to time and enjoying the mild November sunlight.

"How's your nephew?" Valérie asked.

"Good. He's busy writing his novel."

"A novel about you, Poldi?"

"*Madonna,* no! He's a proper novelist. He's writing an impressive family saga covering three generations. It's going to be really juicy, full of twists and turns, shady characters, stubble-chinned villains and ethereal beauties. Lots of flesh, sizzling sex, sweltering days and velvety nights. Parallel historical threads galore. It's his big throw of the dice, his ticket to international bestsellerdom. The only trouble is, the poor boy's making so little progress, him with his constipated jeans-and-navy-blue-polo-shirt look. He's completely stuck, writer's block. And I know a thing or two about getting stuck."

Valérie laughed at her. "But also about starting afresh."

"Because I had to," Poldi said with a sigh. "Letting go is the only thing I've never mastered."

As though on cue, a car was making its way up the winding mountain road. Poldi recognised Montana's Alfa at once. He parked beside Aki's car and came towards her. Poldi rolled her eyes when she saw what he was wearing: jeans, navy-blue polo shirt, brown leather blouson and sneakers.

Valérie got to her feet. "*Mon dieu,* I'm getting cold. See you back at the car."

Montana said hello to Valérie in passing and sat down beside my aunt. Poldi put a finger to her lips and indicated the ethereal Higashi-san, who, having slowly unfurled like an orchid, stiffened like congealing lava.

My aunt and the commissario just sat there for a while, watching the performance artist.

"Incredible," Montana whispered, clearly impressed. Then, "Poldi, what I wanted to —"

"Shh!" Poldi sealed his lips with her finger. "It's all right, Vito."

Montana cleared his throat, moved a little closer to her and then . . . then he held her hand again. And Poldi returned the pressure of his shapely, beloved hand, determined never to let go of it again.

That night, it may be supposed, my Auntie Poldi and the commissario embarked once more on a magical voyage replete with erotic marvels and adventures. At last, Poldi succumbed to the rising magma of Montana's volcano. After all, the man was a detective chief inspector and a Sicilian — in other words, a sexual force of nature. A hurricane of lust raged in Poldi's bed for half the night. Those two less than youthful, slightly shop-soiled lovers entwined like a pair of infatuated octopuses, copulated à la Cyclops and nymph, sometimes tenderly and sometimes with wild abandon. Like a female lobster mating, Poldi discarded her shell — in other words, her wig — and gave herself to Montana utterly, submitting to his passion in a soft and defenceless way, quite without shame or restraint. The Via Baronessa vibrated that night to animal cries of encouragement and delight whenever, after a brief intermission at No. 29, a limp sardine transformed itself once more into a full-grown moray eel, vital and voracious, convulsive and dangerous. Or so I imagine.

Whenever they kissed, Poldi tasted the concentrated flavour of Sicily. Sweet, salty, sour, spicy — the works. Sicilians are a baroque people, so there's no need to roll your eyes in an uptight or embarrassed way. My Auntie Poldi knows a thing or two about Sicily and kissing.

It was hardly surprising, therefore, that Poldi was far too tired to budge when the doorbell rang at around nine o'clock the next morning. And rang again.

Whenever you think "That's that," life demonstrates that the terminal full stop isn't yours to insert.

Poldi had pulled the covers over her head, so Montana got up after the third ring, wound a towel around his waist and answered the door with ill grace.

Standing outside was a tall African in his early forties, Montana estimated. He had a big, broad, watchful face as devoid of false bonhomie as it was of guile — Montana registered this instantly. He was muscular, a head taller than

Montana, and wore pale chinos, a white T-shirt and a green puffer jacket.

The two men eyed each other in surprise.

"Yes?" said Montana.

"I'm looking for Poldi Oberreiter," the man said in English. "Doesn't she live here?"

"And who might you be?"

Montana had switched to commissario mode, and the frown lines in his forehead rapidly deepened.

The African looked wholly unimpressed.

"I need to speak to Poldi Oberreiter. It's urgent."

Montana drew a deep breath and prepared to deliver a retort, but just then he heard a startled exclamation behind him.

Poldi was standing in the passage, naked but for her colourful sarong and her wig. She was holding her hand over her mouth in consternation.

The African caught sight of her. "Poldi!" he cried. "Hey, Poldi, it's me!"

"Can you explain what's going on here?" Montana demanded.

Poldi hesitated for a moment, then uttered a cry and brushed past him.

"Vito," she said as calmly as she could manage, "may I introduce my husband, John Owenya?"

Keep reading for a sample from the
next Auntie Poldi adventure

AUNTIE POLDI and the HANDSOME ANTONIO

Sicily's most glamorous gumshoe returns with a case
that will knock your wig off . . .

Tells of the perils of intercultural communication,
of men, fish cleavers, engine size and Poldi's past.
Poldi is in something of a tight spot, Handsome
Antonio gets noisy, Poldi's nephew burns some rub-
ber, and Montana gets jealous again. And all because
of John.

Handsome Antonio was sick of messing around. He held a fish cleaver to my Auntie Poldi's throat—it resembled a machete and could easily have bisected a mature tuna—and repeated his question.

"Where. Is. It?"

Whereupon my Auntie Poldi repeated her reply. "I've no idea what you're talking about, so put that in your pipe and smoke it!"

Which exemplifies the misunderstandings that were clogging the situation like limescale in a tap. The first one, of course, was lack of communication, because Handsome Antonio put his questions in strongly accented Sicilian Italian, whereas Poldi answered him in immaculate Bavarian German. Misunderstanding number two was the fact that Poldi hadn't a clue where "it" was. Handsome Antonio had hitherto rejected her asseverations to that effect by brandishing his cleaver and yelling, with the result that Poldi had dug in her heels and switched to Bavarian. From her point of view, what aggravated this extremely limited form of communication was misunderstanding number three: the tear-proof duct tape with which Handsome Antonio had secured her to a chair by her wrists and ankles. But the greatest misunderstanding, from my point of view, was . . . me. Like the crucial detail in a spot-the-error picture, I was sitting beside my aunt, secured to a chair likewise and almost wetting myself with terror. Expecting to bite the dust at any moment, I visualised my death as an amusing GIF animation looping endlessly on the internet: the cleaver whistling down, my panic-stricken face, the blade lopping off my head (like a knife through butter), the fountain of blood and finally the Great Light and some weird, plinky-plunky music.

I shouldn't be sitting here, I told myself — no, I certainly shouldn't be sitting here. Nor should my Auntie Poldi, of course, but in her case this series of misunderstandings could justifiably be regarded as an occupational hazard. I, on the other hand, was merely the chronicler of her escapades and investigations. I was the nerdy author of a half-baked family saga, the untalented nephew devoid of a girl-friend or profession. What was the point of slicing me in half? Needless to say, though, this cut no ice with Handsome Antonio. To him, we were both in the same boat.

The unproductive to and fro between my aunt and Handsome Antonio had bred a certain irascibility on both sides — one that was steadily eroding my hopes of a favourable outcome for the situation; they were in fact nearing zero.

However, all of Antonio's threats seemed to trickle off my Auntie Poldi like beads of condensation off a freshly pulled tankard of beer. This was because, unlike me, she had the knack for switching to a belligerent mode that inoculated her against all kinds of everyday tribulations and fears of failure and the future. Admittedly, she could have looked better. Squinting sideways at her, I saw that her camouflage-pattern trouser suit was torn in several places. Her Nefertiti make-up was smudged after our strenuous crawl through the undergrowth, and a small graze was reddening on her forehead. She was still wearing her wig, but this had also suffered quite a bit on our trek; it was dishevelled and partially disintegrating. Although she didn't look her sixty years as a rule, your age tends to show when you're tied to a chair with your wig mussed up and your mascara smudged. That makes it hard to preserve a *bella figura*. I felt momentarily relieved that Vito Montana, the grumpy, chain-smoking, jealous commissario of police, Poldi's light of love and —according to her—a sexual force of nature, couldn't see her in that state, although Montana's presence would have signalled a welcome turn of events. Why? Because my Auntie Poldi and I were in a really tight spot.

"Go on, Poldi, tell him!" I hissed.

"I'm not telling him a thing, the jerk!"

Handsome Antonio now changed his interrogation tactic: he gave up on Poldi and applied the cleaver to my throat instead.

"Poldi!" I whimpered.

"Take it easy, my boy! If I tell him, he'll kill us anyway, you know that, don't you, so calm down, you hear? I know his sort. He's a typical *leone di cancello,* a textbook example of a paper tiger. Big mouth but no balls. Besides, Death hasn't turned up with his clipboard yet, so relax."

"Where. Is. It?"

"I'venoideaI'mjustthechauffeur!" I gasped in bad Italian.

"And a right wimp into the bargain!" said Poldi.

"Poldi, he's going to kill me!"

"Easy, sonny. Where there's a will, there's always a way."

I was nearing the end of my tether.

"Where is it?"

"I don't know," Poldi snapped, "and that's that. *Basta!*"

"I don't know either," I moaned. "I swear!"

"I'm going to kill both of you, starting with you!"

"No, I don't want to die, not yet!"

We were all yelling fit to bust: I squeaking in mortal terror, Poldi barking like a drill sergeant and Handsome Antonio bellowing like a maddened bull. He brandished the cleaver in my face and uttered obscene oaths involving genitalia, the Mother of God and unappetising sexual practices. And as he rampaged around in front of us, I saw something that finally robbed me of speech: my Auntie Poldi had taken on that look again. I refer to the slightly dreamy expression she assumed whenever she sighted a handsome traffic cop. Hard to grasp though I found it, she had taken a shine to Handsome Antonio.

Now it has to be said that Handsome Antonio was not undeserving of his sobriquet. He was an exceptionally handsome young man, even by Italian standards. The fine rib vest he wore with his jeans accentuated his muscular but not overly hairy chest, and his physiognomy, which would have captivated any Renaissance painter, could have been described as classical. His was a sensual face unblemished by any sign of mental acuity, and there was a hint of melancholy in his eyes whenever they weren't, as they were at this moment, blazing with histrionic rage. Even so, Handsome Antonio radiated a kind of — how shall I put it? — animal grace. More suited to the movies than the Mafia, he looked just the way I envisioned Barnaba, the hero of my half-baked family saga.

Animal grace notwithstanding, Antonio was still brandishing his cleaver in my face, and I was getting sick of it. I was sick of his ravings, sick of the hullabaloo, sick of anticipating sudden death and sick above all of my Auntie Poldi's salacious expression. It irked me that her mind dwelt on one thing only — that she never passed up an opportunity to flirt. So Handsome Antonio was sick of messing around? *Benissimo,* so was I!

"That's enough!" I yelled. "*Basta!* Shut up! Pipe down, the two of you!"

Miraculously enough, silence fell at once.

Poldi stared at me in alarm. "What is it, my boy? Feeling all right?"

Struggling to regain my composure, I cobbled together my best Italian. "Look, let's find a solution to this problem that satisfies everyone, OK?"

"Like what?" Poldi said in German. "I'd be interested to know."

"Like some way of getting out of here alive."

"Don't get your knickers in a twist, sonny. Leave this to—"

"Shut up!" I turned to Handsome Antonio and, avoiding

speaking in German so there would not be a fresh outburst, said in Italian, "On certain conditions, my aunt would be prepared to tell you where it is."

"Well I'll be buggered. You've got a nerve!"

"Shut it, Poldi!"

"Hey, I'm still your aunt. I deserve some respect."

Handsome Antonio held the blade to my throat again. "Fuck your conditions," he snarled. "Where is it?"

"It'll do you no good to kill us."

"I'll just kill you, then—very slowly. Your aunt'll spill the beans all right if I cut you into strips."

"You've seen what she's like. You honestly think that'd impress her?"

Handsome Antonio thought for a moment, a process that briefly crimped his harmonious features.

"Yes, I do."

"I ought to mention," I said, lowering my voice, "that she isn't quite, well, all there, know what I mean?"

"Whisperers are liars!" my aunt interjected loudly.

"She's gaga," I went on in an undertone. "Age, booze. I know her. She lives in cloud-cuckoo-land. Even if she told you something, you could never rely on it. It'd confuse her even more if you killed me. I'm the only one who can get her to talk."

"You're just her effing chauffeur."

"I'm her nephew and chronicler, chauffeur and booze destroyer, spiritual adviser and scapegoat, millstone and manager."

"Eh, what's that? Are you crazy?"

I did my best to ignore Poldi and look Antonio straight in the eye. "It's up to you, Don Antonio."

Handsome Antonio's face clouded over again. He even knitted his brow in thought and paced up and down for a bit.

"Not bad, sonny, not bad at all," Poldi whispered in German. "You've obviously picked up some of my know-how. I told you, where there's a will, there's always a way."

"Oh, it's nothing," I said offhand.

But, secretly quite pleased with myself, I thought: *Yeah! Bingo! You cracked it! You're a cool dude, a wizard at empathetic negotiation.*

Handsome Antonio stared at us both with the huge blade dangling at his side. He was looking calm and relaxed.

"You're just messing me about," he said wearily. "You really don't know where it is." He pointed the cleaver at my aunt. "All right, shut your eyes."

And he took a big swing.

I always wake up at this point. It's like a bad film in which the protagonist has to overcome some trauma before he can save the world, his family, his dog and the United States — they always belong together somehow. We don't have to do all that, fortunately; we simply wake up from a nightmare and are happy to be still alive. Then I go down to the kitchen, drink a glass of water, take the first coffee of the day up to the roof terrace and feast my eyes on Etna and the sea. That has been my routine for the past few weeks. It's now the end of March, and I have to admit that in the interim, my dream gave my role in the above predicament a rather more heroic character than it actually possesses.

I've been living on my own at No. 29 Via Baronessa since the beginning of the month. I've cleaned the winter mildew from the corners and whitewashed the walls. I carry out minor repairs on the house, go shopping, water the plants, put out the rubbish, chat with Signora Anzalone from across the way and patronise Signor Bussacca's *tabacchi,* because I've recently taken up smoking. At nine every morning I consume a *granita mandorla-caffè* and a brioche in sad Signora Cocuzza's café bar. Sometimes I visit the aunts or hang out with my cousin Ciro. The rest of the time I write —or rather, spend the day typing a succession of sentences which I usually delete in the evening. I'm busy, in a manner of speaking.

But first things first.

In October last year, Poldi, who had become quite the amateur detective since she retired to Sicily from Germany, had just solved the Avola case. And that was when John appeared at the door like a ghost from the past. To be more precise, John Owenya, Poldi's Tanzanian husband.

My Auntie Poldi had told me very little about her Tanzania episode. As soon as it was mentioned she promptly changed the subject, and she could become quite grumpy if anyone harped on it. As a result, the wildest rumours circulated in the family. My cousin Marco persisted in claiming that Poldi had joined a Masai tribe and had only returned because of its teetotalism—a theory she never explicitly denied. My Aunt Luisa expressed the view that "Tanzania" was merely a code word for Poldi's spell in a rehab centre. Uncle Martino is still firmly convinced that Poldi was working for the CIA during that period and was on the point of uncovering the occult secret of the Knights Templar, a mission that would logically have brought her to Sicily, where the Templars had been based. I sometimes think Martino's theory came closest to the truth.

All that was known for a fact was that three years before her move to Sicily, Poldi had bought a house on the outskirts of Arusha, a Tanzanian town at the foot of Kilimanjaro. Masai country. Why Tanzania, nobody knew, but at that time even my Aunts Teresa, Caterina and Luisa had little contact with Poldi. She returned to Munich less than six months later, relieved of all her savings and so sick at heart that she had to get drunk every night — which, as everyone knows, has bad long-term effects on one's health. Poldi had always been fond of lifting her elbow, but I imagine that this was when she formed the plan to drink herself to death. The following year, both her parents died in quick succession, leaving her their small house in Augsburg. Poldi promptly sold it and used the proceeds to move to Sicily on her sixtieth birthday, intending to enhance her alcoholic suicide with a view of the sea.

We naturally suspected that there must be a man behind the Tanzania episode, and that it was there that Poldi's heart had been so thoroughly broken. We also surmised that she had probably been cheated out of her house there. When Poldi told me about it by degrees later on, however, the truth was even more outrageous than I could have imagined.

I hadn't been back to Sicily for over three months — an eternity, and I was still feeling miffed because her husband's sudden appearance had virtually uninvited me until further notice. John had moved into my attic room with the damp-stained walls and the stuffy, windowless bathroom. Poldi had merely told me to bide my time until she had "settled a few things." It was Aunt Teresa who had first told me about John, but even she had shrouded the precise circumstances of his visit in silence. It wasn't that the aunts uninvited me, but they no longer suggested that I fly to Sicily and look after Poldi for one week a month, and, well, I had my pride.

Feeling offended, I got my job back at the call centre and didn't write a single word of my family saga the whole time, though there were other reasons for that. Total silence prevailed for weeks. Not a single phone call—not even a text.

From November onwards, though, I was preoccupied with other things that kept me relatively busy and steered my thoughts in a quite different direction. I spent Christmas at my parents' place. January got off to a stormy start, unpleasant and really cold.

Early in February my Auntie Poldi called me in the middle of the night and genially invited me back as if nothing had happened. More precisely, she ordered me back to Sicily, having already booked my flight.

"And mind you don't forget your driving licence, OK?"

"Are you feeling all right, Poldi?" I retorted rather sniffily. "You think I've got nothing better to do? You think you only have call me when I haven't heard a word from you in three months—*three months?* You think I'll shout hurrah and hop on a plane at the drop of a hat? No way!"

"Meaning what?"

"Meaning forget it, Poldi. I'm busy!"

She collected me from Catania Airport the next day. No one can say I'm not consistent.

"God Almighty, you look terrible!" were her first words, and who wouldn't welcome such a greeting? "Been fighting?"

She was alluding to the plaster on my broken, swollen, green-blue nose.

I harrumphed sheepishly. "I'd sooner not talk about it, OK?"

"That novel of yours will never come to anything if you don't get over your eternal bashfulness, take it from me. My dear friend and mentor, Simone de Beauvoir, once told me that anyone with pretensions to being a novelist must drop their pants. Make a note of that."

"I've got my little secrets, that's all."

"For God's sake, drop your pants!"

I sighed. "All right, I'll make it short. Two days ago I was buying a currant bun in a bakery when I spotted someone walking past out of the corner of my eye. We were at uni together—"

"A real hottie who always ignored you," Poldi broke in, "or a nice girl who kept giving you the eye and you were too uptight to speak to her?"

"Does that matter, Poldi? Anyway, I catch sight of her and think, hey, maybe she's got time for a coffee. So I grab my currant bun and dash out of the bakery. And—wham! —I run full tilt into this plate-glass door. It's suddenly there out of the blue, freshly washed but clean no longer, and all I can see is stars and my nose is bleeding like a stuck pig."

"And the hottie?"

I shrugged.

"Then it wasn't meant to happen. Still, it suits you some-how, the broken nose—it looks tough, and I know what I'm talking about."

"If you say so."

Poldi was in a hurry. She strode swiftly off to the car park, homed in on a red sports car and opened the driver's door.

I mean, a genuine sports convertible! An old Maserati Bi-turbo Spyder Cabrio from the eighties: six cylinders, 230 horsepower, with cream leather upholstery, an immaculate paint job and a white bonnet.

"Where did you get it?" I said delightedly.

"Don't ask. Did you remember your driving licence?"

"Yes, of course. Why?"

She tossed me the car keys. "Because."

This was something entirely new. Poldi isn't the passenger type, she prefers to be in the driving seat.

"Oh!" I exclaimed. "To what do I owe the honour?"

"I'll explain in due course," she said irritably, and squeezed, swearing, into the passenger seat.

She slammed a prehistoric cassette of eighties pop songs into the slot and turned the volume up full, and we were assaulted by "Africa," "Down Under," "It's Raining Men," "Eye of the Tiger," "Gloria" and "Like a Virgin." Poldi sang along with all of them. When we got to Spliff's idiotic "Carbonara," I eventually cracked and joined in.

Built in the year of my birth, that Maserati was a joke in terms of performance compared with the average sports car of today. But it had charisma. I enjoyed roaring round the orbital motorway in the direction of Torre Archirafi, the sound of the six-cylinder engine, the crash of the gears, the bone-hard steering. I felt like a pop star in an eighties music video. All that irked me was Poldi, who alternated between flooring an imaginary brake pedal and urging me not to dawdle.

"Have you gone senile or something? Step on the gas,

sonny! This car is like a racehorse—it wants to race! Race, not trot, understand? OK, so burn some rubber!"

She surprised me by instructing me to take the motorway exit at Acireale, not Giarre, and directed me onto the secondary road at the Bellavista Bar.

"I know the way," I grumbled.

"We aren't going to Torre," she said.

"Where, then?"

"Femminamorta."

My heart skipped a beat with excitement. At long last, I was going to be introduced to Poldi's secret paradise and to Valérie, Poldi's friend and Femminamorta's ethereal, preternaturally beautiful, utterly sexy chatelaine.

Poldi, who seemed to have read my mind, looked at me askance. "No need to grin in that goofy way. Valérie isn't there. She's visiting her family in France."

"So why are we going there?" I said, disappointed.

"Why? Because that's where I'm living during the changeover."

"What do you mean, changeover? Is something wrong with the house?"

"Stop asking silly questions, I'll explain in due course. Now step on the gas, for God's sake."

And then came Femminamorta.

At kilometre eight we turned off the Provinciale onto the narrow approach road that led across the Piante Russo tree nursery. In the distance I could already glimpse the gateway flanked by two stone lions, and when I got out I found everything just as I'd always imagined it from Poldi's descriptions of the place: the old country house built of volcanic rock, its dilapidated walls lime-washed pink, the sun-bleached sundial, the ornamental eaves, the little bell over the entrance, the pines and palm trees, the enchanted garden. I grasped at once that it was a magical place where friendly spirits roamed and time stood still.

It was very chilly inside and smelt musty. The furniture and antiquarian library exhaled the dust of centuries. Poldi and I appeared to be alone in the house. She showed me a room on the ground floor, a former private chapel whose ceiling was adorned with frescos of saints and the Madonna. There was only one tiny window, the little old bureau against the wall looked decrepit enough to collapse at the slightest touch, the bed creaked and groaned like someone with lumbago, the tiles in the adjoining bathroom were encrusted with at least half a century of lime deposit, and the place smelt even mustier than the living room next door. But I took to it at once. More than that, I sensed I would write some great stuff in there.

"Freshen up a bit and then we'll talk," Poldi decreed before going off to make some coffee.

I took my time. First I smoked a cigarette on the terrace. Waves were pounding lava cliffs in the distance and a cold east wind was driving masses of cloud and spindrift across the sea towards Etna. It was a bleak day. The Sicilian winter had chilled the house and nothing much would change before April. I stubbed out my cigarette but kept the butt in my hand rather than desecrate such a heavenly place.

And then I did something I really shouldn't have done, but something came over me—I simply couldn't resist it. I tiptoed through the house until I located Valérie's bedroom. I didn't root around in her things, I swear, but I wanted at least to take a peek at the place. It made a much lighter and airier impression than the chapel downstairs. The French window led to a stone balcony at the back of the house and afforded a fantastic view of Etna. Everything inside was white, including the painted furniture. There were piles of books and antique knick-knacks everywhere. The bed had been stripped, but lying on it was a pair of big sunglasses Valérie had obviously forgotten to pack. Standing in the doorway, I tried to imagine what she looked like. There were no photos of her anywhere, worse luck. I pictured her as being very petite, with big eyes, laughter lines, sensual lips, bobbed hair, tight jeans and a striped Breton fisherman's shirt. Or in a short, translucent wisp of a summer dress, all elfin and coquettish and as utterly sexy as a girl in one of those French movies with frustratingly unresolved endings —the ones in which the characters merely canoodle and quarrel and make no sense. But all at once I was gripped by a strange sensation, as if someone had come into the room and were eyeing me reproachfully. Feeling uneasy, I shut the door and went downstairs.

Poldi, who was waiting for me in the living room, seemed preoccupied. Beside her coffee stood a glass of grappa. She was looking wearier than usual, it struck me, but she only sipped her drink, which was uncharacteristic. She could easily sink a bottle of Prosecco and half a bottle of grappa a day, not to mention several *espressi* laced with brandy, some liqueur chocolates and a lunchtime beer or two. Quite an intake, in fact, and more than enough to have killed me. Uncle Martino had intimated on the phone that Poldi was going through a bad patch. It was clear that something had gone terribly wrong in recent weeks.

"You feeling OK, Poldi?"

"Don't I look it?"

"To be honest, no."

"Don't treat me like some daft old crone who has to be helped across the street."

I tried to change the subject. "Where's John?"

"Out," she said quietly. "He'll be back soon, but we'll be gone well before then."

"Mind telling me where to?"

"We have to go and find Handsome Antonio."

Whoever that was.

But she'd said "we." It was the first time my Auntie Poldi had actually said "we."

Nobody had known about Poldi's marriage to a Tanzanian man. Neither my other aunts nor Signora Cocuzza, with whom Poldi had recently shared many a spicy secret, nor Vito Montana.

So it was hardly surprising that Montana was dumbfounded when, one fine Sunday morning, Poldi's husband reappeared as if nothing had happened. I often picture various versions of this first encounter. These range from an ultra-cool black-and-white noir scene to the histrionics of a silent film to the emotional explosion of a neo-realist Italian social drama.

The probable scenario: Sunday morning, Poldi and Montana are cuddled up in bed like a couple of teenagers when someone rings the doorbell. *Ring, ring, ring!* It's almost incessant. Exasperated, Montana tumbles out of bed, wraps a towel around his slightly expanding waist, to which Poldi likes to cling during their nocturnal voyages across oceans of lust, and opens the front door. Confronting him is a tall, strapping black man. Mid-forties, alert expression, a head taller than Montana, pale chinos, white T-shirt, green puffa jacket. All very dapper.

Montana: "Yes?"

The man, in English that suggested an East African accent: "I'm looking for Poldi Oberreiter. She lives here, doesn't she?"

"And who are you?"

Montana had switched to commissario mode, not that the man facing him seemed at all impressed. He gets no further, because he hears a smothered exclamation behind him.

Poldi: "Well, I'll be buggered!"

Whereupon the stranger: "Poldi! Hey, Poldi! It's me!"

And Montana: "Will someone tell me what's going on here?"

Poldi has then to explain who the stranger is—namely, her husband John Owenya from Tanzania. And that is when things start to get difficult.

"My husband," she repeats quietly, avoiding Montana's eye. "Husband. Marriage certificate, ring, church—the works, know what I mean?"

Bewildered, she stares at the stranger as if he's a ghost, a revenant risen from the dead.

"Well I'm—"

"It really is me, Poldi." John comes closer and spreads his arms with a beaming smile, but Poldi promptly fends him off.

"Stop! Not another step!"

"What is all this?" growls Montana, who is becoming less and less enamoured of the situation.

Poldi strokes his cheek. "I was just about to tell you, *te-*

soro. Get dressed and make us some coffee, OK?" She turns to John. "No need to stand around, come in." She ushers him into the inner courtyard and points to a chair. "Sit down. Don't budge and don't touch anything."

"Poldi, I wouldn't have come, but—"

"Not a word. My house, my rules, or you can piss off again right now."

John raises his hands in surrender. "*Hamna shida*. Your house, your rules."

Poldi chivvies Montana into the bedroom to get dressed and disappears into the bathroom. Locking the door behind her, she flops down on the lavatory seat, buries her face in her hands and weeps.

Once she has recovered some of her composure, she quickly adjusts her wig and make-up, sprays herself liberally with scent and puts on her favourite caftan, the white one with the gold thread.

When she enters the courtyard, Montana and John are facing each other across the table in silence. Montana, who is filling two espresso cups with coffee from a little aluminium *caffettiera*, never takes his eyes off the newcomer. John seems unperturbed. His expression is serious, but not nervous. He holds Montana's gaze and nods his thanks for the coffee.

Montana naturally wants to fire a thousand questions at the new arrival, commissario fashion, but there's a minor problem: his English is poor, like that of most Italians of his generation, and the *bella figura* principle deters him from trying it out. So he chooses to rely on his celebrated "Montana look," which has been known to crack the toughest of tough nuts. Sadly, John seems impervious to it. Maybe he's a contract killer. Or worse . . . But Montana prefers not to speculate further.

Poldi joins them at the garden table, sweetens her coffee and looks Montana in the eye.

"As I said, Vito, this is John Owenya from Arusha, Tanzania. We got married four years ago. I loved him, but he broke my heart and stole my house. And it turned out he had another family on the side—a woman he had been with for a long time, but never married, and their kids. And now here he is, the bastard, sitting there as if nothing had ever happened. I've no idea what he wants, and I've no wish to know, because whatever he says will be a lie. Oh yes, and there's something else: he's a colleague of yours, a detective inspector with the Tanzanian Ministry of Home Affairs."

Montana sighs. It's just as he feared.

John clears his throat, but Poldi's raised finger tells him to wait his turn. She continues to gaze intently at Montana and takes his hand, the big, shapely hand with the hirsute knuckles. She loves it for its combination of gentleness and strength.

"I'm just as much at a loss as you, Vito," she says. "I'll explain everything later, but first let's get this over with, OK?"

Montana shakes his head and gives a mirthless laugh. "You knock the stuffing out of me, Poldi!"

She kisses his hand and turns at last to John. My Auntie Poldi really is a model of composure.

"All right, I want to know why you're here and how you found me."

"*Hamna shida*, Poldi." John heaves a sigh of relief. "I need your help. Thomas has disappeared."

That, I imagine, was when it revived. The thrill of the chase. The moment when Poldi tasted blood.

"Why come looking for him in Sicily, of all places? Anyway, how did you find me?"

"I have ways of tracing people," John replies rather tetchily. "His mobile phone was logged in to a WLAN in Taormina a week ago. Nothing since then. I managed to trace the hotel he was staying at and checked his room. Thomas purported to be a Tanzanian financial investor. He paid a month's rent in advance but hasn't been seen for over a week, and yesterday, when I happened to see your picture in a newspaper, I thought—"

"You thought you'd drop in and break my heart again."

"Who is Thomas?" Montana interjects.

"His half-brother," says Poldi. "A nice enough fellow, but a bit unstable." She turns back to John. "So he disappeared?"

"Yes, from Arusha, two weeks ago. You know what he's like—he disappears from time to time, only to turn up again sooner or later. Rather the worse for wear, but OK otherwise. Like a stray cat. If you ask where he's been, he always says—"

"Don't worry," Poldi mimicked, "I just got lost in the bush."

John smiles. "Lost in the bush, yes, that's what he always said."

It doesn't escape Poldi that he's already using the past tense.

Montana starts to ask something, but Poldi gets there first. "Because in Tanzania, you never just get 'lost in the bush.' Why not? Because you don't go there on your own in the first place, and you don't get lost because you'll be torn to pieces by lions or hyenas, or, at best, die of thirst. The bush is a big, wild place. It's no fun, and you've no business there unless you're a game warden or a Masai and you really know your way around. Thomas is neither one nor the other—he's a big-city boy to his fingertips. Always looks cool and dapper in some swanky rented car. A likeable show-off who attaches a lot of importance to his *bella figura*. A guy like that never ventures into the bush."

Montana gets the picture. "In other words, a small-time criminal who does the occasional job."

"He really isn't such a bad lot," says Poldi. "But no, one doesn't always want to know exactly where he's been or what he's been up to."

Montana's frown deepens. None of this appeals to him: neither John Owenya's sudden appearance, nor Poldi's secretiveness, nor the sound of this man Thomas, nor the thrill of the chase reflected in Poldi's eyes. He is even less pleased by what John goes on to say.

"So we weren't too worried at first. Not until a week after his disappearance, when four guys with submachine guns pulled up outside our house and—"

"*My* house, you mean," Poldi cuts in sharply.

"I mean *our* house, Poldi. Your house and mine."

"No, you bugger, that's not what you mean! But get this straight once and for all: it's *my* house, just mine. Not yours. You took it away from me, John. You cheated me out of it."

John throws up his arms. "Do we have to thrash this out right now, Poldi?"

"No, but we *will*, believe you me. All right, these four guys—what did they want?"

"They were looking for Thomas."

"Kigumbe's people?"

John nods. "So four guys with submachine guns pulled up outside the house, jumped out of the car and asked for Thomas. All I gathered was that he'd made off with something that belonged to Kigumbe, who wanted it back at any price."

"Like what?"

John gives my aunt a searching look. "They didn't say. I suppose you wouldn't know?"

"Me?" asked Poldi. "Why should I?"

"You know why I'm asking."

"Yes, I know what you're getting at. But no, John, I've no idea what Thomas could have stolen from Kigumbe. If he did, though, it was the height of folly. Kigumbe wouldn't simply let someone rob him. If you ask me, Thomas is in deep shit."

John nods. "You can say that again."

"Who is this Kigumbe?" Montana interjects.

"A boss" is all Poldi says, but that's good enough for Montana. Everyone in Sicily knows what that means.

"I paid him a visit after that incident with his men," John goes on. "He asked after 'Mamma Poldi.'"

"Oh, how nice of him," Poldi says innocently. She mops her brow. "What did you tell him?"

"Only that you'd gone back to Munich and we hadn't been in touch since."

Poldi picks up the *caffettiera*. "More coffee, anyone?"

"Poldi?"

"Poldi!"

Poldi's two very different policemen might have been an

echo. All at once, they sound unanimously suspicious of her, and she doesn't like that somehow.

"What? I honestly don't have a clue what Thomas may have stolen from Kigumbe. What else did the man say?"

"Only that it was something of rather sentimental value." John takes a sip of espresso. "And that it was probably worth ten million dollars on the open market."